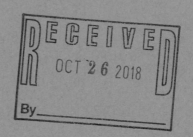

The Oyster Thief

The
Oyster
Thief

SONIA FARUQI

PEGASUS BOOKS
NEW YORK LONDON

THE OYSTER THIEF

Pegasus Books Ltd.
148 W. 37th Street, 13th Floor
New York, NY 10018

First Pegasus Books edition October 2018

Interior design by Maria Fernandez

Library of Congress Cataloging-in-Publication Data is available.

ISBN: 978-1-68177-791-7

10 9 8 7 6 5 4 3 2 1

Printed in the United States of America
Distributed by W. W. Norton & Company, Inc.
www.pegasusbooks.us

To my husband, Aamer, and my parents, Shaista and Amin,

for all their love and support

Contents

The Oyster Thief

ZONE I
Sunlight

1

Fire and Water

"This supper is a special occasion, Coralline," said Trochid.

Coralline frowned at her father. The eighth of July meant nothing to her. But her mother had set the table with their finest limestone plates, which did suggest that it was, in fact, an occasion of some sort. But it was not Algae Appreciation Day or Horrid Humans Day. It was not Coralline's birthday, nor was it either of her parents' birthdays. That meant it had to be . . . Ecklon's birthday—his twenty-sixth! They hadn't been a couple long enough to have celebrated his birthday together, but he *had* recently mentioned the surprise party his fellow detectives had organized for him last year. Coralline had neglected to note the date.

His birthday would explain why he looked particularly handsome this evening, in a jet-black waistcoat with half a dozen large lettered olive shells forming a column of buttons down the center. Coralline's mother was also elegantly attired, in a white corset with wispy sleeves that fluttered gently about her shoulders—as was Coralline's father, in a new, tan waistcoat.

Come to think of it, Coralline herself was also well dressed, though it was not intentional on her part.

She had returned home late from work, swum into her bedroom, and proceeded to do what she usually did at the end of a long day: massage the muscles in the back of her neck with her fingertips, in an attempt to loosen the knots formed over a day of bending over medications at The Irregular Remedy. She had then burrowed under her blanket and, closing her eyes, had thought of her most unusual patient of the day: ninety-one-year-old mermaid Mola, who suffered from dementia and whose memories of her husband kept falling as irreversibly out of her mind as her molars had fallen out of her mouth.

Coralline had been about to drift off into a nap when her mother rushed into her bedroom, flung off her blanket, and, surveying Coralline's corset, pronounced, "You *can't* dress so hideously for supper. Ecklon is coming, remember?" Her mother then handed her a new corset she had sewn for her, with emerald vines that met and separated over a glistening bronze fabric that precisely matched the bronze scales of Coralline's tail. Coralline had slumped on a chair in front of the mirror as her mother had tugged her long black hair into a pillowy mound at the crown of her head and circled the bun with a string of little white spirula shells.

How embarrassing that Coralline had forgotten Ecklon's birthday, especially given how he had spoiled her on her own birthday, a few months earlier. He had taken her to their favorite restaurant, Alaria, where he had presented her with *The Universe Demystified,* the latest book by the stargazer Venant Veritate. Like a telescope into the universe, *The Universe Demystified* had opened brilliant new galaxies in Coralline's mind. Ecklon admired Venant just as much as Coralline, describing him as "the detective of the universe," but she still couldn't imagine how Ecklon had managed to get the book autographed, for the stargazer was known to be just as reclusive as he was illustrious.

It was true that Coralline's wages as an apprentice apothecary at The Irregular Remedy were meager, but she could still have gotten Ecklon a pen as a gift, perhaps an engraved one, which he could use to take notes during his investigations. In the absence of any gift, the least she could do was sing. Clearing her throat, she began:

Happy birthday to you
May you have friends old and new

May life jolt success your way
As grand as a manta ray

Coralline smiled at her parents across the table, encouraging them to join along, but her father's dark-brown eyes squinted at her, and her mother gaped. Undeterred, Coralline continued:

May your sight never fade
Nor your hair gray
Happy birthday to you
May this year all your dreams come true

Coralline clapped—alone.

"My birthday isn't for another month, Cora," Ecklon said, a smile tugging at the corners of his lips.

He had the gall to be enjoying her confusion. Well, she was confused no longer. If it wasn't his birthday, there was just one other possibility that would make this supper a special occasion. But she didn't want to be wrong again; hoping to obtain a hint, she asked, "How was work?"

"Fine."

Coralline sighed. Ecklon had been like this since their very first date. He listened intently to her chatter about her patients but divulged little about his own work until Coralline prodded. The trouble was: He was too modest. His work was *more* than fine, Coralline knew. He had been promoted four times during his six years at Urchin Interrogations, the local Detective Department of the Under-Ministry of Crime and Murder. Just a few weeks ago, his boss, Sinistrum Scomber, a middle-aged merman with an enormous nose and perpetual grimace, had told Ecklon that he was the best detective Urchin Interrogations had ever hired. Sinistrum had sworn that as soon as Ecklon solved his next case, he would tenure him, making Ecklon the youngest detective to ever hold a lifetime position at Urchin Interrogations.

"You got tenured, didn't you?" Coralline gushed.

"Not quite, no . . ."

If it wasn't his birthday and he hadn't been promoted, what else was there to celebrate? Coralline crossed her arms over her chest, in part because she was annoyed and in part to suppress the growls of her stomach. She eyed the scarlet fronds of dulse at the center of the table. Patients had swum through the door of The Irregular Remedy from morning well into the evening, and she hadn't had a bite to eat since her rushed breakfast. Why did she have to work so hard for her supper?

"This day is a special occasion," Ecklon said softly, "because it marks six months since the day we met. Remember the day?" He grinned at her, dimples forming triangular wedges in his cheeks.

She couldn't believe he'd been counting the days, but she smiled back—even if she were to ever have dementia like her patient Mola, she would not forget the day they'd met.

He had swum into The Irregular Remedy with a purple-colored right elbow, the joint stiff and unmoving at his side. Discerning at a glance that it was fractured, Coralline had opened the medical textbook *Splinters and Slings* on her counter. Upon perusing a section titled "Elbow Ligaments," she had directed Ecklon to extend his arm to her across the counter. Warning him that it would hurt, she had felt up and down his arm, pressing into its length with two fingers. Other patients would have whimpered, but he hadn't even winced.

Upon concluding her examination, she had dabbed horned wrack salve onto his elbow, to reduce the swelling. Then, clasping his shoulder with one hand, she had leaned over her counter to crook his elbow at a ninety-degree angle against his chest. She had wrapped the joint with a gauzy bandage of pyropia, and she'd started slinging red strands of spiny straggle around the pyropia, to hold it all in place. But a lock of hair had fallen across her cheek.

Reluctant to recommence her sling, she had shrugged to encourage her hair back behind her ear, but her effort had only resulted in another strand tumbling across her cheek. Ecklon's hand had crossed the counter between them to push her hair back in place. Coralline had drawn her breath; her counter formed a barrier between herself and her patients—he'd crossed the line. She had made the final knot of spiny straggle rather tight around his elbow, then, worried it might restrict blood flow, she had loosened it with her fingers.

"Thank you for your attention, Cora," he'd said.

"*Coralline*," she'd corrected emphatically, wondering how he'd known her name. But of course: He would have read it on the badge pinned to her corset.

"I'll collect you here for supper tomorrow evening," he'd continued.

Don't bother, she'd been about to retort, offended by his assumption that she'd be free for supper (though it was true), but she'd found herself speechless when he'd dropped a scallop shell in the carapace crock on her counter. Patients paid what they could afford—no one had yet given her a ten-carapace scallop shell.

When Ecklon had swum through the door of The Irregular Remedy the next evening, Coralline had been tending a mermaid with pustular calluses across the pale blue scales of her tail. "Wait for me outside," she'd told Ecklon coolly, in part because the clinic was small and in part because he'd arrived at his convenience, not hers. With a nod, Ecklon had slipped outside The Irregular Remedy.

Patients had trickled in one after another for Coralline's attention—a wiry merman complaining of weak gills, a shivering insomniac, a mermaid with hyperthyroidism—and it was not until the waters had started to turn dull and dark and the clinic had been about to close that Coralline had slid out the door. Her tailfin had flicked to commence her swim home, when a voice from behind had startled her. "Ready, Cora?"

She'd whirled around. Ecklon had been leaning against the wall of The Irregular Remedy, his arms crossed over his chest. She had not known then that he was a detective, but the sight of him lurking in the shadows, seeing but unseen, hovering so still that he was almost as hidden as a seahorse, had made her think she was being pursued by a detective. "I'm sorry," she'd said. "I forgot you were waiting."

He had regarded her without impatience, without insult—rather, with respect—and had never mentioned it again.

She smiled at him now, sitting to her left at the dining table. That very first evening they'd met, she had found his face to be a handsome study of contrasts, and she found it to be so still. His jaw was hard but softened by a vertical cleft in the chin. His hair had the varied shades of pebbled sand, but its texture was always sleek and uniform between her fingers. His mouth formed a resolute line, but his lips were tender in shape—they made her think of a poet lost in verse.

In their six months together, not once had they bickered, not once had their opinions differed. Coralline had initially assumed their lines of work to be a world apart, but she had soon gleaned that they were more similar than different. He pursued clues; she pursued cures. He kept merpeople safe; she kept merpeople well. He dealt with murderers in the form of criminals; she dealt with murderers in the form of maladies.

"I've spoken with your mother and father, Cora," Ecklon pronounced, his silver-gray gaze locked on her own. "I've told them what I now tell you: I love you."

That was a notable difference between them—his sense of propriety. His job was to investigate those who broke the law, and he possessed an equal reverence for societal law, in the form of tradition. Coralline, meanwhile, regularly swam out the window rather than the door, even though her mother often told her that to do so was "the hallmark of an ill-bred mermaid." Maybe Coralline should have been elated at Ecklon's declaration of love, but she wasn't, for she already knew in her heart that he loved her, just as she knew she loved him. It felt strange to verbalize it for the first time in front of her parents, though, so she managed no more than to mumble, "Er, thank you."

She then reached eagerly for her stone-sticks, pleased his "special occasion" announcement had been made, and she could finally eat her supper—

"I wish to marry you."

Coralline's stone-sticks clanged against her plate, and her gills fluttered wildly along the sides of her neck. She looked at her parents. Her father's eyes shone with happiness, the lines around them spreading like sea fans. *Don't ruin the best day of your life,* her mother mouthed to her. Coralline tried to pull the muscles of her face into a semblance of normality as she turned back to Ecklon. Fortunately, he didn't seem to have noticed her reaction, for he was extracting something from his waistcoat pocket.

His hand unfurled before Coralline to reveal a shell with a pale pink center melting into smooth alabaster along the edges, like a slow summer dawn. The symbol of engagement, a rose petal tellin.

"Cora," Ecklon began solemnly, "will you make me the happiest merman in the Atlantic by marrying me?"

Before this day, marriage had been a vague concept to Coralline, something in the distance, like the clouds in the sky. Now, she felt as though the clouds had descended suddenly upon her and struck her with lightning. Her mind churning, she considered the changes to her life that would be wrought by marriage. Her name would change, for one; she would go from Coralline Costaria to Coralline Elnath—the new name just didn't have a ring to it. More importantly, she would no longer live in this home with her parents and little brother; she would live with Ecklon and his parents in the Mansion—the largest home in Urchin Grove. But she didn't want to live in the Mansion.

"Cora?" said Ecklon.

His hand trembled under the tellin shell, Coralline noticed through her haze. It was that slight movement that shook her; it told her that, for the first time since she'd known him, he was nervous.

She thought back to the day last week when she'd been sick with a cold. She hadn't told Ecklon, and she still didn't know how he'd learned it, but he'd come knocking at her door with a bowl of buttonweed. "How did you know I was sick?" she'd asked. "I'm a detective—it's my job to know," he'd said. "Well, I'm a healer," she'd countered, "and it's *my* job to not make you sick." His eyes glinting, he'd wrapped his arms around her waist. In contrast to her words, her body had melted against his, and her fingers had tangled in his hair. "I wouldn't care if I was sick every day as long as I was with you," he'd said, and given her a long, languorous kiss.

What was she thinking? Did she have dementia like her patient Mola? This was Ecklon, proposing to her—Ecklon, courageous and kind, Ecklon, as her mother often reminded her, the most eligible bachelor in the village of Urchin Grove. She would be fortunate to marry him. His proposal was a surprise, that was all, and she hated surprises.

"Yes," Coralline said, raising her blue-green eyes to his. Then, more emphatically, "*Yes.*"

Ecklon smiled at her, then at each of her parents. They beamed back at him. Coralline found that, like a star, his smile could swing any satellite into orbit, even her mother and father, who otherwise rotated in opposite directions.

The rose petal tellin was strung on a translucent vine, and Ecklon held it out toward Coralline so he could clasp it around her neck. She turned away from him, grateful to have a moment without her face in full view. His fingers brushed her shoulder blades as they closed the clasp at the nape of her neck. The click of the clasp made her think of handcuffs, and her heart pounded in her ears. Turning back to face the table, keeping her gaze down, Coralline raised the rose petal tellin off her collarbone and ran her index finger over its surface, back and forth. The shell's texture was smooth, its ridges gentle—as their relationship had been.

When Coralline looked back at Ecklon, she found that he had heaped dulse onto his plate, as had her mother and father. Finally, it was time to eat, but, though Coralline was hungry, she had no more appetite for the fronds she otherwise loved. She continued to examine the rose petal tellin, as if it would show her the future.

Suddenly, a tremor distilled into the living room through the window, its pressure that of a drumbeat, its vibrations throbbing through the stone of the house and pulsing through Coralline's very marrow. A stone-stick slipped out of her father's hand. It skittered slowly toward Coralline's tailfin, but she did not dare retrieve it for him.

Her parents and Ecklon sat still and stiff—the standard reaction to passing ships, in order to reduce the possibility of detection—but Coralline clutched the rim of the dining table. Goosebumps climbed from her wrists to her shoulders, and her stomach clawed at itself. She longed to hide under the table, but it would look cowardly. In an effort to distract herself from her terror of the danger above, she started counting her breaths. But she'd managed to count only to five, when the grasp of her fingers started to loosen, and her head started to feel as light and bouncy as plankton. She was beginning to feel faint; it happened to her often. Her father said it was because she did not take the time to eat adequately; her mother said that fainting occasionally was fine, so long as she remained thin.

Coralline tried to anchor her thoughts onto something, for it would help her remain conscious. Her glance fell on her father's right arm.

It was a narrowing rod that culminated not in a hand but in a bony swelling of a wrist. There was a filmy softness to the skin of his wrist, like that of a newborn; though her father was fifty years old, the skin over his stump was just months old. Coralline shuddered to remember the day his hand had been severed: His wrist had been a mangled mess of bone and sinew, blood spurting out of it like the ink of an octopus. Her mother called it his haccident—an abbreviation for "hand accident"—but Coralline considered the term misleading (though she'd grudgingly come to use it as well). What happened to her father had *not* been an accident: Ocean Dominion, its ships ever-present on the waters, had planted dynamite in a coral reef in Urchin Grove, in order to kill and collect schools of fish.

Coralline's father, a coral connoisseur, had been studying the reef with his microscope. He'd made a note on his parchment-pad that coral polyps, the tiny, soft-bodied organisms whose exoskeleton formed the reef, were finding it difficult to absorb calcium carbonate from the waters, due to ocean acidification. When he'd looked up from his parchment-pad, he'd spotted dynamite tucked in a crevice of the reef. Immediately, he'd inserted his hand into the crevice to extract it. He'd managed to wrest the dynamite out and had raised his arm to hurl it away, but it had exploded, taking his hand with it.

Coralline's mother had told him he should have bolted the scene instead of risking his hand and life.

"My hand exploded, so the reef wouldn't," Trochid had replied. "I would do it again, Abalone."

"Well, I don't want a handless husband!" she'd snapped, her amber-gold eyes flaming. "And if you have such poor judgment, I must insist you retire, Trochid."

Applying steady pressure over the next days like a tightly bound tourniquet, Abalone had compelled him to resign from his role in the Under-Ministry of Coral Conservation. In his retirement, he had become a shadow of his former self, in Coralline's opinion. He drifted aimlessly through the living room in the early hours like a ghost. His desk, previously stacked with books like *The Animated Lives of Anemones* and *Love of Limestone*, now sat empty, except for one volume: *Handling a Difficult Adjustment to Retirement*.

Coralline looked at her father's stone-stick on the floor. It divided into two, then three, until it looked like an array of fingers. Her head started to loll, but, just then, the tremors in the waters ended. The ship had passed. Her daze dissipated slowly. . . . Once she was mentally steady again, she bent at the waist, collected the stone-stick, and handed it to her father. He took it, but rather than eat with it, he set it to the side of his plate. He clasped his left hand around his stump, as though his wrist throbbed with a phantom pain in proximity to the phantoms on the waters.

"Humans are a menace," Trochid said. "Our only solace is that they cannot disrupt our lives any more than they already do."

"Why not?" Coralline asked.

"Because they're fire, and we're water. Fire vaporizes water, and water vanquishes fire. The two can never truly meet."

Izar stepped out of his small basement office and looked right and left down the hallway. Satisfied that he was alone, he turned on his heel and strode down the dimly lit corridor to the private elevator, where he flashed his identification card before the scanner. The elevator was right there—Izar was the only person to ever use it—but it was so old and ramshackle that its bars moved as slowly as arthritic knees.

Izar examined his identification card as he waited for the elevator bars to part. A circular bronze-and-black insignia glowed on the back of his card, the letters O and D intertwined over a fishhook that slashed the circle in half. The front of the card stated: Izar Eridan, vice president of operations. Underneath the words was a faded picture of him—light-blue collar, chestnut curls, indigo eyes staring at the camera somewhat anxiously, for the day the photo had been taken six years ago had been his first at the company where he'd decided he wanted to spend the rest of his life.

The elevator bars groaned to a halt. Izar stepped inside the decrepit cage and rode it from the first floor of the basement, B1, down to the second floor, B2. The thirty floors of Ocean Dominion aboveground were sleek and modern—the building formed a bronze glass arrow pointing toward the sky in Menkar—but the three underground floors had always intentionally been excluded from renovation. B1 contained Izar's office and those of other key men in the operations department; B2 was accessible only by this private elevator, to which Izar shared access only with Antares Eridan, the president of Ocean Dominion. But Antares had never descended into B2 after Izar's first day at the company, so Izar considered B2 his private asylum. As for B3, it was accessible only to Antares, but Antares had no use for it, so it lay dark and dusty.

When the elevator opened again, Izar marched three steps to the one door on B2 and stepped inside the room. It was a windowless warehouse with unpainted walls and untiled floor, but he felt as comforted to enter it as though it were a penthouse—this room was his Invention Chamber. Every night, as soon as the responsibilities of his vice president day job were complete, after other employees had grumbled their way out the doors of Ocean Dominion, Izar slinked into his Invention Chamber to start his night-shift: Castor.

Outside the Invention Chamber, Izar existed; in the Invention Chamber, he came alive. But not tonight.

Instead of stomping into his lair like a lion onto a savannah, Izar closed the door and leaned against it, his shoulders sagging. Looking resolutely away from Castor, he took off his pin-striped suit jacket and dropped it to the floor. He then uncuffed his white, starched-cotton shirtsleeves and rolled them up to his elbows. His glance fell upon his watch; the luminescent hour markers told him the time was close to eleven at night. He unclasped his watch and dropped it upon his suit jacket on the floor, finding the concept of time too manacling in a place where sparks of innovation appeared and disappeared as suddenly as the glimmers of fireflies.

Izar continued to stand there, leaning against the door, for how long he did not know. He despised procrastination, but this night, the odds were stacked so high against him that he could not bear to face them . . . not yet. If he succeeded in what he intended, he and Antares would become the richest men on earth; if he failed, his life to date would have been a waste, like the dirt under his shoes. Not only the years of his adulthood but also his childhood would have been a waste, for he had been preparing for this purpose for the last twenty-five years, since the very day Antares had adopted him at three years of age.

Izar still remembered the moment like it was yesterday: Kneeling before him, Antares had lit a match. Izar had been mesmerized by the flame—it was a drop of suspended sunlight, a tiny golden phoenix—but Antares had dropped the match in a glass of water. Izar had plunged his fingers into the water to try to rescue the flame, but it had died instantly. Izar had snatched the glass out of Antares's hand, raised it over his head, and smashed it to the floor. He could still feel the droplets of water splattering his shins.

Antares had not rebuked him. Instead, he had smiled. "I believe you're a very clever boy," he'd said in his hoarse smoker's voice. "When you grow up, I want you to invent underwater fire."

Izar had nodded, and, from that day, become obsessed with the idea of underwater fire. He had played incessantly with matchsticks; he had switched the stove on and off, staring at the crown-shaped blaze for hours; he had torn apart wires and sparked them against one another, reveling in their fumes. Throughout his early childhood years, the question that had driven him was how—*how* he would invent underwater fire; it was not until his adolescence that he had thought to ask Antares why.

"Because trillions of dollars' worth of jewels lie beneath the ocean floor," Antares had answered. "But they lie so deep that they cannot be accessed without blazing a path down. And yet no man on earth has found a way to sustain fire underwater. I myself have hired dozens of scientists at Ocean Dominion to attempt it, men with prestigious degrees and accomplishments, but, without exception, all have failed. *You* will invent underwater fire, boy. Gold and diamonds will form the embers of your flames."

This night, the eighth of July, marked the end of Izar's underwater-fire journey. If a fire didn't flame today, not only would he consider his past to be a dead, dry slate, a barren wasteland, but also his future. It was not written anywhere on his business card, but his true role, the one for which he lived, was not vice president of operations but inventor. He had given the title to himself; this night, he would learn whether he'd earned it.

He longed to know whether he'd succeeded or failed with his underwater-fire mission, but he could not summon the courage . . . not yet. Now that he was at the end of this road, he thought it fitting to pay tribute to the lampposts that had lit his path over the last six years. Most people retained pictures as mementos; he retained implements, which lay scattered all over the floor of his Invention Chamber—ores of iron, sheets of magnesium, rounds of bullets, panes of sensors. An onlooker might view them as dangerous tripping hazards, but Izar knew precisely what each object signified.

He knelt next to a low mound of ash and swept his hand through the granules, watching them trickle through his fingers like black sand. They were the cinders of creators—the cinders of not one person but dozens—and not their bodies but their theories.

Izar had commenced on his underwater-fire journey by consulting scientific manuals, engineering treatises, and technical articles about combustion. They had all asserted, implicitly or explicitly, that underwater fire was an impossibility, a contradiction in terms. "Oxygen is the catalyst for fire," one chemist had stated, "and water does contain oxygen, but it might as well not, for the act of combustion requires oxygen in gaseous form, not liquid." "Even a child recognizes that the role of water is to devour fire," had claimed a physicist, "not to nurture it." "When it comes to fire," had declared an engineer, "water acts as the wolf, not the sheep."

Izar had piled up all the papers and thrown a lit match upon them. A fire had blazed, and its smoke had scorched his eyes but straightened his vision. In his new clarity, he had resolved that the only applicable laws in the universe of his Invention Chamber would be those that he proved or disproved himself.

Now Izar rose to his feet, strode four steps, and, kneeling, thumbed through a crimson-covered notebook that lay half open on the floor with its spine up, like an injured cardinal. Some of its pages were crumpled, others had corners that were softened by water, a few had burnt edges, and all were yellowed, but Izar grinned at the notebook. The night of the cremation itself, he had started scribbling in this notebook. Over the next years, he had written countless chemical and physical formulae into its pages, logging also the outcomes of all his underwater-fire experiments.

Though Izar had chosen the notebook arbitrarily—it had happened to be lying around that night—he seemed to have chosen well, for its length was just right: only one page remained. If Izar succeeded today, he would jot his final note on that page, and it would consist of just two words: *Mission accomplished*. With those two words, the journal would become the most important object in the Invention Chamber, for it would make his work replicable. If he failed, he would destroy the journal.

A burble sounded. Rising to his feet, Izar glanced at the labyrinth of pipes in the ceiling high above. In his first month at Ocean Dominion he had found the sporadic noises of the pipes irritating—they sounded like explosions of dysentery from a maze of intestines (sometimes, he could hear them even from his office upstairs)—but he smiled at the pipes now as at an ailing relative. The pipes had been with him all these years, their sounds his only source of companionship in his Invention Chamber.

His glance landed on the shelves along the walls. The shelves at least were more organized than the floor, though it was more out of safety than any punctiliousness on his part: The shelves were stocked with hundreds of flasks of flammable liquids and powders, potent enough to burn down the entirety of Ocean Dominion, all the way up to the thirtieth floor. Izar had collected them from all over the world and had experimented with each of them in his underwater-fire mission.

But his favorite memento of his journey lay not in the room but in his bone itself, in the form of a platinum chip. He had obtained the chip three years ago, soon after he'd begun experimenting with melting points for all types of metal—lead, tungsten, titanium, cobalt, iron—and had concluded that magnesium was optimal, for it was able to reach and sustain the highest temperature. He had molded himself a torch of magnesium and stuffed it with an array of combustion powders. With his right hand, he had pulled the trigger of the torch in a pail of water, placing his left wrist directly before the barrel to detect viscerally if any heat emerged. With the first iteration of his torch, he had felt no more than a wisp of smoke. The second iteration had singed the hair right off his wrist. He had then doubled the diameter of the internal gas chamber of the torch, to increase its storage capacity for oxygen. When he'd pulled the trigger in water the next time, the resulting flame, though ephemeral, had shot out so sharply that it had burned the inside of his left wrist clean to the bone.

Doctor Navi—the Ocean Dominion doctor from the company's earliest days, a gaunt man with shifty eyes that scurried right and left like a rat's—had replaced the charred inch of Izar's bone with a platinum chip that he'd claimed would make Izar's wrist as strong as an anvil. As Izar examined his wrist now, he smiled dryly to think that he, the wielder of metal, contained metal also within him.

When he looked up, his glance fell on Castor, and he recognized intuitively that it was time. He strode toward the robot. Looming to more than three times Izar's six-foot-four height, Castor stood in an immense tank of water with a bulletproof glass boundary.

Izar knew Castor better than any man he had ever known. So profoundly did he relate to Castor, in fact, that, to his own bemusement, he had taken a knife and carved a hook-shaped scar into the side of the robot's jaw to match his own.

His own hands had laid Castor's flesh with the densest of metal alloys, and his own fingers had shaped Castor's skin with zinc-galvanized steel, to prevent corrosion underwater. He had ensured Castor's legs weighed more than one ton each, to enable the robot to retain his balance on an uneven ocean floor. He had slid magnets into the soles of Castor's feet, in order to attract jewels, and he had also added a sieve of sensors, to separate the valuable materials from the worthless ones. He had inserted suction conduits as nerves inside Castor's legs, to convey the precious metals and minerals to the cylindrical storage vaults in his vertebrae.

He had crafted and embedded a circular bronze shield of Ocean Dominion onto Castor's chest, with Castor's name written atop it. Behind the shield, he had inserted a vault that he'd loaded with hundreds of bullets. They were not ordinary bullets, but bullets that he himself had designed—cylindrical and streamlined, in order to counter water resistance. He had arranged them in concentric circles in Castor's chest, as though artillery were an art.

He had also programmed Castor with a self-defense instinct. For instance, if any merperson were to touch Castor during a mining mission, let alone try to stop him, Castor would shoot the intruder. Izar had loaded long-range cameras inside Castor's eye sockets, so that Izar would be able to view the robot's underwater surroundings on a computer screen and amplify or override Castor's self-defense instinct by remote control, if necessary.

As a lobster has two different claws, one a crusher and the other a pincer, Izar had given Castor two different arms, one a crusher and the other what he called a dragon. At twice the circumference of his right arm, Castor's left arm was the crusher, capable of pulverizing strata into sediment in a matter of seconds. Castor's right arm, the dragon, was intended to blast fire; it was on this arm that Izar's dreams hung.

Mentally, Izar ran through how he hoped it would work tonight.

Upon the push of a button on Izar's remote control, Castor would grow instantly hot, like an electric burner plate. His heat would transform some of his surrounding water into vapor. Catalyst chemicals would fly out of the glands along the sides of his neck, tearing apart the oxygen atoms in water vapor from their hydrogen companions, and compelling them to bond with one another to form oxygen gas. The gas would then funnel into Castor's dragon arm through a one-way distillation chamber inserted in his skin, designed to permit only oxygen gas. The oxygen would spark the combustion chemicals loaded in Castor's arm: sulfur, red phosphorus, potassium chlorate, and the finest of glass powders—the elements of matchsticks. Castor's arm would then crook at the elbow, and a blaze would spew forth. Through the continuous cycle of heat, water vapor, and oxygen distillation, Castor's fire would be self-sustaining, able to continue as long as the combustion chemicals lasted, or as long as Izar permitted through his remote control.

Izar snatched his crimson-covered journal off the floor, then climbed the ladder alongside the tank of water. He disembarked upon the platform above Castor's head, which resembled a wide diving board but had a steel-grid base. Kneeling on the platform, he looked at the two objects lying there.

The first was a battery. Bending forward at the waist, Izar dipped his arm in the tank of water up to his elbow and inserted the battery in Castor's skull. The size of a textbook, it fit perfectly, metal sliding reassuringly inside metal. The second object was a remote control. Grasping it with trembling fingers, Izar held it over Castor's head. In his other hand, he clutched his journal, also above Castor's head. If his attempt at underwater fire failed, he would drop the journal in the water.

He pushed the button on the remote control.

Heat began to emanate immediately out of Castor. The water roiled in disconcerted ripples, and, in the span of a minute, the air above the tank grew as moist and humid as that in a sauna. A bead of sweat trickled down Izar's temple, paused over the scar along his jaw, then dripped off and disappeared into the tank of water. Chains of perspiration dribbled down his back, mingling to form sticky sheets.

Castor's head swiveled side to side. This showed Izar that at least the first part was done; Castor had reached a sufficiently high temperature, and his glands were spraying catalyst chemicals into his surroundings. Next, the process of creating oxygen gas from water vapor also seemed to transpire without incident, evidenced by the streams of bubbles that erupted in the water.

Izar's hands were so drenched with sweat that the cover of his journal felt slippery between his fingers, like a fish trying to escape. He placed the remote control down on the platform but continued to dangle the journal above the tank. Victory was not yet assured, not nearly—the most difficult part remained.

A thunderous rumble sounded as Castor's right arm lifted slowly from his side to crook at his elbow. Izar's jaw stiffened, and he stared at Castor without blinking. In his anticipation, he could not breathe—the fire would blaze forth now or else never—

An orange-red flame pounded through the water. A horizontal cannon of fire, it flowed continuous and consistent like lava, as inextinguishable as a ray of sunshine.

The journal slipped from Izar's fingers. His other hand caught it just before it struck the surface of the water, and he placed it feebly next to his knees.

He had done it. His relief was so tremendous that, closing his eyes, he swayed on the platform on his knees, as though in a hypnotist's trance. "Well done, son," Antares would say when Izar told him. Izar had waited twenty-five years to hear those words.

Izar opened his eyes and gazed at the fire below. A flaming key, it would sear open the door to his future. Within a week, he would set up an assembly line and, using the instructions in his journal, would commence the process of creating thousands of Castors. Each would be a foot soldier in the mission of underwater fire.

Deposits of jewels were richest in the areas where merpeople lived. (Izar had overlaid maps of the ocean floor's topography with maps of merpeople population centers, and the maps matched precisely.) Castor would turn their homes and gardens to rubble in order to extract the precious metals and minerals beneath. Merpeople would have nowhere to live, nothing to eat. By the end of the year, they would be extinct. Their extinction would be an important side benefit of Castor: Merpeople had killed Izar's biological parents, and Castor would kill them.

2

A Matter of the Heart

A mermaid hurried through the door of The Irregular Remedy, a baby in her arms.

"What do you want?" asked Rhodomela Ranularia, glaring at the baby.

"I'm here because my son's tailfin is not flicking yet," the mermaid replied.

"That's because he's too young," Rhodomela snapped. "His tailfin will start to flick in a matter of months. In the meantime, I recommend you stop obsessing over him and develop some ambition in life."

With an insulted huff, the mermaid whirled around and departed.

Coralline looked at Rhodomela out of the corner of her eye. Everything about the master apothecary was efficient: her flesh, which formed a bare coating over her skeletal frame; her shoulders, without an extra tendon; her nose, with its narrow nostrils; her lips, a line as straight and unyielding as her opinions. In the silence of the clinic, Coralline considered asking

Rhodomela about her day but then thought better of it. In her first weeks at The Irregular Remedy, Coralline had tried to get to know her boss in the day-to-day doses of conversation through with which one gets to know anyone, but it had been like trying to befriend a puffer fish. Rhodomela's replies had been prickly or else she hadn't even bothered to respond, leaving Coralline's comments dangling pathetically in the water. Though Rhodomela's and Coralline's counters were just an arm's length apart, there could just as well have been a wall of shale between them.

I'm fortunate to work for Rhodomela, Coralline reminded herself. *I'm the only one who ever has.*

Upon her graduation seven months ago from Urchin Apothecary Academy, and with her rank as valedictorian, Coralline had applied to all the clinics in Urchin Grove—The Conventional Cure, Modern Medicine, Green Rope, The Lone Linctus, and The Irregular Remedy. She'd obtained employment offers from all except The Irregular Remedy. Every acceptance scroll had stated the same role, apprentice apothecary, and the same compensation—one hundred carapace a week. But Coralline had waited an anxious week before sending in her reply. That week, she'd checked the mailbox every few hours, until the slow-moving, mild-mannered mailman had remarked that no one was ever so eager to see him as she.

Coralline had been about to deliver an affirmative reply to The Lone Linctus, when the mailman had delivered a scroll bearing the lime-green seal of The Irregular Remedy. Coralline had wrenched it from his hands, torn the seal, and unrolled the scroll to discover an interview date and time scrawled at the center of the parchment.

Rhodomela had interviewed her in a bare, shabby, dimly lit office at the back of the clinic. She had asked Coralline the standard questions, but her mouth had tightened ominously at the standard answers. Coralline had felt certain she would be rejected from the job, but a letter had arrived the next afternoon, stating:

Role: Apprentice apothecary

Wages: Fifty carapace per week

Condition of Employment: The employee will be subject to a probationary term of six months. If she passes the probation, she will remain an employee of The Irregular Remedy and will earn a hundred carapace a week. If she fails the probation, she will be asked to leave The Irregular Remedy promptly, with or without reference.

Coralline had yelped. Her mother had emerged from the kitchen at the sound and snatched the letter from her hands. Her amber-gold eyes had swept over the words quickly. "Who does the Bitter Spinster think she is," Abalone had scoffed, "to make you such a low offer, half that of other clinics, and to subject you to a probationary term? How ridiculous!"

In her only act of defiance against her mother, Coralline had accepted the offer. Even had the wages been half again what they were, she would have accepted it—for it was Rhodomela who had instilled in her the meaning of healing, the day of her father's haccident.

Coralline and Abalone had brought Trochid to The Irregular Remedy and lain him down on the stretcher next to the door. Rhodomela had injected his arm with anesthetic just above his vanished wrist, and she'd bound a tourniquet of spiny straggle below his elbow. Fresh blood had spurted out, and the pungent smell of it had invaded Coralline's nostrils, making her waver dizzily. "Be useful!" Rhodomela had snapped. "Hold the tourniquet steady." Nodding, Coralline had held the red strings of spiny straggle tight, but she had turned her head away from her father's arm. She'd observed Rhodomela in an effort to distract herself from all the blood and to keep herself from fainting.

Rhodomela had combined smidgens of Clotter Blotter and Un-Infectant in a flask. Bubbles had spewed, then the blend had turned a still, leaden white, smooth as ice. With swift, meticulous fingers, Rhodomela had plastered the paste to Trochid's stump, arresting the bleeding. In that moment, Coralline had understood why she'd always wanted to be a healer: so that she could save the lives of those she loved.

Now, as Coralline continued to look at Rhodomela from the corner of her eye, she contemplated committing her second act of defiance against her mother. She looked at the two scrolls she'd wedged into a corner of her counter, each tied with a golden ribbon—they were the invitations to her engagement party and wedding. She wanted to give one scroll to Rhodomela, though she was not supposed to. She was supposed to give the other scroll to Rosette Delesse—who worked as an associate apothecary at The Conventional Cure clinic next door—but she did not want to.

Coralline wanted to hand the invitation to Rhodomela nonchalantly, without fuss or ceremony, and she wondered how best to accomplish it. Her glance fell upon the tray on her counter, laden with implements—snippers, vials, labels, a mortar and pestle, scalpels, needles. Coralline always took the tray with her into the remedial garden outside the window. She would invite Rhodomela on her way out into the remedial garden, she decided, then she would invite Rosette once she was in the garden. She squeezed the two scrolls onto the side of her tray.

But if she was entering the remedial garden, she might as well snip some algae and refill one of her urns of medication, she figured. She turned to look at the unit of shelves that ran from floor to ceiling behind her counter. She examined the labels of her white-gray limestone urns: Rash Relief, Cough Cure, Swelling Softener, Bruise Abolisher, Gill Gush, Eyesight Enhancer, Headache Healer . . . She opened the Headache Healer urn; as she'd expected, only a spoonful of the gooey gray glob remained.

She'd prepared the medication at least half a dozen times and could probably recite it from memory, but she wanted to be extra certain; flicking her tailfin to rise toward her higher shelves, she ran her index finger over the spines of her medical manuals. *Quick Concoctions for Quick Recovery. Medical Medleys. Heart: The Most Difficult Part. Secrets of the Central Nervous System.* Extracting *Medical Medleys*, she flipped through the thousand-page textbook on her counter until she'd located her favorite recipe for resolving headaches. She scrutinized the short list of ingredients—yes, it was exactly as she remembered.

Gathering her tray, Coralline slipped out from behind her counter and hovered in front of Rhodomela's.

"What is it?" Rhodomela asked, her serpent-like eyes flickering irritably.

"Nothing," Coralline mumbled, losing her nerve. She darted out the window into the remedial garden.

The garden formed a crescent shape around half of The Irregular Remedy. Coralline found herself relaxing as she looked out over the dozens of algae. There were green algae, the most humble and uniform of the algae, the colors of their fronds varying from pale green to deep jade. Then there were brown algae, their strands taller than her, equipped with gas-filled bladders that floated the blades upward for easier photosynthesis. And there were red algae, Coralline's favorite, the colors of their fronds varying widely from scarlet to maroon, pink to purple. Of the three families of algae, together numbering about ten thousand species, red formed the majority because of their ability to photosynthesize at great depths.

Placing her tray on the windowsill, Coralline approached creeping chain, a mat of interlaced blackish-purple red algae. She sheared three blades. Next, she sought the thick, hair-like thalluses of green rope smattering a rock and snipped the four most vibrantly colored fronds. Finally, she snipped just a sliver of iridescent cartilage, admiring its brilliant blue fluorescence. She ground each of the three algae separately in her mortar and pestle, then put all of them in a flask and shook the flask. Only when her arm tired did she hold it before her eyes: Bubbles were sputtering, and sounds were emerging from the flask, as though the algae were whispering to one another. The reaction showed her that the algae were joining, and, through their combination, becoming stronger together than they had been apart. Then, in the blink of an eye, the colors merged completely, and the mixture formed a gray glob. The Headache Healer solution was ready.

Coralline placed the flask on her tray, then grabbed one of the two invitation scrolls. It was time to invite Rosette Delesse, unfortunately. Straightening her shoulders, assuming a stoic expression, she turned to face The Conventional Cure next door.

Rosette was lingering in the remedial garden of the clinic. Her body formed a long, lithe shape, her eyes sparkled sapphire, and her hair, gathered over one shoulder, shone a passionate, fiery crimson. Her corset was woven of a fine, flimsy net and was precisely the same shade as her skin, such that she appeared to be wearing nothing. Coralline swam over to Rosette and handed her the invitation. Rosette's fingers untied its golden ribbon to reveal a small square of ivory parchment filled with cursive gold writing.

The Elnaths and the Costarias request the pleasure of your presence,

along with your family,

at the engagement party of Ecklon Elnath and Coralline Costaria,

at noon on the fifteenth of July in the garden of the Elnath Mansion;

and, pursuant, their wedding two weeks after,

at noon on the twenty-ninth of July at Kelp Cove;

please confirm your attendance as soon as possible,

by scroll to either the Elnath or Costaria home in Urchin Grove.

When Rosette looked up, her gaze fell to the rose petal tellin shell at Coralline's collarbone. Her eyes narrowed, and her face became vicious—she looked like she wanted to snatch off the symbol of Coralline's engagement. Coralline wrapped her fist around the shell, as though she were shielding Ecklon himself from Rosette's gaze.

In the days since the engagement, Coralline had touched the rose petal tellin so frequently that she'd started to worry the shell's delicate ridges would wear. She still didn't understand why she'd had such a cold fin during Ecklon's proposal, but, fortunately, it had evaporated just after supper. Now, she felt so excited about marrying him that she was counting the days to her engagement party (three days) and wedding (seventeen days).

"There's still time to the wedding," Rosette muttered. "Time in which hearts can change. Say, Epaulette hasn't ever invited you for supper to the Mansion, has she?"

"No," Coralline replied quietly. Although Coralline's mother, Abalone, had invited Ecklon for supper often, Ecklon's mother, Epaulette, had never invited Coralline, nor had she once accepted Abalone's invitation to dine at the Costaria home.

"Your shadows aren't good enough to grace the floors of the Mansion," Rosette said snidely. "*My* mother is Epaulette's best friend, and we have supper with the Elnaths in their Mansion once a week. Our standing is similar to theirs; like the Elnath lineage, the Delesse lineage is one of wealth and prestige. It's *my* destiny, not yours, to marry Ecklon."

Epaulette had wanted Coralline and Ecklon's engagement party and wedding to occur many months later; Abalone had fought to set the dates for both as soon as possible. At the time, Coralline had resented the early dates, but now she understood her mother's rationale. "Epaulette wants the engagement party and wedding to take place in the distant future," Abalone had said, "because she's hoping Ecklon will change his mind between now and then and marry Rosette instead of you. We need to reduce the period of time in which Rosette can play her games. . . . How do I know she'll play games? Because I know her type—I *was* her type."

"You've loved Ecklon six months," Rosette said, bending her long neck such that she and Coralline were nose to nose. "I've loved him since I was six years old. I'll steal him away from you before your wedding, mark my words! And I promise I'll ruin you!" Turning on her tail, she bolted in through the door of The Conventional Cure.

Coralline found that her tailfin was quivering, and her hands were clenched so tightly at her sides that her fingers were stiff. She swam into The Irregular Remedy through the window, collecting her tray from the windowsill. Coming to hover behind her counter, she clasped the tellin at her throat anxiously, wondering whether Rosette would succeed in stealing Ecklon away from her. But Rosette couldn't, could she? Ecklon loved Coralline, didn't he?

"Help! HELP!"

A tubby merman entered through the door of The Irregular Remedy, his hands over his heart. Thick, charcoal-gray hair curled around his ears, even as the summit of his head remained as bare as a baby's cheeks. Coralline recognized him as Rhodomela's patient Agarum, but she recognized him only just, for a patchwork of veins now ran across his cheeks, and the majority of his scales had bleached from cobalt to a stark white.

He wrenched off his checkered waistcoat and dropped it to the floor. Coralline helped him onto the stretcher next to the door and surveyed his body of folds. There was no blood anywhere on him, fortunately. She could set bones straight, she could prepare remedies for aching heads and tails, she could knead faltering glands into sudden functioning, but she was terrified of blood. It acted as a sort of tranquilizer for her; as soon as it entered her nostrils, she felt dizzy. Coralline hoped Rhodomela had not noticed her fear of blood, for it could prove fatal for her budding apothecary career.

Agarum was having a heart attack, Coralline concluded from her quick examination of him. Her own heart thudding as though to compensate for his, she asked Rhodomela, "How can we save him?"

She'd expected Rhodomela's hands to be curling around one of her urns, but her knobby fingers were instead drumming a soundless beat on her counter. "As your probation comes to an end tomorrow," she pronounced, "I've been waiting for an opportunity to test you. It has arrived today in the form of Agarum. Whether or not you save him will determine whether you'll have a future at The Irregular Remedy."

Agarum raised his head slightly and mumbled an incoherent protest.

Coralline stared at Rhodomela. Saving lives was not a game, nor was Coralline's career. Also, how could Rhodomela rely on just one case, and such a difficult case, in deciding Coralline's future?

Rhodomela's eyes twinkled, and her onyx tailfin flicked restlessly—she was enjoying Coralline's distress. "You're in a race against time, Coralline," she said. "To help you, I offer you use of my full array of medications."

Rhodomela slid out from behind her counter to create space for Coralline to enter. It was the first time she'd ever invited Coralline behind her counter. Although a healer's medicines appeared to be her most public possession, visible to anyone who entered a clinic, they were actually her most private, accessible to none but her, barricaded from the world by the fence that was her counter. And so, as Coralline slid behind Rhodomela's counter, she felt as uncomfortable as though she were entering Rhodomela's bedroom.

Rhodomela's shelves were so heavily stacked with urns that they'd turned crooked under their burdens. Coralline perused the labels of some of the urns: Temple Tingler, Troubled Tail Tonic, Spine Straightener, Rib Rigidity Release, Appendix Unclencher, Ear Cleaner. From her textbooks, she knew that critical cases often required combining two or three pre-existing medications, sometimes quite unexpected ones. Which urns should she choose?

She pulled out one marked Artery Opener—given that it was intended for the heart, it should be sensible as one of the medications in her blend, she thought.

Agarum's arm dropped off his chest and swung off the stretcher. Practically all residues of cobalt had drained out of his tail by now, Coralline saw, leaving all but a handful of scales a bleached white. He lay just a finger's width from death.

"Hurry!" Rhodomela barked.

What should be the second medication in her blend? Coralline's fingers trembled over the urns, coming to a stop above Rapid Reviver. She looked to Rhodomela for approval, but Rhodomela's expression was flat, her lips straight as a needle. Coralline picked up the urn. She opened Rapid Reviver and Artery Opener on Rhodomela's counter. She snatched three pinches of Rapid Reviver, a fine, deep-green mush, and two smidgens of Artery Opener, a whitish glop. She combined them in a flask and shook the flask vigorously. She then held it before her eyes, hoping to glimpse an alteration in color, a fright of bubbles, a commingling of texture—something, anything, to indicate a reaction.

But there was nothing. The green and white remained separate, lying limply against each other. It was failed chemistry—these two medications were not meant to marry. But this blend was all she had—she could only hope it would prove effective despite indications to the contrary.

Coralline dashed to Agarum. His thick cheeks, contorted earlier, now lay pale and still, but his lips quivered: He was still alive. She cupped his head and touched the flask to his lips—but a hand hurled the flask aside.

Rhodomela's face, before she turned away, reflected bone-deep disapproval. The master apothecary darted to her shelves and, fingers moving as fast as four-winged flying fish, collected Rib Rigidity Release and Troubled Tail Tonic. She deposited pinches of the powders, brown and crimson, in a vial, then shook the vial. When she held the vial before her face, bubbles were frothing, and the brown and crimson colors were combining to form a smooth, brilliant emerald. Rhodomela inserted a syringe through the lid, filled it, then approached Agarum with her needle.

Coralline blocked her path.

"*Simple Recipes for Remedial Success* states that the key ingredients of each of Rib Rigidity Release and Troubled Tail Tonic," she said, "in other words, the pink flaps of halymenia and the brown fronds of lobophora—act as a poison when combined. I distinctly remember reading it in the textbook's appendix."

Rhodomela pushed Coralline aside.

"But you'll kill him!" Coralline cried.

Rhodomela looked at Coralline defiantly as she stabbed Agarum in the heart.

His body shook violently from head to tailfin, his flab rippling like waves. Rhodomela held his face steady in one hand and then swung her arm back and slapped his face. His jowls juddered before settling into a conclusive stillness.

Coralline came to hover to the other side of the stretcher, her breath rasping out of her gills. She'd never seen a dead body before—it was terrifying—and to think that she'd played a role in Agarum's death, first with her failure of a potion, then with her failure to prevent Rhodomela's attack.

But as she watched, Agarum's eyes opened. He looked at the two faces peering down at him, then sat up slowly, as though awakening from a long slumber. With his hand over his heart, he bent carefully to collect his waistcoat off the floor. He slipped his arms through the checkered fabric and clutched it closed with a hand. From his waistcoat pocket, he extracted a slipper limpet and placed the five-carapace shell in the crock on Rhodomela's counter. He bowed his head at Coralline and Rhodomela in silent gratitude, then swam out the door, a new spring in his tail, which was darkening again to cobalt.

"How did you save him?" Coralline stammered.

"I rely on my own judgment more than anyone else's," Rhodomela replied coldly. "I urge you to do the same. Don't believe everything you read in your medical textbooks."

Coralline plopped down on the stretcher vacated by Agarum, her spine limp. What would her inability to save Agarum mean for her probationary review tomorrow? Would Rhodomela fire her? Coralline bit her lip to control her urge to cry; if Rhodomela saw her crying, she would definitely fire her.

"What's that?" Rhodomela asked.

Coralline followed her gaze to the invitation scroll on her tray. Under the present circumstances, with her dismissal all but imminent, she could not bear the thought of inviting Rhodomela to her engagement party and wedding. But nor could she think of a graceful way to bow out of inviting her, now that Rhodomela had seen the invitation scroll. Without a word, Coralline rose and handed the ivory parchment to her.

Rhodomela's fingers untied the golden ribbon, and her eyes scanned the parchment quickly. "You're making a mistake," she said, looking up. "You should not marry."

"Why not?"

"Because love is a farce."

It was not Rhodomela's fault, Coralline told herself, continuing to bite her lip. It was Rhodomela's life that had turned her bitter. Her parents had been mysteriously murdered twenty-five years ago in the middle of the night, when Rhodomela had been twenty-five herself. Rhodomela continued to mourn them to this day; since their death, no one had ever seen her attired in anything but a plain black bodice. Her only living family member was an elder sister, Osmundea, who lived in the distant village of Velvet Horn and who was also said to be a spinster.

Coralline recalled what her mother had once said about Rhodomela: "The Bitter Spinster's pain has numbed her to all emotion."

"I love Ecklon," Coralline said softly. "Have you ever loved anyone?"

Rhodomela's face whitened.

"I'm sorry," Coralline said, a flush creeping up her neck, making the skin prickle. "It's none of my business. You don't have to answer—"

"Once. I loved once, long ago."

A large, circular bronze-and-black insignia glowed on the glass door, the letters O and D intertwined over a fishhook that slashed the circle in half. Antares and Saiph sat to the other side of the glass, laughing so hard that they failed to notice him.

From the other side of the glass, Izar felt as though he were observing a private scene, a father-son moment he had no business witnessing. He knew that if either of them were to turn to see his face at this moment, they would see him staring at them with the desperate loneliness of an orphan—the orphan that he was.

His mind traveled back to the day he had met them. Suddenly, he was three years old again. The moon was glowing like a low-hanging white pear in the sky, and the wind was whipping his hair mercilessly about his cheeks. The jagged gash along the side of his jaw was bleeding a scarlet trail down his neck. He was trying to stanch the flow of his blood with his hands, but he couldn't—there was always more, and then more still—surely, it would all trickle out of him until he was a crumpled sack of skin. Antares's hand on his shoulder had been the only thing that had steadied him that night.

Kneeling to be close to Izar's eye level, Antares had asked, "Do you remember anything of your life before this day, son?"

Izar had tried to remember—he'd tried so hard that tears had squirted out of his eyes—but his mind had been as empty of memories as the sky above of clouds. "Who am I?" he'd asked in a trembling voice.

"Your name is Izar," Antares had said, speaking slowly, as though to aid Izar's comprehension. "You're the son of one of my fishermen. I was passing by in a trawler in the middle of the night, and I saw merpeople attacking your father's fishing dinghy. Merpeople drowned your parents, but I managed to rescue you from their clutches."

"Why did they drown my parents?" Izar had asked.

"Because they're evil. They're vicious savages."

Izar had attempted anew to conjure images of his parents in his mind, but there'd been nothing—not a whisper, not a glimpse, not a scent of them. He had felt as though he was standing before a mirror but seeing no reflection.

"I'm sorry for your loss. From this moment on, you should consider me your father, just as I will consider you my son."

Antares had carted him to the Office of the Police Commissioner of Menkar. The chief police commissioner, a moustachioed man named Canopus Corvus, had written a brief report on Antares's description of the human-merpeople altercation. A reporter from the newspaper *Menkar Daily* had simultaneously interviewed Antares for an article. Meanwhile, Doctor Navi, summoned by Antares, had stitched and bandaged the gash along Izar's jaw.

By the time Antares had taken Izar home, the sky had been bright with morning light. He had taken Izar straight to the backyard. Saiph had been playing in the grass, his hair like smooth, heavy waves of sand—just like Antares's at the time. Izar had gleaned at a glance that Saiph was Antares's son. Two years older than Izar, standing a head taller, Saiph had crossed his arms over his chest and glared at Izar. Meanwhile, Antares had knelt in the grass, unclasped a large wooden box, and turned it over. An assortment of wood blocks had tumbled out—squares, rectangles, triangles, circles, semicircles. "Build me a replica of our home, boys," Antares had demanded.

Izar's shoulders had slumped with tiredness, his jaw had throbbed mercilessly, but he'd sensed that Antares was not a man to tolerate protest. He'd looked at the house, memorized its lines, then commenced his construction. He and Saiph had completed their models at the same time. Izar's had been square, three stories high, as tall as himself, with semicircular windows like half-open eyes, and a roof embedded with a circular skylight; the edifice had been a precise replica of the house. Saiph's structure had risen to his knees, its shape haphazard, its lines crude; it had borne no resemblance to this home or any other. "Excellent work, Izar," Antares had said, beaming.

Excellent work, Izar—perhaps Antares would pronounce the words today as well, when Izar told him of Castor. Izar knocked on the glass door. Antares and Saiph jerked their heads in his direction simultaneously. Izar flashed his identification card against the scanner outside the door and entered.

Striding through a fog of cigar smoke, he pumped Antares's and Saiph's hands in greeting. He then settled into the chair next to Saiph, such that both he and Saiph were facing Antares from across Antares's grand mahogany desk. Antares poured him a glass of whisky and lit him a cigar. Izar took the glass and grasped the thick, dirt-brown stick between two fingers. He didn't care for cigars—he was driven by fumes from his underwater-fire work, not smokes—but cigars and whisky formed a ritual at their weekly meetings, as fundamental as the handshakes preceding them.

He glanced out the thirtieth-floor window. Skyscrapers loomed over Menkar's shores as bright, glassy rectangles interspersed with long-fingered palm trees. Located along the southeastern coast of America, Menkar was among the largest cities in the country, and, in Izar's opinion, the greatest. He had not been born in Menkar but wished he had been, for he loved the dry, dusty city.

He turned back to face Antares, who was sitting deep in his leather chair, a cigar dangling out of the side of his mouth, steel-gray eyes gleaming beneath tufty gray eyebrows. "Updates, vice presidents," Antares commanded.

The atmosphere changed subtly but perceptibly; by mentioning their titles, Antares transformed from their father to their boss. Izar and Saiph sat straighter and patted the buttons of their pin-striped suit jackets. Saiph began with his update first, as always.

"In the last week, I terminated a dozen men whose roles had become redundant. I fired another five who disagreed with me."

"Good." Antares nodded, sipping his whisky. "Everyone's a resource, boys, and every resource has a shelf life. Now, what's the update on Ocean Protection?"

"I'm continuing to keep an eye on the organization," Saiph replied. "They've been rallying dozens of people to their protests outside our building, with signs that say we're murdering the oceans."

"What have those loonies taken to calling the three of us these days?"

"The Trio of Tyrants." Saiph scoffed.

"Those nutcases would have us believe that just because the upper half of the merperson body resembles ours," Antares said, "they are equal to us rather than inferior. But regardless of Ocean Protection's idiotic beliefs, we would be wise to not underestimate them. Their supporters keep growing, not to mention their media coverage. So long as we avoid environmental fiascos like oil spills, though, they won't have anything specific to rally against."

"Agreed," said Saiph.

"And your update, Izar?" Antares asked. Izar wondered whether he'd imagined it, but a note of hope seemed to have lifted Antares's voice at the end.

Izar leaned forward in his chair, his fingers tense around his cigar. He'd waited six long years to make his announcement, but now that the time had come, he found he did not have the words. "Castor's ready," was all he managed.

Antares bolted out from behind his desk and squashed Izar in a hug.

The smell of smoke was strong on Antares, every pore exuding it—it made Izar think viscerally of Castor. He clutched Antares back and breathed deeply, feeling that a massive weight had been lifted off him. So heavily had Castor weighed on his mind that it was as though the twenty-foot-tall robot had been standing on him all these years. But every failure and disappointment Izar had undergone during his underwater-fire mission, each of the thousands of hours he'd spent on Castor—were all worth it, just for this one embrace from his father. He would do anything, invent anything, even another moon, to win Antares's approval.

When Antares returned to his chair, Izar fell into his own seat, dazed with happiness.

"Thirty-five years ago, when I was younger than both of you," Antares said, "I started Ocean Dominion, with no more than the spare change in my pocket. For almost all of Ocean Dominion's existence, the company was a fishing enterprise. Then, two years ago, you, Izar, tripled our revenues when you created our second division, Oil. Our stock price multiplied tenfold in response, such that it sits at an astounding one thousand dollars today."

A warmth flooded Izar's chest.

"From the company's very first days, I dreamt of one day plundering the oceans for precious metals and minerals. Today, you're making my dream a reality, Izar. You're leading us single-handedly to our third bloodline of business. Your underwater-fire breakthrough will enable us to mine for jewels not in depleted mountains but in the depths of the seabed. Think of how much more valuable a pound of gold or diamonds is in comparison to a pound of oil, let alone a pound of fish. We're going to make trillions of dollars, boys—*trillions*—all thanks to you, Izar."

The glow on Izar's face rivaled that on the tip of his cigar, resulting more from Antares's praise than from the prospect of wealth beyond measure. Izar did not particularly care for more money, for there was nothing in his life he would change with it. He viewed excess wealth as an umbrella—useful on rainy days but otherwise unworthy of much contemplation.

Turning to Saiph, Antares asked, "Is Castor's patent ready?"

"Yes." Saiph's teeth flashed white below chiseled cheekbones. "The Patent Office originally gave Ocean Dominion a patent for one year, but I paid an acquaintance to pull some strings and extend it to two years."

The patent was the one area of Castor's life in which Izar had played no role. Antares had assigned the matter to Saiph from the beginning, to Izar's relief. Managing relationships with external stakeholders, associates, and allies was Saiph's territory. Saiph inherently knew whom to talk to, how to get things done, how to keep the right people dancing about his thumbs.

"A two-year patent!" Antares exclaimed. His smile revealed tobacco-stained teeth, and his fist pounded the table, sloshing whisky over the rim of his glass. "Two years, before any other company can start mining the oceans for gold and diamonds. By the end of the patent, there'll be nothing left for anyone else!" Antares guffawed, white smoke surrounding his mirth in the shadows of dusk. "Our stock price will sky-rocket when I announce our third division, Precious Metals and Minerals. When shall I hold the press conference?"

"We're drilling oil again in a few days," Izar said, thinking out loud, "on the fifteenth of July. The day happens to mark exactly two years since we began the Oil division. As such, I think the evening of the fifteenth—the two-year milestone of our second division—would be an opportune time to announce the launch of our third division."

"That sounds fine," Antares said. "But stock prices rumble when press conferences are canceled. A cancelation won't be needed, will it?"

"No. I give you my word."

Izar tried to avoid it, but his gaze traveled to the framed picture of Maia on Antares's desk. There was a perfunctory aspect to her presence in Antares's office—her picture was something necessary but not necessarily wanted, like the coatrack on which Antares's black suit jacket hung. She'd had dark, shoulder-length hair, a haughty chin, and charred-kale eyes that Saiph had inherited. Though he'd been only three when he'd first met her, Izar still remembered how her face had cooled when she'd seen him—it had been like custard hardening. "He belongs to one of your mistresses," she'd said to Antares, without anger, without vehemence, as though she were simply stating a fact.

"He's the son of one of my fishermen," Antares had retorted. "I rescued him from the clutches of merpeople. You'll see an article about it in *Menkar Daily* tomorrow morning."

Maia had been opposed to Antares's desire to adopt Izar, but, for a reason Izar still didn't understand, Antares had insisted. Maia had nonetheless continued to resent Izar's "illegitimate" presence in her home. To keep him out of her sight, she'd given him a storage closet in the basement as a bedroom. She'd hired the best tutors money could buy for Saiph; Izar had had to make do with Saiph's old school textbooks and uniforms. But Saiph's grades had still rarely exceeded mediocre, whereas Izar's had always been stellar, without his actively trying.

At school, Saiph and his friends had chased Izar as cats chase a mouse, and Izar had escaped like a mouse, darting into any alley, into any trash can, into any corner he could fit in. Antares had been the only one who'd been kind to Izar in those childhood years, but he'd rarely been home, returning home late every night, sometimes smelling of stale perfume. Izar's moments with him had felt coveted and stolen, like crumbs of bread rather than a slice; he'd always felt hungry after, but crumbs were all he'd had.

By the time Izar had become an adolescent, his intellectual curiosity had shifted from his textbooks to the way things worked. He would sit on the floor of his storage closet, ringed by a fortress of rubble and parts. One night, when he was sixteen, Maia discovered him with his head and hands in the hood of her luxury car.

Tugging his hands out, she'd slapped his face.

"I just wanted to know how the engine works," he'd protested in a hurt voice.

Antares's car had pulled onto the cobblestone driveway just then.

"Your mistress's son is trying to kill me," Maia had snapped at him.

"I'm losing patience with you," Antares had said in a tightly controlled voice, stepping out of his car. "I think you should visit a psychiatrist. I'll take you to one myself tomorrow."

"Don't bother! I'm going to meet with a divorce attorney first thing tomorrow morning."

But she'd never made it to a divorce attorney's office—her car had exploded on the highway. She'd died instantly.

The Office of the Police Commissioner of Menkar had opened an investigation into the case. The prosecution had fought to send Izar to jail for life, but Antares had settled the case out of court: He'd paid moustachioed chief police commissioner Canopus Corvus half a million dollars to bury the case. Izar had felt as small as a worm in those days. Not only had he killed Antares's wife, even if by accident—though, to this day, he could not fathom how his brief exploration had resulted in an explosion—but Antares had had to spend heftily to save him.

Now, Izar met Antares's gaze across the mahogany desk. Antares's steel-gray eyes wore a strange look—Izar knew they were both thinking of Maia's funeral.

Antares had wept that day as Izar had never seen a grown man weep, as he hoped to never again see a grown man weep. It was at Maia's funeral that Izar had learned that love could be contradictory and conflicting and flawed, and it was then that he'd determined that his love, if he were ever to love a woman, would be neither contradictory nor conflicting nor flawed—it would be a pure, clear river flowing consistently over both rocks and shallows.

3

A Constellation of Stars

Coralline tucked Naiadum's blanket around his shoulders.

"Read me a story!" he demanded, his pudgy cheeks pink with anticipation.

"Yesterday, I read you *The Wandering Cardinalfish*," she said, tousling his golden hair, so like their mother's. "What would you like me to read you today?"

She ran her index finger over the spines of story books stacked on his bedside table: *The Sneaky Snipefish*, *The Sly Sergeant Major*, and *The Legend of the Elixir*.

Turning his head to examine the titles, he piped, "*The Legend of the Elixir*."

Coralline had been hoping he'd select one of the other two, but she nodded and opened the requested book on her lap.

"The story of the elixir is the oldest legend of the ocean," she read aloud in a deep voice. "The elixir is a life-saving potion made of starlight, prepared by a magician named Mintaka. Over the millennia, countless individuals have embarked on quests for the elixir, in order to save the life of a loved one, but only a rare few have succeeded in finding Mintaka and her elusive elixir. Even those who have succeeded are said to have been doomed, in a sense, for the elixir is a blessing that comes accompanied by a curse—"

"Is this legend a true story?" Naiadum asked, his amber-gold eyes wide.

"No one knows for certain, but I can't imagine how it would be a true story. I can't imagine how an elixir can be made of starlight."

"Me neither."

Coralline smiled. Though he was only eight, Naiadum sometimes thought like a detective, reminding her of Ecklon.

"Do you know anyone who's found the elixir?" Naiadum pursued.

"No one has found it in my lifetime, but I did hear someone found it about thirty years ago. . . . Now, let's continue with the story: The curse varies based on the individual—"

"I don't like *The Legend of the Elixir*," Naiadum pouted.

"I don't blame you. I don't understand why it's even considered a children's story." Coralline fell silent for a moment, then said, "Do you know who I'm going to miss more than anyone else when I get married and leave home?"

"Who?"

"You." She wouldn't watch him grow up a little every day, she wouldn't help him with his homework, she wouldn't read him bedtime stories every night.

"I'll miss you too." Frowning, he pulled his blanket up to his chin.

"What's the matter, Naiadum?"

"I can't sleep these days."

"Why not?"

"Because you're leaving."

He looked suddenly deflated, smaller under his blanket. Tears welled in Coralline's eyes, and her lower lip quivered, but, manufacturing a smile, she said conspiratorially, "Want to know my secret to falling asleep every night?"

"What?" he asked, his eyes bright again.

"Looking at the stars."

"But there are no stars in the ocean."

"There are."

Coralline looked up at the luciferin orbs traversing the low, dome-shaped ceiling like slow-motion comets. Strings of light pulsed within the glassy spheres, casting a white-blue glow over the room. "You know a story I tell myself every night?" she whispered.

It created the effect she'd desired. "What?" Naiadum whispered back.

"I pretend each luciferin orb is a galaxy of stars, and the galaxies are traveling the universe."

Naiadum contemplated the orbs newly, his eyes reflecting their glow. "How do luciferin orbs create light?" he asked. "Is it magic?"

"Not quite. The orbs are full of a bacteria that contains luciferin, a compound that generates light in the presence of oxygen, assisted by an enzyme called luciferase. Luciferin light is a form of bioluminescence, which means light created by living organisms. You know, I've always found it fascinating that among the smallest entities in the universe, bacteria, can produce what is otherwise produced by the largest entities: stars."

Naiadum looked hopelessly confused. She should have provided him with a simpler explanation, Coralline thought, one more suited to his age. He pondered the orbs, then his gaze returned to hers. "I've never seen the sky before," he said. "I want to look at real stars, not pretend-stars. Can we go up to the surface now and look at the stars?"

"*No!*" Gathering her breath, Coralline tried to hide her alarm at his suggestion. "The surface is not safe. Humans are often there in their ships, with fishnets ready to trap and kill."

"But I want to crest," he whined. "When can I crest?"

"In eight years, when you turn sixteen."

"Why can't I crest sooner?"

"Because the Children Anti-Cresting Act of the Under-Ministry of Youth Matters forbids it."

His face fell.

"You're not missing out, Naiadum. I crested when I was sixteen, and I certainly never want to return to the surface again."

Coralline hadn't even wanted to crest, but her mother had insisted, for it was tradition to crest on the day one turned sixteen. Her parents had cheered her nervously from below as her head had broken out over the waves, her neck remaining submerged so that her gills could continue to breathe. The sky had been empty and the sun piercing, and the rays of light had pricked her pupils and wrung hot tears from her eyes. The waves had thrashed her about, and she'd found their temper appropriate—the surface was violent, like the men who trod upon it.

"But how will anyone know if I swim up to the surface?" Naiadum asked. "I'll know."

"Not if you're not looking," he said, a mischievous glint in his eye.

"I'll always be looking for you." Coralline brushed his hair off his forehead. "Dreams are for *after* you sleep, not before. Now, admire the stars in your room and close your eyes, you dreaming crester."

"I adore Yacht," gushed Ascella Auriga. "It's such an artfully designed restaurant. I even love the name. Did you know, I practically grew up on yachts? Daddy owned such a large fleet of them."

Izar cast a glance about him. The restaurant's dark, gold-specked floor tiles were polished enough to double as mirrors. Black pillars soared toward the ceiling, vaulted with birds perched on leafless branches, poised to fly but caged into sculptured stillness.

His chair was wide and cushioned, but he sat as stiffly as though upon an iron bench. He had no choice but to be here; it was the most expensive restaurant in Menkar, and thus Ascella's favorite restaurant. Their first date had been here. Since then, the place had become a monthly ritual for them; now, they sat across from each other at their twelfth dinner here, celebrating Ascella's birthday.

On their first date, Izar had glanced at the patrons at other tables and felt ashamed of his crinkled suit, with its faint smell of combustion fumes, his shoes, their soles filthy and scraped, and his belt, its leather wearing like rubber from an old tire. He'd almost choked to see the tab at the end of the dinner—two thousand dollars. Their next visits to Yacht had seen him gradually changed, with clean nails, creamed hair, and tailor-made suits.

His transformation had been aided by a morbidly obese etiquette consultant who, over the course of several tedious hours-long sessions, had instructed him on the pairing of wines with food, the utensils to use for different courses, and the advantages of setting up advance tabs at restaurants. Izar had never told Ascella about the etiquette consultant. To her, etiquette and social graces happened naturally—there was no more need to teach them than to teach walking. But indulgent dining was not Izar's first language the way it was hers—the consultant had helped him interpret some of its mysterious undertones.

As Izar had invented Castor in his Invention Chamber, he had reinvented himself in order to be admitted to Yacht. At his Chamber, he flashed an identification card to gain admittance; at Yacht, he flashed a credit card. As Castor had had many iterations, Izar had improved himself each time he'd been here. And each time, he'd hoped to feel comfortable, as though he belonged, but it had not yet happened. At the moment, he felt as constrained as though his silver-gray tie were a noose. He would much rather have eaten take-out dinner on the floor of his Invention Chamber than dine at Yacht.

"This coming week will be incredibly busy and eventful for me at work," Ascella said.

In the champagne glow of the chandelier, Izar thought her ear-length hair resembled pale gold silk. He found himself admiring her silver-sequined, floor-length designer gown, held up by a single strap.

"Tarazed arrives tomorrow—"

"Tarazed?" Izar asked.

"Yes, remember? I told you." Ascella's eyes glimmered the cold, pale blue of morning frost, and her poppy-red lips puckered. "We're hosting a special exhibition for Tarazed next week at my art gallery, Abstract. Tarazed is the world's most renowned modern expressionist."

"Right. Of course. I remember Tarazed now."

Izar had seen pictures of the flamboyant forty-year-old painter in newspapers. He had dark hair and dark eyes and cheeks that sprouted with stubble like a profusion of weeds. He wore shirts that resembled the jarring lines of his artwork, but little of their design was visible in the photos Izar had seen—numerous women were always hanging over his arms.

Izar had forgotten about Tarazed only because he was distracted by thoughts of Castor. Throughout dinner, he'd been waiting for an opportunity to tell Ascella that he'd invented underwater fire, but they were now on their dessert course, a square of cocoa-dusted hazelnut tart, and she'd been speaking incessantly about art.

"I'm going to be Tarazed's escort while he's in Menkar," Ascella continued.

Izar's dessert fork paused mid-air. "His escort?"

"Yes. His personal escort. I'll show him all the sights the city has to offer."

"Is it usual for a curator to serve as an escort to an artist?"

"It's not, but the relationship with Tarazed is an important one for Abstract, given his artistic status."

"I see."

"I've admired his work for so long," she said dreamily. "I've been counting the days to his visit."

Though Ascella worked at an art gallery, Izar had never been to an art gallery. In his field of invention and engineering, precision was key—every bolt mattered, and a single misplaced screw or nail could ruin the whole. In abstract art, in contrast, there were no standards of value that he could discern; the concept of value itself seemed subverted, for the most absurd pieces seemed to fetch the most absurd prices.

Izar's world and Ascella's were entirely different, and they would never have intersected if not for Saiph. Saiph had met Ascella while requisitioning a Tarazed art piece for his office. The next day, he had introduced Izar and Ascella at a cocktail party he'd organized at a bar. Izar hadn't known how Saiph had guessed Izar would be infatuated with Ascella immediately, but he had known it, and Izar had been. Izar still remembered how Ascella had looked that night, a year ago, her hair lustrous, her nose pert, her neck long and smooth. An ivory dress had caressed her long curves and an ivory purse had dangled at her elbow, as she'd sipped a cloudy drink. She'd been surrounded by men, but she'd also stood apart from them, as conspicuous in their midst as a gazelle among rhinoceroses.

The scar along the left side of Izar's jaw had, for the first time, prickled with self-consciousness. He'd hoped she wouldn't notice it, but her eyes had traced its hook-shaped line from his earlobe almost to his lip. She'd frowned at it, as at chipped nail varnish. It was not just the physical mark of the scar that had given her pause, Izar thought, but the fact that it hinted at harshly different upbringings. Yes, Izar had been adopted by Antares, a wealthy businessman, but his biological father had been an impoverished fisherman; Ascella, meanwhile, was the daughter of a billionaire real estate tycoon.

A lanky waiter bowed obsequiously before refilling their glasses with the thousand-dollar vintage red wine they'd ordered. Upon his departure, Izar grasped the stem of his glass close to the base and swirled the wine just as his etiquette consultant had taught him to do, bringing his nose close for a whiff. The wine smelled a little like his old sneakers, but, smothering the thought, he took a sip.

"Happy twenty-seventh birthday, my love," he said, putting his wineglass down. He extended Ascella a black velvet box across the eggshell tablecloth.

She opened it. Even from across the table, Izar could see the brace-let's rose-cut and princess-cut diamonds flashing thousands of shards of brilliance across the restaurant, across the smile crescenting her face, across her shoulders, which glowed just a shade fairer than snow, and across her eyes, which sparkled like frost melting in the spring sun. She extended him her hand, and their fingers intertwined over the tablecloth.

But it was ironic, he thought for the first time: Jewelry was the most expensive thing in the world, yet it was also the least functional thing in the world. Now that he thought about it, jewelry posed, for him, a similar contradiction as abstract art, with its dichotomy between price and value.

"Ascella," he said softly, leaning forward, "I've invented underwater fire."

She sat back and stared at him, her eyes cooling. "You can't have," she said. "Underwater fire is impossible, a fantasy."

Izar neutralized his expression so that she would not learn how deeply her words hurt him. He looked at the candle flame at the center of the table, at how delicately it flickered. At one point in the history of humanity, even this miniature flame would have been considered a miracle.

Avoiding her eyes, he clasped the bracelet over her wrist. Beaming at it as at a friend, she tilted her wrist this way and that, and the diamonds shimmered even more brightly.

He would prove his breakthrough to her soon enough, Izar told himself. After all, the thirty-thousand-dollar diamond bracelet he'd just given her formed a paltry substitute for what he truly wished to give her: a ring that would make other rings look like gaudy trinkets, a ring of the sort to which no other woman could lay claim, a ring that would be mined by Castor from the depths of the ocean and fashioned by Izar's own hands in his Invention Chamber—a ring that would glitter like a constellation of stars upon her finger.

4

Intellect and Intuition

Coralline dawdled outside the door of The Irregular Remedy. She saw red from the corner of her eye and turned toward it. Rosette Delesse stood staring at her from the remedial garden of The Conventional Cure. There were no flasks or snippers in her hands—it seemed to have been the sight of Coralline that had drawn her out among the algae. She stared at Coralline's rose petal tellin as though a magic spell could rip it off and transfer it to her own throat. Closing her hand over the shell, Coralline hurried through the door of The Irregular Remedy.

Coralline knew Rhodomela was waiting for her in the back office, but Coralline was alone in The Irregular Remedy only rarely, and she looked about the small space with the hunger of a trespasser. Her gaze caressed the shale walls, the low ceiling, the two counters crisscrossed by scratches, the narrow stretcher, and her beloved unit of shelves, stacked with white-gray limestone urns. How little the sight of the urns meant to a passerby, but how much it meant to her, the contents of each prepared painstakingly by her own hand.

She lingered before an article in a scuffed sandstone frame close to the door. Its ink was faded, as was the portrait accompanying it, but Coralline recognized Rhodomela by the hooked angle of her nose. Her cheeks had been full then, and there'd been a softness about her eyes that had alluded to an ephemeral beauty. Titled "A Young Master," the article from *The Annals of the Association of Apothecaries* stated that Rhodomela was the youngest person in the whole nation of Meristem to ever have achieved the title of master apothecary, at a mere twenty-five years of age.

Five rungs defined a typical healer's path: apprentice, associate, senior, manager, then, only for some, the coveted title of master. The Association of Apothecaries typically awarded the title of master not on the basis of experience but of invention: A healer had to devise a novel, life-saving medication to attain the title. Rhodomela had invented a solution called Black Poison Cleanser, which had propelled her in rank from associate to master apothecary, skipping the two rungs in between.

Rhodomela had founded The Irregular Remedy within a week of attaining her new title. Most healers started practices at a respectable distance from other clinics, in order to reduce competition, but Rhodomela had started The Irregular Remedy next door to The Conventional Cure, which had always rejected her on account of her nontraditional techniques. Though Rhodomela was just one person, and healers at The Conventional Cure numbered half a dozen on a typical day, The Irregular Remedy had, over its twenty-five years of existence, slowly but steadily supplanted The Conventional Cure to become the best regarded clinic in Urchin Grove, the place where the most confounding medical cases were solved.

Taking a deep breath, Coralline knocked on the door to the back office. "Enter," called an imperious voice.

Coralline slipped inside the back office. It had a low ceiling and two tiny windows that formed circular tears in the abraded walls. It was intended to be a supplies room, but it was not used as such, nor was it quite furnished as an office. Its minimal windows made it almost as dark as a cave, yet only two luciferin orbs traveled the ceiling.

Rhodomela frowned at Coralline from a high stool behind a tall slate desk. Coralline perched on the stool across from Rhodomela, feeling as though she'd been summoned to the school principal's office for misbehavior.

Her elbows resting on the desk, Rhodomela leaned forward, her snake-like eyes peering at Coralline. "You're diligent and hard-working," she said. "You arrive early, and you leave late. But, other than yesterday, during Agarum's heart attack, have you ever prepared medication without relying on a textbook? Have you ever devised anything of your own?"

"No." This was not how Coralline had expected her probationary review to begin.

"Precisely. That's because you rely on your intellect, but you reject your intuition."

"What does intuition have to do with anything?" Coralline asked, pronouncing the word "intuition" like it was the name of an algae she was encountering for the first time.

"Everything. It was my intuition rather than my intellect that led me to save Agarum during his heart attack. Intuition thrives in the presence of courage and conviction but falters in the face of fear—fear, such as that of blood."

Coralline flinched. How long had Rhodomela known?

"I noticed your fear of blood in your first week here. I didn't say anything, because I hoped you would rid yourself of it. But you didn't. You don't understand that in order to heal others, you have to first heal yourself. You don't understand that fear and success cannot co-exist any more than can day and night. The reason you consult your medical textbooks endlessly is that you fear being wrong or looking foolish. You think that by doing what other healers have done, you will become as good as them. But success is an outcome not of imitation but of authenticity—of not abiding by the rules but changing them. The questions are more important than the answers."

"What does this mean for my future at The Irregular Remedy?"

"The Irregular Remedy is a place for those who think irregularly. You don't. As such, I'm sorry to say that you have no future here."

Just yesterday, Coralline had been snipping algae in the remedial garden and treating patients at her counter. How could it all end so suddenly? "I rejected offers from other clinics to work for you," she stammered. "I rejected jobs that paid twice what you offered me."

"I'm sure other clinics would still be happy to have you. I believe your style and personality would be most suited to The Conventional Cure. I'd be happy to refer you."

It was a slap to the face, Rhodomela's recommendation to refer Coralline to the clinic she reviled.

"You never told me why you hired me," Coralline said, tears pricking her pupils, "when you'd never hired anyone else."

"You never asked."

"I'm asking now."

"Your father was an extraordinary coral connoisseur. Even though he's now retired, he continues to know coral reefs better than anyone else in Urchin Grove."

"What does that have to do with me?"

"I hired you because I was hoping you'd be your father's daughter. I've discovered, however, that you are your mother's."

Red, blue, and yellow flashed before Coralline's eyes—primary colors that reflected her primary emotions. How dare Rhodomela speak to her as such? How dare Rhodomela look down on Abalone?

"My mother is right about you!" Coralline snapped. "You truly are a Bitter Spinster. Your meanness drives everyone away. Everyone in Urchin Grove hates you!"

"I know."

Coralline's cheeks flamed at her own vitriol, and tears trickled from her eyes, water meeting water, salt meeting salt. She erupted out of her stool and whirled around to leave. Her hand was on the doorknob, when Rhodomela called quietly, "Coralline."

She turned. She hoped Rhodomela would apologize, then Coralline would also apologize. She admired Rhodomela; she didn't care what anyone else said about her; she owed Rhodomela a lifetime of gratitude for having saved her father—these were the things Coralline would say, and then Rhodomela would say that she wanted Coralline to continue to work at The Irregular Remedy, that there'd been some horrible misunderstanding.

"Your medical badge, please."

Coralline glanced down at the sand-dollar badge pinned to her corset just above her heart. The shell was a smooth white circle engraved with the words, in small black letters: *Coralline Costaria, Apprentice Apothecary*. With trembling fingers, she unpinned the badge from her corset, turned it over, and read the words on its back: *Association of Apothecaries*. Printed and provided by the Association, it was this badge that gave Coralline license to practice. She was required to wear it anytime she was treating anyone other than herself.

As she handed the badge to Rhodomela, she felt as though she were handing over part of her own palpitating heart.

Izar did not know what had compelled him to Mira on this day specifically, but he had canceled his meetings, boarded a cabin cruiser, and steered himself to the one place Antares had warned him to always avoid: the island of his birth. *The ghosts of your past will only haunt you*, Antares had said.

And so, as Izar disembarked on the brittle sands of Mira, he could not help feeling he was betraying Antares. But he swallowed his guilt and, hands on his hips, looked about him. His nose wrinkled—there was a powerful stink of rotting fish and a sense of death and decay among the flaking palm trees. Children emerged out of doorways and stared at him, their knees knobby and faces sweaty, their arms dirt stained. Izar must have looked just like them before Antares had adopted him.

Mira had been flooded some years ago—Ocean Protection had decried the flood as a symptom of climate change—and the paltry population of fishermen had plummeted. Fewer than a hundred families lived on the scrappy sands today, compared to three hundred families a decade ago. And so, as Izar strode on the sands, he had the sense that he was walking in the shadow of a place rather than the place itself. Spotting a fisherman on the shore, he stopped to ask the bedraggled old man, "Where can I find the home of Heze and Capella Virgo?"

The man squinted suspiciously at Izar's sunglasses, cleanly shaven face, and collared shirt. But his gnarled hand pointed, and Izar followed. When he reached the house in question, he identified it by a sign on its door: *The Virgo Residence.*

The formality of the sign seemed an attempt at self-deprecating humor, for the place was a hovel that had rusted upon itself. Its tin roof was dented in the center, and its doorway was so low that Izar had to bend his neck to fit through. He came to stand in what he supposed was the living room, but it was the size of his childhood basement storage closet. The floorboards squished beneath his feet, spongy and frayed like limp asparagus.

Izar fell to the floorboards on his knees, in order to be closer to the eye level of the toddler he once had been. He stared at the fissures in the walls and ran his hands over the scabs on the floor. He hoped to recognize something, anything, that would tell him that this hovel had been his home until the age of three. Often during the last twenty-five years, he had felt hollow and unmoored, like an empty shell, and he'd longed for some memories to clam onto when tossed about by the currents of life, but he'd had nothing. He'd hoped desperately to find something here, in his childhood home, but it could just as well have been a stranger's home—no recollections flew forth in his mind.

Even the meteors that crashed into the surface of the earth could be traced back to where they'd begun, their trajectories plotted with a degree of accuracy. How could his own past be such a black hole? It was as though his memory had been systematically wiped clean the night of his parents' death, like a computer's hard drive erased upon a command.

He had often been told he was fortunate to have been adopted by Antares, and he had often thought it, but he had never felt it as he did now, in his very pores. He had often thought about the trials he himself had undergone, but only now, as he knelt on the floor of his childhood home, did he properly consider the trials Antares had undergone on his behalf. Antares had risked his life to dive into the ocean and rescue Izar from merpeople, and he had carved a wedge in his marriage with Maia by adopting Izar.

Izar found himself irritated by the lone furnishing in the hovel, a bright blue pail. Water dripped into it slowly but steadily from a leak in the roof; the splash of the droplets, low though the sound was, grated on his nerves by its incessance. He watched a droplet as it struck the surface of water in the pail. The surface fragmented then settled, becoming smooth and flat as a mirror, only to be shattered by the next droplet. As Izar watched, a reflection materialized in the pail, a reflection of a thickset man with a sun-sizzled face as furrowed as downtrodden leather.

Jumping to his feet, Izar whirled around.

The man narrowed his eyes at Izar, but the effect of the narrowing was lost—his deep-blue eyes had squinted so much that they'd become permanently narrowed, the pupils unable to expand or contract even indoors.

"Who are ye?" he slurred, his breath smelling of stale beer.

"I'm Izar, the son of Heze and Capella Virgo. Who are you?"

"Rigel Nihal. I lived beside Heze and Capella Virgo for a decade before they died." Rigel pointed his thumb in the presumed direction of his own hovel. "Ye cannot be their son."

"Why not?"

"Because that boy is dead. I buried him meself."

Izar blinked, stunned.

"Most kind folk I ever met, Heze and Capella Virgo," Rigel continued. "Most mysterious death I ever saw. Heze never fished at night, but the night he died, someone forced him out onto the water—forced him to drag Capella and the boy with him. Capella cried and screamed, and I came out of me home at her shouts, but Heze dragged her and the boy onto his fishing dinghy. I asked him why he was taking his wife and boy onto the sea, when he otherwise never did. He said he couldn't tell me, but it was important, said his job with Ocean Dominion depended on it.

"When I woke up in the morning, I saw that all the fishermen of Mira had gathered on the shore. They told me that Heze, Capella, and the boy were all dead. I steered meself into the water and found the three bodies. I brought them back in me dinghy and buried them next to one another. I called the chief police commissioner of Menkar, Canopus Corvus, the man with the handlebar moustache. I told him he should investigate the deaths. He told me he already knew what had happened: Heze and Capella Virgo had been drowned by merpeople, while their son had been rescued. I said that Heze and Capella looked like they'd been bludgeoned by a man, not drowned by merpeople, as did the boy himself—who was dead. Canopus had the nerve to tell me I was lying, but I put aside me dignity"—Izar couldn't imagine him having any—"and begged him to come see the bodies. He said he would send someone to take a look the next morning. But the next morning, all three bodies had been stolen from the grave—someone stole them overnight!"

"You're lying."

Izar's fists clenched and unclenched compulsively at his sides, and blood pounded into his head, turning his eyes bloodshot. Perhaps the degree of his anger was irrational, but everything that he knew about his past was little enough to be wrapped in a handkerchief, and Rigel was tearing holes in that meager fabric. How dare this drunkard fabricate stories about his parents, such farfetched and absurd tales?

"*I* am Heze and Capella Virgo's son," Izar reiterated through gritted teeth.

"That yer not! That boy is dead—dead as his parents, dead as this home, dead as this island. I held his dead body in me own hands!" He held out his hands, fingers splayed, palms dark and grainy. "Yer not who ye think ye are—"

49

"Stop talking."

"Don't ye see, through that thick skull of yers? Yer a pawn in a game, the same game that killed Heze and Capella, the same game that will kill ye—"

Izar's left arm curled, and though he recognized he shouldn't follow through, the realization dawned too late: The punch landed along the side of Rigel's jaw.

The man fell flat on his back, toppling the pail along the way. Water splattered Izar's shoes and seeped into Rigel's shirt. It also spread over the floorboards, which absorbed it as readily as a sponge. Cursing, Izar bent down to reinstate the pail below the leak. It was probably Rigel who'd placed the pail there, he thought now—in his own way, maybe Rigel *had* cared about Heze and Capella. Maybe Rigel had been unable to help the things he'd said—maybe he was not only drunk but mentally deranged, unable to comprehend the nonsense spewing out of his mouth. Yet there had been a lucidness to his voice.

Shaking out his fist, Izar examined it with regret. His punch was strong, too strong, because of the platinum chip in his wrist—it carried the strength of an anvil, Doctor Navi had told him. Izar had expected Rigel to stagger back, but not to collapse unconscious on the floor. Glancing at him one last time, Izar strode out the door, wishing he'd taken Antares's advice and never set foot on the island of Mira.

5

Friend

The next collision will be your last!" Pavonis growled. With his snout, he tossed up the merboy who'd happened to be lingering in his way.

The familiar sights around Coralline blended together in a blur of color as she clung with both hands to the dorsal fin on Pavonis's back. She saw homes of shale, standing encompassed by small, crescent-shaped gardens. She saw the majestic columns of the bank called Grove Trove, where her parents stored their conchs and whelks, shells worth fifty and a hundred carapace each. She saw Alaria, her favorite restaurant, where Ecklon had taken her for their first date and her birthday.

She breathed a sigh of relief when Pavonis came to rest in a kelp forest.

Sculpin fish rose at their sudden entrance, then settled again among the holdfasts of giant kelp—the shorthorn sculpin, dark and rock-like, and the longhorn sculpin, with long cheek spines and fan-like fins.

Pavonis had been circling The Irregular Remedy during Coralline's probationary review, so he already knew much of what had transpired, but Coralline recounted it to him nonetheless in a hushed whisper. "I'm so ashamed. . . . My dreams are dead. . . . And I feel awful for the things I said to Rhodomela in anger. . . ."

She leaned against the five vertical gill slits along Pavonis's side. Five feet long, they flared open and close in synchrony with her sobs. She wrapped her arms around as much of him as she could, which was not much. From the tip of his tailfin to his snout, Pavonis stretched to thirty feet, five times Coralline's length. He was a whale shark, the largest sort of shark in the world. Whale sharks were part of the shark family, not the whale family; the first half of their name related merely to their size and filtering pads—screens inside the mouth through which food filtered into the throat.

"You're the only one I've ever told of my fear of blood, but Rhodomela guessed it."

"For the life of me, I still can't understand your fear of blood," Pavonis drawled. "There's not a smell in the world to which I am more attuned than that of blood. That's how we met, in fact—through your blood."

When she'd been two years old, Coralline's mother had plopped her down on the window seat in the living room and had swum away to bustle about the kitchen. The currents had risen and, unseen by her mother, Coralline had drifted out among the dahlias and jewel anemones of the reef garden. Unable to swing her tailfin at that age, she'd been blown about the waters like a young snail, the currents lifting her higher and higher as they swelled. A golden mesh from an Ocean Dominion ship had descended like a delicate blanket from the surface, and her dimpled fingers had curled around it. But something sharp in the net, a flint of a hook, had scratched her arm, and a drop of blood had sprouted. A force larger than life itself had tossed her away from the net just in time, for the net had been tightening around her, about to haul her up to the waves. Upon Pavonis's push, she'd rolled and tumbled through the froth, giggling, her stomach tickled by her own speed. When she'd come to a stop, she'd marveled at his yellow-spotted back, and her tiny hands had clasped trustingly around his dorsal fin.

Pavonis had dived down vertically, and Coralline's stomach had churned at his descent, and she'd squeezed her eyes shut. When she'd opened them, she'd found that the two of them were at the center of a scene of confused commotion. Dozens of merpeople were gathered outside the Costaria home, for Abalone had been knocking on doors and shouting that her daughter had been abducted.

As soon as she'd seen Coralline with Pavonis, Abalone had pried her off his fin and fled with her indoors.

Undeterred, Pavonis had arrived at the living room window every afternoon to visit Coralline. Months later, when Coralline had grown a little and learned to flick her tailfin and swim on her own, she'd ambled out the window one afternoon while her mother was in the kitchen. She'd grabbed Pavonis's dorsal fin and he'd taken her for a turbulent, rumbling ride through Urchin Grove.

He'd returned her home in time for supper that evening, and every evening after over the next fourteen years, even when she enrolled at Urchin Apothecary Academy at sixteen years of age. When she'd bite her lip in trepidation before a test, he'd pull faces outside the classroom window, opening his mouth five feet wide, as only a whale shark could. His tunnel of a mouth, columned with three hundred teeth, would make her giggle.

Now, Coralline laid her cheek flat against Pavonis's side, her hands patting his ridges. "You also detected Father's blood the day of his haccident," she reminded him.

"Ah yes," Pavonis said. "We had another dream that day, remember? We were going to traverse the Atlantic from top to bottom. Our North-to-South Expedition was to be the greatest adventure of our lives. We were to leave immediately after your graduation from Urchin Apothecary Academy and to travel to places with deeper waters and wilder waves, before returning to Urchin Grove, forever changed by our adventure. . . ."

Coralline nodded guiltily. On this day, Rhodomela had crushed her dream of healing; on that day, seven months ago, Coralline had crushed Pavonis's dream of travel.

The day after her graduation, Coralline had waited at the window seat in the living room for her father to return home from work, so that she could tell him and her mother that she and Pavonis wished to embark on a North-to-South Expedition. Pavonis had lingered outside the window next to Coralline to ensure she didn't lose courage before the conversation—they both knew her parents would require considerable convincing to agree to the Expedition.

Together, Coralline and Pavonis had scanned the darkening evening waters for a hint of her father's copper tail. But Coralline's gaze had shifted to her family's reef garden, as new inhabitants had emerged one after another. A seven-foot-long conger eel had glided across the sediment, then a tiny cardinalfish had erupted from a crevice underneath an overhang, then a horseshoe crab had clambered onto a rock. The three heralds of the night had made her wring her hands and forget all about the North-to-South Expedition: Her father was a beacon of punctuality. Why was he late returning home from work? Had he been injured—or worse—by humans?

Suddenly, Pavonis's snout had twitched, and he'd departed with a sharp swing of his tail. He'd sniffed blood, Coralline had known from his reaction. She'd paced the living room, swimming back and forth, her glance flitting repeatedly to the sand-clock on the mantel, watching the trickle of sand from the upper to the lower ampoule. Most of the sand was collected now in the lower ampoule, for most of the day was gone. She only hoped the same could not be said for her father's life.

When Pavonis had returned, it had been with her father. He had been on the verge of unconsciousness, his left hand clutching Pavonis's dorsal fin just barely, his right hand creating a shroud of blood that surrounded him like an expanding cape, his tail as lusterless as the sand gathered underneath the doorjamb.

Had Pavonis not smelled his blood, her father would likely have died of blood loss at the site of the coral reef dynamite blast. As such, both Pavonis and Rhodomela had saved Coralline's father, Pavonis by finding him, Rhodomela by treating him. And yet Coralline had just spoken rudely to Rhodomela.

"You know I couldn't leave, Pavonis," Coralline said softly, brushing aside the large, bright-green fronds of kelp to look into his eye. "My family needed me."

"I understand," he rumbled.

"But I do still owe you an apology. I haven't been there for you when you've most needed me, in the last nine months since Mako's death. First, it was my graduation, then it was Father's hand, then I started at The Irregular Remedy, then I met Ecklon. None of this is any excuse, of course."

Pavonis was Coralline's only best friend, but, just nine months ago, Pavonis had counted two best friends: Coralline and Mako. Mako had been a whale shark like Pavonis himself, but his birth name hadn't been Mako; in adulthood, he'd renamed himself after the shortfin mako, among the fastest sharks in the world. Pavonis and Mako had been similar in personality—irreverent and adventurous—and they'd even looked similar, to an uncanny extent. Individual whale sharks could be distinguished by the yellow spots on their skin, but Pavonis's and Mako's patterns had borne such a strong resemblance that they were often mistaken for each other.

One day, a merman had arrived at the Costaria home. Coralline had been perusing *The Ultimate Apothecary Appendix* at the window seat in the living room, but the stranger had looked at her with such alarm that she'd thrown the book aside and followed him outside immediately. He had taken her to the scene of a mob. At the center of the mob had been Pavonis, slamming his great white belly down onto rocks until they fragmented into pebbles. The mob had kept a safe distance from Pavonis, but Coralline had dashed over to Pavonis's side.

"Mako's dead," he'd wailed.

With that admission, the anger had drained from him, and he'd lain in the rubble, as still as though he himself had died. She'd asked him how Mako had died; he'd refused to say. That day, by the time he'd arisen, he'd changed permanently. He'd started snapping and snarling at children, smacking them with his tailfin. Worse, from Coralline's perspective, he'd developed a habit of falling into long, brooding silences, sometimes for days at a time.

"Will you tell me how Mako died?" Coralline asked Pavonis gently. She peered into his orb of an eye, whose dark color looked partly green in reflection of the surrounding kelp.

"I can't," he hissed in a pained voice. "But don't trouble yourself. My issues are my own problem."

"Well, my issues have always been your problem, so it's only fair for your issues to be my problem as well. What can I do to help you?"

"I've always longed to travel, but especially since Mako's death. Everywhere in Urchin Grove, I'm haunted by memories of him. But I cannot leave Urchin Grove without you—you're all I have left." His eye sparkled suddenly; Coralline knew it meant he had an idea. "We failed to leave Urchin Grove after your graduation," he said, his voice high with excitement, "but we could leave today!"

"What? How?"

"You can view your dismissal from The Irregular Remedy as an unexpected gift. You don't have to be anchored to Urchin Grove anymore!"

"But I do. My engagement party is tomorrow, and I'm marrying Ecklon two weeks after."

"Well, you don't have to."

"You don't approve of him?"

"Approving of him and approving of your marriage to him are two different things."

"Don't speak in riddles," she said, slapping his side in reprimand. With his thick skin, it would feel like a pat.

"Fine. Ecklon will most likely get tenured at work soon. To marry him means to marry Urchin Grove."

Coralline's gaze fell upon a rock below smattered with acorn barnacles. The arthropods had grown their round, bumpy beige shells directly onto the rock and would spend the rest of their lives there, utterly sessile. Would that be the rest of her life, unbudging from Urchin Grove? If so, would it be so bad? "Life is peaceful here," she said at length.

"Oh, *please*, who are you kidding?" If Pavonis could roll his eyes, she knew he would. "People here are not at peace; they're fast asleep."

"Life is safe here," Coralline persisted. "Year after year, Urchin Grove is ranked the safest settlement in Meristem in the annual Settlement Status rankings prepared by the Under-Ministry of Residential Affairs—"

"Stop it. You sound like a salesperson for the Under-Ministry. Safety is an illusion. Anything can happen anywhere at any time. I learned that when Mako died."

Coralline fell silent.

"You face two choices today," he continued, in the voice of a lawyer closing his case. "You can clam yourself to Urchin Grove for the rest of your life, like those acorn barnacles you're looking at, or the two of us can pick up and leave today."

"But where would we even go?"

"We could start with . . . Blue Bottle."

The capital of the nation of Meristem, a long swim south. There, no one would know of her professional humiliation. There, she would be able to start over, in another clinic—a better clinic. "Blue Bottle," Coralline whispered, her heart lifting out of her chest, as light and airy as the fronds of kelp all around her.

Izar looked about his drillship, *Dominion Drill I*, which stretched one-hundred-and-sixty feet from bow to stern. Fifty or so men shuffled aboard it under the blazing sun, a mass of denim-clad legs and sun-scorched arms, their shirts and caps featuring the bronze-and-black insignia of Ocean Dominion. A ninety-five-foot-tall derrick ascended to the sky at the drill-ship's center, its towering height and structure intended to provide the strength to haul oil out of underwater wells and into the storage tank below deck. The oil drill was tomorrow morning; this evening marked the routine drillship check that preceded every oil drill. *Dominion Drill I* was anchored to shore but bouncing lightly with the currents.

Izar stood where he always stood, in the shadow of the derrick—a circle could have been drawn to mark the spot—for it was the one position that afforded him a three-sixty-degree view over the entire drillship. He stood with Zaurak Alphard, the fifty-seven-year-old director of operations. Zaurak's large, shaved head was shaped as a boulder, with a flap of flab lining the back of his neck. A drop of sweat dangled off the tip of his lumpy nose before splattering onto his boot. After Antares, there was no man on earth Izar trusted more than Zaurak.

"I apologize for interrupting," said Deneb Delphinus, arriving between Izar and Zaurak.

Deneb had a chest as built as a bison, but his tread was light as a mouse's. A tattoo of a mermaid marked his ebony forearm, twirling all the way from the inside of his elbow to his wrist, the mermaid's tailfin billowing over his veins. Many workers at Ocean Dominion were stamped with ink, but their tattoos tended to feature fishhooks, nets, trawlers, ships, sometimes even the Ocean Dominion logo. A mermaid tattoo was a first in Izar's experience; he frowned at it with distaste.

"I just wanted to let you know that I've checked the drill pipe and monkey-board," Deneb said. "They're ready for our oil drill tomorrow."

Nodding, Zaurak placed two neat tick marks on the checklist he held, tacked to a clipboard. His pen glinted in the sun, its black surface engraved with the bronze-and-black insignia of Ocean Dominion as well as his name, Zaurak Alphard, in block letters.

"Thanks," Zaurak said. He thumped Deneb's strapping shoulder, but the playful gesture almost unbalanced him. Clutching Deneb's arm, Zaurak leaned on his left foot, his right all but ornamental, the toes lifted. His arms were thick, hairy, and sinewy like a gorilla's, as though to try to compensate for the limp in his right leg.

"May I ask you a personal question, Zaurak?"

Izar raised his eyebrows disapprovingly at Deneb, but the twenty-two-year-old derrickhand did not notice.

"Ask away," Zaurak replied cheerfully.

"What happened to your leg?"

"That's a personal question," Izar interjected coldly. Zaurak fraternized with the men, but Izar wished he would keep them at a distance, as Izar himself did—Ocean Dominion was a corporation, not a community collective. He was, however, surprised that Deneb did not already know the story of Zaurak's leg; all the other men did. It must be because Deneb was new, hired by Zaurak just two months ago.

"I'm sorry." Deneb removed his cap and fidgeted with it, his eyes downcast.

"It's fine," Zaurak assured him with a swift smile. "I'm hardly sensitive about it. When I was thirty, and a manager of operations at Ocean Dominion, I was skinning a whale shark, and my leg got caught in the skinning equipment—which quite resembled a shark's jaws, as a matter of fact. My shin bone split in half horizontally across the middle. Doctor Navi said I would lose my leg below the knee, and he was prepared to saw it off himself, but Antares hired the best specialists money could buy and paid for my medical care and rehabilitation out of pocket—a total of a quarter million dollars. The sum enabled me to retain my leg. When Antares visited me in the hospital after my surgery, he gave me this pen."

Deneb looked at the pen as incredulously as though it were a wand. "That's a beautiful story," he said, whistling. "Antares sounds like a great man."

"He is," Izar said.

Continuing to whistle, Deneb slipped away.

Workers arrived at Zaurak's elbow one after the other to tell him which parts of the drillship they had checked: stand pipe, draw works, turn table, rat hole, crown blocks, suction line. Zaurak nodded, smiled slightly, and made tick marks steadily in his clipboard. He commanded a natural loyalty and deference from the men, as he did from Izar.

"Is the drillship check almost complete?" Izar asked him.

"Almost, *boss*," Zaurak replied.

Izar laughed at the word that formed a running joke between them.

Six years ago, when he'd been Deneb's age, Izar had begun as a lowly but spirited assistant engineer at Ocean Dominion. (Antares had been willing to give Izar any role he wished, but, unlike Saiph, who'd decided he wanted to start off in senior management, Izar had wanted to start at the very bottom—that way, he would earn each of the promotions he aimed to get.) On Izar's very first day, Zaurak had hobbled over to him and pumped his hand. His black eyes had glinted like he knew him—like he was greeting a long-lost nephew, not a young, replaceable worker. Izar had had the strange sense that Zaurak had been waiting years for him to arrive.

Like the other assistant engineers at the company, Izar had kept his hands perpetually in machine parts, grime blackening his nails, grease smearing his elbows. Within a year, however, in addition to performing his ordinary workload with extraordinary quality, he'd also managed to invent an ultra-lightweight fishnet. The net had doubled Ocean Dominion's catch of schools of small fish, and Zaurak had promoted Izar to the role of Engineer.

Soon after, Izar had informed Zaurak that he wished to widen Ocean Dominion's focus from fishing to oil. "Commence your research today," Zaurak had said, "and meet with me in my office every week to provide me an update." Every week, Izar had arrived in Zaurak's office with stacks of papers—articles, early drillship designs, scraps of calculations. Zaurak had offered suggestions, never directions, for Izar's consideration.

A year after he'd commenced his oil research, Izar had a detailed drillship blueprint in hand, three feet in length. He'd shown the blueprint to Antares and Saiph during his weekly meeting with them in Antares's thirtieth-floor office. Antares had beamed so widely that even his tufty eyebrows had appeared to be grinning. "I promote you to director of operations," he'd said.

"Thank you," Izar had said, "but I have to decline."

Antares had nearly choked on his cigar, clouds of smoke billowing from his lips. "Why?" he'd asked, coughing.

"Because Zaurak is director."

"Do you think he'll be in his office right now?" Antares had continued, sipping his whisky.

Izar had nodded. Zaurak was an eternal bachelor, married to Ocean Dominion's fleet of ships. He worked steadily through the evenings like a train making its rounds.

"Good. I'll call Zaurak up here and dismiss him straightaway." Antares had started dialing the phone, but Izar had placed his finger on the dial, his arm almost displacing Antares's whisky.

"Zaurak mentored me through all aspects of the drillship blueprint," Izar had said. "I wouldn't have been able to do it without him. If anything,

Zaurak and I can be *co*-directors of operations. I can lead our new Oil division, and he can continue to lead the Fishing division."

Antares's steel-gray eyes had pondered Izar from across the wisps of cigar smoke. "Zaurak was among my very first men," he'd said. "He started at Ocean Dominion thirty-five years ago, in the first month of the company's founding itself. I like him well, and I'm not opposed to paying two director salaries for a single role, but that's not how the world works, son. He would be competing with you every step of the way, undermining you, in order to protect his position and maintain his influence. I cannot give you his position while he still has it."

"He'd turn the men against you," Saiph had added, charred-kale eyes gleaming. "He wouldn't let you succeed, not over his dead body."

Izar had removed his finger from the dial.

"I'm glad you finally understand—" Antares had begun.

"If you fire Zaurak," Izar had pronounced, "I'll resign from Ocean Dominion this moment."

Antares's fist had slammed down on his desk, and his face had jutted forth through his cigar smoke, the reddening color of his cheeks making Izar think of a tiger. Izar had been startled at his own declaration, for he had nowhere else to go—his walking away from Ocean Dominion would have been equivalent to a penguin waddling away from ice. There was no habitat he could imagine to which he was as specifically suited as to Ocean Dominion. Antares had waved his cigar reproachfully until its embers had dusted his mahogany desk like black pepper, but, eventually, he'd relented.

A year later, when *Dominion Drill I* was built and had conducted its first oil drill, tugging twenty thousand barrels of gurgling black bubbles out of the ocean floor, Antares had promoted Izar to vice president of operations and informed him that he'd gotten a new office built for him next to his own on the thirtieth floor.

Izar had insisted on remaining in his present office, next to Zaurak's on the first floor of the underground, B1. He had done it in part so that Zaurak would not feel that Izar had risen above him not only in title but also physically, in the level of the building. Another reason was that Izar viewed Ocean Dominion as a giant with wide feet and a gargantuan head. He'd always resided in the feet of the giant—both his office and Invention Chamber were underground. The feet of the giant were a place he understood, a place where respect was earned through diligence and effort.

The head of the giant was populated by men recruited by Saiph, men with expensive degrees but obscure duties. The head of the giant was perpetually in the clouds, Izar had come to conclude—he wanted to do his best to ensure the giant's feet remained steadfast on the ground.

Antares had promoted Saiph to vice president of strategy in the same meeting. Izar's sense of his own accomplishment had been diluted, for Saiph had done nothing to deserve his promotion—he simply would have resented Izar's rise over him.

When Izar had informed Zaurak of his promotion, Zaurak had said, "Congratulations, *boss*," and they'd both laughed.

Atop *Dominion Drill I*, the sun was so bright that Izar could see every mote of dust between himself and Zaurak as a suspended golden particle. He waved a hand before his face to watch the particles dance, then settle again—the laws of physics continued to amaze him even long after he understood them.

Serpens Sarin, a large, red-bearded man, shuffled up to Zaurak's elbow. He had cloud-gray eyes and an energetic manner, like a tense violin string. Each of his ears was studded with one-inch-long spears, arrows that pointed at the face of anyone to whom he spoke. Thirty-five-year-old Serpens had started off in the oil-drilling business at a competing firm, Seven Seas, at the lowest level, roustabout, and had risen steadily through the ranks of motorman, derrickhand, then driller. He'd been a driller for four years when, two years ago, Zaurak had poached him to be manager on *Dominion Drill I*. Serpens was in charge of supervising oil drills, including the one planned for tomorrow. Increasingly, he had become Zaurak's right-hand man.

"The drill bit and conductor casing are checked," he said.

"Good man," Zaurak said. Upon making two quick tick marks in his checklist, he placed an arm around Serpens's shoulder and started whispering in his ear. A chorus of waves and cackling seagulls drowned out his voice, such that, though Izar's ear was keened, he could not hear a word.

"What was that about?" Izar asked when Serpens shuffled away.

"Nothing worth your time."

Returning to his clipboard, Zaurak scribbled along the margins of his checklist, while Izar's gaze roved over the workers, surveying their activity.

"Zaurak," said Deneb, arriving between Izar and Zaurak, "I've checked the lifeboats; they're all in good shape—"

His face froze, and his eyes widened as his gaze flew over Izar's head. Izar felt a shadow darkening over him, but before he could crane his neck to look, Deneb had flung himself onto him with the force of a grizzly bear. They hit the floor together with a smack and tumbled toward the opposite rails of the ship. A crash sounded just where Izar had been standing.

He rose to his feet and stared incredulously at the derrick that had, just moments ago, stood stalwart at the center of the drillship. A tower of power and stability meant to withstand extreme winds and waves, it now lay flat on its side like a fallen tree. It had almost splintered the floor of the three-thousand-ton vessel; if not for Deneb, it would surely have splintered Izar from head to toe. Someone must have secretly traipsed below deck and loosened its foothold—someone who wanted Izar dead. But who?

Izar looked suspiciously at the workers, assembled now to the other side of the derrick. They stood with their arms wrapped around themselves, their faces distressed, as though someone had just pointed a gun in their midst. Standing next to Izar, Deneb examined the collapsed derrick, his brow as puzzled as at a spaceship that had landed before him.

"You saved my life," Izar said, pumping Deneb's hand.

"Good man," Zaurak told Deneb, slapping him so hard on the back that Deneb coughed. "Now, derrickhand, lead the men in re-erecting the derrick."

Deneb ambled over to the crewmen, appearing equally excited and flustered by the responsibility assigned him.

Zaurak beckoned Izar over to the rails of the ship, his eyes like black ice. Their heads together, their elbows on the highest rail, they looked out over the sea, deliberately facing away from the workers.

"We have to cancel the oil drill tomorrow," Zaurak hissed.

"We can't. Antares asked me when to schedule a press conference, and I suggested tomorrow. The drill tomorrow is meant to mark two years of oil exploration for Ocean Dominion. The Marketing department has already written it into the press release."

"Blast the press release! There's a traitor among us, someone trying to kill you. We can't go out onto the ocean until we learn who. Trust me, cancel the drill."

"I trust you with my life, but I've given Antares my word. We have to proceed as planned tomorrow."

"If you insist," Zaurak muttered, chewing the lid of his pen. "I'll dismiss the crew for the evening as soon as the derrick is re-erected. Then I'll double-check the whole ship myself, down to the lowliest corkscrew. Tomorrow, in the middle of the ocean, any mistake will be fatal for all of us."

6

Muse

Abalone carried a limestone tray into Coralline's room, with two covered bowls upon it and a pair of stone-sticks.

Her stomach rumbling, Coralline eagerly uncovered one of the bowls. Rich red clumps of pepper dulse tangled with bright-green tubular fingers of velvet horn. The contrasting colors created a tornado effect—the dish looked like a work of art. Coralline's mouth watered; she particularly loved pepper dulse, the truffle of the sea. She reached for the stone-sticks.

"The algae in this bowl is not for you to eat," Abalone said.

"What's it for, then?"

"Once you're married, Ecklon will expect you to prepare supper for him. This is the kind of beauty and complexity you should be aiming for in the dishes you prepare. The algae in the other bowl is for you."

Coralline uncovered the other bowl. It contained light-green sheets of ulva. She looked questioningly at her mother.

"I know sea lettuce is tasteless, darling, but it'll help you lose weight between your engagement party and wedding. I remember that in the weeks before my own wedding, my only goal in life was to become wispy, just barely visible, like a moon jellyfish. Until your wedding, consider ulva your only friend—after me, of course."

Coralline reluctantly ate a few fronds of ulva. They tasted like sand.

"Now, let's get you ready for your engagement party, starting with your hair!"

Coralline plopped down in the chair her mother placed in front of the full-length mirror behind the door. Abalone brushed Coralline's long black locks briskly, using the olivine-encrusted comb she'd gifted Coralline for her twentieth birthday. Coralline examined her mother's reflection in the mirror.

Abalone's cheekbones were aristocratic, and her neck was long and regal. Her bodice was woven of a fine white brocade; long, translucent tendrils of white swayed off its hem and swirled about her hips like a school of eels. The white bodice above the golden scales led Abalone to resemble the beautiful white-and-yellow butterfly fish darting about the coral reef outside the window. As a mergirl, Coralline had hoped she would resemble her mother when she became a mermaid, but they looked nothing alike. In addition to a difference in hair color, there was a difference in tail color—Coralline's bronze scales were closer to her father's copper than her mother's gold. Coralline's shoulders were also narrower, and she was half a head shorter. As she sat in front of the mirror, she felt herself very much in her mother's shadow.

Abalone put the comb aside and began fashioning Coralline's hair into a fishtail side braid.

"I wonder why her eyes look puffy and her cheeks splotched," said a shrill voice.

Coralline's glance flew to her mother's shoulder, and she groaned. She had not detected Nacre because of her mother's side bun, but two finger-length tentacles were poking out through the golden locks now. Nacre, a medium-sized snail with a thick, solid shell carrying a high spire and five rounded body whorls, looked down on Coralline from Abalone's shoulder. She was a scotch bonnet snail, her shell cream in color, with a pattern of red rectangular patches. Most snails were beautiful, but Nacre was more beautiful still than most. Even within her scotch bonnet species, she was particularly bright—others tended to have orange, brown, or tan patches rather than a vivid red. Her location on Abalone's right shoulder was not coincidental; she claimed to always be right.

"She looks sullen and ungrateful," Nacre continued, speaking of Coralline to Abalone as though Coralline were not there. "She's forgetting that no one likes a bleached coralline."

"You're right, my dear muse," Abalone said. Raising cautionary eyebrows at Coralline in the mirror, she tugged Coralline's hair sharply, making her wince. "There's no excuse for you to not be smiling from ear to ear, Coralline. You're marrying the sole heir of the wealthiest family in Urchin Grove—an heir who happens to also be handsome and intelligent. You're the envy of all young mermaids in the village. You'll spend the rest of your life in the Mansion, as cozy as a clownfish among anemones. Unlike your mother, with her continuously toiling fingers, carving stitch upon stitch into fabric, you'll never have to work a day again in your life."

Well, Coralline could not work even if she wanted. She had cried all night about her firing, hence the puffy eyes and splotched cheeks Nacre had mentioned. She was planning to tell her parents about her firing tonight, after the engagement party, when things were less busy, and, hopefully, she would be able to talk about it without bursting into tears.

Abalone knotted Coralline's fishtail braid at the end. It formed a black rope that draped Coralline's left shoulder, falling to her waist. Abalone then embedded a dozen cloudy periwinkles within the plait, the tiny shells glistening in the braid like a constellation of fog-draped stars in the night sky.

She asked Coralline to rise, then whirled Coralline about by her shoulders. She traced two circles with a stick of rouge over each cheekbone, then smeared the color outward with her index finger. "I want you to look prettier than Rosette just this one day," she said. When Coralline looked again in the mirror, she found that her blotchiness from crying had transformed into a rosy glow.

Abalone's eyes met Coralline's in the mirror, glimmering as brightly as globules of knotweed. "Your engagement party bodice is modeled after the latest fashion in Blue Bottle, the kind of sensational high fashion Urchin Grove has never seen before. Aren't you just itching to see it?"

Coralline nodded, a little unnerved by her mother's enthusiasm.

Abalone slipped out of the room, returning with a corset in her hands. Diagonal stripes of orange-and-purple sequins traversed it like full-body bandages, as though intending to mummify its wearer in shimmer.

"I can't possibly wear this—"

"Of course you can. I took precautions to ensure you fit."

Before Coralline could protest, Abalone swept the bodice over her and proceeded to button it. It had a high collar that reached Coralline's throat and long sleeves that reached her wrists. Its buttons, a medley of bright, mismatched shells, formed a column along her spine. As Abalone closed the buttons one by one, the sequins pricked Coralline's skin like hundreds of blunt needles, and the stiff fabric constricted her ribs. She shivered with itchiness, wishing she could scratch her back by sliding up and down against a wall. But she remained in front of the mirror, her reflection making her think of a puppet being prepared for a mysterious sacrifice.

"I have another present for you, too," Abalone announced. She handed Coralline a book, *Appropriate Muses for Mermaids*. "We must speak about the Ogre."

"Please don't start on Pavonis, Mother."

"I can't help it. I should have stopped your silliness when you were young. I pleaded and scolded for you to find a more feminine muse, but I should have placed my tail down and insisted upon it. I know you're attached to the Ogre, but only mermen, never mermaids, have sharks as muses. It's a breach of convention for a mermaid to be accompanied by such a large creature. You know the rule of thumb: A mermaid's muse should never be more than half her length. The Ogre is five times your length. I think you should try to find yourself a pretty little snail, like I have, or maybe a seahorse, like your father's muse, Altair. Another possibility is to be un-mused, of course, like your brother and the vast majority of merpeople."

"Pavonis has always been there for me," Coralline said crossly. "I will never leave him."

"Well, what if Ecklon leaves you because of him?"

"What?"

"Ecklon's mother, Epaulette, is even more traditional than I am. I've heard that she jeers at you behind your back because of the Ogre. As soon as you're married to Ecklon, Epaulette will urge you to replace the Ogre with another animal. You have to consider the wishes of your mother-in-law-to-be from now on, and place them before your own."

"I don't care what Epaulette thinks," Coralline snapped. "My animal best friend is my own business."

"Don't be disagreeable. It doesn't suit you." Abalone left Coralline's bedroom in a flutter of gold.

Coralline swam to the window and looked out over the reef garden; Pavonis wasn't there, fortunately, and so he wouldn't have heard what her mother had said. Despite the stiffness of her bodice, she managed to fold herself into the cradle of the windowsill, and she sat there gazing out over the garden, hoping its sight would calm her.

Cultivated by her father, the reef garden sprawled around the house in the shape and colors of a painter's palette. Loose green tentacles of snakelocks anemone danced together, their lilac tips undulating gently. Green sea urchin crawled along the reef; Coralline remembered the time she'd pricked her fingers on their spikes as a mergirl—they were sharper than her mother's sewing needles. A blanket of colorful jewel anemones grew along an overhang, with brilliant, golden-tipped tentacles. Coralline algae carpeted several rocks in bright pink; coralline was her father's favorite algae, because its encrusted strata indicated the health of a coral reef. It was her father who had named her Coralline.

The Costaria home was ordinary, an inverted bowl in shape, but the coral reef just outside its windows was extraordinary—it was said to be the most beautiful in the village. Everyone said Trochid had a reef thumb—he had only to look at a reef for it to flourish. As a coral connoisseur for the Under-Ministry of Coral Conservation, he had been responsible for the well-being of most reefs in Urchin Grove; now, in his retirement, this was the only reef he tended. The thought made Coralline sad.

"Congratulations on your upcoming wedding," said a low, tremulous voice.

Coralline looked down. Just beneath the windowsill swayed a small, brilliant orange form, his tail coiled around a tuft of turtle-grass. Her father's muse, the lined seahorse Altair.

Trochid had found Altair as a fingernail-sized baby seahorse, living in a bleached coral reef where he would almost certainly have died from a lack of sustenance. Trochid had brought him home and deposited him in his own thriving coral reef. The two of them had bonded immediately; part of their bond related to their preference for quiet and solitude, Coralline thought. Altair had never once left the reef, believing the world outside to be full of "moral confusion and peril," as he'd once told Coralline.

"Congratulations to you as well," Coralline said with a smile. "Father told me yesterday that you're expecting."

Altair camouflaged, becoming indistinct among the grasses. When he glowed orange again, the lines that outlined his neck area—and served as the source of his species name—shone particularly white. He bobbed his coronet, a tiny, star-shaped crown atop his head. He then cast a glance about for his mate, Kuda, red in color. Coralline looked at Altair warmly: Seahorses could change their color, brightening and dulling at will, but they never changed their mate. If either Altair or Kuda were to die, the other would likely never seek another mate. They cemented their bond with a quivering ritual dance every morning, in which they spun around and swam side by side, their tails entwined. Seahorses were the most romantic animals in the ocean, Coralline had always thought.

"You're looking rather shapeless, Pole Dancer!" Nacre cackled.

Looking about, Coralline found the snail clammed to the wall, her tentacles pointing at Altair's pregnant, slightly protruding belly. Nacre called him Pole Dancer because he, like other seahorses, needed to wrap his tail around something, usually a strand of grass, in order to avoid getting blown about by the currents. But what was Nacre doing in her room? Coralline wondered with a flash of irritation. She must have climbed off Abalone's shoulder without Coralline noticing. It was not the first time Coralline had caught the snail in her room, spying and snooping. Coralline didn't know Altair well but liked him well enough; Nacre, she found as galling as nails on shale.

The waters outside the window swelled and shifted, and they would have pushed Coralline away from the window had she not wrapped her fingers around the windowsill. Pavonis came to a stop before her, the size of a ship. She extended a hand through the window and patted his yellow-spotted back.

"Have you decided to leave the apothecary field in favor of becoming a clown?" he drawled, his orb of an eye roving over her gaudy corset. Coralline chortled, then stopped, as the sequins pricked her ribs. "What are the Minions doing here?" he said.

Nacre, smaller than Pavonis's eye, hid in her shell. Altair, the size of Coralline's hand, camouflaged, vanishing as completely as a ghost.

"Minions is not their name," Coralline said, giving Pavonis a warning look.

"I have no reason to know their names. They're beneath me."

Coralline sighed. How could she and her parents have such different muses, all three of them disliking one another?

"*Coralline!*" Abalone called from the living room. "It's time to leave for your engagement party!"

Coralline's vertebrae sagged in the frame of the windowsill. In the aftermath of her firing from The Irregular Remedy, all she wanted was to lie in bed under her blanket. She didn't want to greet a hundred guests at her engagement party. She particularly didn't want to greet Ecklon's mother, now that she knew Epaulette jeered at her behind her back.

"You know, we could have avoided all this if we'd left for Blue Bottle yesterday," Pavonis said in an I-told-you-so voice.

"Oh my," Altair gasped from among the grasses, even as he remained invisible. "Leaving your love Ecklon . . ."

"I couldn't leave him," Coralline said.

The water formed a sheet of turquoise embroidered with white, and the breeze was heavy with brine evaporated from the froth. A seagull with gray wings cackled as it flew over the drillship.

"Any word yet from Zaurak?" Izar asked Deneb. "Or Serpens?"

"I've tried both of them every ten minutes since we left Menkar," Deneb replied.

Zaurak had a written checklist for the oil drill; Izar had a mental one, with just one word upon it—Zaurak. Zaurak was like a cane upon which Izar relied—without the cane, Izar could still walk, but his feet felt precariously unsteady. Yet the director of operations was missing today.

Izar had phoned him repeatedly before the drillship had departed Menkar. The phone had rung continuously, but there'd been no answer. Zaurak was always at least a quarter-hour early; where could he possibly be? Izar had wondered. On the other side of the ocean, the sun had scurried into the sky in limpid pink fragments that had dissolved to a burning gold. Izar had reluctantly given the crew an order to unlatch the ropes and hoist out to sea. It was the first time an Ocean Dominion drillship had departed on its mission an hour after schedule.

It was not just Izar who felt Zaurak's absence—and, to a lesser extent, Serpens's, who was also missing. The workers seemed to feel it, too, for their legs and arms moved robotically, mechanically, as they proceeded about their tasks. Izar looked at them with distrust: One of them had attempted to murder him yesterday. *Dominion Drill I* was an immense, sturdy ship, but Izar could just as well have been out at sea alone on a raft—that was how unsafe he felt. His gaze flew up to the derrick, in whose shadow he stood. His toes trembled in his steel-toed boots, prepared to leap out of the way in case the tower collapsed on him again. At any point, one of the workers could attempt to murder him, one of them might be plotting it at this very moment. . . .

The schedule for the day had been tight and had been tightened further by their delayed departure. The press conference was this evening, and Izar had to return to Menkar in time for it. With the constricted timeline he himself had established, he felt as though he'd buckled his belt two notches too tight and just couldn't feel comfortable. Too many things could go wrong, and he had too little control over them.

"May I ask you something?" Deneb asked.

He was standing on the lowest rail of the ship, balancing somehow without holding onto the higher rails. Much of his face lay in the shadow of the sun, such that it appeared a dark oval. The mermaid tattooed across his forearm shone brightly. The only worker with whom Izar was speaking this morning was Deneb, for he had saved Izar yesterday, and so Izar trusted him and was trying to like him.

"Ask away," Izar said.

"After the fall of the derrick yesterday, Zaurak was supposed to have double-checked the drillship. If we haven't seen him today, how do we know he completed his check?"

"He left his clipboard on my desk. Everything was checked off." Izar recognized the swerving handwriting, the spelling mistakes, the deep-blue flow of Zaurak's engraved pen.

"But why would Zaurak and Serpens not be here? *Both* of them?"

"I can't speak for Serpens, for I hardly know the man. As for Zaurak, maybe he's sick."

Izar was lying—he knew Zaurak could not be sick. In all of Izar's six years at Ocean Dominion, he'd never once seen Zaurak so much as cough. Even in the weeks after his leg injury twenty-seven years ago, Zaurak had continued to work—from the hospital. Zaurak was like Izar; even had his leg been amputated, he would not have shirked work. His absence today went deeper than the water, deeper than the riser pipe the crew would soon drive into the ocean floor.

"I haven't drilled oil before without Zaurak or Serpens," Deneb persisted, "let alone without both."

"Me neither."

"Ocean Dominion's competitor Atlantic Operations went bankrupt three months ago after its oil spill and the resulting loss of shareholder confidence. The entire crew died in the spill. What if that's us, today?"

"We're *not* Atlantic Operations." Izar's gaze shifted to the lifeboats. He could see part of two lifeboats over the rails, clinging to the sides of the drillship.

"As manager, Serpens's role is especially crucial during an oil drill. He leads the men—"

"*I* will lead the men today," Izar interrupted. "I alone designed the drillship and supervised its construction. I know the functioning of every nail and screw on this vessel, just as a biologist knows the functioning of every cell of the human body. Do you not trust me, Deneb, although I trust you?"

"But I do!" The derrickhand jumped down from the rails and strode over to Izar. He braced his feet hip-distance apart and crossed his arms, his stance paralleling Izar's. His face gleamed under the morning sun, his ebony skin coated with a fine spray of froth. "May I ask you a personal question?"

"If you must."

"When you take the private elevator down from your office, what do you do?"

Izar's lips tightened. He only ever descended into his Invention Chamber late in the evening; the time of day was intentional, for the workers would have gone home by then. He supposed a few workers may have seen him step into the elevator once or twice, but all of them had the sense to not ask him about it.

"I cannot answer that," he said. From Izar's first days at Ocean Dominion, Antares had made him promise to not tell anyone of his underwater-fire work until an announcement was made publicly, in order to keep competing firms at bay. Other than Antares and Saiph, only Ascella knew about Castor, and she did not believe him.

Deneb was about to return to his position on the rails, when Izar said, "I now have something to ask you."

The derrickhand squared his shoulders and stared at Izar like he was a one-man firing squad. "Anything!"

"Why is there a mermaid tattoo on your arm?"

"Oh, this." Deneb smiled sheepishly at the tattoo, as at a crush. "I think mermaids are beautiful. I've always wanted to see one but have never been so fortunate. I wish they wouldn't avoid ships, but I can understand why they do. Have you ever seen a mermaid?"

"I haven't, and never want to. You're trying to catch sight of a mermaid—is that why you insist on perching like a pelican upon the rails?"

Deneb's eyes sparkled, as though Izar's words were an indication of prophetic perception. "Yes," he whispered.

"In that case, your loyalties seem troublingly confused. The company for which you work is called Ocean *Dominion*. The ocean and all its inhabitants are ours to dominate. I recommend you erase your tattoo at once—mermaids won't exist on earth for much longer anyway."

"Why not?" Deneb asked in an alarmed voice.

"You'll see soon enough. Now, please try Zaurak and Serpens again."

7

Absence

"How very unseemly of Ecklon to be late to his own engagement party," said Sepia Selene.

She waved a small, cushiony hand in an attempt to signal a waiter. The rings that adorned each of her fingers clanged against one another, and the flesh of her arm swayed loosely.

Coralline's gaze roved over the garden of the Elnath Mansion. Much of it was planted with paddle-grass, the stalks shorter than those of other grasses, the leaves bright green. Scarlet bushes of berry wart cress and crimson stalks of siphoned feather grew in bright columns, interspersed with the dreamy, silvery concentric bands of peacock's tail. The whole garden was hemmed with sea fans, large, lacy sheets of beige and lilac that swayed like fanning servants. The garden was twice the size of the Costaria home.

People glided about smoothly underneath trellises and cloud-like arches erected intermittently among the grasses. Coralline did not recognize most guests; they were friends of her mother and mother-in-law-to-be—strange acquaintances, acquainted strangers, that was how she thought of them. Her heartbeat rose when she caught a sliver of a silver tail, but when the merman turned, she saw it was not Ecklon. She yearned to tell him about her dismissal from The Irregular Remedy—he would understand her devastation; he would console her. But where was he? She rarely found herself agreeing with her mother's best friend, Sepia, but it was true: It was unseemly of him to be late to his own engagement party.

"You know," Sepia continued, giving Coralline and Abalone a conspirational look from beneath raised eyebrows, "I cannot help but notice that Rosette Delesse is missing from the party as well."

An image floated into Coralline's mind: Rosette and Ecklon tangled in an embrace, her crimson scales against his silver, her red hair draping his chest, her long neck craned up to his. . . . She shook her head so hard at the thought that a periwinkle shell tumbled out of her fishtail braid.

A waiter arrived, bearing a tray. His breast pocket was inscribed with the word *Caulerpa*; the most expensive restaurant in Urchin Grove was catering her engagement party, Coralline realized with a measure of surprised alarm. It must have been Ecklon's idea; it would not have been his mother's. Even simple suppers of colander kelp or velvet horn at Caulerpa cost no less than a slipper limpet—a hefty five carapace.

"I have all four kinds of wine," the waiter said, gesturing smoothly to the decanters lining the tray he clutched close to his shoulder. "Oval sea grape, bell sea, beaded cushion, and parasol." The color of each wine he mentioned was a darker green than the previous, in reflection of its greater strength. "Which would you like?"

Sepia picked off a bright-green decanter of oval sea grape wine, Abalone chose a medium-green bell sea wine, and Coralline's fingers snatched up dark-green parasol wine. She tilted the decanter at her lips; if Ecklon decided to leave her for Rosette, she would need all the bolstering she could get. The sweet, pungent wine stung her throat, leaving a lingering relish.

"Coralline!" Abalone reprimanded. "Mermaids don't drink parasol wine. And please stop swigging!"

"Yes, Mother." Coralline took a smaller sip, trying to be daintier.

She looked at the Elnath Mansion, in whose shadow the three of them hovered. Other houses in Urchin Grove were low, rounded, single-story homes, shaped as half-bubbles or sea-biscuits, walls turning smoothly into ceiling; the Elnath home, in contrast, was a wide rectangle looming three stories over the seabed. The walls of other homes were ordinary shale—usually variations of gray but otherwise dull brown, rust, or gray-green; the Elnath Mansion was a stark black shale, the most rare and expensive of the fine-grained laminated sedimentary rocks. In keeping with the hard angles of the structure, the windows were rectangular rather than the usual oval shape, and they had ornate golden borders that looked like portrait frames. Coralline tried to imagine herself looking out at the world from within those frames, but she couldn't imagine it. She quivered, wishing she could scratch her itchy, sequin-covered back against the wall of the Mansion.

"Coralline has triumphed over Rosette as winner of the marriage mart," Abalone told Sepia. "She will soon become princess of this palace!"

Coralline cringed. Last year, Sepia's daughter Telia, as fuchsia-tailed and voluminous as her mother, had married a wiry, low-level legal clerk who worked at the law firm of Ecklon's father, Erizo Elnath. The law firm, Rights and Justice, started by Ecklon's great-great-grandfather, was what had made the Elnaths the wealthiest family in the village. In the same way that Erizo's station was above that of Sepia's son-in-law, Coralline knew her mother viewed her own station as being above Sepia's, now that Coralline would soon be Erizo's daughter-in-law.

"Well, no matter the princess," Sepia rejoined smoothly, "Epaulette will always be queen of her Mansion—an iron-fisted one."

Coralline could not help but silently agree.

"My stomach is rumbling for a morsel," Sepia said, rubbing the expansive area.

"Epaulette really should have hired more waiters," Abalone said. "We had to wait an era for wine, now we must pine unto infinite for a bite—"

Sepia's lips parted at the sight of two mermaids who'd just come to hover behind Abalone.

One of them had a silver tail, and her bodice dangled with long, confetti-like crimson-and-white tendrils that resembled the fins of a red lionfish. An elaborate matching headdress of quills crowned her silver bun. It was Ecklon's mother, Epaulette. The mermaid who accompanied her was also flamboyantly red, but more naturally so, in the form of both her hair and her scales. It was Violacea, Epaulette's best friend and Rosette's mother.

Coralline hoped they hadn't overheard her mother's complaint; if they had, she hoped they would be polite enough to not mention it.

"I'll send a waiter to you shortly with plenty of devil's tongue," Epaulette said.

Abalone's amber-gold eyes lowered, and her cheeks flushed with embarrassment. No fault lay with the service, Coralline knew—the truth was that her mother felt inferior in her new environment and wished to conceal it with a ploy of superiority in the form of a complaint.

"We've been admiring your garden," Sepia gushed.

"I'm sure you have," Epaulette said, but her gaze remained on Abalone.

"Everything seems to grow here," Sepia continued enthusiastically.

"Everything except coralline algae."

Coralline felt her face reddening. She sipped her parasol wine; the liquor seeped through her veins like hot steam. Epaulette frowned at the decanter. Her silver-gray eyes then swept over the orange-and-purple sequins swathing Coralline from neck to hip. "What terrible tailorship," she remarked.

Abalone's lips drew into a thin line.

"We've never worked a day in our lives, have we, Violacea?" Epaulette said, without turning her head to Violacea.

"We certainly haven't," she said, giggling.

"How goes your sewing, Abalone?" asked Epaulette.

"It goes well."

"Strange, the way things are in your humble home," Epaulette drawled. "The wife with overworked hands, the husband without a hand."

Violacea laughed uproariously, as though she'd never heard something more original.

Abalone's eyes narrowed to slits. "How smug—"

Coralline laid a hand on her mother's arm. Her mother's temper was like a corset with loose strings; any provocation, and it would unravel; once it did, the strings could not be rejoined, and the outcome would be a scandal, even if undeserved.

"Your family will never be good enough for ours," Epaulette snapped. Her gaze turned to Coralline. "*You* will never be good enough for my son. There are still two weeks left to the wedding; there's still time for Ecklon to come to his senses and choose Rosette over you."

"Yes, it is my daughter who deserves him!" Violacea said.

"If I have my way," Epaulette continued, "this garden will be as close as you and your family"—her gaze darted between Coralline and Abalone—"ever get to my Mansion!"

Coralline had never cursed before; to avoid doing so now, she bit her lip so hard that she tasted blood.

Epaulette and Violacea fluttered away arm in arm to greet other guests, the pace of their swim slow and ambling, as though no unusual words had been spoken. Coralline, Abalone, and Sepia sipped their wines in silence. Sepia rarely stopped talking, in Coralline's experience, but even she seemed to find herself at a loss for words.

A waiter arrived, bearing a platter of devil's tongue. Coralline loved the red algae, but she shook her head—she had no more appetite, knowing that Epaulette would have sent him over. Sepia collected a fistful of the slippery red flaps, and Abalone plucked up two. "Naiadum loves devil's tongue," she said, casting a glance about the garden. "Hmm . . . where is my little angel?"

Coralline looked for Naiadum's tawny tail. There were only a few children in the garden, clustered together noisily, but her eight-year-old brother was not among them. She turned her head to look at her mother again; though her neck swiveled slowly, the movement felt lightning fast, as though her head might come unhinged.

"Now, we have to look for your brother." Abalone sighed. "Will you find him, or shall I ask your father to search for him?"

Coralline's gaze found her father on the other side of the garden, beside a pair of swaying sea fans. He was laughing with a merman she did not know, gesturing animatedly with both arms, a care-free aspect to his manner she hadn't seen since his haccident. "Let's not trouble Father while he's enjoying himself," she said. "I'll find Naiadum."

"Do you promise?"

"I promise."

"Good. Now, excuse me while I swim up to your father and remind him to conceal his stump behind his back. I don't know why he can't remember my social etiquette instructions—oh, goodness! What is the Bitter Spinster doing here?"

Coralline followed her mother's gaze toward an emaciated mermaid arriving at the fringe of the garden. Her decanter almost slipped from her fingers. How dare Rhodomela attend her engagement party after firing her!

"I can't *believe* you invited the Bitter Spinster!" Abalone shrieked. "And I can't believe she's wearing black, the color of mourning, even at this time of celebration. Oh look, she brought her older sister, Osmundea, with her."

Osmundea shared Rhodomela's dark hair but otherwise bore little resemblance to her. Her tail was indigo rather than black, and her face was more pleasantly contoured, with wide-set eyes and full cheeks. A short, faded scar lined the side of her lip.

"What a sorry spinsterly pair," Sepia said.

No one greeted Rhodomela or Osmundea. Instead, mermaids cleared out of their way, forming a vacuum around them, as though spinsterhood were a disease contractable by proximity.

Rhodomela's black gaze found Coralline.

Coralline slid aside and away, without a word to her mother or Sepia. She placed her now-empty decanter on a passing waiter's tray and snatched up another decanter of parasol wine. Swerving around a corner of the Mansion, she found herself behind it. There was no one there. She saw only juvenile red crabs skittering among the pebbles and a common cuttlefish propelling itself upward by its frilly fin, camouflaged partially by its zebra-like stripes. Relieved to find herself alone for the first time all morning, Coralline leaned against the wall, closed her eyes, and shifted up and down sharply, feeling a pleasure-pain from scratching her sequined back against the smooth black shale.

Love is a farce, Rhodomela had said. Perhaps the master apothecary was right, Coralline thought now. After all, Ecklon still wasn't here, long after all the guests had arrived, all the guests except Rosette—Coralline's eyes flew open. Ecklon was likely somewhere in the Mansion. If he was with Rosette, Coralline might be able to catch him red-handed by peeking through the windows. If he was cheating on her, it would be better for her to know it now, so that she could leave him—though the thought of leaving him made her heart feel like it would shatter into a million pieces. . . . Could she bear to see him cheating on her? No, but she had to know.

He wasn't the only one who could be a detective.

She shifted to the nearest window, along the bottom left of the first story. The room was a guest bedroom, and it was empty. Her tailfin flicking ever so gently, she crept toward the window next to the first—its shutters were drawn. She continued on to the next window, and the next. Half of the Mansion's windows were open, featuring guest bedrooms or spacious armoires, and the other half were shuttered.

But then, *there*! Through a window on the third story, she saw him. He wasn't alone.

A few clouds had gathered overhead, softening the glare of the sun, dampening the day.

His hands on his hips, Izar continued to stand where he had all morning, in the shadow of the derrick. Men bustled about *Dominion Drill I* all around him, making him think of bees buzzing about a hive.

Their sun-roasted faces bent to the equipment in concentration, they anchored the drillship in Zone Ten, the site of the oil drill today. In Ocean Dominion's map of the Atlantic, neat squares divided the entire ocean from north to south pole. Izar had chosen Zone Ten for this day because Ocean Dominion had done little in the area in recent years, except for a coral reef dynamite blast about seven months ago—a failed project in which they'd caught few fish, but a merman's hand.

Through a borehole in the moonpool on the base of the hull, four men lowered a riser into the water, a high-tension steel pipe with a diameter of close to two feet. The eight hands of the four men moved with the symmetric collaboration of a spider's legs. Machines aboard *Dominion Drill I* shrieked and shouted as the riser powered deeper and deeper into the ocean. Many men wore earmuffs to block out the racket, but Izar didn't mind it. Despite the clamor aboard, the penetration into the ocean floor would be smooth and soundless below; he'd designed it that way, to reduce the possibility of interference from merpeople.

A vibration soon rang through his elbows; it meant the riser had collided with the seabed and was on its way in.

Earlier, Izar had told derrickhand Deneb that he'd be directing the crew; he saw now that they did not need direction—together, they formed a well-oiled machine. He was redundant—the thought made him smile, for it meant Zaurak had trained them well.

Slowly, in ones and twos and threes, the crewmen completed their tasks and turned to face him. Izar strode to the base of the derrick, his knees stiff and creaking, protesting their first movement in hours. He looked down through the four-foot-wide borehole through which the men had passed the riser pipe. At the top of the borehole, on level with the floor of the drillship, lay the ram blowout preventer; below that, just underneath the hull, in the water, lay the annular blowout preventer. The two valves were more crucial than their size would suggest: Their donut-like rubber seals, reinforced with steel ribs, would prevent the riser from exploding under the erratic pressure of oil. Essentially, they formed the security guards of the drillship.

When Izar had been designing *Dominion Drill I*, a crucial decision had related to choosing blowout preventers. "Most oil spills are caused by malfunctioning preventers," Zaurak had told him. "Don't assemble your drillship of shiny new toys from the most expensive manufacturers in the world. And don't trust anyone or their streams of warranties. Test everything yourself." Izar had nodded and tested many makes of preventers, subjecting them to double the pressure they'd be subjected to during even the most tumultuous of oil drills. Only two had passed the test—he'd placed an order for both immediately. These were the two he stood examining now.

And yet the annular blowout preventer looked slightly different than usual, its metal less gray. It must be because of the clouds overhead, Izar thought.

"Any word from Zaurak or Serpens?" he asked Deneb. He did not need to turn his head to know that the twenty-two-year-old stood just behind him, like a stray puppy who'd found an owner.

"No," came the reply from just over Izar's shoulder, as he'd expected.

Izar stepped away from the borehole and did what he always did just before the commencement of an oil-drill—he wrapped his hand around a rung of the derrick. The ninety-five-foot-tall turret of metal would momentarily supply the strength to haul thousands of barrels of oil from the depths of the ocean, and Izar would obtain a measure of power from grasping its power. Were Zaurak here, he would have stood next to Izar, but, rather than clasping a rung of the derrick, he would have leaned against it, to alleviate some weight from his right leg. Their ears would have been instinctively keened below, even though they'd both learned on their very first drill two years ago that the rush of oil was something felt rather than heard, like a heartbeat.

Izar did not need to give an order to start the drill; the workers knew it from his clasp of the derrick, and they put the levers in motion. The floor of the drillship vibrated, and the pressure radiated up the soles of his boots until it swirled in his knees. It resembled the vibration of an airplane before takeoff, except much stronger. He closed his eyes and rested his head on the inside of his arm. He knew he wouldn't be able to see oil flowing into the storage tank below, but he still craved to feel it—and he did. He never knew how he knew, but he smiled as he identified the precise moment when oil started surging up the riser pipe, flying past the blowout preventers, and settling into the storage tank beneath the hull.

He continued to stand there, eyes closed, in a meditative silence, losing track of time. When he eventually glanced at the luminescent hour markers on his watch, he saw that more than an hour had passed, as smooth as any he'd ever spent on the drillship.

Then, a sudden tremor shot through his fingers. He frowned, lifted his head from his arm. The tremor vibrated through the fingers wrapped around the derrick. He withdrew his hand, as though burned. Staggering away from the tower, he frowned down through the borehole at the two blowout preventers. The flow of oil seemed to be turning temperamental and uncontrolled, but its pressure could not possibly exceed that of his laboratory tests. But then he heard it—sputters and chokes, like a man coughing to death. The riser pipe that connected the drillship to the seabed was shaking manically, he saw through the borehole, so manically that it was creating huge waves. The floor of *Dominion Drill I* shuddered like a dog shaking off fleas.

Losing his balance, Izar tumbled forward and would have plummeted straight down through the borehole into the ocean had a hand not grasped his arm and pulled him back. "Watch out!" shouted Deneb from behind him.

"This is the second time you've saved my life in as many days," Izar said, turning his head to flash a brief smile at him.

Then, in a single, fluid movement, Izar fell to the platform in the position of a push-up, his hands beneath his shoulders, his fingers clutching the round rim of the borehole, his head peering down. He placed both hands upon the ram blowout preventer. It was cool and strong and steady—nothing was the matter with it. He gazed farther down at the annular blowout preventer, close to the top of the riser pipe, in the water. It should have been still as an iceberg, but it was shivering like a man in the throes of a final fever, the steel ribs around its rubber seal beating violently.

He hadn't been able to tell while he'd been standing, but he recognized now that the annular blowout preventer *was* different than the one he'd had installed on the drillship two years ago—that was why its color looked duller. Someone had switched out the original, and the new one looked similar enough to go unnoticed unless one stared at it closely. But who could have switched out the preventer?

It would have been the man who'd tried to kill him yesterday, through the collapse of the derrick. But who was that man?

"Shut everything down!" Izar hollered, raising his head from the borehole. "There's a problem—"

The steel ribs of the preventer exploded like a dozen belts, the rubber seal beneath them dissolving into flaccid fragments. The vertical, two-foot-wide riser pipe that connected the seabed to the storage tank cracked open, as smoothly as though struck by a saw. Blackness gushed out in all directions like blackberry juice. Izar felt as though he'd been stabbed and was watching his own blood spill out of him. But who had stabbed him?

Even if it killed him, he would learn the answer, he determined. He thought of what the drunkard Rigel had said on the island of Mira—that he was a pawn in a game. Could it be true? If so, who was playing this game against him, and to what end?

The platform quivered, as the earth might just before an earthquake. With the preventer broken, the drillship would sink in a matter of minutes, Izar recognized.

The workers, who did not have his background in engineering and physics, sensed it instinctively. With bull-like bellows, they leapt into a stampede of activity, hauling lifeboats onto the platform from over the rails. Working in pairs, they connected the lifeboats to mechanical pumps. The boats should have started inflating automatically, like tires connected to bicycle pumps, but they remained flat. One of the men knelt on the platform and thumped his hand along the fabric. "Someone knifed the material!" he cried.

Similar cries erupted from bow to stern throughout the drillship. All sixteen lifeboats had been ripped, it turned out. Like pin-pricked balloons, they could no longer be used.

"But I checked every one of them yesterday!" Deneb said.

"I believe you," Izar muttered. Zaurak had checked them as well, for the "lifeboats" line-item, like all the others, had been marked off on the checklist he'd placed on Izar's desk. Whoever had knifed the lifeboats must have done it in the middle of the night, when no one was there.

Whoever wanted Izar dead wanted it badly enough to be willing to kill the entire crew. As such, whoever it was, he was not on the drillship. That left only two men: Zaurak and Serpens. It could not be Zaurak, and so, by elimination, it had to be Serpens. But why? Why would Serpens want him dead? He hardly even knew Serpens.

A judder sounded underfoot, and the drillship fell by several inches. Losing their footing, men tumbled and rolled about the platform.

"We're all going to die!" a motorman yelled.

"I knew we shouldn't have left without Zaurak and Serpens!" Deneb said to Izar. He came to imitate Izar's position, such that he also lay sprawled on his belly, peering down through the borehole at the cape of blackness below. He squeezed his cap in both hands until it was as shapeless as a rag. "What should we do?"

Izar alone knew the drillship inside and out, the whole in addition to the parts. But there was nothing that could be done. Trying to save the drillship would be like trying to save an airplane whose engine was dead.

But he had to try. They would all die otherwise. The only way to save the drillship and the men aboard it would be to detach the rig from the ship. With the rupture of the annular blowout preventer, most of the rig was already detached, but it would be essential to detach it fully. The rig was like a limb that had torn off unevenly instead of being cleanly severed; its gangrenous tissue would infect and kill the whole. Izar would have to dislocate the ram blowout preventer and plug the borehole, otherwise oil would lap onto the platform soon, and *Dominion Drill I* would sink under the weight of the very oil it was supposed to have collected. But to remove the preventer was a job that would take at least an hour, not minutes—yet minutes were all Izar had.

"Do exactly as I'm doing," he directed Deneb.

He wrapped both hands around the ram blowout preventer. Deneb placed his hands next to Izar's. They tried to turn the preventer, to rotate it clockwise, and then counterclockwise, but the valve didn't budge. Meanwhile, the ocean continued to darken below, the oil like a sticky, thickening cake of tar. The drillship continued to lower, several sudden inches at a time; Izar felt each lurch in his belly. A gush of grease washed onto the platform through the borehole. Gooey, stinky, it rolled underneath Izar on the platform, through his shirt and pants, and Izar thought of himself as a cutlet in a frying pan. And then another wave of oil hijacked the ship. The drillship fell again; this time, the fall was by more than a foot, and Izar felt as though a string connected to his navel had jerked him down.

Time was almost out.

A sweat broke out on his brow. Deneb was also sweating, so profusely that the mermaid across his arm seemed to be weeping, her tears falling into the ocean through the borehole. Izar shifted in position slightly, such that his left hand, with the platinum chip, bore most of the pressure of the attempted rotation. He clenched his teeth so tightly that he thought the two rows might shatter against each other. But then it happened: The preventer started to loosen.

A froth of oil splashed his face and Deneb's; they managed to shut their eyes just in time. They continued to rotate the valve together, their eyes opening cautiously. The blowout preventer came off, their hands released it, and it fell into the oil, where it disappeared instantly, like a clove in a stew. Their hands working in unison, Izar and Deneb slid the stopper out from just underneath the platform and rotated it upward through a handle in its center. It was like a bathtub drain plug, except with a diameter of four feet rather than four centimeters. They rotated it repeatedly until it was on level with the platform and could be tightened no further, like the lid of a jar.

Oil could no longer get onto *Dominion Drill I*—which, now, without the rig, was no longer a drillship, but just a ship. The thought made Izar feel both safe and sad as he laid his cheek against the stopper. The stopper was greasy, filthy, but it did not matter—he would live; they would all live.

Through oil-smeared eyelashes he saw rows of steel-toed boots; he had not realized it, but the men had gathered around him and Deneb while the two of them had been working. Now they tugged Deneb up to his feet, lifted him onto their shoulders, and tossed him up and down, cheering raucously. They knew better than to be so informal with Izar—he would view it as an infraction. As the men celebrated their survival, Izar continued to lie there on the platform, in the midst of others but pleasantly alone.

Something rolled over to his cheek, coming to a stop along his scar. Narrow and cylindrical, it was blackened with oil, such that he could identify nothing beyond its shape. It must have gotten lodged in the stopper, otherwise he would have noticed it before. He picked it up and dabbed the oil off with his thumb.

It was Zaurak's engraved pen, he saw with a start.

Its location all but stated that Zaurak had been at the borehole and that he'd been there after having placed his checklist on Izar's desk, for he'd have used the same pen to complete the checklist.

But why would Zaurak have visited the borehole specifically? Izar tried desperately, but he could think of no reason Zaurak would have for visiting the borehole other than to switch out the annular blowout preventer. But

Zaurak had a crippled leg; he could not plunge into the water through the borehole himself. The thought did not bring Izar the relief he expected, though, for Zaurak could have done it with his right-hand man, Serpens. Relatedly, Serpens would have been the one to lean out over the rails and slash all the lifeboats. Was that why they were missing together—because they were working together to try to kill Izar?

It could not be, yet it had to be . . . the pen in his hand told him so. It must have slipped out of Zaurak's shirt pocket and gotten lodged in the stopper by accident.

Yesterday, Zaurak had whispered in Serpens's ear during the drillship check—he must have been telling Serpens to loosen the foothold of the derrick and make it fall upon Izar. When that ploy had failed—Deneb had rescued Izar—Zaurak and Serpens must have started hatching this second plan, to sink the ship.

Izar wrapped his arms around himself, feeling as though invisible feet were kicking him in the ribs. Three years ago, when Antares had wanted to fire Zaurak upon promoting Izar, he had fought fiercely for his friend and mentor, even threatening to leave Ocean Dominion for him. He would give his life for Zaurak; why would Zaurak want to take his life?

He shook the pen in his hand, as though he were shaking Zaurak by the shoulders. *Answer me!* he implored the pen. But it remained silent. His neck hot and red, Izar dragged himself to his feet and lumbered over to the rails. With all the strength of his arm, he flung the pen as far away as he could and watched it fall and disappear in the flood of blackness below.

8

Black Poison

I caught you!" Coralline cried.

Ecklon whirled around.

His companion was very much not Rosette, Coralline saw. It was a grim, diminutive merman with an enormous nose, fossil-gray eyebrows, and deep lines through his forehead: Sinistrum Scomber—his boss. Sinistrum grimaced at her, then swam past her out the window with such haste that his tailfin practically knocked her decanter of parasol wine off the windowsill.

Ecklon swam over to Coralline, wrapped his hands around her waist, and pulled her into his room through the window. His hands lingered over her tailbone, his fingers loose and light. He was wearing a stiff, deep-green waistcoat with a high collar encrusted with translucent-green olivine stones. Coralline's arms draped around his neck, her fingers strumming through his hair. She saw her face in his silver-gray eyes and tried to concentrate on her reflection, but it melted and vanished as fast as a sea pen. She should not be drinking so much, she thought, as she took another sip.

Turning her head slowly, she looked about his bedroom—in two weeks, it would be *their* bedroom. His floor was laid not of the usual dull gray gabbro stone, nor even the more fine-grained basalt, but limestone. White and smooth, streaked gently with pale gray, it formed a sharp contrast to the black shale exterior of the Mansion. A large, bright rug sprawled in the center of the room, its pile filaments carrying the red, blue, and yellow tones of a flame angelfish. Beside the rug stood a bed, twice the size of Coralline's, its posts pointing as pinnacles toward the ceiling. Its frame was slate but not the traditional gray slate used for furniture—rather, a rare, handsome green slate. A sky-blue blanket with shimmering golden threads lay upon the bed.

She could get used to life in the Mansion.

There was a nonchalance she noticed in Ecklon's manner, an indifference to the opulence around him, as though no matter the superiority of his surroundings, they could not be superior to him.

"Who exactly did you think I was with, Cora?" Ecklon asked.

"No one," she said, looking away.

"Rosette?"

Her gaze darted to his. It seemed to provide him his answer, for he threw his head back and laughed, dimples carving triangles in his cheeks. Coralline tried to cling to her hapless sense of indignation, but she found herself smiling at him. "I'm sorry," she said sheepishly.

"I'm sorry, too. I should have been with you instead of Sinistrum. But he requested to speak with me urgently."

"What about?"

"He'd promised me he'd tenure me when I solved my next case. I solved it last night—a poisoning by the acid kelp, desmarestia." Ecklon's eyes glittered so brightly that Coralline had the illusion of looking at twin stars. "Sinistrum tenured me today! I now have a lifetime position with Urchin Interrogations. Isn't that wonderful?"

Coralline's fingers stilled in his hair. Pavonis had been right in saying that marrying Ecklon would mean marrying Urchin Grove. Just when she'd become somewhat unmoored to the village, through her firing, he'd become especially moored to it, through his tenure.

"What's the matter, Cora? I thought you'd be happy for me—for us."

"I am. . . ." she said, studying the array of olivine stones studding his collar.

"Talk to me." He tilted her chin up with a hand, such that she had no choice but to meet his eyes.

"What if we don't want to spend the rest of our lives in Urchin Grove?"

He blinked. "Our families live here. We want for nothing here. Why would we ever leave?"

"To see more of the world."

"Urchin Grove is our world."

"I guess you're right. . . ."

Coralline rested her cheek against his waistcoat, so he could not see her face. The village of her birth would be the village of her death—surely, there were worse things in life than that. Earlier she'd longed to tell him about her dismissal, but she could not tell him now, not when he was celebrating his tenure. Here he was, the superlative detective of Urchin Grove, marrying a mermaid fired from her very first job.

A blue-striped grunt fish snorted as it passed outside the window. Coralline's head rose from Ecklon's chest, her eyes pursuing its path.

"We should go see our guests," Ecklon said, sighing.

Coralline nodded, though there was nothing she wished to do less. As she and Ecklon swam over the rug, its kaleidoscopic colors fractured into a thousand fragments, then assembled again just as swiftly—the parasol wine was really muddling her mind. Hand in hand, she and Ecklon emerged from the window, swerved around the rear of the Mansion, and swam into the garden.

All eyes turned to them, and a crowd started to form. People looked at her differently when she was with him than without him, Coralline noticed, their gazes carrying more respect.

A figure hurtled toward the front of the crowd. Her corset formed a wisp of low-cut sapphire blue, minimalist both at the top and bottom, for it culminated at her ribs, revealing an enviably slender waist. With her sapphire bodice and flaming hair, Rosette Delesse formed a stunning vision. Batting her eyelashes at Ecklon, she wrapped her arms around him. A long moment passed, and whispers started among the guests, and Coralline cleared her throat loudly, before Rosette managed to untangle herself from him. Turning to Coralline, she asked with a smirk, "How's work?"

Coralline gulped. From Rosette's tone, it was clear Rosette knew of her firing, but how could she possibly know?

From the window of The Conventional Cure, she must have seen Coralline leaving The Irregular Remedy in tears, and she must have guessed the reason for it. How humiliating—at Coralline's own engagement party, Rosette must have told many guests about the firing, perhaps fabricating colorful rumors as well.

Just then, Coralline overheard one mermaid say to another, "Do you think it's true Coralline got fired for stealing carapace?" Her companion whispered back, "Oh, I thought she stabbed a patient who was having a heart attack."

Coralline felt her cheeks burning. Fortunately, Ecklon did not seem to have heard the two mermaids, for he was looking politely between her and Rosette. This was not how Coralline wanted him to find out. He did not yet know; she hoped her parents, and his parents, didn't either.

Abalone arrived in front of Coralline, displacing Rosette, who left grudgingly. But Coralline's relief at her mother's arrival was short-lived. Grasping Coralline's wrists, Abalone hissed, "I've been looking everywhere for Naiadum and I don't see him. You promised you'd find him. Where is he?"

"I'm sorry. I forgot to look for him." In her haste to escape Rhodomela (whom she could not see at the moment), then her snooping on Ecklon, Coralline had neglected to search for Naiadum. She scanned the throng now for a tawny tail, but the darting of her eyes made her as dizzy as though she were spinning in circles. Where could her little brother possibly be?

Coralline looked up. A tornado of large silver cod were descending so rapidly from the surface that the lateral line along their sides looked like single arrows. Above them, along the waves, a band of blackness seemed to be settling. Because of the band's position, far behind and above everyone, she seemed to be the only one to see it, but she must be wrong, she had to be imagining it, it had to be a lingering effect of the parasol wine, for she'd never seen a band of blackness before.

Coralline looked down. A yellowtail flounder buried itself in the sediment until no more than two of its rusty red spots remained visible. Half a dozen hogchokers smaller than a finger settled into the sands until their tiny, dark-brown forms were fully covered.

Something was wrong. Very wrong.

Coralline looked up again. The black was a growing blanket, rippling menacingly close. She should point and scream. Her lips parted, but her tongue remained glued to the roof of her mouth. What if she was wrong? Wouldn't she look foolish then? Wouldn't everyone know she was drunk?

"*BLACK POISON!*" a voice yelled. Coralline could not see Rhodomela—she must be at the hem of the crowd—but the voice was distinctively hers.

All necks craned up simultaneously. Shouts began, then blended, such that they became a deafening roar. Guests started scrambling into the Elnath Mansion through the windows. The black blanket, now directly above, was descending continuously, its path blocking sunshine and shrouding the waters. Coralline clutched Ecklon's elbow. The ocean was closing in around her. No place could offer a superior refuge to the Mansion, and her tailfin flicked in her readiness to swim through a window herself, but she had to find her brother first. "Naiadum's missing," she told Ecklon.

Within a minute, all guests were indoors, and only Coralline and Ecklon remained in the garden, their eyes scanning the waters for Naiadum. An immense bow shape circled above and descended with a powerful swell of water—Pavonis. Coralline sagged against him and asked him whether he'd seen Naiadum. "I haven't," he huffed. "Your brother tends to always be under-tail; how can he have vanished?"

The sands agitated, and velvety, navy-blue wings patterned with white spots emerged like bedsheets lifting—Menziesii. He nodded his head at Coralline in greeting, and she nodded back at him. Spotted eagle rays were often taciturn, but Ecklon's muse, Menziesii, was more taciturn than most—a nod usually formed the extent of his communication with her.

"Did Naiadum give any hints about where he could possibly be?" Ecklon demanded, grasping Coralline by the arms.

"The day before yesterday, when I was reading him a bedtime story, he told me he wanted to crest. He threatened he might venture up to the waves when I wasn't looking."

Coralline, Ecklon, Pavonis, and Menziesii looked up as one at the dark swath. Opaque and indiscernible, descending continuously, it was by now almost upon them. Coralline shrank and shuddered in its shadow.

Ecklon raised his arms such that they formed arrows to either side of his head and, without a further word, he dove upward into the blackness. Before Coralline could even blink, he'd disappeared in the swirl, vanishing as fast as a tube anemone. Menziesii disappeared after Ecklon, just as completely and wordlessly, his long whip of a tail slapping the waters behind him. Pavonis fixed a grim eye on Coralline and then angled himself up and vanished also.

Part of the reason they were entering the black poison so readily was that they were not apothecaries. From her medical textbooks, Coralline knew the precise perils of black poison: gill slits could close, causing suffocation, and ingestion of the poison could cause blood contamination. The difference between the two forms of death was speed—fast versus slow. Those who were prone to fainting were particularly susceptible during a black poison spill, because, when unconscious, their bodies were limp and defenseless against the poison. And Coralline was more prone to fainting than anyone she'd ever known.

What if she died in her attempt to save Naiadum? In fact, what if Naiadum was already dead? But he could not be dead, she told herself. Had he died, his body would have sunk down to the seabed—as merpeople bodies did in death—and a passing mermaid or merman would have spotted him. Unless, of course, black poison caused flotation, in which case his body would not sink.

Coralline's hands rose to her gill slits, as she imagined them closing like window shutters in the slime. Smacking her forehead to clear her thoughts, she scolded, *Stop being a coward!* Then she raised her arms over her head, pressed her lips together, and, tail quaking violently, arrowed her way into the black poison.

The blackness coated first her fingers, then her arms, then her shoulders—a slippery, stinking layer—then it covered her scales and slipped steadily through the sequins of her corset to swathe her skin. It constricted her breathing—her gills were no longer flaring open and closed freely, but were fluttering weakly along the sides of her neck. It weighed down her tail, such that she had to swing with all her strength in order to move at all.

She sought Pavonis's wide tailfin in the blackness but could see no farther than her own fingertips. Knowing she wouldn't last long in the low-oxygen environment, she swung her tail harder in order to arrive at the surface faster. The blackness became increasingly impermeable, a part of the water but also apart from it. . . . Her eyes closed, her head lolled, and her arms flopped down to her sides. *I can't afford to faint now*, she whispered to herself. Both her life and Naiadum's depended on her remaining conscious. Opening her eyes, she managed to force her arms back over her head. All of a sudden, her head erupted over the waves.

She kept her neck submerged, so that her gills could continue to breathe (to the limited extent that they could in the black poison). The air whipped and parched her greasy cheeks and desiccated her eyes, turning her vision as gray and heavy as the sky that stretched above. A wave of blackness crashed over her head. She shivered uncontrollably, feeling as vulnerable as a turtle without a shell. She considered the ocean itself a shell—like a roof over the head, it formed a dense layer of protection, as well as separation, from humans.

"Coralline!"

The voice was unfamiliar, as was the face in the distance. It took her a moment to recognize Ecklon, for his face was smeared black; she probably looked the same to him, she thought. And his voice sounded different because he'd called her name in the air rather than water.

Behind Ecklon, Coralline made out the triangular shape of Pavonis's dorsal fin, as well as one of Menziesii's white-spotted wings. Far behind them was a ship, retreating into the distance, a tower rising to the sky at its center. From her position, the men trodding about the ship looked like black sticks against the sun. She'd never seen humans before—their legs truly were as stodgy and graceless as she'd always heard. A bronze-and-black Ocean Dominion insignia glowed on the side of the ship.

An object floated over to Coralline's nose. Narrow and black, it was a pen engraved with the Ocean Dominion logo and a name next to it in block letters: Zaurak Alphard.

She squeezed the pen with both hands, as though it were the villain's throat.

"*Coralline!*" Ecklon cried again.

She slashed toward him, her head still over the water. But her progress was stalled, for she bumped into countless carcasses along the way: a northern puffer fish, floating with its yellow belly pointing skyward; a patch of tripletail fish floating on their sides; a leatherback sea turtle, the length of its carapace rivaling her own length.

Only when Coralline reached Ecklon did she see that his arms were cradling a body. A small, limp form with a pudgy, blackened face. Only the edges of his tailfin still hinted at its earlier tawny color. Naiadum.

The wall-to-wall carpet was not the standard, scratchy office floor covering; rather, it was an extravagant beige rug with an immense, bright-pink chrysanthemum blooming at its center. The walls of the press conference room were not a cold white, but were covered in a wallpaper of flying fish. And the chandeliers imparted a warm golden glow rather than an unfeeling fluorescent one. Floor-length windows stretched over one whole side of the rectangular room, and a slow sunset crept over the faces of the assembled men and women, bathing half of their faces in long, orange shadows.

Reporters are like "rabid dogs," Antares often said, like "a hissing herd of hyenas," and the press conference room, with its spongy colors and soft swaths of light, was designed to try to sedate their senses.

Antares stood at the center of a small stage at the front of the room. Saiph and Izar flanked him, standing along the two back corners of the stage, their hands folded before them in the manner of security guards. It had always been the role of the three of them to protect Ocean Dominion, but Izar had failed today, and his failure had endangered them all. The company he loved more than life itself stood liable to burst into flames all around him.

Directly in front of the stage, reporters sat at the edge of their seats, their raised hands rupturing the air above them at abandon. It was not a scene Izar had seen before. At most Ocean Dominion press conferences, most chairs were empty; today, each chair was occupied, and a surplus of reporters crowded together along the fringes of the room. There must be two hundred of them, Izar estimated, their faces forming a sea of scorn waiting to drown Ocean Dominion. Izar felt as though he, Antares, and Saiph were defendants standing trial before a smug, self-appointed jury.

Izar had spoken to Antares and Saiph just before the three of them had climbed onto the stage. Antares had hugged him and, with thick tears shimmering in his eyes, had said, "It's too bad about the spill, but I'm happy you're safe, son. I don't know how I'd live if anything happened to you."

Izar had hugged him back, but shame had lingered along the corners of his mouth. Speaking crisply, he'd given Antares and Saiph a detailed recounting of what had happened, mentioning both the collapse of the derrick yesterday and the explosion of the blowout preventer today. Antares had immediately given his assistant an order to dispatch a Secret Search team of five black-clad men to locate Zaurak and Serpens, neither of whom had been seen in the Ocean Dominion building or harbor all day.

"You won't be safe until they're locked behind bars," Antares had said to Izar, "and so I will not rest until that moment. Guard your life at every step, son."

Now, Antares nodded at a young, thin-lipped woman in the front row, whose hand was tearing through the air. "Your company spilled more than ten thousand barrels, or about four hundred thousand gallons, of oil into the ocean today," she said. "The spill is so substantial as to be visible by satellite. Your market capitalization has collapsed by half a billion dollars. Do you think your fate will resemble that of Atlantic Operations?"

Izar felt himself bristling like a copper wire sparked end to end. It was insulting—comparing Ocean Dominion to a defunct competitor.

"We hope not," Antares answered evenly.

From the streets thirty stories below, a chant floated up as a faint tremor: "Death to Ocean Dominion! Life to the ocean!" Nonprofit organization Ocean Protection had rallied hundreds of placard-wielding protestors on the streets below. They'd been chanting so incessantly that, to Izar's ears, their mantra now sounded like a hymn with a catchy ring.

Antares nodded at a middling reporter. "Who is to blame for the oil spill?" the man croaked.

Izar had expected the question, but his knees still turned to jelly, and a sheen of sweat broke out across his hairline. The world would now know he was responsible.

"I, and I alone," said Antares, "am to blame for the spill—"

Izar heard a suppressed choke; it had sputtered out of his own throat. He realized he'd crossed the stage to Antares only when Antares's steel-gray eyes were staring at him impatiently—it was unprecedented for either Saiph or Izar to interrupt Antares during a press conference. They were sentries, not spotlights, their function ornamental.

Pens scribbled frenziedly upon notepads as Antares wrapped a ham-like fist over the microphone and turned it away from his face.

"*I* am vice president of operations," Izar hissed in Antares's ear, a hand cupping his mouth to conceal the movement of his lips. "Any error in equipment, or the men who manage it, is my fault. Tell them the truth."

"Return to your place, son," Antares said in a barely constrained voice, "and never question my judgment again."

Resuming his location, Izar stared stoically at Antares's back.

"In light of today's events," Antares boomed over the microphone, "I announce my resignation, effective immediately."

Cameras flashed, one after another, lighting up shadowed pockets of the room like fireflies in the woods.

It was fortunate there was a wall behind Izar; otherwise, he would have keeled to the floor. His shoulder blades sagged against the wall, and an airless vacuum formed in his chest. Izar had once, years ago, asked Antares what he would do when he retired. "I'm not the sort of man who sits around and goes fishing, boy," he'd guffawed. "I'll retire when I'm in my coffin."

Twenty-five years ago, Antares had saved Izar's life by rescuing him from drowning by merpeople; today, Izar had paid Antares back by carving his coffin. Antares would live physically, but his professional death could just as well be his physical death. It had taken him thirty-five long years to build Ocean Dominion into the force that it was; it had taken Izar a single day to stab it. The oil spill was like a gash to the face of Ocean Dominion—even if the company survived the attack, a scar would always remain, as would Izar's knowledge that it was he who'd wielded the knife.

How different the press conference had turned out to be from what they'd planned in Antares's office just three days ago. Antares was supposed to have announced Castor and proclaimed the beginning of a new division at Ocean Dominion and a new era for the world—one lit with underwater fire. He was also supposed to have mentioned the two-year milestone for the Oil division.

"I will be succeeded by my son, Saiph Eridan," Antares continued over the microphone. He began to ring out Saiph's accomplishments—Saiph's knowledge of the levers of government, his experience in management, his appreciation of the patent process—but the words floated over Izar's head. His ribs felt as stiff as though they'd been flattened under Castor's feet.

He glanced at Saiph on the other side of the stage. He was smiling courteously at the crowd, the corners of his lips edged with humility, his charred-kale eyes gleaming.

Since the day Antares had rescued Izar and kindled in him a fascination with fire, Izar had known his destiny lay with Ocean Dominion. Throughout his studies, in both school and university, he had moved from one assignment to another with impatient efficiency, excelling at them not because of any illusions of their having intrinsic value but because he'd believed they'd serve as stepping-stones for the purpose he'd start to obtain as soon as he arrived at Ocean Dominion. Saiph's fondness for Ocean Dominion did not match his—Saiph's feeling was like a swimming pool, pleasant but shallow; it was not the sea that sang daily through Izar's veins.

But, of course, Izar had never expected to become president. He had always known that if there were to come a time when Antares retired, Saiph would assume the role of president. Saiph was Antares's biological son, but it was more than that: Saiph *wanted* to be president; Izar had never once wanted it—the endless meetings, the appeasing of egos, the management of politics. At university, Izar had studied engineering; Saiph, management. Izar had found his niche in the engineering realm; Saiph, in the interpersonal. Izar was a technical man, with a tactical bent; Saiph built relationships strategically, like every day was a game of chess.

It did not bother Izar that Saiph would be president. What bothered him was that Saiph's first executive action would, almost certainly, be to fire him. Izar could not expect Antares to know this, for Antares had never known Saiph as Izar had. Antares did not know, for instance, about Bumble.

In the first week that Izar had arrived in Antares's home as a three-year-old, Saiph had descended into his basement storage closet bedroom and offered him a teddy bear, Bumble. Izar had accepted the round, mud-brown form gratefully and fallen asleep with Bumble in his arms. Over the next month, he had come to consider Bumble his comfort, his safety, his only source of familiarity in his unfamiliar new world, and had spent every minute, awake or asleep, with the bear. But then, one night, just as suddenly as Saiph had arrived in his storage closet to give Bumble to him, he had arrived to snatch him away. Izar had wailed for the bear, but Saiph had grinned and slammed the door shut behind him.

The next morning, Izar had sneaked upstairs into Saiph's bedroom while Saiph had been practicing piano with a tutor in the library, Maia hovering over him like an eagle over her nestling. Izar had discovered Saiph's bedroom to be a zoo of stuffed animals—tigers, giraffes, pandas, leopards, on shelves that ran from floor to ceiling—but there was no Bumble anywhere in sight. Izar had nonetheless felt appeased by his visit: Given Saiph's menagerie of animals, surely, he would not mind Izar's keeping one. Surely, he would return Bumble soon.

That night, Saiph had returned to Izar's storage closet and, eyes twinkling like fresh-cut grass, had handed Bumble back to him. Izar had grasped the teddy bear for only a moment, before dropping him with a gasp. Bumble's button-nose had been dangling from a thread, one of his eyes had been missing, and white fuzz had been streaming out of his belly like rotting innards.

Izar's hands clenched on stage in the press conference room, as though they continued to clutch Bumble's remains. Saiph had destroyed Bumble because he'd known how much the teddy bear meant to him; Saiph would fire him because he knew how much Ocean Dominion meant to him.

9

Brother

As Coralline observed from a shadowed corner, her mother and Rhodomela eyed each other at the door with a marked vehemence. They were the same age, fifty, but Rhodomela—wiry as a strand of eel-grass—looked a decade older, Coralline noticed for the first time.

Rhodomela swept into the Costaria home, trailed by Trochid, whom Abalone had sent to The Irregular Remedy to fetch her. He had left home for the clinic hours ago; patients must have streamed in one after another for Rhodomela's attention, Coralline thought, hence the delay in his return with her. He could easily have gone to another clinic, such as The Conventional Cure just next door to The Irregular Remedy, but he had waited, Coralline knew, because Rhodomela was the foremost black poison expert in Urchin Grove. It was her Black Poison Cleanser solution that had led to her achieving the title of master apothecary.

Rhodomela's gaze fell on every part of the Costaria living room: the settees, Trochid's desk in the corner, the dining table in the alcove, the large arched window overlooking the reef garden, the row of three bedrooms. Her glance seemed to cling especially to the wedding-day portrait of Abalone and Trochid on the mantel. Trochid's hair had grayed at the temples in the two and a half decades since the wedding, but Abalone still looked just as golden as she had then. Perhaps Rhodomela was wondering how her own life might have looked had she married, Coralline thought.

Abalone led Rhodomela to Naiadum's bedroom. Rhodomela brushed past Coralline without even greeting her, as though they'd never met.

In her black bodice, Rhodomela had been the only person inappropriately attired at the engagement party, but she was the only person appropriately attired in the aftermath of the black poison spill. Coralline's orange-and-purple sequins dangled off her corset on loose threads. The tendrils trailing the hem of Abalone's bodice had been white earlier but were black now and hanging straight down upon her scales instead of swirling about her when she moved.

"Black poison has gravely sickened at least two dozen people in Urchin Grove so far," Rhodomela said in a monotonous voice, "and has rendered at least four terminally ill. In addition, there have been a minimum of three deaths. . . ."

Rhodomela was speaking of death and illness like it was a part of life—because it was a part of her life—but her staid recounting of casualties caused Abalone and Trochid to shudder. Coralline frowned at her former boss, wishing she would be more sensitive.

Rhodomela perched on Naiadum's blanket exactly where Coralline always sat when she read him a bedtime story. She unlatched the clasps of her apothecary arsenal, her out-of-office medical kit. Coralline watched her anxiously, from the row she formed with her parents against the wall behind Rhodomela. Coralline glanced at the books on Naiadum's bedside table—*The Wrong Wrasse, A Little Merboy Named Anthias*. She had not yet read these stories to him.

"Coralline," said Trochid, "will you not bring your own apothecary arsenal to help Rhodomela?"

"That won't be necessary," Rhodomela replied, before Coralline could stammer out a response. Her head swiveled around, her nose looking especially hooked in profile. "Didn't Coralline tell you? She doesn't work for me anymore."

Trochid's mouth fell open. Abalone gasped. Coralline's cheeks flamed, and she stared mutely at the opposite wall. It was the first secret she'd ever kept from her parents, and for only a short period of time—since yesterday. Her father, she knew, must be especially hurt, because he had always advised her on her career, but she had blocked him out as soon as something had gone wrong.

"Did you fire her out of revenge?" Abalone snapped, amber-gold eyes narrowed.

"Revenge for what?" Rhodomela asked, sounding as surprised as Coralline felt.

"Abalone!" Trochid said. "Let's focus on our son. His life lies in Rhodomela's hands."

Rhodomela turned back to Naiadum somewhat stiffly. Just before Rhodomela's arrival, Abalone had attempted to rub the grease off Naiadum—scrubbing him with the same ferocity with which she stitched fabrics—but she had only succeeded in smearing the slime deeper, such that Coralline hardly even recognized her brother. Rhodomela opened a vial of Black Poison Cleanser, lathered the salve onto gauzy pink swaths of pyropia, then rubbed it all over Naiadum, starting with his face and proceeding down to his tailfin. Everywhere it touched, it wiped spotless like magic.

The secret of her solution was that it was oil-based, Coralline remembered Rhodomela telling her, for only oil could conquer oil—water was too pure to dissolve it. The solution consisted primarily of derbesia's green tufts ground with spatoglossum's brown fronds, both of them among the most oleaginous of the algae.

When Rhodomela sat back, Coralline wished she hadn't done such a thorough job with her brother, for it was impossible to mistake anymore that the yellowed, waxen figure on the bed was Naiadum.

Her cleaning complete, Rhodomela proceeded swiftly with her medical examination. She turned Naiadum's wrist and pressed her fingers to it, to check his pulse. She pried open each of his eyes and scrutinized their whites. She turned his head and ran her index finger over his neck—his gill slits flickered, but just barely. She inserted a needle into the vein at his elbow and watched blood gush into the syringe. Holding the syringe under a microscope, she flicked it three times with her fingernail, then studied it.

"Black poison has contaminated his blood," she announced. "It has clotted his organs, disabling their effective functioning. He will die within two weeks—before your wedding, Coralline."

Izar buzzed his identification card in front of the scanner and pushed open the glass door, then paused midstride at the sight in the room.

Saiph sat in Antares's black leather chair, behind Antares's grand mahogany desk, in Antares's office. Izar's hands balled into fists—he had a mind to grab Saiph by the collar and hurl him out of the chair—but it was not Saiph's fault, he reminded himself. It was Izar who had forced Antares out of his own office and put Saiph in.

Izar didn't feel his legs stride across the cream carpet—they were silent wheels, conveying him to his hanging. He collapsed in the chair across from Saiph's desk.

Saiph slid a glass of whisky toward him. Izar shook his head. He wouldn't engage in the weekly ritual they'd both shared with Antares; he wouldn't pretend things were as they had been, when they never would be again. "Any update on Zaurak or Serpens?" he asked hoarsely.

"I spoke with the Secret Search team just minutes ago. They have nothing."

Izar nodded, then swallowed hard before blurting out the hardest words he'd ever uttered: "Did you call me here to request my resignation?"

"I wouldn't accept your resignation, even were you to offer it."

So, Saiph wished to humiliate Izar by firing him.

"I've always envied you," Saiph said.

"What for?" Izar asked, his eyes widening with astonishment.

"Your mind. I've envied you ever since that day we met, when you built a precise replica of our family home, and I couldn't."

Izar's ear caught on "*our* family home." Saiph had never before indicated he considered it their shared home; he had always made Izar feel like an unwanted guest, especially after Maia's death.

"I'm sorry," Saiph said. The word seemed to have cost him something, for he tilted his head back and gulped down his full glass of whisky. He then looked Izar unflinchingly in the eye. "I'm sorry I made your life miserable. I'm sorry I never accepted you. I'm sorry for everything. Will you ever forgive me, brother?"

"Yes," Izar said at length, though he continued to gape at Saiph. Then he found himself grinning from ear to ear. A brother. After twenty-five years of intersecting with a stranger, he would finally have a brother. He'd never even thought he wanted a brother until now.

"Good," Saiph said. He leaned forward until his elbows rested on the desk, his navy-blue suit jacket taut over his shoulders. His hair, gelled back, glistened like a dune of sand. "I want you to join me in the role of president. I would like for us to be co-presidents of Ocean Dominion."

Izar had always recognized that it was at his adoptive father's company where he worked, and he'd always known that Antares watched over him as an invisible, omniscient god even through the many floors that separated them—but he'd deserved each of his previous promotions, for they'd followed on the heels of specific accomplishments. There was no reason for him to be promoted from vice president to co-president today. "I almost drowned the company," he reminded Saiph.

"But you didn't. And we both know it wasn't your fault. It was an attack on your life, for goodness's sake. *I* might well unintentionally drown the company, however, if I work alone. Our skill sets complement one another. I have the soft skills; you have the hard skills. I build connections; you build machines. You're the motor of Ocean Dominion; I'm the grease. The company needs you. *I* need you. I know I'll fail as president without you. I beg you to join me as co-president. Will you?"

"Yes!" Izar beamed. Whatever he'd expected in this meeting, it was not this. He'd been wrong about Saiph. He'd judged Saiph as an adult on the basis of his actions as a child.

"Good." Relief swept over Saiph's chiseled cheekbones.

Izar gulped down the whisky Saiph had poured for him, relishing the trail it burned from his throat to his belly. His only regret was that Antares was not here, with him and Saiph, at this moment.

"In a few months," Izar said, "when the oil spill is old news, when reporters are chewing the bones of some other carcass, let's find a way to bring Father back."

Izar realized only belatedly that he'd referred to Antares as his father. When they were boys, Saiph had punched him every time he'd used the word, threatening also, "I'll cut your tongue out if you ever call him Father again." The word had assumed a ponderous, prophet-like quality for Izar since then; it had meant too much to actually pronounce.

Saiph sat back in his chair and smiled at Izar; he must have noticed Izar's use of the word. "It's a good idea to bring Father back," he said agreeably. "We can be the Trio of Tyrants again!"

They chuckled.

"Let's you and I reconvene here first thing in the morning to devise a strategy," Saiph said. "Also, I've gotten your office cleaned for you."

He was referring to the office Antares had had built for Izar two years earlier on this very floor—the office Izar had rejected in favor of remaining Zaurak's neighbor in the basement, like a mole rat. Izar had foregone sunshine and status for the man who'd tried to kill him. His windowless underground office had been so dilapidated that he'd never thought to show it to Ascella. He would show her his new office next week, he decided.

"How's Ascella?" Saiph asked.

"Well. We went to Yacht two days ago for her birthday. I got her a bracelet."

"Are you planning on a ring as well?"

"How did you guess?"

"You're more predictable than you think, Izar." Saiph grinned. "I'm afraid I've taken after Father myself in the fidelity department!"

"Will you be my best man?" Izar heard himself ask.

"I'd be honored."

Saiph stepped out from behind his desk and hugged Izar. They'd had a fragmented childhood, but they'd have a companionable remainder of their adulthood, Izar thought to himself. Side by side, they would conquer any challenges Ocean Dominion faced.

Coralline stared at the luciferin orbs traveling the ceiling, imparting a white-blue glow to her room. Just the day before yesterday, she'd explained to Naiadum how luciferin orbs worked. There were so many more things she wished to explain to him over the years, so many more bedtime stories she wished to read to him.

A sob broke out of her, and she pressed the palms of her hands into her cheeks to squelch its sound. But the stink of black poison was strong in her fingernails. Disgusted, she moved her hands away and pressed her face into the pillow.

She could not shake the images from her mind: her father crying after Rhodomela's diagnosis, his shoulders quaking—not even when he'd lost his hand had he cried, yet he'd wept inconsolably at the thought of losing his son; her mother yelling, "It's all your fault, Coralline! You promised you'd find him, then you forgot all about him!"

Coralline had become an apothecary so that she could save the lives of those she loved, but she was now no longer an apothecary, nor, even had she been, could she have done anything to save Naiadum—his was a fatal case. Prevention is always better than cure—that was the primary precept of apothecaries—but Coralline had neglected it. She alone had had the power to prevent everything that had happened. If only she'd found Naiadum instead of edging away upon Rhodomela's arrival—like a coward. If only she'd screamed when she'd seen the band of blackness, instead of remaining silent—like a coward.

A thump sounded at her window. She turned to the shutters, her eyes round with alarm. Who could be visiting her after midnight, when all of the village lay in a perturbed sleep? The thump was pursued by another, then another, hard and insistent. She saw no choice but to answer the visitor, otherwise her parents, who'd fallen asleep only with difficulty, would wake up, their room adjoining her own. With a tremulous hand, Coralline pushed back her blanket and crept out of bed. Unfastening the shutters, she blinked through the horizontal slits.

"Took you long enough!" a voice hissed. "Black poison has made this horrible village even more horrible."

Pavonis. Coralline could hardly see him because of the darkness, but she would have recognized him even had he not spoken, from the strong ripples created by his arrival. She reached a hand through the shutters to touch his face and felt comforted when her fingers found his snout. His head itself was larger than the window frame, so he angled himself to it diagonally, such that one eye was looking at her through a slit in the shutters. She would normally have pulled open the pane of shutters and stayed with him at the window, but, drained from the events of the day, she returned to her bed and pulled her blanket up to her chin.

"I have an idea," Pavonis announced.

"What?" she asked with little interest.

"We can save Naiadum through the elixir."

"The elixir is just a legend, Pavonis."

"We don't know that."

"Well, I don't understand how an elixir can be made of starlight. And a quest for the elixir is known to be foolhardy."

"Foolhardy is a league above cowardly."

"I am a coward, Pavonis! When a ship passes above, my first inclination is to hide under a table."

"That may be your inclination under ordinary circumstances, but not necessarily under extraordinary circumstances. You saw the ship from the waves today, the ship that spewed the black poison—you didn't hide; you stayed."

"I suppose," Coralline said glumly.

"Beyond saving your brother, I have another motive for my elixir quest recommendation, as I'm sure you've guessed."

"I haven't."

"I'm itching to leave Urchin Grove. We never managed to make it on our North-to-South Expedition after your graduation from Urchin Apothecary Academy, but we can make it on this expedition, this . . . *Elixir* Expedition, let's call it. Let's leave tonight, before anyone rises."

"But where would we even begin our quest? How would we find Mintaka, the magician who makes the elixir?"

"Hmm. Let's begin by swimming over to that fiancé of yours and enlisting him in our Elixir Expedition. Given that he's a detective, I'm hoping he can make himself useful—"

"Well, I wouldn't dream of leaving without him!"

"That makes one of us. Now get out of bed, Coralline."

Coralline thought back to a day at Urchin Rudimentary, when she'd been summoned to the principal's office. She'd been fourteen, and a merboy in her class had shoved Naiadum, then two years old, during playtime. Naiadum's arm had gotten scratched against a stone, and he'd wailed to draw Coralline's attention away from her lunch of felty fingers. Despite being a head shorter than the bullying merboy, Coralline had hurled herself at him and pushed him down into the sand. Her face had been just as startled as his—she hadn't known she'd been capable of aggression until then, when her brother had been hurt.

Now, while Naiadum was hovering on the brink of death, she was lying comfortably ensconced in her bed. *She* was responsible for Naiadum's condition. Therefore, even if it killed her, it was her responsibility to find a way to save him. Flinging off her blanket, she leapt out of bed.

From the doorway, Izar looked about his office: the staid black desk, its surface scratched; the chairs, new but already worn; the faded blueprint of *Dominion Drill I* tacked to the wall with pushpins. For the first time, he understood why he'd always found himself comfortable in this shabby, underground space—it resembled the basement storage closet from his childhood.

His conversation with Saiph had been a shot of adrenaline. His legs pulsed with energy, but his office seemed too cramped to contain it, so he continued to hover in the doorway. There was a gray tin on his desk, he noticed suddenly, just a little bigger than a tissue box.

His neck swerved right and left so sharply that a muscle creaked across his shoulders. But the dimly lit corridor was empty. It was the middle of the night; the men had long gone home. He turned back to the tin, his breath turning low and deep, blood pounding in his ears. The tin must be a third murder attempt on his life. But he'd just spoken with Saiph, who'd just touched base with the Secret Search team, and they had not yet found Zaurak or Serpens. That meant there must be another man involved—a Third Man.

Izar shrugged out of his gray suit jacket, dropping it to the floor. He uncuffed his blue, starched-cotton shirtsleeves and rolled them up to his elbows.

In three long strides, he was behind his desk, in his chair, his gaze unveering from the tin. Its weight would give him a clue. He picked it up gingerly, his fingers leaving tracks in the dust. It was light; from all the dynamite he'd designed for coral reefs, he knew it was unlikely to contain an explosive device. Placing the tin in front of him, he flicked its lid up with a thumb.

A half-shell lay there, with long, flaunting beige ridges and dark-pink fan-like ribs. The shell would have been somewhat heart shaped had it not been broken precisely in half. The line of the break was sharp enough to maim; it was a crude version of a dagger, Izar decided. He had never seen this half-shell before, and yet he had . . . but where? And when? Holding it up to his face, he swept its point just over the ridge of his scar. Could it have been this very half-shell that had gashed his jaw, twenty-five years ago? If so, perhaps the Third Man was telling Izar that, just as his biological parents had died, so he would soon die. As his jaw had been cut open then, his throat would be cut open soon.

Placing the half-shell on his desk, Izar returned his attention to the tin. An amber scroll lay in it, its material as thick as cardboard but, fortunately, a little more flexible than cardboard. He unrolled it carefully. Words were written upon it, but they were as indecipherable as washed-out scratches on a tree trunk. He'd never seen material like this before—that meant it must have come from the water. But what could merpeople have written upon it? And why was it on his desk?

Maybe it was a death note. In fact, in all likelihood, it was.

Izar picked up the final item in the tin: a small card, the size of a business card, but without any words—just coordinates, latitude and longitude. It could be the location of the Third Man. Maybe he was taunting Izar to come out and find him. Maybe the contents of this tin were clues for Izar to solve his own murder mystery.

His feet tapped the wheels of his chair until the half-shell beat a faint tune on his desk, until the scroll started to roll away. His hand caught the scroll before it rolled off his desk—in that moment, a thought flew across his mind: Merpeople paper should be legible underwater! He raced to the restroom one door away from his office and held the bottom-right corner of the material experimentally under the spray of the faucet. It started bleaching a yellow pigment into the sink, like it was bleeding a pus-filled death. He yanked the scroll away from the sink, cursing. How could water damage that which was meant to be read underwater?

He heard a thud—it sounded like someone somewhere in the building was slamming himself against a wall. But between Izar, in the basement on B1, and Saiph, on the thirtieth floor—though he would have gone home by now—there should have been not a soul. Where could the sound have come from? And who could it be?

The Third Man. Perhaps he was trying to leave the building, now that he'd placed the tin on Izar's desk. Izar would not let him leave Ocean Dominion alive.

Quiet as a panther, he stepped out from the restroom into the corridor, and looked about, beads of sweat sprouting on his brow. But the hallway was empty—not a shadow, neither to right nor left. Izar heard another sound—a rattle, like someone was wrestling against his chains. It had come from below. He strode into his office, placed the scroll on his desk, then fell flat to the floor in the position of a push-up, as he had on *Dominion Drill I* when he'd been looking down through the borehole. He pressed his ear to the floor and, eyes shut tight, listened. A faint clang again—definitely from below.

That made even less sense than if it had come from above.

Hurrying out of his office, Izar stomped to the end of the hallway. He flashed his identification card in front of the scanner to the private elevator. Jumping into the ramshackle cage, he pressed B2. As soon as the bars parted, he bolted into his Invention Chamber. But no one was there except for Castor. He breathed a sigh of relief, for the Invention Chamber was the most vulnerable part of the company—a raw, open kidney—because of its shelves of flammable fluids.

A sputtering sound—Izar's gaze flew up to the maze of intestine-like pipes in the ceiling. But this gaseous noise was different than the sounds he'd heard earlier.

He shut the door to the Invention Chamber and returned to the private elevator. His index finger hovered over B1, then dropped down to B3, the floor accessible only to the president of the company.

With a small shock, Izar realized that *he* was now president of Ocean Dominion, along with Saiph, and so the floor should now be accessible to him. He pressed the B3 button so hard that its crimson light flickered out. The ramshackle cage closed and descended. When the elevator came to a halt, Izar flashed his identification card against the interior scanner, but the bars did not part.

Of course. His identification card was still that of vice president. In order to obtain a higher level of access, he would first need to get a new card from the security department. He nonetheless stood there, listening intently, trying to catch a whisper, a rustle. And there it was again, a sound—this time, like a sigh.

The Third Man was here, on this floor. He might have a gun; he might spring out of the shadows at any moment and point it at Izar's head. Trapped in the elevator, Izar would be unable to defend himself. He should flee immediately up to the safety of B1. But though his finger poised over the button, it refrained from pressing it. He continued to stand there, listening with both his ears and body.

But all fell silent. Not even the air swirled anymore on this deserted floor. The only sound he heard was the grating of his own breath. Clutching the bars of the elevator, he banged his head against them, like a caged bear.

It had been a long day; the noises he'd heard must have spewed from the pipes in his Invention Chamber.

10

The Night Assailant

Her decision made to find the elixir, Coralline felt a reservoir of eel-like electric energy building in her tail. She changed out of her chemise into an iridescent-green bodice with thick straps. She then lifted her hair to the top of her head and made a big, loose bun, tying it all with a rope of sisal. Next, she grabbed her satchel off a hook on the wall and laid it open on her bed.

Darting to her armoire, she pulled out a handful of corsets from a drawer. One she held up and examined whimsically—it was the sky-blue bodice she'd worn on her second date with Ecklon, with lace along the neckline and cloud-white ribbons down its center. She remembered how admiringly he'd appraised her that evening. It remained his favorite item of her wardrobe, she believed. Folding it delicately, she placed it in her satchel, along with the other corsets. Then she packed an ivory chemise in which to sleep, carefully tucking into its folds the olivine-encrusted comb her mother had given her.

"You're going on an Elixir Expedition, not your honeymoon," Pavonis called. "Only the bare necessities, please."

Ignoring him, Coralline clutched the pen she'd discovered in the midst of the black poison spill, with the name Zaurak Alphard engraved upon it. She held it close to her nose and stared at it so fiercely that her eyes crossed. It would serve as the funnel for her anger, a motivator if she ever lost courage. She added it to the contents of her satchel.

She then shifted to the shelves lining the wall next to her bedroom door. Her fingers traveled over the spines of some of her favorite medical text-books: *A Reference Guide for the Diligent Apothecary's Bedside, The Medical Relationship Between Happiness and Healing, The Age-Old Amalgamation of Alleviating Algae*. She wanted to pack them, but there was no space in her satchel for books. She rose toward the ceiling to look at her most precious medical item, sitting lofty and self-important on the highest shelf, its case a pretty, pearlescent white: her apothecary arsenal.

Collecting it off the shelf, she slid aside its twin clasps. The apothecary arsenal consisted of two sections: one for algal experimentation—with polished flasks and vials in precise compartments, snippers with shining blades, a blue-shale mortar and pestle, a long-handled microscope; and another section for patient treatment—soft swaths of pyropia bandages, fine filaments for stitches, a scalpel, even a vial of anesthetic.

Her father had given the medical kit to her on her twentieth birthday. It was intended to be used outside of a clinic, when one didn't have all of one's implements at hand. But Coralline had never used it before, because she'd never treated anyone outside of The Irregular Remedy before. Plus, she'd been saving it for a medical emergency.

"As I examined anemones with a microscope during my career as a coral connoisseur," her father had said as he'd handed her the apothecary arsenal, "you will examine algae with a microscope during your career as a healer. My career was shorter than I would have liked"—he'd looked down sadly at his stump—"but I hope yours lasts as long as you live. No joy is more rejuvenating than that which springs from the work you love."

Coralline hugged her apothecary arsenal to her chest. She longed to pack it in her satchel but wondered whether she should. Without a medical badge from the Association of Apothecaries, she would be in defiance of the Medical Malpractice Act if she were found to be treating anyone other than herself. But she was legally permitted to *experiment* with algae—it was just that no one could consume her preparations other than her. Also, since she'd packed a memento of her mother—the jeweled comb—the apothecary arsenal could serve as a memento of her father. Yes, that was fair, reasonable.

She added it to her satchel, packing it vertically, to one side, so its case would not get scratched. It consumed almost half the space of the satchel, but it let her entertain the illusion that she was still an apothecary, and just for that, it was worth it.

Coralline added two small jars of salve to her satchel: toothed wrack salve, for open wounds like cuts and gashes, and horned wrack salve, to reduce swelling and bruising. She'd applied toothed wrack salve every night to her father's stump in the weeks after his haccident, and she'd applied horned wrack salve to Ecklon's fractured elbow the day he'd arrived at The Irregular Remedy for the first time.

"You're taking too long!" Pavonis hissed through the window. "Time waits for no one."

Ignoring him again, Coralline sat at her desk. She examined the streaked red-brown sandstone jar standing in its corner—her carapace crock. Holding the crock next to her ear, she shook it, listening intently to the jingle of shells. She hadn't told anyone except Ecklon and Pavonis—she hadn't even told her father—but she was saving to start her own clinic one day, Coralline's Cures.

She unlidded the crock carefully. The shells within would clang if she were to empty the crock directly onto her desk, so she gathered the shells in her hand and placed them one by one on the gray-slate surface of her desk. When she'd arranged them all in a neat line, from smallest to largest, she started counting them eagerly. She had one moon snail shell, luminous even at night—equivalent to one carapace. One wentletrap, a lovely, spiraled little white cone—two carapace. One slipper limpet, smooth and rounded—five carapace. One scallop, patterned calico—ten carapace. And, thank goodness, one cerith, pigmented and pointed—twenty carapace.

She did the math; the total came to thirty-eight carapace. It was much less than she'd hoped. How she wished she had a conch or whelk in hand—shells worth fifty and a hundred carapace each! But Rhodomela had paid her only fifty carapace per week at The Irregular Remedy, and Coralline had spent much of the amount in household expenditures, for she'd wished to ease her family's financial burden in the wake of her father's retirement. Her decision to work at The Irregular Remedy had been a wrong one in every way, she now admitted to herself.

She piled the shells in a golden drawstring pouch her mother had stitched for her, embroidered with her first and last name in cursive letters. She then extracted a pen and small parchment-pad from the first drawer of her desk. She ran her fingers lovingly over the cover of the pad, embossed as it was with the armored, branching shape of coralline algae. Naiadum had given it to her on her twentieth birthday, and she'd adored it the moment she'd laid eyes on it. She'd considered using it for medical instructions and pre-scriptions to patients, but she had decided it was too beautiful and special for such a mundane use.

Biting a corner of her lip, she tore a page out of her parchment-pad and wrote:

> Dear Mother and Father,
>   I'm leaving to find the elixir to save Naiadum. I'll return as soon as I can.
>   Love, Coralline

She read it over. The note's brevity gave it an unintended sense of for-mality and finality. She thought of writing a new note, but tears rose to her eyes and her hand trembled over the parchment. She had never left her family before. Not one night had she spent away from her home. Could she truly leave her parents and brother, and that, too, in the middle of the night? Why did she feel like she was abandoning them, like she was trying to escape the circumstances she herself had created? Was leaving home the courageous thing to do, or the cowardly thing?

"Don't, Coralline."

She didn't know how he knew, but Pavonis always knew what she was thinking.

Coralline hurriedly placed a starfish-shaped parchment-weight atop the note. Her parents would see the note as soon as they entered her room in the morning. She added the pen and parchment-pad to her satchel—the parchment-pad would serve as a memento of Naiadum.

"The Elixir Expedition may be the journey of a lifetime," Pavonis drawled, "but it will not last a lifetime. Your satchel is as thick as two pillows. We haven't even left, and we're already stalled with your sentimentalism."

Coralline drifted up to the ceiling and collected a luciferin orb. It was warm in her hands—its heat and glimmering white-blue light consoled her. She connected the orb to a rod—thus connected, the luciferin orb transformed to a luciferin lantern. It would guide her at night during the Elixir Expedition.

Zipping her overflowing satchel with difficulty, she slung it over her shoulder.

"You've forgotten the most important thing," Pavonis called. "A dagger."

Ecklon had tried to teach her how to wield a dagger, but after trying a few swipes with his dagger, she'd handed it back to him, saying, "The only sharp instrument I need to be able to wield with any level of skill is a scalpel."

"Fetch your father's dagger," Pavonis directed.

Coralline could picture her father's dagger precisely; it would be hanging in a sheath above his desk in a corner of the living room. He would never miss it—it was largely ornamental—nor would he begrudge her borrowing of it. But her bedroom door would creak if she were to open it, and if either of her parents awoke from the sound, the Elixir Expedition would end before it could begin. They would not want her to leave home, not like this, not on a quest to find something that may be no more than a legend.

"You're better than any dagger, Pavonis," Coralline said, intending it as a compliment.

"You need to be able to defend yourself—" His voice cut off, and his body slammed against the wall. Coralline's desk rattled, her bedside table quivered, and several books tumbled off her shelves. "Something's attacking me!" he bellowed. "Help, Coralline, *HELP!*"

The gray tin under his arm, Izar rang the doorbell for the fifth time, keeping his thumb pressed to it until his nail whitened. From the entryway in which he stood, decorated with a glass foyer table and a porcupine-like spiky ball balanced precariously atop it, Izar could hear the bell echoing to the other side of the door. Was she asleep? Or was she not home? But where could she be in the middle of the night?

He'd never arrived at her penthouse unannounced before—it felt a little like arriving for dinner at Yacht without a reservation—but he'd had an impossibly tumultuous day and would feel steady only when he held her in his arms.

Footsteps pattered on the other side of the door, soft as reindeer on snow. The door opened a wedge. Izar stared at Ascella with open-mouthed astonishment.

The lids of her frost-blue eyes shimmered with sultry shadows, like an early-morning sky topped with swirls of smoke. Her lips were as crimson as poppies—it was the same lipstick she'd worn during their dinner at Yacht. She wore a low-cut powder-blue slip that ended at her thighs, with a slit rising up to the hip on one side. A matching silk robe covered her loosely, then tightly, as her fingers knotted its sash at the waist.

"Were we supposed to meet here tonight?" Izar asked, chagrined. "Am I late?"

"No. You're not."

"Good."

Izar stepped inside Ascella's apartment, closed the door behind him, and wrapped his arms around her. She smelled of lavender, the fragrance sweet and purple, delicate and subtle. "I've missed you more than you can imagine today," he said softly.

"Er, thank you—"

"How come you didn't call me after the oil spill?" he said, his voice a gentle reprimand. "Didn't you hear the news smearing all the channels, spouting poison at Ocean Dominion?"

"I did hear it. I'm sorry, but I've been busy with Tarazed all week. Abstract hosted an exhibition for him this week—"

"I know, I know. You told me. Never mind. Let's not talk about work now."

Izar ran his thumb over the third finger of her left hand, the finger that would soon wear a ring mined by Castor from the depths of the ocean. He leaned forward to kiss her but pulled apart abruptly at the sight behind her. Forgetting her momentarily, he strode farther into her living room.

There was her glass coffee table that he recognized, with an icicle-shaped quartz vase standing in its center like a glacier in a transparent sea—Ascella loved diamonds, and quartz and crystals were as close as home decorations could get to diamonds. Behind the coffee table was something he didn't recognize: a purple-and-black painting, five-by-six feet. A series of jagged black strokes over a violet canvas, it made Izar think of a massive bruise. As his scar marred one part of his jaw, he felt that this bruise marred one part of her home, which was otherwise white and glassy, much like her complexion.

The painting, in Tarazed's signature style, seemed to make the entire apartment an advertisement of the artist. Worse, like the other senseless work Tarazed produced, it must have cost a fortune, at least a quarter million dollars. "How did you afford it?" Izar asked, turning back to her.

"I didn't. It was a gift."

"From Tarazed—?" Just then, he heard a splatter like a waterfall, coming from her bedroom, whose door was closed.

Someone was in her shower.

Izar's gaze ran with new understanding over Ascella's slip, smoky eyes, and poppy lips. His insides felt as though they were being slowly extracted out of him with burning tongs. He'd been prepared to give Ascella the world, but she'd wanted it from another man.

Tarazed must be the man. Hence the gift of his artwork, which served to mark her penthouse, and her, as his territory.

Izar's eyes glazed over, such that he seemed to be looking at Ascella from across a screen of bubbles over a pot of boiling water. She became no more than a blur of powder blue. He turned back to Tarazed's painting. The black lines on the violet canvas shifted, as though the bruise were bleeding, festering, just like his heart.

He opened the gray tin that he'd discovered on his office desk. He'd brought it here to show it to her, to ask her to help him interpret its contents. His intention now changed, he extracted the half-shell and staggered into her bedroom.

He'd expected to see some evidence of Tarazed in the room, but not a scrap of clothing littered Ascella's lily-white sheets. He crossed the room until he stood just outside her bathroom. He became dimly aware that his body was shaking as severely as though he was in the throes of an epileptic fit. Ascella was flapping about him, the sleeves of her robe swaying like the wings of a blue jay. Her mouth was moving—she was talking to him, perhaps trying to get through—but he couldn't hear a word.

His hand felt warm and wet. Looking down mechanically in its direction, he saw droplets of red splattering the white floor tiles—he was clutching the half-shell so fiercely that he'd cut himself on its ragged edge. Tarazed's blood would soon join his on the floor, except that it would be not a drip but a gush like a shower.

114

Pavonis wriggled and tossed, creating a powerful current that shoved Coralline back from the window. But she pushed through the swell, pulled open the pane of shutters, and leaned out. She placed one hand on his snout and, with her other hand, held her luciferin lantern nervously out over the reef garden in an effort to identify his assailant.

Tentacles of snakelocks and jewel anemones cast shifting shadows in the darkness. Spikes of green sea urchin and purple sea urchin looked twice as long and sharp as they ordinarily did, like needle-thin pens. A marble cone snail, with its white-spotted carapace, crawled slowly in search of a victim to poison with its single, harpoon-like tooth.

"I beg your pardon, Pavonis," said a low, tremulous voice. "I was trying to reach the window, and my strand of grass must have rubbed you the wrong way."

Coralline slipped out the window and lowered her lantern toward the voice. Her father's muse, Altair, gazed up at her and Pavonis from among dense, bright-green tufts of turtle-grass, his tail coiled around one of them. His dorsal fin fanned as he ascended haltingly to the very peak of the tuft, his color darkening to orange. "I've never eavesdropped in my life," he said, as though defending himself against an unstated accusation, "but I was unable to sleep and could not help overhearing your conversation about the Elixir Expedition."

"Go to sleep, Minion," Pavonis growled, "unless you want me to *put* you to sleep."

Coralline stroked the side of Pavonis's face. She knew he was embarrassed by his strong reaction, by the fact that a thirty-foot-long creature such as him had been so rattled by the movement of one the size of her hand.

Altair trembled but did not lower himself among the grasses. "It's life-threatening to venture out into the unknown," he said. "Think about your parents, Coralline. When they wake up in the morning, how do you think they'll feel to find that not only is one of their children dying before them, but the other is quite possibly dying away from them—in some unknown place?"

Coralline flinched.

"She will come to no harm as long as I live," Pavonis rumbled. With the wide shape of his head and eyes set to either side of it, the whale shark could not examine anything with both eyes, and so, as though to compensate, he fixed a particularly cold eye upon Altair.

The seahorse shrank, camouflaging partially. "And what if you die, like your friend Mako?"

Coralline gasped. If silence had not been advisable, in order to avoid waking her parents, Pavonis's tail would have smashed against the wall of the house to wring out his wrath. "Minion, you're a coward who's never once left this coral reef," Pavonis retorted. "Let's go, Coralline."

"But your father will never forgive me for letting you go, Coralline!" Altair implored.

Coralline vacillated, her tailfin flicking like a pendulum.

"Tell him you were asleep, Minion," Pavonis suggested.

Altair's dorsal fin ceased its fanning. "I've never lied in my life!" he sputtered.

"That's your problem," Pavonis said. "You face two choices at this moment. You can join us on our Elixir Expedition, or you can get out of our way."

Altair's tail loosened from around his tuft of turtle-grass. "Trochid rescued me when I was a baby seahorse," he said, speaking to himself, "and so I owe him my life. I cannot let anything happen to his daughter." His gaze climbing back to Coralline, he said in a barely audible voice, "I will join you on the Elixir Expedition."

"When I said you can join us or get out of our way," Pavonis hissed, his snout approaching Altair menacingly, "I obviously didn't mean it. You'll be of no use to us whatsoever."

"What Pavonis means is that we greatly appreciate your desire to help," Coralline said hurriedly, "but we'd hate to separate you from your lifelong home, especially at this . . . *familial* juncture in your life." She glanced pointedly at his pregnant belly. "And your mate, Kuda, would miss you terribly."

"Not as much as I would miss her. I regret only that I cannot say goodbye to her. She's sleeping in another reef tonight, to care for a sick friend. But I know that, given our family values, she would understand."

Coralline hadn't wanted it to come to this, she hadn't wanted to point out the obvious, but there was a glaring flaw with Altair's plan to join the Elixir Expedition. Pavonis would point it out far less delicately, so her words tumbled out as a stream: "Because seahorses swim vertically, you're among the very slowest swimmers in the ocean. As such, I don't understand how you'll accompany us."

"Do you think we plan to travel not in leaps and bounds," Pavonis sneered, "but finger widths?"

"I'll slip in there," Altair whispered, looking at Coralline's satchel with the injured look of one squeezed of the last shreds of his dignity.

Coralline tried to think of any other reason Altair shouldn't accompany them, but she couldn't think of any. Shrugging at Pavonis, she helped the seahorse slide into an outer pocket of her satchel. Then, luciferin lantern in hand, she began weaving a path through the darkness.

Lightning rent the sky. Rain pounded Izar, slipping through his collar, forming ice-cold chains down his back, but he hardly noticed. His feet landing as gently as a hare's, he clambered over the rails of the trawler. He examined the coordinates listed on the card in his hand, the card he'd found in the gray tin on his desk—yes, this was the precise location. If the Third Man was here, Izar would find him.

The trawler's platform, about fifty feet long, was empty. A narrow set of stairs led to an area below deck—the sleeping quarters. Like a trailer, the trawler was a home, and the secluded, rocky enclave in which it was anchored, whose surrounding stones looked like swords protruding over the waves, acted as a private trailer park.

With all the noise of the storm, the Third Man would be unable to distinguish Izar's footsteps on the platform. Walking on the tips of his toes, Izar crept toward the stairs, his body partially crouched. Dangling low like a white-gold pendant, the moon cast a long, quivering spotlight at his feet. He wished it would not shine so bright this night.

He paused at the mouth of the stairs. The path down was dark. He wondered whether Zaurak and Serpens could be belowdecks as well—that would explain why the Secret Search team had not yet found them. But if they were belowdecks, waiting for him, he would be walking directly into a trap.

A seagull cackled overhead. He jumped. The tin under his arm rattled, the shell within clanging. Losing his balance, he steadied himself with a hand on the railing of the stairs. But when he looked ahead again, he was facing the barrel of a gun.

The gun was pointed at him so smoothly, so naturally, that he asked himself whether he'd almost expected it. He became conscious of every breath entering and exiting his lungs. Strange, he'd never stopped to contemplate his breathing before—how deftly lungs moved, how miraculous it all was—his life, life itself.

The gun touched the bridge of his nose. The trigger cocked. Izar stumbled back.

Out of the shadows, a giant loomed onto the platform. He had a grizzled beard into which an entire body could have disappeared, and into which one of his front teeth seemed to have. His lashes were sparse, absent in clumps like deforested patches, as though they'd decided to abscond to his beard. Belonging to a man of his girth, the gun in his hand seemed ornamental, like a crocodile protecting itself with a fake set of fangs. With his bare hands, the giant could crush any man he encountered, including Izar.

His brown-gray eyes glinted in the moonlight as flat, impassive slits, their expression so still that Izar wondered whether the giant was even human—he could just as well have been a lizard. And yet his face looked distantly familiar; it was not the sort of face one could forget—looking, as it did, like it belonged on a wanted-for-murder poster. Frowning, Izar tried to clutch at a memory, but it was not even remotely close enough to grasp—it was like a song he'd heard as a child, of which he recalled only one or two words—insufficient to whistle a tune. He hated wispy memories—they were like flies buzzing around his head, irritating but impossible to swat.

"The name is Alshain Ankaa," the giant said, the movement of his lips barely displacing the thicket around his mouth. "I've been waiting for ya, Izar."

Izar's eyes widened at the mention of his name. So, he *had* walked directly into a trap. He'd been so impatient to uncover the identity of the Third Man that he'd arrived unarmed and unprepared.

"Why is yer hand bleeding?" Alshain asked.

Izar looked down at the scrape that tore through the palm of his hand like a straight, orderly earthquake. He had shed no blood other than his own this night. He had planned to kill Tarazed, but he'd been unable to bring himself to open Ascella's bathroom door and see him in her shower. He'd whirled around and walked out of her apartment and her life.

"Never mind my hand," he said.

Alshain dropped his gun, such that it dangled at his side. But Izar's exhale of relief caught in his throat, for Alshain stepped closer, such that their shirts were almost touching. His face was perfectly still, as though even the veins beneath his beard had cooled.

"I brought ya to Menkar that day," Alshain said, "when ya were a boy. Antares and I were on this very trawler."

That was why Alshain's face looked familiar—Izar had seen it as a three-year-old! He had gone to the island of Mira yesterday to try to remember his past, but he'd remembered nothing and had heard only the lies of his biological parents' neighbor, the drunkard Rigel Nihal. Now, most unexpectedly, by means of the mysterious tin under his arm, he had arrived at a bridge to his past—this giant, Alshain.

Was it possible that, in the state of paranoia pursuing the two attempts on his life, he had wholly misinterpreted the tin? Could it be that the man who'd placed the tin on his desk was not an enemy but a friend? After all, the card with coordinates had led him here; the half-shell could be construed as a tool to defend oneself rather than a threat; as for the amber scroll, although he had no means to decipher it yet, perhaps it contained a helpful message. Feeling suddenly better, Izar straightened his shoulders.

"Thank you for helping save me that night," Izar said. "Can you tell me more about that night?"

"I can take ya to the area where we found ya. Do ya want to go?"

Izar looked up at the sky, but he could make it out just barely, for rain was lashing his eyes. The clouds were emptying bucket upon bucket over the ocean, and he was as soaked as though he was sitting in a bathtub. There was a fury to the night, a challenge to its tempest. To set forth on a night like this, even on a ship much larger and sturdier than Alshain's, would be dangerous. And Alshain, a giant with a gun, could not be said to inspire trust. He could easily shoot Izar and hurl his body overboard. But Izar needed to know—all his life, he'd wanted to know who he was, how Antares had found him in the ocean, how he'd come to acquire the scar along his jaw. Maybe by going to the stretch of water where Antares and Alshain had found him, he would remember something.

"Let's go," he said.

11

Salt and Sea

I'm nauseous," Altair moaned.

Coralline looked down at her side. The strap of her satchel lay tight and diagonal over her torso, the satchel itself at her hip, as she swam horizontally. She lowered her luciferin lantern over the satchel's outer pocket. Altair looked a dull, sickly brown. She patted his star-shaped coronet gently and then returned the lantern in front of her, but it was too late: Her forehead bumped into Pavonis's tailfin. He muttered irritably, but she found the collision comforting—it showed her physically that, even though she could make out no more than his size and shape in the dark, he was there with her.

He was navigating the way to the Elnath Mansion, his tail swerving sharply around houses. The swim would have been faster had they been traveling in the waters above Urchin Grove instead of weaving among the village's homes, but they'd found earlier that black poison was more concentrated in higher waters. They'd consequently sought the safety of the seabed, notwithstanding that it was darker there, hundreds of feet below the waves at night, and the swim would take longer because of all the maneuvering.

They hadn't counted on being lost, though, which Coralline now had to admit to herself that they were. The swim to the Mansion should have taken half an hour, but they'd already been out at least two hours by her estimation. Pavonis, an unerring navigator by day, was a poor navigator by night. It was not his vision—he could see at night, even if not as well as during the day, and he could see better than merpeople—but it was the fact that he, unlike most sharks, liked to navigate in part based on the sun, as it traveled from east to west, and he got confused about direction once that compass was gone. Yes, like other sharks, he relied on a whole slew of other data as well—currents, temperatures, smells, mental maps, magnetic fields—but the sun was his favorite navigational tool.

From a shuffle in the sands below, Coralline thought she discerned a brown-striped octopus scuttling over the sediment. Then she saw something glowing directly ahead of her and Pavonis. It was a spotted lanternfish the size of her hand, its iridescent head flashing with blue-green light. Spots of bioluminescence sparked suddenly and intermittently throughout the waters, momentarily cracking the blackness. They were manifestations of nocturnal creatures lighting their paths through the night—eels, octopuses, crabs. The biological mechanism of their light matched that of the bacteria in her lantern: light created through the reaction of the compound luciferin with oxygen. Coralline liked seeing the sparks—they made her feel like she was traveling through the night sky.

She looked around her, at the homes she passed, the gardens, the shops. She must have seen them countless times before, but she could recognize not one of them in the dark. Her own village felt foreign to her; she could just as well have been in any other part of the Atlantic Ocean. She didn't like the feeling of unfamiliarity in a place that should have felt familiar.

Suddenly, Altair lurched out of her satchel. "Something's moving in there!" he cried.

Pavonis whipped around, his massive head appearing where his tailfin had been. "You're just a spineless Minion," he scoffed, "spooked by everything."

But Coralline felt it, too—a minor movement against her hip. And Pavonis heard it—a jangle from within her satchel, as though something was traveling over her pouch of shells.

"Open it," Pavonis commanded.

"But what if there's a snake inside?" Coralline said, trembling.

All sea snakes were venomous. They were never muses, in part because of their venom and in part because of their proclivity for the surface—as marine reptiles, they breathed air rather than water.

"We have to find out," Pavonis insisted.

Holding the satchel away from her, Coralline unzipped it quickly. Tentacles came waggling out above a red-and-white scotch bonnet carapace. It was her mother's muse, Nacre. Coralline would have preferred a snake, for Nacre's tongue was more venomous still. "How did you get inside my satchel?" Coralline asked.

"My last recollection is of having been curled up in one of your corsets."

Coralline had tossed a handful of corsets into her satchel and must have neglected to notice Nacre among them. "Why were you in my bedroom to begin with?" she demanded.

"I was snooping, of course."

"That's unacceptable—"

"Why are we out in the middle of the night like hooligans—even the Pole Dancer?" Nacre interrupted, in the imperious tone of addressing a servant.

Altair stiffened.

"We're on our way to find the elixir to save Naiadum," Pavonis said.

"I'm not in favor of the idea myself," Altair added.

"For the first time, the Pole Dancer and I are in agreement," Nacre said. "Now, Coralline, return me home and place me on your mother's shoulder!"

"I'm afraid I can't do that," Coralline said apologetically.

"We're not returning home until we find the elixir," Pavonis growled. "Now, get back in the bag, Minion, or we will leave you on the seabed here!"

"You're just a big, mean Ogre!" Nacre retorted. "As for you, Coralline, you're in big trouble. When I do eventually return home, you'll see all the things I tell your mother!"

Nacre vanished inside her shell. Sighing, Coralline zipped her satchel most of the way to try to create a separation between herself and the snail.

"Things are starting to implode," Altair remarked, in a voice directed at everyone and no one, "as often happens in irrational and ill-considered situations."

The Elixir Expedition had barely begun, but Coralline was already anticipating the struggle to her sanity that would be wrought by the three muses together.

Izar stood at the bow of the trawler. A wave shot over the rails, like saliva out of the mouth of a rabid hound. Its froth soaked him freshly from head to toe, plastering his clothes to his skin. He shivered, teeth rattling.

Alshain Ankaa's trawler was ill equipped for depth, and great beasts were lapping at it hungrily from all directions—big, black-bodied waves with white heads. The storm was rousing them to ever-greater heights like a snake charmer. The sky and sea together formed a single, wet, tumultuous layer; there was no horizon but only a great swath of empty darkness.

It had been a mistake to venture out onto the ocean this night.

The trawler started to slow. Izar heard footsteps as heavy as a bull's and turned his head slowly, his hands continuing to grip the rails for balance. Alshain, who'd emerged from the cockpit, came to stand beside a small table nailed to the center of the platform. Alshain's gun lay diagonally over it; he had placed it there when they'd set out two hours ago. The giant crossed his log-like arms over his chest, his feet spaced apart, his stance making Izar think of an undertaker posing over a grave.

Izar staggered over to him on legs that felt as pathetically wobbly as a fawn's.

"There was a third man with me and Antares that night, twenty-five years ago," Alshain said.

"Who?"

"A man with a limp." Izar's blood congealed in his veins, for there was only one man he knew with a limp. His heart raced—he could hear it even through the downpour. "Zaurak Alphard," Alshain continued.

Izar placed his hand on the small table for support. "I remember nothing before that night," he said, "but I remember that night. How come I don't remember Zaurak in it?"

"Because Zaurak went belowdecks."

Izar found himself believing Alshain, because when Izar had first met Zaurak at Ocean Dominion and they'd shaken hands, Zaurak had looked at him like he knew him. But why had Zaurak been there that night, twenty-five years ago? And why had no one ever told Izar?

"Everything ya know about yerself is a lie," Alshain said. He gripped the handle of his gun and pointed it at Izar's forehead.

Not again. Izar's feet remained under him, but he had the sense he was floating in the air even while standing. His original thinking had been right—Alshain *was* the Third Man. In alliance with Zaurak, he had brought Izar here to kill him. This would be the third murder attempt on Izar's life, a successful one. Upon shooting Izar, Alshain would dump Izar's body overboard, where no one would ever find it. People would think he'd simply disappeared.

The barrel of the gun came to rest on Izar's forehead, its steel cold. Izar closed his eyes.

The Elnath Mansion's black-shale walls loomed before Coralline like great boulders. After hours of searching in the dark, it was a relief to have finally arrived at her destination. She rapped on the shutters of Ecklon's golden-framed window. She knocked again, then again, before the shutters turned to slits and silver-gray eyes peered out at her. Ecklon pulled the pane open, and Coralline flew into his arms.

"Is everything all right, Cora?" he asked, his hands caressing her hair.

She told him about her firing from The Irregular Remedy, then about Rhodomela's diagnosis for Naiadum. Her voice was dispassionate, the voice of a journalist stating facts, but tears trickled down her cheeks in contradiction.

"I'm so sorry," he said softly. "But what are you doing here in the middle of the night, my love?"

"We're embarking on a quest for the elixir to save Naiadum."

"What? Am I dreaming?"

"You're not, unfortunately," Altair said. "I'm glad your stance seems to parallel mine. I only hope your influence exceeds mine."

Ecklon looked about for the voice, bewildered. Coralline pointed out the seahorse, his head sticking out of her satchel. Altair looked somewhat embarrassed at his presence in the midst of their embrace.

"Cora, you're forgetting who you are in the wake of the black poison spill," Ecklon said, his gaze returning to her. "You've never left Urchin Grove before. You're delicate—like the algae after which you were named—"

"I'm not delicate."

"I'm sorry, I didn't mean it in an offensive way. What I mean is that you're fragile, feminine. You don't know how to wield a dagger—"

"Tell me about it," Pavonis commented dryly.

Ecklon looked toward the whale shark's face in the window, then, turning back to Coralline, continued, "You can't honestly believe the elixir exists. You have a scientific mind, Cora. The whole concept of the elixir is ridiculous—the magician, the starlight. Doesn't it sound absurd even as I say it? I mean, *The Legend of the Elixir* is a children's story—that's because adults shouldn't believe in such things. But for the sake of argument, let's say that the elixir does exist. Even if so, no one has found it in our lifetime. What are the chances that you will find it, in the short time frame that you have? And if *The Legend of the Elixir* is true, that means the elixir comes accompanied by a curse—which is hardly something to be excited about. Finally, those who do try to find the elixir often die over the course of their quest. My point is: Don't chase a legend. It'll be equivalent to chasing your own tail—except imagine that your tail is equipped with a stinger, like a stingray's. Please, I beg you, don't venture out into the unknown and risk your life, all for nothing."

"It's not for nothing," Coralline said, her voice as pleading as his expression. "It's for Naiadum. I can't just let him die. My only question is: Will you accompany me on the Elixir Expedition or not?"

Ecklon clasped her hands and held them to his heart. "I would like to accompany you on your quest, if only to keep you safe. But my mother has fallen sick in the aftermath of the black poison spill. I cannot abandon her."

"How can you side with your mother over me!"

Coralline's face flushed at her words. She was acting like a haranguing wife before she was even a wife. She had not told Ecklon what his mother, Epaulette, had said to her and Abalone during the engagement party. She found herself bristling at Epaulette's words even at this moment, but this was not a time for pettiness, she told herself. Either way, Ecklon didn't deserve to be punished for that unpleasant exchange.

"I'm sorry," Coralline said. "I should thank you, not blame you. It was you who waded first into the black poison; it was you who located Naiadum. Of course, I understand completely that you want to stay here and care for your mother."

Ecklon nodded and pulled her close. She fingered the rose petal tellin shell at her collarbone, the symbol of her engagement to him. It would serve as a memento of him during her quest, but it wouldn't be enough. "Give me a portrait of you so I can look at it every time I miss you during the Elixir Expedition."

He rummaged through a dresser drawer and returned with a miniature portrait. His face was somber in the little black-and-white sketch, his hard jaw softened by a vertical cleft in the chin. He formed just the image of a dashing detective, Coralline thought, as she tucked the portrait carefully in her satchel.

"I promise I'll return as soon as I can," she said, clasping hands with him again. "Can you do me a favor while I'm gone?"

"Anything."

"Try to stay clear of Rosette. With me gone, she'll be stalking you day and night, thinking this is her once-in-a-lifetime opportunity to get you to pick her over me."

He threw his head back and laughed.

"I'm only partially joking," Coralline said, smiling.

"I must say, on the verge of marriage," interjected Altair, "the two of you separating—I don't like it."

"I can't wait to marry you, Ecklon," Coralline said, trying to pretend they were alone.

"I love you, Cora."

"I love you, too."

He bent his head and kissed her, but she found the taste of his mouth disconcerting—it was the taste of finality.

Izar's head throbbed, and his eyes opened groggily. Fog circled him in spectral gray wisps, and he shuddered in its grasp. The rail behind his shoulders was cold; he was half-sitting, half-leaning against it, every pore of his body soaking wet.

He tried to place his hands to either side of him and jump to his feet, but he couldn't summon his hands. They were tied behind his back, he realized drowsily. But how was he even alive? When Alshain had pointed the gun at him, Izar had thought the giant would shoot him, but, instead, Alshain had knocked the butt of the gun against Izar's temple. Where was the giant now?

A beard erupted through the fog, high above him, then dropped down to his eye level.

"What do you think you're doing?" Izar sputtered.

"Yer tin is in this satchel." Alshain held out a bag weaved of a stiff, murky-green fabric—an ocean variation of a duffel bag, it seemed. "The Ocean Dominion identification card I found in your pants pocket is also in here."

Alshain dropped the satchel diagonally over Izar's chest, such that the top of the strap rested on his right shoulder and the bag itself lay on his left hip. The giant tightened the strap over Izar's torso. Only then did Izar look down to find that he was naked.

"I took yer clothes off because they'd get in the way," Alshain explained.

"In the way of what? Drowning? You don't want to waste a bullet on me, so you're throwing me overboard to the sharks. Is that it?"

"The privates of merpeople are sheathed in their scales, ya know," Alshain continued calmly, as though Izar hadn't spoken.

"Why would I care to know that? Have you lost your mind?"

The hairy hands reached forward. Izar retreated into the rail behind him, despising the powerlessness of his position. But Alshain gripped Izar's biceps and pulled him up to his feet as easily as though Izar were a sack of cotton. Then, with a single push, he shoved him out over the rails.

The moment of contact with water made Izar gasp and convulse from head to toe. Waves lashed him like cold whips, freezing the blood in his veins. He tasted salt on his lips, in his mouth, in his nostrils—harsh and tangy. It pricked his eyes like dozens of pins. He was facedown in the water, he realized belatedly. He knew how to swim, and his arms fought to loosen his hands from their binds, but couldn't. Using the power of his shoulders, he managed to turn over onto his back.

He coughed out the salt water he'd swallowed, then inhaled cautiously. But just as his lungs began to inflate, a wave smashed over him. Waves crashed over him one after another in quick succession, pounding him mercilessly, like hammers over a nail.

His eardrums felt on the verge of explosion, like fizz attempting to escape from a bottle. The air in the cavities was being compressed by the pressure of water, he acknowledged to himself—a fact that meant he was sinking. His face scrunched, and he pressed his lips together to keep water out of his lungs, but his mouth opened of its own volition.

He choked. He thrashed. Then he was attacked.

Teeth as sharp as butcher's knives slit open the sides of his neck, carving one painful gash after another on each side. He wished the creature would just swallow him whole, but instead, it broke the bones in his legs, starting with his toes and ankles, which gave way as easily as toothpicks, then his shins and thighs, which held up no better than rickety chairs.

Slowly, agonizingly, he died.

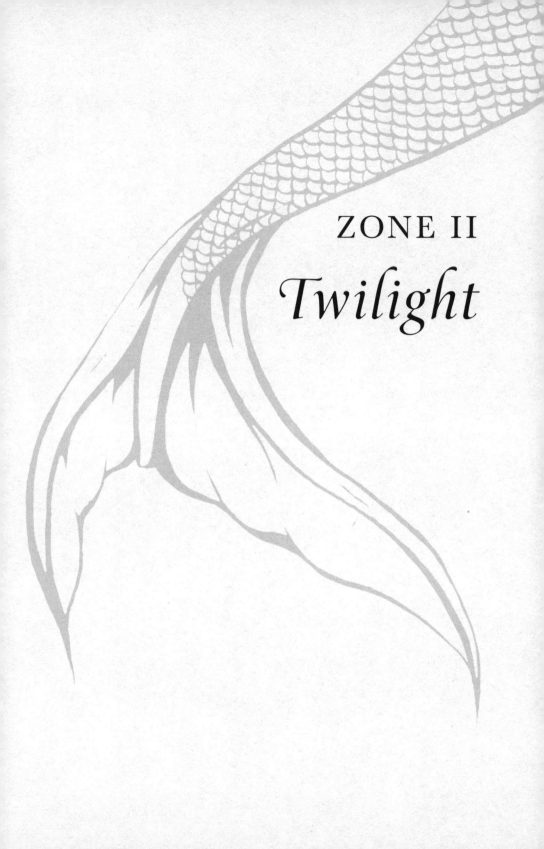

ZONE II
Twilight

12

Dead or Alive

Sunshine refracted into the water slowly but steadily, in thick segments and spurts. Octopuses and eels retreated into their lairs, and rays and snails emerged slowly from their crevices.

Grateful for the daylight, and for having survived her first night out of doors, Coralline stuck the rod of her luciferin lantern in an outer pocket of her satchel.

Houses no longer sprouted out of the seabed, there were no shops or lanes, just clear, uninterrupted expanses of ocean. Urchin Grove was now behind her. At twenty, she had finally left the village of her birth. She hadn't known what she'd expected to see, but what she did see was that, if not for the lack of dwellings, the vista before her quite resembled Urchin Grove—the water, the algae, the rocks, the sands—yet it somehow also looked different.

She'd hoped to feel something inspiring or poetic as she examined novel surroundings, but all she felt was the sleepless tiredness of her muscles. She continued to follow Pavonis's tail, flapping right and left in front of her, but there was an aimlessness to its swing. During the night, their goal had been to leave Urchin Grove; now that they'd accomplished that basic feat, they did not know where to actually begin the Elixir Expedition.

Pavonis came to a sudden stop. Coralline bumped into his tailfin. But the collision was different than usual, for his tail was now stiff, and Coralline felt as though she'd bumped her head against a door. She'd seen such stop-and-stiffen reactions in him before—they happened when he smelled blood.

"Let it go, Pavonis—" she began, rubbing her forehead, but he was already cutting through the waters at breakneck speed. She trailed him with a sigh. He was the detective of blood—where there was blood, he could not rest until he knew its source. Generally, the source was someone with a minor cut across the hand or arm—nothing particularly interesting—and Coralline apologized to the person on Pavonis's behalf; his sudden arrival, with its great swell of water, tended to alarm. The only serious case Pavonis had ever encountered had been her father's hand.

But now, when Pavonis came to a stop, Coralline's hands flew to her mouth.

A dead merman hovered vertically before them. His eyes were closed, his gill slits lay flat and unfluttering along the sides of his neck, and his tail was as bleached as though it had never once held a spot of color. Goosebumps prickled all over Coralline's arms. She'd always been terrified at the idea of encountering death; now, she realized why: There was an eerie stillness and finality to it.

There was also a mystery to it, in this case: The merman's body should have descended to the seabed instead of hovering as it did, almost precisely midway between the waves and the ocean floor. The descent to the seabed should have happened naturally, for surplus water should have filtered into the body through the gills, making it heavier. Humans, she had heard, were different than merpeople in this regard. Just as they lived differently than merpeople, they also died differently—on the rare occasions that they died in the ocean, their bodies floated up to the waves. This person had died like he was neither a merman nor a human, or else was both.

"It's a bad omen to be near a dead body," Nacre said quietly, emerging at the top of Coralline's satchel, "especially one in such an unnatural position."

"Let's go," Pavonis said, his tail starting to swish.

"But what if he isn't dead?" protested Altair. "It's our moral duty to help him, in that case, especially given that Coralline is a healer."

Coralline nodded in Altair's direction, her gaze unveering from the merman. She should at least examine him perfunctorily—that way, she could tell herself she'd done what she could. She approached him cautiously.

His face was angular, with a hard jaw and a set line to his mouth; it was similar to Ecklon's in structure but there was nothing to offset the severity in this case—no traces of dimples, no cleft in his chin. Rather, a hook-shaped scar ran from his earlobe almost to his lip, making his face harsh.

Also, disconcertingly, he was bare chested. At The Irregular Remedy, Coralline had sometimes examined mermen without their waistcoats—such as Agarum, during his heart attack—but never outdoors had she encountered a merman without a waistcoat. There was a vulgarity, as well as a strange intimacy, to being in such close proximity to him. Coralline proceeded with her examination swiftly. She placed two fingers just below his jaw; there was no pulse, as she'd expected, but his temperature was high—so high that her hand almost flew back to her side. He must have died of a fever, she decided, though she'd never come across such an extreme fever before.

There was no blood on him that she could see, yet there had to be some, otherwise Pavonis would not have smelled it. "Take a look at his hands," Pavonis drawled from above.

There were red marks along his wrists, as though his hands had been tightly bound, but he'd managed to wrest them free just before dying. She turned the palms of his hands gingerly. A gash cut through the palm of his right hand—it did not seem to be bleeding anymore, but it must have been just a short while ago.

Toothed wrack salve would soothe the wound. And yet to apply a salve to a dead merman, it was ridiculous. It was not against the law, however: The Association of Apothecaries required Coralline to possess a badge in order to treat anyone other than herself—anyone *alive*. There was no law against treating a dead person, for the obvious reason: Why would anyone want to? Recognizing that what she was doing was idiotic but at least not illegal, Coralline extracted her jar of toothed wrack salve from her satchel and quickly dabbed the balm onto his cut.

"You've got to be kidding me!" Pavonis bellowed. "I'm starting to think your sentimentality borders on insanity."

Pavonis's tail flicked sharply in disapproval. The gush of water pushed Coralline toward the dead merman, until their scales and shoulders touched.

She did not know what drew her, but her hand rose to his cheek, and her finger traced the ridge of his scar.

His eyes snapped open.

Izar was flooded by water—it was in his ears, nose, eyes, and mouth—yet he somehow remained alive. A girl with turquoise eyes was staring at him, her lips just a kiss away from his, but before he could so much as blink, she slipped away, tail flashing—she was not a girl but a mermaid.

He looked down at himself. He had a tail similar to hers. Commencing abruptly at the hips, below the navel, the monstrosity that had swallowed his legs divided him into two bodies—his own upper body and an alien lower body. The scales of his tail were white, but the color indigo was streaming steadily into them, as with an invisible paintbrush. He touched his scales with a tentative hand and shuddered—they were slimy, coated with a film of mucus like oily soap. That was how fish scales were, he knew, in order to help fish escape; merpeople belonged to the class of fish, and so, he supposed, it would make sense for their scales to be similarly slimy.

His tailfin, meanwhile, was long and gauzy and close to transparent at the tips. It made him about seven feet in height, as tall as that blasted giant Alshain Ankaa, who'd thrown him overboard.

But Izar should have died. How had he transformed into a merman instead?

Whatever the reason, Alshain must have somehow expected the transformation. When he'd told Izar that clothes would get in the way, he must have meant they would get in the way of his transformation into a merman. And when he'd said the privates of merpeople are sheathed in their scales, it was because he must have thought that would be the most alarming aspect to Izar about his transformation.

Izar was a pawn in a game—of that, he felt by now certain, but it was a bizarre game with rules he couldn't understand. He wished he'd died rather than transformed. He would rather be anything than a merman, even a slug or stone, for merpeople had murdered his biological parents.

He fixed his attention on the mermaid, who was staring at him from about ten feet away.

He'd known in theory how merpeople looked, but he'd never seen one before. She was a little over six feet tall—the heights of most merpeople ranged from six to seven feet, he knew, just as that of most humans ranged from five to six feet. Her scales were bronze, and they shimmered like hundreds of pennies arranged close together. Her immense blue-green eyes gave a look of fragility to her face, of youthfulness—hers was a face that would never grow old—yet he found her eyes unsettling, like two beams turned upon him with unflinching brightness.

Along the sides of her neck fluttered light layers of skin, buoyed by the currents like window blinds in a breeze. Izar raised his hands to his neck and groaned—his neck was lined with exhaust fans just like hers, his gills slippery and supple, like slices of peaches. When he'd felt his neck being slashed, as with a butcher's knife, gill slits had been forming on either side.

He glanced down at his chest. It neither rose nor fell; his lungs, if they still remained in his chest, were now defunct. That helped explain the statuesque stillness to the mermaid. He supposed he had it, too. It was due to the absence of lungs, which created that steady rise and fall to which his mind and body were so accustomed.

Not even his body hair had been spared in his hideous transformation—not the hair on his chest, nor even the stubble on his cheeks. Body hair would slightly increase water resistance, he supposed, and so, from an evolutionary perspective, it would make sense that merpeople would not have any, but he still found his new smoothness emasculating. He passed a hand over his skull and found that the hairs on his head remained but had a different texture than before—they were thicker and heavier. The mermaid's hair seemed similarly thick and heavy, for the tendrils that had escaped her bun were not blowing about in all directions with the ripples of water but were framing her face.

His skin had also altered in his transformation. It was no longer suntanned but, like the mermaid's, was so pale as to be practically translucent, and so fine, he could almost make out the capillaries. Merpeople had no direct exposure to the sun, and so, from an evolutionary perspective, he could understand that they would lack melanin, the pigment that darkened skin and provided sun protection—but that did not mean he liked his new paleness.

A shadow shifted behind the mermaid. Izar had noticed it before but had not paid it any heed—he frowned at it now, for he saw that it was not a shadow at all but a thirty-foot-long beast. The mermaid was leaning against it—but then the beast emerged from behind her and started to approach him. It was a gargantuan, yellow-spotted shark the size of a ship, its head wide and flat, its tailfin the size of a curtain. It opened its mouth to reveal a great big cavern lined with hundreds of teeth, a black tunnel ready to swallow him.

After all the sharks Izar's ships had killed, it was now his fate to be killed by one of them.

He lurched away from the shark, but the waters swirled, and the shark arrived in front of him, blocking his path like a tree. He thought the shark would bite off his arm and chew upon it as a dog chews a bone, but instead, the monster circled him in loop after loop. The waters churned around Izar, pressing him in from all four sides—he wasn't spinning, but he felt like a whirling dervish, like his head might dislocate at any moment. That must be how it would feel to be trapped in the eye of a hurricane—the shark was torturing him before it would eat him.

"Enough, Pavonis!" called the mermaid.

The shark ceased. It angled its body such that it pushed Izar toward the mermaid, rounding him up as a policeman rounds up a criminal. Izar found himself face-to-face with the mermaid. She was slight, pretty, beautiful even, he observed, but his lip could not help curling with revulsion: She belonged to the ranks of those who had orphaned him.

The shark returned to its position behind the mermaid, and she leaned against it again, as trustingly as though it were a wall. Then, as Izar watched incredulously, she patted its back. It looked the equivalent of a mouse patting a cat with its tail. Could the beast be a pet of some sort? he wondered. It was certainly possible—savages would keep savages as pets.

"Try to escape again, and I'll crush you against the sediment!"

The mermaid's lips had not moved, yet the voice was loud and clear. There were no other merpeople nearby, though—just plenty of fish in all kinds of colors. His ears were still likely adjusting, Izar concluded. Earlier, while he'd been drowning, his ears had felt as though they might explode; now, he felt nothing, no more pain or pressure, because there would be no more air in his ear cavities. Even parts of him that were the same were different.

"Who are you?" the mermaid asked. Her voice was soft and sweet and clear, like the glaze of a donut.

"Izar Eridan. I'm a human." Lower, more bass, his voice was unrecognizable to him in the water. Like his body, it was hardly his own.

"I guess that's why your skin was hot, because you're a human."

He became vaguely aware of a tingling sensation in his veins—it must be because his blood was cooling. In a matter of minutes, he would be fully cold-blooded, like the mermaid, like the fish all around them. He laughed without mirth. The sound was that of a gurgle, like he was rinsing his teeth out with mouthwash.

"How did you transform from a human to a merman?" the mermaid asked, squinting at him suspiciously.

"I was just about to ask you that myself."

"I've never heard of such a transformation before."

A snail was creeping steadily up her arm, Izar noticed. The size of a little tree ornament, it had a smooth, rounded, red-and-white shell. It ascended to perch upon the mermaid's right shoulder. She did not flick it away with a hand—perhaps she would eat it, he thought.

"Let's learn more about him," said a haughty voice. Again, the mermaid's lips had not moved.

"The human's nudity suggests a penchant for indecency." This was a low, tremulous voice, a voice that seemed to have strong opinions but a fear of voicing them.

"Who's speaking?" Izar asked sharply.

"Let me introduce you to everyone," the mermaid said. "I'm Coralline Costaria, and this"—she patted the shark—"is my muse, Pavonis." Crossing her eyes to look at the snail on her shoulder, she continued, "This is my mother's muse, Nacre, and in here"—she tapped the satchel gently—"is my father's muse, Altair." A tiny orange head, the shade of marigold, peeked out from over the pocket of her bag.

"What's a muse?" Izar asked, looking from the shark to the snail to the seahorse in confusion.

"An animal best friend."

Why would she think he cared about her family zoo? "Who's speaking?" he repeated impatiently.

"*We* are," she said gently, with a pitying expression, as though he might be mentally deficient. "All of us."

But of course they were, Izar thought—merpeople could speak with animals because they were just a bare breed above animals themselves. It was strange, this new world below the waves, but he should focus, he told himself—merpeople-animal friendships were the least of his concerns at present. "Do you know how I can become a human again?" he asked Coralline.

"No."

"If I knew how you could transform back to your hideous self," Pavonis snapped, "trust me when I say I'd be the first one to tell you."

How would he transform? Izar wondered. What if he remained like this for the rest of his life? The thought made him feel as trapped as though a rock lay upon his tail. His glance fell to the satchel at his hip. Its color had deepened from murky-green to bottle-green, and the fabric was flappable rather than stiff. It quite resembled the satchel at Coralline's hip, except that hers looked ready to burst at the seams. He should show Coralline the gray tin he'd found on his office desk, he thought. Perhaps she could make sense of the half-shell and amber scroll in it. In fact, maybe the scroll would hold some clue about his transformation!

Excited at the thought, he hurriedly unzipped his satchel. He saw the gray tin, but it was accompanied by a large drawstring pouch. Izar opened the pouch to discover that it was full of shells. He collected several in the palm of his hand—they were round and spiraled, pigmented and pointed, of various sizes and shapes. Did Alshain think that Izar, like a little girl, was a collector of shells? Cursing, Izar released the pouch, wishing he could slam it against the giant's head instead.

"Perhaps you've lost your mind in your transformation," Pavonis said.

Coralline caught the pouch before it could drift away with the currents. "Why are you throwing away your carapace?" she asked.

"My what?"

"Your currency."

"Oh. How much is it in total?"

She extracted shells from the pouch one at a time and placed them in his hands, which he joined together. "You have four moon snail shells, worth one carapace each," she said, in the slow, instructive tone of a school teacher. "Three wentletraps, worth two carapace each. Two slipper limpets, worth five carapace apiece. One scallop, worth ten carapace, and one cerith, worth twenty carapace. And you have one conch, worth fifty carapace, as well as one whelk, worth a *hundred* carapace."

She did not hand these two large shells to him but examined them with reverence, clutching one in each hand. She must be poor, Izar thought.

"In total, you have two hundred carapace," she said.

Izar had calculated the same, using the denominations she'd mentioned. He was more comfortable with numbers than most people, but she also appeared to be able to do sums fast. He'd hired dozens of men over the course of his career, but never a woman—there were hardly any at Ocean Dominion, except for a few lethargic, middle-aged creatures in the marketing department. Had Coralline been a woman rather than a mermaid, and had he ever interviewed her at Ocean Dominion, he would likely have hired her.

The carapace pouch provided further evidence that Alshain had known Izar would transform rather than drown. With this currency in hand, Izar would be able to pay for his own food and water in the ocean—just food, rather: There would be no need to drink water, of course, given that it was filtering through his gills.

Coralline returned the whelk and conch rather reluctantly to his pouch. Izar funneled his hands and poured in the remainder of the shells. Putting the pouch away, he then opened the gray tin and showed her the half-shell. "Is this a weapon?" he asked.

She ran her index finger over its ridges, then over its ragged edge. "No," she said at length. "It's half of a lion's paw scallop shell, but I can't imagine why it's torn in half."

Izar showed her the scroll next. It was no longer as starchy as cardboard but was instead as malleable as a banana leaf. It unrolled smoothly in his hands and, in the water, was easily legible.

Find Tang Tarpon. He will guide you to the elixir.

—O

Coralline read the note with him—out loud, seemingly for the benefit of her zoo. The name of the author, scribbled in the bottom-right corner, had gotten washed out by the tap water to which Izar had subjected the note. Only the first letter of the name remained, the letter *O*. The reason the note had started to bleach under tap water must relate to osmosis, Izar thought now, a process by which molecules pass across a membrane in order to equalize the concentrations on each side of the membrane. The salts within the material of the note must have leached out in the salt-deficient environment of tap water.

"How strange!" Coralline cried, her eyes the size of quarters as they met Izar's. "We're searching for the elixir, too. We're on an Elixir Expedition!"

"This is one bad coincidence," Pavonis muttered.

"What is the elixir?" Izar asked.

"A legendary life-saving potion made of starlight," said Coralline, "thought to be prepared by a magician named Mintaka."

Izar considered himself a man of level-headed rationality, but his possessions at present did not indicate it; rather, they were the belongings of a palm-reading mystic: a pouch of colorful currency, a half-shell, and a note about a magical elixir. He looked down at himself: at his slippery scales, now fully indigo. Was his current state not some inexplicable magic trick itself? And could this inexplicable form of magic, the elixir, revert the horrendous trick?

"Do you think the elixir can transform me back to a human?" Izar asked.

"I'm not sure," Coralline said. "Its purpose is to save life."

Well, to transform him back to a human would be to save his life—so he would take that as a *yes*. He touched his left wrist—the platinum chip embedded beneath his veins bonded him to Ocean Dominion by blood and bone. Even if it killed him, he would find a way back to the company he loved, the company he was to lead with Saiph.

There was an olive-brown paste on the palm of his right hand, he noticed, sticky and adhesive, covering the gash he'd acquired when he'd clutched the half-shell in Ascella's apartment. He looked at Coralline questioningly.

"The toothed wrack salve will help your cut," she explained.

"Don't get me started on your sentimentality again, Coralline," growled Pavonis.

Izar didn't care about his cut, he didn't care whether he had a hand or not, he just wanted to be human again. Pavonis was right—Coralline did seem sentimental despite being smart. "Where can the elixir and the magician be found?" he asked her.

"That's the big question," she replied. "No one knows."

"Well, this note mentions a Tang Tarpon. Where can he be found?"

"Hmm . . . We could find him in the Register of Residents of Meristem, a central directory—"

"Meristem?"

"Yes, you're in the nation of Meristem. The word *meristem* refers to the part of an algae where the stem meets the frond. The nation of Meristem, which stretches throughout the Central Atlantic Ocean, consists of various settlements in the form of villages, towns, and cities."

"Continue."

"By law, every settlement in Meristem has a Ministry office. We could go to the nearest settlement from here—a village called Purple Claw, I believe—and speak to an administrator in the Under-Ministry of Residential Affairs. We would ask that person to look for the name Tang Tarpon in the Register of Residents of Meristem. . . ."

He would use Coralline, Izar decided, reaching the conclusion as swiftly as he made his business decisions. She could help him get his bearings underwater—he had no more orientation in his new environment than a grain of pollen wandering on the wind. She could be his compass, she could help him find the elixir that would give him his life back. She even carried medicine with her—like the balm she'd applied to his hand—and so he could also view her as a first-aid kit.

He could not have encountered anyone better.

But what if there was just one of these elixirs? In fact, wasn't that likely? If so, how would he ensure that he kept the elixir instead of her?

He would buy it from her. There was not a man or woman he'd met who was not motivated by money. And given how she'd looked at his conch and whelk, she'd probably be eager for some carapace. Upon finding the elixir, he would give her all the carapace he had left in his drawstring pouch, Izar decided. And if she wanted more still, he would find a way to get it to her after transforming back to a human.

"Why are you searching for the elixir?" he asked.

"My eight-year-old brother is dying of black poison."

Maybe she and her menagerie should have been watching what the merboy ate, Izar thought. Regardless, if she was motivated more by love than money, things could get tricky. He would deal with the situation when it arose.

"What do you do?" Coralline asked.

"I work at Ocean"—he began, but stalled at the word *Dominion* and finished with—"Ocean Protection." The name of the enemy organization tasted bitter on his tongue.

"I've heard of Ocean Protection," Coralline said enthusiastically. "My father told me it's a small group of humans who care about the ocean. Unlike the people at Ocean Dominion."

"I think everyone at Ocean Dominion should be beheaded," Pavonis drawled.

"I think so, too," Izar said with a gulp. "'Death to Ocean Dominion! Life to the Ocean!' is our motto at Ocean Protection. My ocean advocacy has led me to become an enemy of Ocean Dominion." His face tightening, he added, for extra measure, "In fact, it was someone from Ocean Dominion who threw me overboard."

"Looks like we share a common enemy," Coralline said.

"We can also share a common aim," Izar said, trying to sound nonchalant. "We can work together to find the elixir. It'll increase our chances of success."

"Not a chance in hell!" Pavonis boomed, tossing Izar up with his snout.

"Let's talk, Pavonis," Coralline said, just as he was about to toss Izar up again.

Pavonis glared at Izar one last time before arriving at Coralline's side. They turned away from him.

"Izar's scroll is the first clue on our quest!" Coralline bubbled. She knew from Ecklon's detective work that any clue on any quest should be cherished, no matter how casually it was stumbled upon. "Do you think we should let Izar join our Elixir Expedition?" Coralline asked the three animals.

"It cannot be a coincidence we met him," Nacre quipped from Coralline's shoulder. "I think it's fate. Let's work with him."

"We can work only with someone we trust," Pavonis said, "and we can never trust a human."

"Not even a human who works on behalf of the ocean?" Altair said.

"We should not believe a word he says," Pavonis retorted, "for we have no way to verify it—as he well knows. And no matter where he claims to work, we should not forget that it is humans who sickened Naiadum. It is because of humans that we're searching for the elixir in the first place. Humans are our enemies, not our allies."

Coralline thought of the men she'd seen aboard the Ocean Dominion ship during the black poison spill, looking like sticks against the sun. Her hands rose to her neck as she recalled the slime that had encased her gills, almost suffocating her, the same slime that had contaminated Naiadum's blood. Pavonis was right; they could never trust a human.

"We have the clue now," Pavonis continued. "We can find Tang Tarpon on our own."

"But what if Tang demands to see a note?" Coralline said with a sigh, thinking out loud. "To be on the safe side, maybe we should work with Izar until we meet Tang; then, as soon as we meet him, we can go our own way with whatever information he provides us. What do you think?"

"That's a good idea," Altair said.

"You're cleverer than you look, Coralline," said Nacre.

"Fine," Pavonis said, his gaze swiveling to Izar. "But I won't take my eye off him for a moment. One mistake, and I'll crush him to death."

13

The Serpent

S almon, tuna, shrimp, what do you have?" Izar asked.

The voluminous yellow-tailed waitress, who'd introduced herself as Morena, fingered the mole above her lip and said, "Very funny."

Izar returned to scanning the menu at the restaurant, Taieniata. The words read like hieroglyphics to him: colander kelp, dulse, undaria, velvet horn, pepper dulse, ulva. Moments ago, Coralline had told him which of these algae were red, brown, and green, as though their scientific classifications should make some difference to him. "I'll have ulva," he said, for no other reason than that it was the last item on the menu, and so his eye hovered over it last.

"The same for you?" Morena asked Coralline.

"No way!" Izar stared at Coralline, as did Morena. "I've been eating it at home to please my mother," she explained. "Undaria for me, please."

"Anything to drink?" Morena said.

"What do you have?" Izar asked.

"All four wines."

Wine, underwater? Who would have thought? "The strongest," Izar said.

"Parasol, then." Morena's thick chin jiggled as she nodded, then turned to Coralline.

"No wine for me," Coralline said.

Morena soon returned with a shapely flask that had a wide base and narrow neck. A sliding stopper on top prevented the dark-green liquid from mingling with the waters. Izar lifted the decanter tentatively to his lips and tilted his head; the stopper slid back automatically upon the angle, and a sweet, pungent liquid seared his throat. It tasted like something between wine and whisky, and it made Izar think of his weekly whisky-and-cigar meetings with his father and brother. They now felt as distant as though they'd occurred on another planet.

"What is underwater wine made of?" Izar asked Coralline.

"Fermented sea grapes. Each of the four wines is prepared of a different grape—oval, bell sea, beaded cushion, and parasol—so it's of a slightly different shade of green."

Izar nodded. He braced his elbows apart on the table, sitting straight with effort. They had swum all morning to reach this Purple Claw village, and the swim had been equivalent to jogging steadily for hours without a break. Izar had slowed a few times, but the shark had turned his huge head to smirk at him—yes, he'd actually smirked—and Izar had bit his tongue and continued to keep pace with the monster and the mermaid.

Upon arriving in Purple Claw, they'd obtained directions from passersby to the Ministry of Meristem. Coralline had asked to speak with an administrator in the Under-Ministry of Residential Affairs. But there was a long queue of people seeking addresses, and Coralline and Izar had been given an appointment for an hour later. Izar had concluded that the government process was just as slow and bureaucratic underwater as on land.

With nothing to do during their hour of wait, they'd decided to get lunch at Taeiniata, the nearest restaurant to the Ministry. Coralline had deposited Altair and Nacre in a neighboring patch of grass, and Pavonis had rushed off to explore Purple Claw, saying he was fulfilling his "dreams of travel." Izar preferred it this way: without the three nuisance animals.

He looked down at his dark-gray waistcoat. Its buttons were thirty small white shells called baby's ears. It had taken him an eternity to do up the column of buttons. He had not seen a need for a waistcoat, but Coralline had said, "No one will serve us if you're not dressed," and her seahorse had added, "Nudity is inappropriate and unacceptable." Izar supposed it was similar on land—he would be unable to gain entrance to any decent restaurant without a shirt—but he didn't view his current body as his own, so he didn't care to tend it in any way. Conceding to Coralline and Altair nevertheless, he'd purchased a handful of waistcoats from a little shop called Panache, located around a bend in the lane from Taeiniata.

Morena arrived with two plates. She placed one in front of Coralline, brimming with soft flaps of olive-green leaves, and the other in front of Izar, towering with light-green sheets that he thought looked awfully like lettuce. She handed them each a pair of stone-sticks, which Izar thought resembled chopsticks. Coralline attacked her plate enthusiastically while Izar found himself chewing as thoroughly as a rabbit. Appearing to take pity on him, Coralline placed a leaf from her plate onto a corner of his. Sampling it, he found that it was flavorful and fragrant, melting on his tongue, much better than his bland ulva.

Sipping his parasol wine, Izar asked Coralline questions about life in the ocean. She answered him patiently.

Merpeople settlements tended to be located at a depth of anywhere from one hundred to six-hundred-and-sixty feet below the waves, she said. The minimum range was determined by safety—keeping a distance from humans and ships—and the maximum range was determined by sunlight—almost no light penetrated beyond six-hundred-and-sixty feet, the boundary of the Sunlight Zone. Because most parts of the ocean went deeper than six-hundred-and-sixty feet, while some were shallower than one hundred, merpeople settlements tended to be scattered throughout Meristem as isolated pockets, she said. The rest of Meristem consisted of open ocean and deep sea. Constituting half the surface of the earth, the deep sea commenced at about five thousand feet below the surface (or one mile). Entirely pitch-black, it was almost as foreign an expanse to merpeople as to humans, Coralline said.

Izar concluded that as birds flew high but not extremely high, generally staying within a few hundred feet of the surface of the earth, so merpeople lived deep, but not extraordinarily deep, staying within the Sunlight Zone. As birds never crossed the ozone, merpeople never entered the deep sea.

Merpeople told time in two ways, Coralline told him: the hue of the waters and sand-clocks. She pointed out a sand-clock to him on the mantel of Taeiniata. It was an hourglass filled with fine white sand, with twenty-four notches carved onto its lower bulb, one for every hour of the day. The time was a little after noon now.

He glanced at the menu and asked Coralline what it was printed upon. Parchment, she said, made of treated, pressed sargassum, a tall, common brown algae that tended to grow in thick masses near coral reefs. He asked her how ink didn't run in water. Because it was formulated from any of a variety of oleaginous algae, she said—fatty, oil-filled algae—and oil and water could not dissolve in each other.

Perhaps it was the wine, but Izar found himself relaxing. Things could be a lot worse than they were. For one, she was not half bad to look at, his mermaid companion. More importantly, his enemies, led by Zaurak, would be unable to find him in the ocean. They would not know he had transformed into a merman. And even if they did know, even if Alshain had told Zaurak, it would be impossible for them to locate him in the Atlantic, hundreds of feet below the waves.

Izar breathed deeply—for the first time in days, he was safe.

Doubt beset Coralline as she hovered with Izar before Tang Tarpon's door.

The roof of Tang's house was partially caved in, and the gray walls were decrepit, their shale deeply scratched, as though someone had taken a dagger to them. And yet Tang's home looked no worse than the others in his town of Hog's Bristle.

There was a stagnancy in the waters themselves of Hog's Bristle, a restless unhappiness—Coralline sensed it as clearly as she sensed the day morphing from late afternoon to early evening, the passage of time evident to her in a dulling of the waters. Loiterers were everywhere, lingering among worn shops and dilapidated homes, staring at passersby. A thickset loiterer with a square face hovered directly across from Tang's home, staring openly at her. Coralline could see at a glance why Hog's Bristle was ranked the most unsafe settlement in Meristem year after year in the annual Settlement Status rankings prepared by the Under-Ministry of Residential Affairs. The safety situation in Hog's Bristle seemed so dire, in fact, that even the structure of homes appeared impacted: Most houses had tiny windows, perhaps so that thieves could not squeeze in through them.

Coralline looked up as a shadow traveled above her—Pavonis. He was tingling to explore Hog's Bristle, she knew, exhilarated by the town's "dangerous edge," but she had asked him to stay overhead while she and Izar met with Tang—just in case. Nothing could happen to her so long as he was there, she believed. As for Altair and Nacre, she'd deposited them all too gladly in a rocky alcove close by—they'd bickered incessantly throughout the three-hour swim from Purple Claw to Hog's Bristle.

Coralline knocked on Tang's door . . . and waited . . . and waited. The administrator in the Under-Ministry of Residential Affairs in Purple Claw had looked through the Register of Residents of Meristem and had told Coralline and Izar that Tang Tarpon lived in Hog's Bristle. He had provided them an address, which Coralline had scribbled in her parchment-pad, but she thought now that perhaps the address had not been updated. Maybe Tang had moved. Izar was about to knock as well, when the door flew open.

Tang Tarpon's hair fell to his shoulders in thick gray clumps. His nose was globular and pocked in places. His scales were a limp-brown color and his waistcoat was so stained that Coralline could not tell its original shade. The grooves around his mouth and eyes suggested he was about sixty years old.

His gaze shifted from Coralline to Izar and back, and he blinked, as though trying to prevent their faces from blurring in his vision. "Why are you bothering me?" he slurred, clutching the doorknob for support.

He was drunk in the middle of the day. Hiding her alarm, Coralline introduced herself and Izar, and continued, "We're looking for the elixir, and a note guided us to you."

Tang's gray eyes expanded beneath straggly brows. "Show me the note," he demanded.

Izar handed it over. Tang's eyes scanned it, then he said, "Come in." No sooner had they entered through the door than he looked about surreptitiously outside and slammed the door shut behind them.

It was good she'd decided to work with Izar, even if briefly, Coralline thought. Had she arrived at Tang's door alone, without a note, he would likely have turned her away. But as she heard the lock click in place behind her, the feeling in her heart was far from relief. Half a dozen empty decanters of wine cluttered the living room floor in the shape of a semicircle. Tang seemed to have been lying among them, for he smelled like a life-sized decanter as he swept past her and Izar. How could such a mess of a merman possibly help them?

Despite her doubts, Coralline felt somewhat appeased to see a bookshelf on the wall; a merman who liked to read was a merman to whom she could relate. She smiled to see that the most prominently displayed book on the shelf was *The Universe Demystified* by Venant Veritate, her favorite author. Other book spines stated the name Tang Tarpon; he was a writer, much to her surprise. His books included *The Case of the Confusing Conch*, *The Vanished Whelk*, *The Under-Minister's Assassination*, and *Death by Desmarestia*. Their names suggested to Coralline that they were murder mysteries. She herself did not read murder mysteries, but she knew that Ecklon enjoyed them; she wondered whether he'd read any of Tang's books.

Tang staggered into a chair and beckoned them to sit on the settee across from him. It was narrower than Coralline would have liked; her scales touched Izar's at the hips as they sat down together.

Tang turned the elixir note over and studied the back of the parchment, running his hand over it slowly, deliberately. His thumb paused over the top-left corner; something seemed embossed there. Holding the note up to his nose, he squinted at it. "P&P," he pronounced softly. Returning the note to his lap, he looked at Coralline and Izar, and continued, "I believe P&P refers to a stationery shop called Printer & Parchment, located in the settlement of Velvet Horn. I know Printer & Parchment because I've had a few of my book manuscripts printed there in the past."

Tang was smarter than he looked, Coralline thought with a flicker of hope. He'd noticed a logo that had slipped both her attention and Izar's.

"Do you know who wrote the note?" Izar asked Tang. "Is there anyone you can think of whose name starts with the letter *O*?"

"I'm afraid not, no."

"Either way, why do you think the note would lead us to you?" Coralline asked.

"Because I found the elixir."

Coralline gasped. This was so much better than she'd expected. Tang's words showed that, at the very least, the elixir was not just a legend—it *actually* existed! And given that he'd found it, who better to guide her to it? Clasping the armrest of the settee, Coralline perched at the edge of her seat and asked breathlessly, "How do you propose we find it—"

With a heave, Tang started sobbing. His face itself appeared to be disintegrating, the lines twisting and turning. "I'm sorry," he said eventually between hiccups. "I found the elixir for my wife, Charonia."

Coralline looked about the living room newly, at all the decanters littering the floor. How could any mermaid worth her salt live like this? Coralline would have been willing to bet every shell in her meagre carapace pouch that Tang was a dedicated bachelor.

"Thirty years ago, just a month after our wedding," Tang continued in a breaking voice, "Charonia was diagnosed with a malignant spinal tumor. Apothecaries said she would die in a matter of weeks. I couldn't bear the thought of it and decided to find the elixir for her—and I did. I still remember the moment as clearly as if it was three days, rather than three decades, ago: The moment she swallowed the elixir, Charonia glowed brightly, and her tumor simply vanished, like it had never existed. The elixir saved her life, but, as it appears, it could not save our marriage. We were together thirty happy years, but she left me last week for another merman."

He keeled forward, his head collapsing in his hands, long clumps of hair falling around his face like dead kelp.

How selfish, Coralline thought. Tang risked his life to save Charonia, and she repaid him by leaving him. No wonder he looked so miserable.

Suddenly, a merman's shadow passed a small window to one side of Tang, a window overlooking an empty alley. Coralline turned to Izar, wondering whether he'd noticed the shadow, too, but he was staring unwaveringly at Tang, a touch of sympathy in the set of his face. Had he recently been betrayed himself? Coralline wondered. But his features hardened before her eyes, and he said, in an expressionless voice, "Where did you find the elixir?"

"I'm afraid Mintaka made me swear to keep her location a secret."

Izar muttered a series of curses.

Tang scowled at him. Coralline also glowered at him. She tried to warn Izar with her eyes—Tang was doing them a favor by speaking to them, they needed him on their side, Izar should not address Tang like he was a sluggish employee—but Izar was not looking at her.

Coralline turned back to Tang with an apologetic smile. "We really appreciate your speaking to us despite the difficult time," she said. "We're trying to find the elixir ourselves. Would you mind our asking you a few questions about it? You can answer those that allow you to remain true to your oath to Mintaka."

"Fine," Tang said sullenly.

"Is the elixir made of starlight, as the story *The Legend of the Elixir* states?"

"Yes."

"And is it made by Mintaka?"

"Yes."

"And is it true that the elixir is a blessing that comes accompanied by a curse?"

"Yes."

"May I ask what your curse was?"

"Mintaka told me: *Beware of the serpent.*"

"What does that mean?" Izar asked.

"I can't imagine. I never managed to figure it out."

"How do you suggest we proceed with our elixir quest?" Coralline said.

"There's someone who might be able to help you, someone who helped me. Take a look at that scroll."

He pointed an index finger at a scroll lying on the mantel. Coralline rose and picked it up. Stars sparkled brightly over the parchment, their glitter smooth and indelible. It was an invitation to the Ball of Blue Bottle, taking place in an auditorium called The Cupola. Coralline knew the Ball to be the most prestigious annual event in Meristem—a gathering of its most successful and esteemed people. She sympathized newly with Tang—considering the level of accomplishment he must have had to be invited to the Ball, his fall in life at the loss of his love was all the starker.

"The Ball of Blue Bottle is in three days," Tang said. "I was planning to attend with Charonia, but, given the current state of affairs"—his gaze roved over the empty decanters—"I won't be attending. The two of you can take my invitation and attend instead of me. Now, read the back of the parchment."

Turning it over, Coralline read the one sentence scribbled upon the back: *Meet me at the center of The Cupola when the music ends.* She looked at Tang quizzically.

"The merman you should meet is—"

A dagger flew past Coralline's scales and stabbed Tang in the chest.

Her head whirled toward the small side window from which the dagger had flown in—she caught the barest glimpse of a head as it vanished. Had the dagger been aimed at her? But who would aim it at her?

Coralline trembled. She wanted to cower, to take shelter behind the settee, but her nerves seemed frozen. All she managed was to shield her torso with her arms.

Tang tumbled off his chair to the floor, his hands encasing the dagger. It had stabbed him in the heart—the precision of its location suggested to Coralline that it was meant for him, not her. But that provided little consolation. Blood was spurting out of him, spewing through the waters, accosting her nostrils. His tail started bleaching, scale upon scale turning a dead white, a disappearing act of color.

It was Coralline's fault. She'd seen a shadow pass the window, but she hadn't said anything—just as she hadn't said anything when she'd seen black poison spreading above Urchin Grove.

"Look at the dagger," Izar said quietly, next to her.

Its hilt was encrusted with translucent-green olivine stones in the pattern of a serpent. *Beware of the serpent*, Mintaka had told Tang—*this* was that serpent. To know in theory that the elixir came accompanied by a curse—to read of it in a story book, to hear of it through Tang—that was one thing, but to see the curse in action was yet another. It seemed unbearably cruel, the way it worked, the blessing and the curse. If Coralline found the elixir, this could well be her own fate—a dagger in the heart, or death in some other way.

Focus on Tang, Coralline told herself. She dug her nails into the palms of her hands to bring her attention back to her present environment through pain. She had to do something—but what could she do? She was a disbarred apothecary. If she tried to save Tang, she would be in trouble legally under the Medical Malpractice Act for practicing without a badge; in that case, she would be forbidden from practice for the rest of her life. If she let Tang die, she would be in trouble morally—how would she live with herself?

"I'll find you a back door," Pavonis hollered through a window.

Coralline turned her head in his direction mechanically. He must have smelled the blood. And the reason he wanted to find a back door was that Tang's body lay so close to the front door that it would be impossible to open the door without passersby seeing.

"Be ready to beat a hasty retreat as soon as you hear my dual thumps, Coralline!" he hissed, before vanishing around the corner.

It was a game they'd played many years ago, when she was a mergirl, called A Hasty Retreat. She'd enter a place such as a library, he'd find a back door, and she'd try to reach it as quickly as possible upon hearing the dual thumps of his tail, the private alarm signal between them. Over time, he'd become faster at locating exits and she'd become more accurate at locating the beat of his tail. But it had always been just a game; she'd never once thought she'd actually have to beat a hasty retreat.

"Let's go, Coralline," Izar said. "We can't do anything for Tang."

Tang's eyes were closed, and his face was still, but its lines were set in pain—that meant he remained alive. Regardless of the Medical Malpractice Act and what it might mean for her future, she could not just let Tang die, she decided.

Her fingers fumbled with the zip of her satchel. She extracted the pouch of carapace sitting atop her apothecary arsenal, deposited it on the floor with a jangle, then took out her arsenal and unclasped it. She unrolled thick swaths of pyropia to stanch the flow of blood and put pressure on the wound. She then turned to the dagger: She would have to pull it out. But that would cause more blood to flow. The thought made her fingers jitter and her stomach turn somersaults.

She heard two consecutive thumps; Pavonis was tapping his tail against the back door he'd found.

Coralline wrapped her hands around the hilt of the dagger, its encrustations hard and cold beneath her fingers. Closing her eyes, leaning forward, she mustered all her strength to wrench it out—

"*Murderess!*" a voice yelled.

Coralline's head whirled toward the shout. A square face was staring at her through a window—it belonged to the thickset loiterer she'd noticed as she'd hovered at Tang's doorstep. She looked down at the dagger in her hands, then she looked at Tang: Each and every scale of his tail was white, and his face was blank—he was dead. Just minutes ago, he'd been alive—thinking, feeling, breathing—telling her and Izar about his wife, about the elixir, and now, as fast as a snap of her fingers, he was dead. It was dizzying, the speed of it.

"Let's go, Coralline!" Izar said. "We can't remain here. . . ."

The wide movement of his lips told her he was yelling, but she could hardly hear him through her daze. His words were arriving to her as though from across a great distance.

The living room doorknob turned. The door did not open—thank goodness Tang had locked it. And the windows were too small for the loiterer to fit through—earlier, she'd disliked the tiny windows of Hog's Bristle; now, she felt grateful for them.

Izar shook her by the shoulders, stopping only when her teeth rattled. It snapped her out of her stupor. Shrugging his hands off, she returned her apothecary arsenal to her satchel and added the invitation to the Ball of Blue

Bottle on top. She then stopped in her tracks and closed her eyes, trying to listen to Pavonis's dual thumps not just with her ears but with her body. "This way!" she called to Izar. Trailed by him, she fled through a narrow corridor, swept past a few bedrooms, and erupted out a back door.

"*Murderess!*" screamed the square-faced loiterer, speeding toward her from within the alley outside Tang's home.

Pavonis's tail cut a mighty diagonal streak above, and Coralline followed it resolutely.

14

A Shady Place

B ristled Bed and Breakfast looked like a wide, crooked, coarse-grained rock, misshapen in places, with haphazard crevices carved throughout to serve as rooms. Even algae seemed to have given the place a wide berth, for its surroundings consisted of bare, brittle sands.

Two mermen lingered next to the door like weeds, both with orange tails. One of them was obese, his belly pushing against the seams of his waistcoat, and the other was gaunt, with concave cheeks and hollow eye sockets. A dagger glinted in the hand of the fat one.

"I feel sick to even look at this place," Altair moaned from Coralline's satchel.

"Everything makes you sick, Pole Dancer!" Nacre said from Coralline's shoulder.

"To think what your father would say, Coralline, at the prospect of your staying here," Altair persisted.

Coralline tried not to think of it.

"Regardless of its aesthetics," Pavonis said, "Bristled Bed and Breakfast is our safest option for the night. Located along the southern perimeter of town, this hotel is as far as we can get from Tang's home, in the north, while remaining in the same settlement. The distance from Tang's home is important in case any constables are searching for you, Coralline. We face two options at this moment: We can swim through the night to reach the next settlement, far away, or you can stay the night here."

Coralline's scales quivered at the thought of a second night without sleep. Her gills had fluttered profusely all day during their swims between settlements, and there was an airy lightness to her body. It took all her effort to even keep her shoulders straight. And even if she were willing to swim through the night, she knew from her visit to Ecklon last night that Pavonis, despite his strength as a daytime navigator, might well lose his way in the dark.

"You'll be staying here just one night," Pavonis continued, "not the rest of your life. I don't know why you're even hesitating."

"I'm hesitating because Bristled Bed and Breakfast was the site of a brutal murder just two weeks ago." She had heard of it from Ecklon. As a detective, he knew of practically all murders committed anywhere in Meristem. Whenever he'd told her about them, they'd sounded distant and foreign, in faraway places, but now here she was—at her second murder scene of the day.

"Tell you what, Coralline," Izar said, "I'll sleep next to you, if you're afraid."

Altair gasped.

"How dare you, you vulgar human!" Pavonis hissed. His tail slapped the waters, creating turbid ripples, and his snout tossed Izar up. Coralline tried to follow Izar's trajectory with her eyes but could make out little past the narrow radius of her luciferin lantern's white-blue glow.

Long moments later, when Izar managed to return to her side, his hair was disarrayed and his expression bewildered. "I meant I would sleep in the *room* next to you," he clarified.

"Thank you for the thought," Coralline said, only to be polite.

"It's irrelevant where you sleep, human," Pavonis growled. "My eyes are always open."

He meant it literally, Coralline knew: Sharks did not have eyelids. Many types of sharks, including whale sharks, didn't truly sleep, not the way people did. Sharks experienced rest periods, turning off one side of their brain like whales and dolphins, but they were always partially conscious and aware. Some sharks, including whale sharks, continued to swim while resting, so that water would continue filtering through their gills, providing fresh oxygen. If they stopped swimming for even a short period of time, they could die of hypoxia, or oxygen loss. Coralline had always found it a lucky thing that merpeople didn't need to move in order to breathe—imagine, nights without sleep! Yes, merpeople had five sets of gills like most sharks, but merpeople gills were finer and floatier than most, such that even the barest of ripples let water, and oxygen, pass through. Pavonis's lifestyle had its own advantages, though—his incessant swimming meant that tiredness was an alien concept to him.

"Think of it, Coralline," Pavonis persisted. "Instead of wasting time in indecision, you could be fast asleep at this moment, cocooned comfortably in a bed."

A blanket covering her up to her chin, a bed beneath her back, her tail resting—Coralline could not resist the vision. "You're right, Pavonis," she said, tucking the rod of her luciferin lantern in her satchel.

She deposited Altair in a spot he chose in the shadows of Bristled Bed and Breakfast. He camouflaged himself immediately, as though to hide from the world that he was in the vicinity of such a place. She deposited Nacre on the exterior wall of the hotel, upon Nacre's order of such. "I'll entertain myself by eavesdropping through open window shutters," the snail said cheerfully.

"Keep your shutters open, Coralline," Pavonis said. "I'll drop by before you sleep."

Coralline nodded. From his tone, she knew there was something he wished to say but could not say in front of the others. Trying to suppress her sense of foreboding, she took a deep breath and forced herself across the threshold of Bristled Bed and Breakfast with Izar. A dagger continued to glint in the hand of the merman just outside the door.

Fissures marked the walls of the lobby like acne, and the whole place looked like it might collapse into a pile of rubble at any moment, but Izar felt relieved that he and Coralline were finally inside Bristled Bed and Breakfast. No one had asked him for his opinion outside, so he had not bothered to offer it, but it was his opinion that Coralline took too long to make simple decisions and that everything affected her too deeply—Tang Tarpon's death, the feelings of each of her ridiculous pets, the appearance of this motel-like place. She was like a sponge—absorbing everything around her and letting it steep through her skin.

The two of them approached the concierge, a pudgy, slack-faced merman with pores on his nose that made Izar think of sprinkles of black pepper. A square stitched onto his breast pocket stated his name as Bream. A placard on his desk announced: "If you want breakfast in bed, sleep in the lobby."

"Did you send us a scroll to make a reservation?" Bream asked placidly, his arms lifting and landing softly on his desk.

"No," Coralline answered.

Izar could not help but scoff. He thought of the many reservations he'd made at the restaurant Yacht through an act as simple as picking up the telephone. But merpeople were primitive, living without long-distance communications such as phones and cables, without electricity—with nothing but running water. Even their clothes were old-fashioned, the corsets and waistcoats. Izar had traveled a few hundred feet below sea level but felt as though he'd traveled a hundred years back in time.

"Here's the key to your room," Bream said, dangling a single key before their faces. Long and weighty, it made Izar think of a relic from the sixteenth century. "Your room number is—"

"*Separate* rooms," Coralline pronounced.

"You could have said," Bream muttered in an injured voice.

"Rooms next to each other," Izar said, remembering his promise to Coralline outside, not that it had seemed to matter much to her.

As Bream poked about a drawer for another key, Izar felt a slight current at his back. He was now attuned to currents, he realized—a current was like a breeze, except that a short-lived current was usually created by movement rather than the elements.

He turned around. Two mermen came to hover behind him and Coralline, the same two who'd been lingering outside the door. Their orange tails made Izar think of a cantaloupe and a carrot. Despite the discrepancy in their shapes, he could tell at a glance they were brothers: An identical circle of baldness brewed at the center of their skulls, and their complexions looked like pallid lumps of powder.

Though Izar stared at them now, they did not seem to notice him. Their eyes were traveling up and down Coralline's iridescent-green bodice and bronze scales, as she leaned over the counter. "Let's get a room next to hers," the fat brother said to the thin one.

"Your room numbers are forty-one and forty-two," Bream said, dangling one key before Izar and the other before Coralline.

Izar grabbed his key, then asked, "Is there anything to eat around here?"

Bream opened a drawer conspirationally. "I can offer you a snack of devil's tongue from my personal stash," he said in a low voice.

Izar did not know what to make of the offer.

"Devil's tongue is my favorite snack!" Coralline said, her eyes sparkling.

Bream handed them each a set of thin red strips, knotted also with a red strip. It looked like a packet of tongues—it was a sort of red algae, Izar supposed. Coralline snatched her packet from Bream's hand, extracted a tongue, and began to munch on it enthusiastically. Izar tried a tongue more gingerly. The bite was rubbery, with the taste and texture of jerky—he liked it and took another bite.

"Three carapace each, please," Bream requested.

Recalling Coralline's counting of his carapace earlier, Izar placed two shells on the counter, one of them small and round—she'd called it a moon snail shell—and the other ridged and pointed, shaped like a miniature ice-cream cone—she'd called it a wentletrap. Coralline dipped her hand into an outer pocket of her satchel, extracted the same two shells as him, and placed them on the counter. After lunch, Izar had noticed that she'd given her cerith, worth twenty carapace, to the yellow-tailed waitress Morena, and had requested smaller denominations. Morena had given her a fistful of moon snails and wentletraps. Coralline had placed most of them in her golden carapace pouch and had inserted a couple into an outer pocket of her satchel for easy access.

Following Bream's directions, Izar and Coralline entered a shadowed, bumpy corridor to the side of the lobby. Room numbers started at one and continued onward, with ten rooms to a corridor. After they'd turned their fourth corner, Coralline slipped her key into the keyhole of a door marked forty-two, said good night to Izar, and closed the door abruptly. Izar fumbled with his key at length—he was used to flashing a card for entry, not wielding a museum-variety object.

There was a current at his back again. He turned around. It was the same two mermen from the lobby, the carrot and the cantaloupe. They inserted their key into the keyhole for room forty-three, next to Coralline's, and looked at her door with longing. The fat merman licked his lips.

Izar squared his shoulders and clenched his fists. He considered confronting them, but then thought: What would he confront them about, precisely? And why should he confront them about anything? Coralline meant nothing to him. She was simply a pathway to the elixir, to his becoming a human again.

The brothers entered their room and shut their door. Izar managed to pry his own door open, and swam in.

It was a small, cave-like space with a slanting floor, equipped with three items of furniture: a topsy-turvy desk with cracked pillars; a narrow bed somewhere between a twin- and a full-size; and a dented dresser, upon which he immediately tossed his satchel. His nose wrinkled—the room had a musty odor. In water, smell was just as pronounced as on land, but the specific source of the odor was harder to pinpoint—smell was similar to sound underwater, in that sense. But other than its smell, Izar didn't particularly mind the shabbiness of his room—he'd grown up in a storage closet, after all. He swam to the three little round, submarine-like windows and pulled their shutters over them.

Breathing a sigh of relief at being alone at last, he unzipped his satchel and pulled out the gray tin he'd found on his desk at Ocean Dominion. He unrolled the scroll inside the tin, turned it over, and ran his thumb over the logo Tang Tarpon had indicated in its top-left corner: P&P, referring to a stationery shop in Velvet Horn. Who knew where within Meristem that settlement might be, but, if time and circumstances permitted, he would like to go there, Izar decided. It might give him context on how the elixir note and half-shell had ended up in his possession, and, more importantly, how he'd transformed into a merman.

Eager to sleep soon, he turned his attention up to the half-dozen luciferin orbs meandering over the ceiling. Pulses of light within the glassy baubles cast a white-blue glow over the room. Luciferin orbs were always there, in all indoor spaces, journeying slowly over the ceiling, Coralline had told him at the restaurant Taeiniata. The orbs sought the ceiling automatically because, bubbling with nothing but bacteria, they were practically weightless and thus had a tendency to travel up. The orbs were not noticeable during the daytime because their bacteria glowed only in the dark.

The principle of the orbs was not different than that of his Castor's dragon arm—both depended on oxygen. In the case of the orbs, the spark of light was obtained from a trick of biology: the reaction of oxygen and luciferin, a naturally occurring compound. In Castor's case, the spark of fire was achieved through a trick of chemistry: the meeting of oxygen and combustion chemicals.

But how to dim these luciferin orbs at night? Izar wondered with irritation.

Flicking his tailfin, he ascended toward the orbs, but he moved so fast that he bumped his head against the ceiling. Movement indoors was different than outdoors, he'd just learned the hard way. Indoors, merpeople seemed to move slowly, vertically, the tailfin flicking gently to prevent collisions. Outdoors, merpeople swam horizontally, the tailfin flapping hard right and left to generate speed.

Izar grabbed a luciferin orb in his hands. Countless tiny pores smattered its surface to permit the flow of oxygen, just as the skin of Castor's dragon arm was fitted with a distillation chamber to permit oxygen. Izar ran his hands over the orb; his fingers discovered a tiny switch and rotated it. The pores closed, and the light within the orbs dimmed, then eventually died, as the quantity of oxygen dwindled. Izar rotated the switches of two other orbs. He decided to leave the three other orbs in the room aglow, so that some light would remain. He did not trust the darkness of the water.

He collapsed on the bed but winced—the mattress was more of a plank than anything else, just a couple of inches thick. The blanket, meanwhile, was heavy—so that it wouldn't float away, he supposed.

In an effort to become more comfortable, he tried to unclasp the baby's-ear shells buttoning his waistcoat. The tight fit of a waistcoat made sense while swimming—so the fabric wouldn't fly up due to water resistance—but it was constraining when lying down. His fingers fumbled with the shells, but they were too tiny and cumbersome to maneuver through buttonholes. Cursing, he conceded to sleeping in his waistcoat.

Chewing on his strips of devil's tongue, he then aired his frustrations to himself.

He hated wasted time; every day was supposed to prove its use in the form of a tangible, precise accomplishment. But the feeling he'd had all day had been of wandering about with an animal circus. He still knew no specifics of the elixir; the conversation with homeless-looking Tang had only made him skeptical. Tang's murder had also confirmed his suspicions about merpeople—given their bloodlust and eagerness to kill, it was no surprise they had murdered his parents.

How differently the day would have passed had he been on land. At Ocean Dominion, each hour of his day fell immediately upon the next, like a domino. And this day would have been more fast-paced than most, for it would have been his first as co-president. He'd never taken a single sick day from Ocean Dominion, let alone a day of vacation, and now, on his first day as co-president, he was missing. It was shameful. Saiph and Antares must be worried sick about him. What would they think if they saw him like this?

His gaze shifted to the scratched, full-length mirror on the wall. He'd swept past it intentionally when he'd entered the room. He hadn't encountered any mirrors over the course of the day, and it had been for the better, for he hadn't been able to bear the thought of looking at his reflection. But now, he crept out of bed and sidled toward the mirror.

His reflection was that of a stranger. A scaly tail started at his hips, narrowed where his ankles had been, then flared out, turning transparent at the corners. Gill slits formed diagonal cuts on both sides of his neck, opening and closing in parallel.

In the restaurant Taeiniata with Coralline, he had lulled himself into thinking he was safe, that he'd left his enemies behind on land, but he saw now that his enemies were not the primary danger he faced; his body was—the possibility that he might be like this for the rest of his life. He punched the mirror with his platinum-chipped fist.

The luciferin orbs glowed too mildly for Coralline's tastes—their bacteria had probably not been recently replenished. Most merpeople slept in the dark, or nearly dark, but she liked her luciferin orbs bright all night long—they were the galaxies she admired as she drifted off to sleep. She'd loved watching them ever since she was a mergirl, but she hadn't understood why until she'd read *The Universe Demystified*. "The stars tell us that no matter what happens to us," Venant Veritate had written, "no matter whether we live or die, the universe will continue to exist." Coralline found there to be something steadying and humbling in that fact.

A thump sounded at the window.

She turned her head sharply, her heart in her throat. But then she remembered: Pavonis had said he would visit. She moved toward the central of the three tiny windows, extended a hand through, and felt soothed when her fingers found his snout. Luciferin orbs needed oxygen to glow; she needed him.

"The nefarious human's windows are closed, but I'll speak softly in case he overhears." In a voice just above a whisper, Pavonis continued, "Do you have Tang Tarpon's invitation to the Ball of Blue Bottle, or does he?"

"I do."

"Good. It's the guiding clue we have on our elixir quest at this stage. Izar has served his purpose by getting you through Tang's door, just as we'd planned. We don't need him anymore. In the morning, I'll tap on your window to wake you up, and we'll leave Hog's Bristle without him. When he wakes up, he'll find all of us gone."

"But it doesn't feel right to abandon him," Coralline said hesitantly.

"Doesn't it? Not only is he a human, but he's a human competing with you for the elixir. Do you think Mintaka has a shop full of elixirs, one for each visitor? I think not. And *you* must get the elixir instead of Izar. Our only goal at this stage is to save Naiadum—not to worry about whether Izar will get his hideous legs back. But that's not the only reason I want to be rid of him."

"What else?"

"As I told you when we met him, I wouldn't take my eye off him. And I didn't. I kept one eye trained on him practically continuously throughout the day. There's something he's not being honest about; I feel it in my bones. He's keeping a secret from us, one that would change everything."

"If you say so." Coralline yawned.

"Fine, don't believe me. Who do you think killed Tang?"

"I can't imagine. But it related to his elixir curse: *Beware of the serpent.* Oh, Pavonis! When I was trying to save Tang, I was worried about being in defiance of the Medical Malpractice Act; I never once thought there might be a murder charge against me."

"Has Ecklon told you the investigative process for murder cases?"

"Yes," Coralline said, picturing Ecklon as she spoke. "If that loiterer truly suspects me of murder, he's required by law to visit his local Constables Department within twenty-four hours and fill out a form with my colors—black hair, blue-green eyes, bronze scales. With the form in hand, the constables of Hog's Bristle would visit the local branch of the Under-Ministry of Residential Affairs and sift through the Register of Residents of Hog's Bristle. They would make a list of all mermaids in Hog's Bristle with my colors. Only upon ruling out each of them would they move on to mermaids from other settlements."

"Phew. That means we have time on our side. Constables may take a few days to even start investigating the mermaids of Hog's Bristle, let alone finish."

"Yes, but if they were to somehow come in possession of my name, that would change the nature of the investigation. With my name in hand, they would find my details in the Register of Residents of Meristem, including my home address and portrait. They would share my information with all Constables Departments across Meristem. In that case, I would be safe nowhere—because they would have my portrait, constables would be able to recognize me from one look at my face."

"That won't happen," Pavonis said quietly. "But, for the sake of argument, let's say it does. Let's assume the worst-case scenario: that you're found guilty of Tang's murder. What then?"

"Then I'll spend the rest of my life in the Wrongdoers' Refinery." Coralline shuddered.

She'd never been inside the Wrongdoers' Refinery but had heard plenty about it from Ecklon. The prison windows were tiny, he had said, and there were five bars across every window, like gill slits across the neck, to make escape all but impossible.

"Can we pin Tang's murder on Izar?" Pavonis suggested.

"I hadn't thought of that," Coralline said, both impressed and perturbed by his thinking. "But I was seen holding the dagger, so I can't see how we'd pin it on him. At worst, because he was with me, he would be considered an accomplice. But even if constables were to catch him, they wouldn't be able to find any information about him in the Register of Residents of Meristem. If unable to identify him, they would have to release him within twenty-four hours. It's a law of the Under-Ministry of Crime and Murder, Ecklon told me, called the Identification and Anti-Detention Act."

"What a tragic law. Anyhow, enough of crime and murder for one night. What do you think you'll learn at the Ball of Blue Bottle?"

"I don't know. Tang was stabbed mid-sentence, just as he was about to utter the name of the merman we should meet at the Ball."

"That's too bad, but I hope you'll be able to identify the merman once you get to the Ball."

"I hope so, too."

"Regardless, our mission now is to get to the Ball. Blue Bottle is a long distance south, and the Ball is in only three days. Be prepared to swim energetically tomorrow."

With that, Pavonis departed, and Coralline fastened the shutters across all three windows.

15

A Dagger

A thump sounded. Again and again.

Coralline sat up in bed. The blanket around her was not the lush, black-and-white one of her bedroom but a scratchy, stuffy, mildly odorous thing—she was not at home but at Bristled Bed and Breakfast. She darted to the shutters of the central window and tugged the pane open.

"Took you long enough!" Pavonis hissed. The waters behind him, the little of them that Coralline could discern behind his girth, were not yet bright—the time of day was early morning. "There's a problem," he pronounced. "A big problem."

"What?"

"Constables. They're here, looking for you."

Coralline's heart skipped a beat then resumed at a frantic pace. "What do you mean—"

"Who saw the constables first?" said Nacre, crawling onto the windowsill from the exterior wall.

"Nacre was the first to see the constables," Pavonis acknowledged impatiently, "and she alerted me. The constables swam into the lobby of Bristled Bed and Breakfast and spoke to the concierge, a different merman than the one last night—a fortunate thing, otherwise he might have directed them straight to your room. I can't fit anywhere, but I asked the Minions to enter the lobby through a window and eavesdrop on the constables—"

"*Asked?* More like ordered!" a voice protested. Coralline couldn't see him, but Altair's voice was coming from somewhere in Pavonis's shadow, at the level of the seabed. "I eavesdropped not because I enjoy stooping to the level of snoop," the seahorse continued, "but as a sacrifice for the good of the team."

"Stop pretending you're above everyone and everything, Pole Dancer!" Nacre scoffed. "I, for one, am loud and proud about my two interests in life: snooping and snoozing."

"Enough with your nonsense, Minions!" Pavonis snarled. The glassy circle of his eye hardened as his gaze swiveled to each of them, before rushing back to Coralline. "The constables have a warrant out for your arrest for the murder of Tang Tarpon."

"B-but how?" Coralline stuttered. "How do they even know my name?"

"I don't know," Pavonis replied.

"If they know my name," Coralline said hoarsely, "it means that they have my portrait, or will have it soon, which means they'll recognize me on sight." Her mind was whirling, but she tried to calm down and rationalize through the situation as Ecklon would. "They have no motive," she said.

"But they do," said Nacre. "They believe you were trying to rob Tang and stabbed him when he refused to give you carapace."

"But that's absurd!"

"I agree," said Pavonis, "but we have to stay focused if we want to make it out of here. They're checking all the rooms, starting with room number one."

Coralline was in room number forty-two; that bought her a little time to escape.

"I looked for potential exits last night," Pavonis said, "but it was dark, and it was tough to tell. I'm going to circle this place now and try to find you a back door. Once I find it, you'll hear my dual thumps in the corridor outside your door. Slip out of your room as soon as you hear them, then

I'll guide you out of this labyrinth through further taps on the walls. In the meantime, pack your satchel and close your shutters, in case constables decide to peek through windows."

"What about us?" Altair said. "Where will we go?"

"Given the murder charge," Nacre said, her tentacles waggling down in his direction, "we're safer with the Ogre than with Coralline. Bring your snout to the wall, Ogre, so I can climb on it. As for you, Pole Dancer"—she laughed—"you'll have to get inside the Ogre's mouth!"

Pavonis glowered at them but touched his snout to the wall, so Nacre could crawl atop it. When she was settled, she looked like a red-and-white bump on his head. He then opened his mouth for Altair to enter; the seahorse did so tremblingly.

"Don't worry, Altair," Coralline said. "You'll be separated from Pavonis's throat by the filtering pads in his mouth."

That didn't seem to bring Altair any consolation. Pavonis closed his mouth, gave Coralline one last look, then left. She closed her shutters with quivering fingers. Then she swam to the dresser in a daze and changed out of her chemise into the sky-blue bodice with cloud-white ribbons that Ecklon so liked. It was an outfit for a happy day, a happy time—ill-suited to today—but she wore it so she could pretend he was with her.

She packed and closed her satchel, finding that its zip moved as smoothly as an eel. Something was wrong—missing, rather. When she'd first packed the satchel in Urchin Grove, it had been so full that she'd had to tug at the zip to get it to budge at all. What was missing?

She opened the satchel and rummaged quickly through its contents. She should have heard the jangle of carapace, but there was not a sound. Her carapace pouch was missing.

When had she last seen the golden purse? Not last night, when she'd paid for this room, because she'd paid with a moon snail shell and wentletrap shell that she'd kept aside, in an outer pocket, for easy access. No, she'd last seen the pouch in Tang Tarpon's home: She'd taken it out of her satchel in order to extract the apothecary arsenal beneath. In her rush to leave Tang's home, she must have forgotten it there. Her full name was stitched onto the fabric of the pouch; that must be how the constables knew it. And the pouch must be the reason they thought she'd tried to rob Tang.

How could she have forgotten the pouch there? And what would she do now over the remainder of the Elixir Expedition? Not only was she suspected of murder, but she had not even a moon snail shell to her name anymore. Where would she sleep? What would she eat?

The doorknob turned. Her head swiveled toward it. How could the constables be here already? Could someone have given them a clue, leading them to skip most other rooms and arrive directly at her door? But the door did not open, despite their efforts with the doorknob—she'd locked it, of course. She thought the constables would rap on the door and announce themselves, in which case she would be required by law to open the door—but not a word transmitted through the oval slab of slate. Instead, the doorknob kept moving—were they picking the lock?

They were—the door opened suddenly. Coralline put her hands up.

Two orange tails filled the doorway, then the door closed. The mermen were not attired in the deep-purple waistcoats of constables; their breast pockets did not carry the circular black seal of the Under-Ministry of Crime and Murder. These mermen were not constables. Instead, they were the mermen Coralline had seen lingering just outside the door of Bristled Bed and Breakfast last night. Their eyes traveled over her now in parallel, from the tip of her tailfin to the top of her head and back down again.

"There are constables in the corridors," Coralline said, trying to control the tremor in her voice. "They'll arrest you if you try anything."

"I think they'll arrest *you*, mermaid," said the fat merman, his jowls juddering. "I reckon she's a criminal on the loose, Sparus; otherwise, she wouldn't have put her hands up when we entered."

"I reckon you're right, Eliphus," said the skinny merman, Sparus. "Otherwise, she would also have screamed by now. Go ahead, mermaid, scream if you dare."

Coralline's lips parted, but no sound emerged. If she were to scream, constables would hear her and arrive at her door. But at no cost could she risk capture—if they caught her, she'd be detained at the Wrongdoers' Refinery indefinitely, awaiting trial for days or weeks, unable to continue on the Elixir Expedition, unable to save Naiadum. No, she could not scream. Now that she was suspected of breaking the law, she could no longer expect it to protect her.

Eliphus's and Sparus's mouths prickled into smiles.

"What shall we do with her?" asked Sparus.

"Let's start by slashing her corset off," Eliphus suggested. He extracted a dagger from his waistcoat pocket and rotated it in his hand. "We can kill her after we're done with her."

As stealthy as squids, the two brothers approached Coralline from out of the shadows of the doorway.

Every nerve in her strained to flee, but there was nowhere for her to go. As an apothecary, she'd focused so resolutely on enhancing the survival of others that she had never bothered to learn any survival skills herself. She retreated slowly through the small room. All of her senses were alive. She felt acutely aware of every object in the room—her satchel, the desk, the bed, the mirror, the luciferin orbs, the pillows. But nothing could help her. She had no dagger, no voice, no Ecklon, no Pavonis.

But there was Izar, in the adjoining room. She'd been planning to leave before he awoke, but what if she woke him up now? He might help her. But how could she wake him up? She would have to make a noise loud enough for him to hear but low enough not to draw the attention of anyone else at Bristled Bed and Breakfast. But how? She looked at the wall separating their rooms. The topsy-turvy desk stood against the wall. If she hit the desk repeatedly with her tailfin, the desk might thud against the wall, and the noise might wake him up.

She sidled toward the desk and jumped when her shoulders grazed the wall behind. The shale was cold, but she pressed her back to it in order to get as far away from Sparus and Eliphus as she could. They arrived easily to either side of her, though, clasped one of her arms each, and jerked her forward, away from the wall. Sparus positioned himself behind her and grabbed both her wrists in one hand, pinning her arms to her sides. But her tailfin remained close to the edge of the desk, fortunately. She slapped the desk. It didn't thud against the wall. She flicked her tailfin harder. The desk thudded gently against the wall this time. She flicked her tailfin twice more; the desk hit the wall with a light, grating tempo.

Eliphus hovered in front of her. His stubby fingers twirled with the lace along her neckline, a swollen smile across his lips. His other hand landed on her cheek, sticky and clammy, and his lips pressed upon hers. She turned her head away, but he caught her chin and pressed his mouth to hers again. She bit his lip.

His face separated from hers. His eyebrows formed shaggy swaths, and a vein throbbed in his temple. The back of his hand landed hard across her jaw. Her neck turned so sharply, it creaked. Her head reeled; the room spun. But, trying to focus, she continued to flick her tailfin against the desk. Her tempo was weakening, though, as she herself was.

"I'll teach you a lesson," Sparus hissed into her ear from behind. He squeezed her wrists so hard, a small scream escaped her lips. Her wrist bones were close to splintering in his grasp.

Where was Izar? Could he not hear her? Or could he hear her but didn't care?

Eliphus thrust his dagger forward. Coralline drew her ribs inward; the point of the dagger landed on her navel, just a hair's breadth away from drawing blood. It split into two—Coralline blinked hard, and it became one again. A wave of dizziness was sweeping over her, clouding her vision. Her shoulders sagged, and her vertebrae went limp. She no longer had the strength to continue to flick her tailfin against the desk.

Eliphus clasped the hem of her bodice with his thumb and forefinger and started cutting upward. The cloud-white strings gave way one after another, as he undressed her stitch by stitch. When he was halfway up, his hand landed on her belly from underneath her loosened bodice. His fingers toyed with her navel, then traced each of her lower ribs.

The door flew open.

Izar entered the room, his gaze flying from Eliphus to Sparus to Coralline. "You can take your turn with her after us," Eliphus said, turning toward him, dagger in hand.

Coralline's lips were the crimson color of bitten apples, Izar saw, and her eyes were drowsy and staring, their expression shell-shocked. Tears sprawled thickly over her lashes, making him think of raindrops over window panes. When her hair had been up in a bun yesterday, she'd been pretty; now, with her hair falling to her waist like a blanket of darkest night, she was striking.

The merman behind her, the carrot, sneered at Izar as he placed a hand on her belly and tugged her against him.

Blood pounded into Izar's eyes, turning them bloodshot, and streamed into his hands, which folded into fists. He would kill both brothers, even if it killed him.

He focused his attention on the cantaloupe, whose sideways smirk made his mouth look like a centipede. Izar darted to him, his fists extended before him. The plump arm thrust forth with the dagger, flesh swaying like a loose rope. Izar leaned back at the waist—the dagger slashed through the waters where his neck had just been.

Izar punched in the direction of the cantaloupe's face. The merman skirted out of the way. His dagger flashed forward again, toward Izar's chest—it tore off one of the baby's-ear shells. The dagger approached Izar's face. Izar knocked the cantaloupe's hand with an elbow, and the dagger slipped out of his grasp. On land, it would have clattered to the floor, but in the water, it floated between their faces. The cantaloupe's hand shot out for it, as did Izar's. Izar's reached first. Clasping the hilt of the dagger, he faced the cantaloupe. The cantaloupe started to retreat cautiously through the room, but Izar put the dagger aside, on a corner of the dresser. He was still planning to kill the cantaloupe, but not yet—he would punish him first.

The carrot flung Coralline aside. She would have hit her head on the desk had she not placed her hands in front of her. Her wrists were pale blue from their constriction, Izar saw, and her eyes formed large, frantic coins in her face.

Turning back to the cantaloupe, Izar punched him in the gut. The big belly wobbled, and the merman slid aside, gasping. The carrot took his brother's place. He jabbed at Izar, first with his right fist, then his left. Izar retreated slightly. Appearing emboldened by Izar's withdrawal, the carrot advanced and gave Izar the opportunity he'd been waiting for: Just as the carrot was about to level his next punch, Izar grabbed him by the scruff of the neck and slammed his head on the dresser. A crack sounded, whether of his head or the dresser, Izar didn't know.

Izar slammed the carrot's head on the dresser again, harder.

"We'll go!" said the cantaloupe, putting his hands up. "We're sorry. But don't kill my brother!"

"Don't kill him, Izar!" Coralline cried.

Izar looked down at the carrot, whom he continued to clutch by the back of the neck. The lanky merman was now unconscious, his body horizontal. Izar slammed his head against the dresser again.

Suddenly, the cantaloupe flew at Izar and shoved him against a wall. He pummeled his shoulder—once, twice, thrice. Streaks of pain radiated through Izar, as though an iron rod were branding his bone, sinews, and muscles together. Trying to ignore the pain, Izar extended his hand to the dresser. His fingers found the dagger, grasped its hilt. He slashed it toward the cantaloupe's face.

The cantaloupe leapt off Izar, started to retreat again. Izar lunged toward him, but Coralline caught Izar's arm. "Don't kill them!" she pleaded.

Her grasp on his arm was like a parrot's claws on a branch. The grasp did not loosen easily, but, managing to shake it off, Izar cornered the cantaloupe against a wall. He jabbed the dagger toward the fleshy neck. But a pair of hands stayed him again. This time, their grip on his arm was not a parrot's but an eagle's. The eagle compelled the tip of the dagger to stop at a vein in the cantaloupe's neck, just a hair's breadth away from slicing the neck open. "Let's not stoop to their level," she implored.

Izar flung himself off the cantaloupe. The merman sidled away, clutching his throat. He grabbed his still-unconscious brother by the elbow and hurried out the door.

Coralline's hands fumbled to close the folds of her corset over herself. Appearing to concede defeat, for the strings were in tatters, she bolted to the bed. Izar was aware of her crying not through any sound but because, with her loosened corset, much of her back was visible, and he could see her individual vertebrae shifting like waves. "Constables are here, looking for me," she told him in a muffled voice from over her shoulder. "They think I killed Tang. We have to leave."

"I'll be back with my bag," Izar said. With a hand on his throbbing shoulder, he left for his room.

There seemed a gap between Coralline's mind and body: Her mind realized Eliphus and Sparus's violation was over, but her body didn't seem to quite believe it. Her teeth chattered, and tremors vibrated through her ribs.

She heard a dual thump. The sound came from the window in the corridor outside her door. It would be Pavonis—he must have located a back door. Coralline longed to snuggle under the blanket, to fall into a long sleep, but his tail continued to clobber the wall, insistent, impossible to ignore. Dragging her tailfin over the side of the bed, she sat up, but her back continued to slouch like a snail's, and her shoulders formed listless triangles.

She straightened with effort and shifted slowly to the dresser. Fumbling through the contents of her satchel, she pulled out the most conservative of the bodices she'd brought with her: a heavy, durable scarlet piece with elbow-length sleeves and a high, rounded neckline. She donned it numbly and buttoned the column of large beige pitted murex shells that ran down its center.

She stashed the remains of her sky-blue bodice at the bottom of her satchel. She wished she hadn't worn Ecklon's favorite bodice today; she wished she'd worn anything but. Propriety and tradition were important values to Ecklon. What would he think if he saw her now? Certainly, if his mother, Epaulette, ever came to learn of what had happened, she would insist on canceling the wedding. Coralline clutched the rose petal tellin shell at her throat anxiously.

She glanced at herself in the mirror. Her shoulders looked as stiff as though pins were embedded in the blades, and her face looked stricken—and struck. An angry gray smudge was forming beneath her right earlobe, a souvenir of Eliphus's backhand across her jaw. Coralline wound her hair into a long side braid and curled it up over her ear to conceal the mark. She was fortunate there was no blood anywhere on her, for Pavonis would otherwise detect something to be the matter as soon as he saw her. She couldn't bear to tell anyone, not even him. Only Izar would know, because he'd been there.

Coralline started to slip away from the mirror, but a glint on the floor caught her eye. Eliphus's dagger. She bent down to pick it up, discerning her reflection in it as a faint, frowning wedge. She rotated the dagger between her fingers. It was such a simple implement—just larger than her hand, its hilt carved of sandstone—but whoever held it wielded power. She'd made the mistake of leaving her home without a dagger; she wouldn't make the mistake of leaving this dagger behind. If ever she were assaulted again, she would not hesitate to kill. She was accused for murder; if necessary, she would live up to the charge.

Coralline often knew how ill a patient was as soon as the patient swam through the door; Ecklon often knew how difficult a murder case would be as soon as he swam through the door of the murder scene. This would be a difficult case, he recognized, as he swam through the door of Tang Tarpon's home.

His gaze roved over the half-dozen empty decanters of wine forming a semicircle on the floor. His attention then shifted to Tang's bookshelf. Ecklon had read two of Tang's murder mysteries, *The Vanished Whelk* and

The Under-Minister's Assassination, and he'd liked them, finding them to be full of uncanny surprises and unexpected twists.

Tang's body was no longer in the living room—it was being examined by the Forensics Department of the Under-Ministry of Crime and Murder—but the smell of his blood lingered. The murder-mystery writer had, ironically, become the subject of his own real-life murder mystery.

Most people wanted to have an interesting life, but Ecklon also wanted to have an interesting death—a death of the sort for which a detective like himself would be required. He wondered whether Tang had felt similarly; probably not.

Ecklon slipped away from the bookshelf and looked about the small, shabby space. His gaze dropped to the murder weapon on the floor, a dagger with a serpent-encrusted hilt. He collected the dagger, ran his hand over its hilt. He had a passion for daggers, as did many at the Detective Department of the Under-Ministry of Crime and Murder. He was attentive to the style of dagger carving, just as mermaids were attentive to the style of their bodices; he evaluated dagger blades on the basis of their shine and sharpness, just as mermaids evaluated fabrics on the basics of their sheen and softness. The merman who'd owned this serpent-encrusted dagger seemed to have a passion for daggers as well.

Ecklon would begin his murder investigation by interviewing dagger carvers in an attempt to learn the identity of the owner of this dagger. Dagger carvers were often ancient mermen, for dagger carving was an art that was becoming lost over time—a shame, in Ecklon's opinion. The elderly age of dagger carvers meant two things: Their memories were often weak, and they may have sold a dagger decades ago, making recollection of the purchaser difficult. But Ecklon would have to try nonetheless. Once he had an identity, it wouldn't take long to find a motive, he knew from experience. Placing the serpent-encrusted dagger carefully in his satchel, he extracted his own dagger.

His dagger had been designed by the most elderly dagger carver in Urchin Grove, an eighty-five-year-old merman with arthritic hands, and it featured an eagle ray wing across the hilt, because his muse, Menziesii, was an eagle ray. He had not told Coralline, but, soon after their wedding, Ecklon planned to return to the same dagger carver and have a new dagger designed for himself, one encrusted with the precious olive-green gemstone peridot in the branching shape of coralline algae. That way, Ecklon would think of Coralline every time he wielded his dagger—and he would wield it always to protect her, to protect them.

He remembered the day he'd tried to teach her how to wield a dagger. After some half-hearted flicking of her wrist, she had handed his dagger back to him, making some comment about a scalpel. He had put his dagger away patiently, deciding to try to teach her again after they were married. He carried a dagger and a pair of handcuffs in his satchel at all times, to defend and to intercept, respectively; it was imperative to him that his wife know how to wield the former and stay out of the latter. His boss, Sinistrum Scomber, had alluded to that when informing him of Coralline's murder charge.

His enormous nose wrinkling, Sinistrum had handed Ecklon a scroll from the Constables Department of Hog's Bristle. Ecklon had read it and, after a stunned silence, announced, "I'm going to be the detective on Tang Tarpon's murder case."

"That's a bad idea," Sinistrum had said with a grimace. "Credibility comes from neutrality, and you have no neutrality in this case. Whether or not your fiancée is a murderess, I suggest you refrain from murdering your career for her."

"Now that I'm tenured," Ecklon had said, in a sharper tone than he'd intended, "I can choose my own cases. And I choose to investigate Tang Tarpon's murder."

"Don't make me regret my decision to tenure you!" Sinistrum had snapped. "Unfortunately, though, you're right that I cannot stop you from choosing your own cases and, in this case, making your own mistakes. Who will you choose as your associate detective?"

Detectives usually worked in pairs, a lead and an associate, because, when criminals learned the identity of a detective, the detective's life was often under threat. Two detectives working together offered the advantage that, if one of them was murdered, at least the other would know the specifics of the case. But Ecklon did not want to share this particular case with anyone, because he did not want to share Coralline with anyone.

"I'll work alone," he'd said. He had then burst out of his chair, pushed past Sinistrum, returned home, and hurriedly started to pack a satchel. He'd tried to deflect his mother's questions, but she'd read the scroll he'd placed on his dresser, from the Constables Department of Hog's Bristle.

"You have to cancel your wedding to Coralline!" she'd said. "Think of the terrible headlines in *Urchin Examiner* and *The Groove of the Grove* once it becomes public knowledge that she's a murderess."

"Coralline is not a murderess, Mother," he'd said, without looking up from his satchel.

"The truth matters in your profession, son, but nowhere else. In the eyes of society, it does not matter whether or not Coralline actually committed the murder—an accusation is as good as a conviction."

"Well, in my eyes, it's not. Also, I've never asked you this, but why have you always hated Coralline?"

"Because she and her family are beneath us."

"It appears that everyone is beneath you, Mother, and no one beneath me."

Ecklon had zipped his satchel and swum past her, but, just as he'd reached his bedroom door, she'd said sadly, softly, from behind him, "I'm still ill from the black poison. Don't leave me, son."

Trained to detect lies, he had not needed to turn around and look at her face to know she was lying—she was no longer sick; she was fine. "Father is here for you," he'd said. "And your life and liberty are not at risk, but Coralline's are." Speaking to himself, he'd muttered, "I should have left with Coralline on her elixir quest for Naiadum; had I done so, she would not be in this situation."

He had swept out of his room and to the front door, where he'd bumped into Rosette. She was wearing a lacy, bright-pink corset with a hem that ended at her navel. Batting her eyelashes at him, she'd said, "I made you a casserole set with carrageenan," and she'd thrust the dish in his hands. Nodding politely, he'd been about to turn around to take the casserole into the kitchen, when she'd leaned forward and kissed him on the lips. He'd drawn back, looking at her with surprise. Then he'd swum into the kitchen, deposited the dish on the counter, and, to avoid bumping into Rosette again, had left his home through the back door rather than the front door. Accompanied by Menziesii, he'd swum straight to Hog's Bristle, pausing not for a moment along the way.

A knock sounded at Tang's door. Ecklon pulled it open.

A thickset merman with a square face hovered there. He was the loiterer, Wentle Varice, who'd given a statement to the Constables Department of Hog's Bristle. It was he who had claimed to have seen Coralline's hand wrapped around a dagger; it was he who had insisted she'd committed the murder—in other words, it was he who was responsible for the murder charge she was facing. Ecklon tightened his grip around his dagger; it took all his self-restraint to not point the dagger at Wentle. After all, it was he who had summoned Wentle here.

"I'm Ecklon Elnath, the detective on Tang Tarpon's murder case," he began coldly. "I read the statement you gave the Constables Department of Hog's Bristle. Is there anything else you noticed? Anyone else you saw?"

"Yes." Wentle gulped, eyeing Ecklon's dagger. "There was another merman here with her. I didn't get a good look at his face, but he had an indigo tail."

Ecklon frowned. He could think of no one whom he or Coralline knew with an indigo tail. He would uncover the identity of this merman sooner or later, he knew, as he continued to investigate Tang's murder. "Anything else?" Ecklon asked.

"No," Wentle said, and left.

Ecklon closed the door. He saw Coralline's small, golden drawstring pouch on the floor and picked it up. Holding it to his nose, he sniffed. It did not smell of anything, as he'd expected, but it still helped him remember the sweet fragrance of her.

He found himself thinking back to their first date, at the restaurant Alaria. It was her favorite restaurant, and he pretended it was his favorite as well, simply because it was her favorite. After their main courses—undaria for her, buttonweed for him—they'd shared a custard of devil's apron, a saccharine kelp that had melted on their tongues. Their stone-sticks had accidentally bumped against one another in the bowl of devil's apron, and Ecklon had found it to be the most strangely romantic of sounds. They'd lingered at their table long after finishing the agar-gelled dessert, taking their leave of Alaria only when the waitress had said apologetically that the restaurant was closing for the evening.

Ecklon had insisted on escorting Coralline home. They'd swum in a companionable silence, trailed above by Pavonis and below by Menziesii. After Ecklon had dropped Coralline at her door and was swimming back to his own home, Menziesii had told him that his silver tailfin had swayed in exact tandem with her bronze tailfin, as though their swim together had been not an informal amble but a synchronized dance. Ecklon, who'd never danced before, had laughed at the thought.

At their second date, at another restaurant, Lacerata, Coralline had worn a sky-blue bodice with cloud-white ribbons, and Ecklon had found himself unable to look away from her. In murder investigations, there was often an *aha!* moment; in his relationship with her, the *aha!* moment had arrived that evening. Asking him to tell her about his day, she had rested her chin on her hands and looked at him with her big blue-green eyes. As a detective, his purpose was to uncover truth in a world that lied constantly, seamlessly. There had been no guile in her gaze, he had found. He had seen the ocean itself in her eyes, and he had seen himself, as part of the ocean, as part of her. He had decided then that he wanted to marry her.

Ecklon touched his lips, hoping to remember his last kiss with Coralline, but the taste on his lips remained Rosette's.

16

Silk

P avonis, can we please swim closer to the seabed?" Coralline asked, turning her head to look at him.

"No," came the reply.

Izar looked at Coralline to his left and, past her, at Pavonis, to her left.

"But the surface is dangerous," Coralline wheedled.

"No kidding. Thanks to humans." Pavonis's dark orb of an eye, the size of a golf ball, swiveled pointedly to Izar before returning to Coralline. "But we have to remain up here, because constables might be looking for you below. Right now, constables pose a greater danger to us than ships, so we won't be descending to the seabed until we stop for the night, somewhere far, far away from Hog's Bristle and on the way to Blue Bottle."

Listening to Pavonis's thumps along the walls of Bristled Bed and Breakfast, Coralline and Izar had followed the convoluted corridor to a broken-hinged back door. But the constables had spotted Coralline just as she and Izar were slipping out the door, and they'd given chase. Thanks to Pavonis's swerving and maneuvering, they'd managed to lose the constables, but it had not been easy.

Izar looked at Coralline from the corner of his eye. Her rolled-up braid looked like an ant mound atop her ear, like a little pincushion, and the effect was not unpleasant, but Izar hated to look at it, for he knew the bruise it concealed. Her wrists were still pale blue from how tightly the carrot had clasped them. They must be sore, Izar thought, but Coralline seemed aware of any pain only subconsciously, when she massaged them at intervals.

He was aware of his shoulder pain much more consciously—he felt as though forks were stabbing the socket. On land, he would not have been aware of his shoulder pain the way he was in the water. When he swam in the water, it was primarily his head and shoulders that combated the force of water resistance for his body, just as, when he'd walked on land, it was primarily his legs that had combated the force of gravity for his body. But water resistance was not easy to combat—water was eight hundred times denser than air. As such, to swim with an injured shoulder was worse than walking with an injured leg.

"Are you a human or a turtle?" Pavonis growled.

Izar saw that he'd fallen slightly behind Coralline and Pavonis, and he swung his tail hard to arrive at their eye level, his hand covering his shoulder to soften the impact of water against it. Coralline looked at him but didn't say anything.

A small white fish fluttered past Izar. A black dot on the fish's tail, and black lines along its face, made him think of a magician with a pencil-thin moustache. He thought of yesterday, when he and Coralline had passed all manner of animals during their swims. In an encyclopedic voice, Coralline had told him their names: bluehead wrasse, fairy basslet, green razorfish, gray angelfish, roundel skate, turbot, tarpon. He'd nodded at her occasionally, curtly, until she'd discerned his disinterest, and her voice had trailed off.

She had spoken more broadly about other things and had used certain expressions while doing so. Izar had managed to interpret the expressions as follows: *Alewives circling the stomach* was equivalent to the human expression *butterflies in the stomach*. *A snake in an eel's crevice* was the parallel of *a square peg in a round hole*. *Collecting two shells with one hand* was equivalent to *killing two birds with one stone*.

Coralline's analogies to animals had been less easy to interpret, and Izar had asked her for explanation. To be a sinistrum whelk meant to be different, she'd said, because sinistrum whelks were in the one percent of snails whose shell coiled exclusively to the left. To be a starfish meant to rebound quickly, because they regrew limbs that were hacked off. To be a rockfish meant to live a long life, for they lived more than a century. To be an octopus meant to be defensive, for they had plenty of defenses, including black ink and camouflage. To be a jellyfish could mean one of multiple things—to be short-lived, flimsy in loyalty, or skinny in form. To be a whale did not mean to be large but to be confused about one's identity, for whales straddled the boundary between water and air: They lived in water but breathed air.

Now, Izar wished Coralline would say something, anything, no matter how confusing it might be. But she hadn't spoken a word to him since he'd left her room.

"This is the fourth time today I've had to yell at you to keep pace, human!" Pavonis bellowed. "I'm not going to say it a fifth time—if you fall behind again, I'm going to start tossing you around. Is that clear?"

"Yes," Izar muttered, catching up again with Pavonis and Coralline.

He looked up at the waves crashing just above him. Two otters frolicked among them—sleek, slippery, long-whiskered. Through the waves, Izar could make out the sky. When seen through a screen of water, the sky looked like a series of photographs taken one after another, forming an animated film of disparate pictures; every time a wave landed, the sky broke and reassembled. Just as uncomfortable as Coralline seemed to feel at the waves, Izar felt comfortable. He could almost convince himself that he'd simply tumbled off an Ocean Dominion ship and would climb back aboard any moment, his legs braced apart firmly below him.

Something fell over him, a lightweight fabric. He fingered the mesh-like material curiously. Smooth and strong, it seemed to be the fishnet he himself had invented when he'd been an assistant engineer—the net that had doubled Ocean Dominion's catch of schools of small fish. But how could his own net ensnare him? He flung his arms and tail in all directions but found that he could not move forward; he was simply flailing in the confines of the net. The net was utterly inescapable—it had to be his own.

The net jerked him up through the waves. For the first time since he'd been hurled into the ocean, his head erupted over the surface. He gasped at the glare of the sun, a torturing flashlight that parched his eyes and fragmented his vision. Without the buoyant medium of water, his head felt loose upon his neck, as though it might detach and float away. Blinking profusely, he focused his gaze on the ship about twenty-five feet in front of him.

It had a bronze-and-black insignia along its side, but it was not an ordinary Ocean Dominion ship—Izar recognized it as part of his Silk fleet. Upon his having become co-director of operations, Izar had designed the Silk fleet—fifteen narrow, light-bottomed, streamlined watercraft, intended to be as sleek in their movement as sharks, creating hardly a ripple. Like the lightweight fishnets he'd invented, the Silk fleet had increased Ocean Dominion's fish catch. Beyond that outcome-based evidence, however, Izar had had no way of knowing whether they truly were as stealthy as he'd intended. He saw now that they were, for he hadn't sensed this ship's presence at all.

Two men stared at him from the bow of the Silk ship, men with large, shaved heads and over-muscled arms. Izar did not recognize them. That was not surprising—hundreds of men worked in operations at Ocean Dominion, and he could not possibly recognize all of them. They did not seem to recognize him either, though. Perhaps it was because he was in the form of a merman, he thought.

From behind and between the two men emerged a third, one with blood-red hair and beard, and spears through his earlobes: Serpens Sarin, the thirty-five-year-old manager who, in alliance with Zaurak, had tried twice to kill him—through the fall of the derrick on the drillship, then through switching out the blowout preventer and almost drowning *Dominion Drill I.*

Serpens's arms held a gun, aimed at Izar.

Izar knew he should try to escape, but he could not move, even if he hadn't been trapped in a net. How had Serpens known he was in the ocean, in the form of a merman? he wondered. Serpens must have learned it from Alshain—which meant that Zaurak knew it, too. Zaurak did not seem to be aboard this Silk ship, but he must be directing Serpens from a distance. This would be the fourth attempt on Izar's life. It would be successful, air-tight—no one in Menkar would know he was dead, not even Antares and Saiph.

But how had Serpens located him in the Atlantic Ocean? It was the equivalent of locating a needle not in a haystack but in a forest. The chances were so low as to be negligible. There was something vital Izar did not know, there was more here than was meeting his eye—

Serpens fired his gun. A bullet roared past Izar's shoulder, missing him by an inch. But Izar still felt injured: Ocean Dominion was so much a part of him that it was as though his own body was attacking him in the form of an autoimmune disease.

Another bullet fired, traveling past his ear.

Floundering within the net, Izar pushed his weight down in an attempt to sink, but he found that he could descend no more than two feet—it was he who'd designed the net to enable flotation. But with his head again submerged, even if by only two feet, his first feeling was relief—his eyes were again moist, their vision crisp. In his present form, as much as he disliked it, he belonged underwater.

A bullet careened through his hair, hot against his scalp.

Where was Coralline? he wondered, his eyes seeking the scarlet color of her bodice. He'd forgotten all about her and Pavonis when he'd seen the ship. Now, he discovered her and the whale shark far below, at least a hundred feet down. Her eyes were staring straight at him, a dagger glinting in her hand.

Coralline's heart beat so turbulently that she felt certain the men aboard the ship could hear it.

"Let's get out of here!" Pavonis said, his tailfin billowing.

But Coralline remained in place. As she watched, a bullet zoomed past Izar's scar, a finger's width away from grazing his jaw. Upon missing its mark, the bullet slowed, then glided about as haplessly as plankton. It made Coralline think of birds who swooped down into the ocean to catch fish—their flight was always fast at first, then slowed rapidly with water resistance. The greatest protection any creature of the ocean had was the ocean itself.

She thought of the day when, as a fourteen-year-old mergirl, she'd discovered a bullet among the pebbles of Urchin Grove. She had not known what it was, a fact that had told her it did not belong to the waters. Clutching it gingerly between her thumb and forefinger, she'd shown it to her father. "I believe this is a bullet," he'd said. "It ruptures through the flesh when shot out of a gun at high speed. You and I will never understand this, but humans have more ways of killing one another than an octopus has arms." Coralline had placed the bullet on a corner of her bookshelf, to remind herself of the lesson she'd learned that day: When it came to humans, even things that looked innocuous were dangerous.

"The Ogre is right!" Nacre cried from within Coralline's satchel. "We have to leave right away."

"The ship might try to find us and kill us next," Altair said tremulously.

A bullet whizzed over Izar's head.

Coralline rotated the dagger in her hand.

"We'd planned to leave without Izar in the morning," Pavonis rumbled, "but, somehow, he's still with us. This ship attack is the perfect opportunity for us to get rid of him. Let's leave him here to die, at the hands of his own bloodthirsty people. What could be better? What are you even thinking, Coralline?"

She was thinking that Izar had fought for her at Bristled Bed and Breakfast. She was thinking that if not for him, she would likely be dead—the two brothers had said they would kill her.

A bullet swept in front of Izar's nose.

Soon, within minutes, the men on the ship would manage to kill him. Then it would be his blood she would be smelling in her nostrils, like she had smelled Tang's yesterday.

Raising her arms over her head, Coralline started cutting a path straight up like a swordfish, until she reached Izar and the fishnet. A bullet flew past her chin, so close that she momentarily froze. Then, swinging her tail, using all the strength of her arm, she started gashing through the bottom of the net with her dagger. As Izar dodged to avoid bullets, the net lurched and shifted continuously between her fingers, but she kept slicing, snipping filaments with the same meticulousness with which her seamstress mother joined them.

Honeymooners Hotel swelled three stories above the seabed like the Elnath Mansion, and it had similar golden-rimmed windows, but its shale was not the stark, imposing black of Ecklon's home—rather, it was a rare, pale pink, like a new blush.

The hotel was encompassed by a brightly colored garden of siphoned feather, red comb, and berry wart cress. It was just the sort of fairy-tale-like place Coralline had admired in mergirl story books like *Haptera's Happily Ever After* and *The Adventures of Agarose*. The mergirl in her longed to swim through its doors, but the mermaid in her was stayed by the fact that she was not here on her honeymoon; she was here with Izar.

The town of Rainbow Wrack was a honeymoon destination, though. Almost all accommodations had sappy names, including the two, Romantic Retreat and Couples Corner, that flanked Honeymooners Hotel. Neither of them had availability. "It's wedding season," Coralline and Izar had been told in explanation.

Coralline followed Izar through the arched doors of Honeymooners Hotel. The lobby had a high, rounded ceiling with continuous arches that merged with twirling pillars like a broad set of shoulders. The architecture was strong and masculine, but frills scattered throughout the lobby—mirrors and heart-shaped tables—made the place also feminine. Even the concierge, whose breast pocket stated his name as Plaice, seemed suited to the hotel, for he had a large hulking form, but his scales were as lushly pink as a horse conch shell.

"We have a room available," Plaice said in response to their unasked question.

"Separate rooms," Coralline said, though she did not know how she would pay for her room without any carapace.

Plaice looked at her with surprise. Coralline supposed it didn't happen often that a mermaid and merman requested separate rooms at Honeymooners Hotel, given that most people would be here on their honeymoon. "I'm afraid we have just one room available," he said apologetically.

Coralline turned on her tail to leave, but Izar's hand landed gently on her elbow. "Can we speak, please?" he said, gesturing to a little alcove off to the side. Coralline nodded and trailed him into the nook. "I can sleep on the sofa," he said.

"The what?"

"The thing on which one sits in the living room, like in Tang Tarpon's home."

"Oh, the settee?"

"Yes, that. I'll sleep on the settee."

It was strange, the idea of sleeping on a settee, but if they shared a room, he might pay for it, and that would solve the problem of her carapace crunch. "Fine, thank you," she said.

They returned to Plaice. Coralline inhaled sharply when he requested twenty-five carapace for the room. The sum was half as much as she'd earned for a full week of work at The Irregular Remedy. But Izar handed Plaice a cerith and slipper limpet shell rather casually, as though he'd never once experienced a shortage of currency.

She and Izar then trailed Plaice down a spacious corridor with limestone adornments along the walls. He opened the door to their room, bowed, and departed.

The room was divided into seating and sleeping areas. The seating area was furnished with a coral-pink settee, a large mauve rug embroidered with bright-pink halymenia algae, and a white-slate dresser with a framed oval mirror. The sleeping area, located deeper in the room, contained an immense bed covered with an orange-pink blanket. The room was luxurious by any standards, but especially after Bristled Bed and Breakfast, Coralline found it as opulent as a palace. She swam in enthusiastically.

She placed her satchel on the dresser. In the mirror, she saw Izar fling his satchel onto the settee, then plop down next to it; from his wince, he appeared to have expected the settee to be cushiony. Their eyes met in the mirror. Only then did it properly sink in to Coralline that she was sharing a room with him, when she'd never even shared a room with Ecklon before. When she'd agreed outside to sharing a room, she had been thinking practically—her lack of carapace—she had not been thinking of propriety. She looked away from Izar now.

Turning back to her satchel, Coralline extracted her jar of horned wrack salve and dabbed the balm onto the bruise next to her earlobe. She then unwrapped the braid she'd curled around her ear, loosened the strands with her fingers, and, jeweled comb in hand, fell gladly into her nightly routine: She ran the comb through her locks from one end to the other, pulling meticulously at her knots. For her, the nightly sweep of her hair was not just therapeutic but symbolic—if, with systematic effort, she could untangle all the knots in her hair, she could do the same with all the knots in her life. And this day, the knots had been many.

At last putting her comb away, she dug her ivory chemise out of her satchel. She'd never slept in a bodice before—they tended to be stiff and fitted—and she longed to change out of her bodice into her chemise—as smooth and soft as anything in the world—but it would be inappropriate for her to sleep in a chemise tonight, with Izar there. Sighing, she tossed the chemise back in her satchel.

In the mirror, she saw Izar rubbing his shoulder. She'd noticed him fiddling with it earlier as well, during their swim.

"Take off your waistcoat."

"Excuse me?" He raised an eyebrow at her.

Assuming a commanding tone in an effort to hide her flush, she said, "I mean, something's clearly the matter with your shoulder. Let me take a look."

Izar's fingers fumbled with his baby's-ear shells, turning and twisting but unable to get them out of their buttonholes.

"Let me help," Coralline said impatiently.

Perching next to Izar on the settee, she commenced with the top-most shell, at his collar. Her hands traveled steadily down his chest, one shell after another, and her flush traveled steadily down her face, coming to encompass her neck and throat. She'd never unfastened Ecklon's buttons before, nor had he ever unfastened hers. It was the sort of simple but domestically intimate act she'd always associated with marriage.

By the time Coralline had undone Izar's buttons, her face was fiery. She avoided Izar's eyes, but he was smiling.

He slid out of his waistcoat. His chest was finely sculpted, and his shoulders were broad, she saw, each one as wide as her whole hand. But his right shoulder had a bruise over it the size of Pavonis's eye and the color of a purple sea urchin.

"Why didn't you tell me?" she demanded.

"You had plenty to occupy your mind," he said, his indigo eyes pondering her.

Coralline didn't want to think of the morning. Nor did she want to think of the fact that Izar had seen her mostly undressed, in her slashed corset. Rising, she shifted to the dresser, grateful for the slight distance that the movement created between them. When she returned, it was with a neutral expression and two jars of salve.

With her fingers, she dabbed his shoulder with horned wrack salve, a pale-green paste. "This will reduce the pain and swelling," she explained. Then she turned his hand over and examined it. The gash along his palm still remained, but it was less pronounced than at the time she'd discovered him, yesterday morning. She applied the olive-brown balm of toothed wrack salve to it. When he turned his hand over, she saw that his knuckles were red and inflamed, the skin across them chafed. She applied toothed wrack salve carefully to each knuckle, asking, "Is this from the fight with the two brothers?"

"Partially."

"What else?"

"I broke the mirror in my room last night."

"Why?" She looked up at him.

"I didn't like my reflection."

Assuming he was joking, Coralline started to laugh, but she stopped when she saw that the set of his lips was serious. "Humans legs are hideous," she said. "We merpeople are so much more beautiful. Why would you dislike your reflection?"

Izar threw his head back and laughed. It was the first time Coralline had seen him laugh. She found that his merriment changed his face, softening his jaw, vanishing his scar, making his indigo eyes sparkle like violet opal. It was no longer a harsh face, but a handsome face.

Covering her salves with their lids, she made to rise, but his hand wrapped around her wrist. She glanced at it sharply; the fingers unraveled. "Thank you for cutting me out of the fishnet," he said.

"You don't need to thank me. By saving you, I also saved myself."

He gave her a quizzical look. She could not explain it to him, nor even properly understand it herself, but after the morning assault, she'd felt herself a victim, and after she'd cut him out of the net, she'd felt herself a victor. By wresting him out of the net, she'd lifted herself out of her temporary daze of powerlessness.

"You saved me as well, from the two brothers. Thank you for that."

"That was my fault," Izar said, a shadow crossing his face.

"How so?"

"I saw them looking you over last night and should have confronted them then. Had I done so, this morning would not have happened. I'm sorry."

"It's not your fault," Coralline said. "You couldn't have known their intentions. But if it makes you feel any better, I have a confession to make, too."

"What?"

"I was planning to leave you behind this morning."

Izar shook his head, as though to clear out his ears. Now it was Coralline's turn to burst out laughing.

"Pavonis and I were planning to leave Bristled Bed and Breakfast before you woke up. But then, when those two brothers appeared, I decided to wake you up by rattling the desk against the wall."

"Well, I'm glad for that!"

"I have another confession to make," Coralline said, in a more serious tone, "and a favor to ask."

"Anything."

"I have no carapace left. I forgot my pouch in Tang Tarpon's home. May I borrow some carapace from you?"

"Of course."

"Thank you. I'll pay you back, I promise."

"There's no need."

"But I will."

Coralline returned the jars of salve to her satchel, then swam to the bed and crawled under the blanket.

Izar now understood why Coralline had given him a strange look when he'd offered to sleep on the settee. A settee no more resembled a sofa than would a stone bench with armrests. It was also far too short—his head lay on one armrest, while much of his tail dangled out over the other. He turned to look at Coralline, to the far side of her bed.

He knew he shouldn't—he even clasped the armrest to prevent himself—but he found himself rising from the settee. Watching Coralline's form with acute attention, he moved toward her vertically, slowly, like her seahorse, his tailfin flicking so lightly that, even had the floor been covered with sand, not a grain of it would have stirred. When he neared her bed, he paused, tried to dissuade himself from approaching any more—if she were to wake up, she would be alarmed—but he could not keep away. He came to hover just over her, his body horizontal, parallel to her own.

Coralline was lying on her side, with her tail curled up, the equivalent of knees pressed into the chest. Her blanket was pulled up to her chin, and her long hair draped over it like a cape of dark velvet. Her shades—her black hair, her bronze scales—formed his favorite pairing of colors, Izar realized, because it was the pairing of colors of Ocean Dominion's insignia.

He had come within a hair's breadth of killing the two mermen who'd accosted her. He would have killed them had she not stopped him. But why should he have been so upset? What did she even mean to him?

She and he were opposites in every way. She was a healer, he a destroyer. She was driven to rescue; he was driven to raze—he, Antares, and Saiph were called the Trio of Tyrants after all.

He smiled to remember her promise to pay him back for the carapace she borrowed from him. In Menkar, he had more money than he could count. He would have even more once he launched Castor.

Oh, how his Castor would light the ocean on fire! Whenever he and Coralline had entered a settlement—Purple Claw, Hog's Bristle, Rainbow Wrack—Izar had looked down at the seabed and thought: Perhaps here—no, here!—would be a good place to launch Castor. But his thought exercises had been largely hypothetical. From his studies of the ocean floor, he knew that each and every settlement of merpeople would be a good place to launch Castor.

As soon as he returned to Menkar and created his army of Castors, he would become rich—so rich, Ascella would regret her affair with Tarazed. Gold and diamonds—he'd wanted to collect them from the bottom of the ocean for her. But what was it that he'd so loved about her? he asked himself for the first time.

He found himself comparing Ascella with Coralline. The differences between them were like day and night: Ascella, with her pale gold hair, Coralline, with her dark locks; Ascella, with her eyes of cold frost, Coralline, with eyes of the flowing ocean. In appearance, Ascella was like a rose, immediately noticeable; Coralline was more of a lily, simple but beautiful.

Like the art she liked, Ascella's personality was abstract, artificial, and Izar had created an artificial version of himself for her, with his pressed suits and polished shoes, with their extravagant dinners at Yacht. It was not Ascella's fault but his own—artifice had marked his intentions from the beginning with her. He had sought a future with her in order to escape his past as a scarred orphan raised in a storage closet. *That* was what he'd most loved about her, he saw now—the idea of escaping his past through a future with her.

A strand of hair strayed over Coralline's cheek. He twirled it around his finger—it was as soft and plush as a silk thread.

17

The Doom of Desmarestia

Coralline's eyes opened leisurely. She turned around in bed to glance at the settee—Izar was not there. She sat up and looked about; from a snatch of indigo, she saw that his long form was sprawled on the mauve rug. She breathed a sigh of relief. Somehow, it brought her a sense of safety to see him there, in the room with her. Slipping off her blanket, she crept out of bed. She swept past him to a window and peered out over the town center of Rainbow Wrack.

Places have their own character just like people, she had read somewhere once but failed to understand before now. Her home village of Urchin Grove was, if she considered it objectively, a yawn inducer, as Pavonis often suggested. Purple Claw, the first settlement they'd visited on the Elixir Expedition, had appeared to have a similarly slow pace of life. Hog's Bristle, meanwhile, could be considered a gangster town, with all its loiterers. Rainbow Wrack, in contrast, was picturesque and pretty, with homes and hotels built in pastel shades of shale. Coralline smiled to see an elderly couple swim past her window, hand in hand. She and Ecklon would be like that one day.

Coralline swam out the window. Pavonis had told her he'd come find her somewhere in the town center sometime in the morning. (Yesterday evening, he'd unceremoniously dumped Altair and Nacre in a coral reef, then had left to explore the town.) Coralline hoped Pavonis would collect her late in the morning, for the last two days had been exhausting, and all she wanted was to luxuriate in the relaxed looseness of an aimless morning.

She looked at shops with a wanderer's carefree curiosity. Personalized Parchments, a tiny stationery store. Lobata, a casual restaurant. Devil's Apron, a dessert bistro. Pyropia, a clinic named after the gauzy algae used for bandage.

Coralline turned away from Pyropia, but not before tears sparked in her eyes. She'd wanted to start her own clinic one day, Coralline's Cures; the dream now felt a delusion. Swimming away from Pyropia, she entered a colorful public garden alongside a row of small homes. But even among the bright columns of algae, she found she could not sheathe herself from her profession—what she most missed about The Irregular Remedy was its remedial garden.

In the public garden, she saw a patch of coralline algae splattering a rock, its branches congealing and separating like networks of capillaries. The sight of her namesake algae made her inordinately happy—it was something familiar in an unfamiliar world—and she found herself staring at it as she never had before, even though it carpeted the rocks in the reef garden outside her own home in Urchin Grove. Coralline algae was parchment-thin, she noticed now, but coated with a fine, articulated armor. Like everyone else, she'd always considered coralline algae fragile, but now she thought it looked resilient. Similarly, everyone had always considered *her* fragile, but perhaps she wasn't—perhaps she was resilient but hadn't had the opportunity to show it before the elixir quest.

She hadn't snipped algae for a few days, and it felt as unnatural as not having eaten for a few days. A longing to snip made itself felt as a pressing ache in her tail. Most clinics cultivated their own remedial gardens, but healing algae did not have to come exclusively from a remedial garden. It could grow anywhere. She looked about the public garden and noticed the thick, coarse, hair-like strands of green rope. She was badge-less, disbarred, unable to use any medications she prepared for anyone other than herself—but that did not mean she could not prepare them. It would be like preparing supper despite being unable to serve it—most would consider it pointless—but it would still offer her a measure of gratification and happiness. Who was she to deny herself?

Racing back to Honeymooners Hotel, Coralline darted into her room through the window. Izar was sitting on the settee, dark circles underlining his eyes, as though he'd hardly slept. He flashed her a smile, but she'd already picked up her apothecary arsenal and was out the window again.

Swimming back to the garden, Coralline placed her apothecary arsenal neatly on a rock, being careful to not scratch its pearlescent case. She started her medicinal preparations by snipping the vesicles of horned wrack, in order to refill her jar of horned wrack salve. Next, she cut iridescent cartilage, admiring its brilliant-blue hue so fervently that she almost cut her fingers. Then, she sheared the straggly golden-brown strands of sea oak, followed by the olive-brown fronds of dabberlocks.

Pulling out her blue-shale mortar and pestle, she ground all the algae she'd collected in separate batches, then stuffed them neatly in individual vials. She'd forgotten to bring her pen to the garden, so she would label the vials later, she decided. She rose to hover horizontally again over the garden, seeking her next suspect, when she spotted desmarestia algae.

Coralline had snipped desmarestia just once in her life, upon mistaking its olive-brown fronds for dabberlocks. She'd learned her error only when people had gathered around her and screamed, "Who are you trying to poison? Whoever it is, remember that the Doom of Desmarestia will settle upon you!"

Desmarestia was a poisonous algae, an acid kelp that killed its consumer in a matter of minutes. Its telltale symptom was writhing. Everyone was so afraid of it that, since time immemorial, it was a source of superstition: The Doom of Desmarestia was said to settle on those who dared swim over the acid kelp, leading them to grow as bitter as its fronds over time. Had she been in Urchin Grove, Coralline would have skirted the bush; now, she considered it. At the moment, she possessed just one weapon against the world, a dagger; desmarestia could serve as a second weapon. The more weapons she possessed, the stronger she would be during her elixir quest.

Her hands rising and falling as fast as the heads of garden eels, she snipped some fronds of desmarestia, reveling in their rough, forbidden texture.

As they swam southward to Blue Bottle, Izar admired Coralline in profile. Her scales were shimmering like newly minted coins, and her hair was swishing down her back like a mare's tail. She wore a pale-pink corset with ruffles for shoulder sleeves and a dozen tiny cream shells for buttons—it made him think of a scone.

"Do you know what the world needs?" she said, turning to look at him.

"What?"

"Corsets with pockets."

"Hmm. How did you think of that?"

"Waistcoats always have pockets, but corsets don't. It's disadvantageous to mermaids."

"What would you put in your pocket, if you had one?"

"A dagger."

Izar didn't know what to say.

Coralline turned to Pavonis, on her left, and said, "Can we please swim closer to the seabed?"

"Just because we didn't encounter any constables after leaving Hog's Bristle yesterday," the whale shark said, "doesn't mean we won't encounter any today. You're safer up here."

"But what if we're attacked by a ship again today?" she persisted.

"If we were attacked yesterday, what are the chances we'll be attacked again today?"

Izar swallowed his twinge of guilt. None of them knew that the ship attack yesterday had been not a random incident but a targeted attempt to kill him. But Izar shared Pavonis's rationale toward probability—Serpens had caught him yesterday by a stroke of sheer luck. The chance of another such capture today would be no greater than that of two meteors striking the earth on consecutive days.

Glancing again at Coralline, Izar tried to think of something to say. . . . What had he ever talked about with Ascella during their dinners at Yacht? Art, jewelry, Castor.

"From an early age," he said, "I've had a fascination with fire."

"That's an odd fascination," Coralline said, frowning. "My father says that fire vaporizes water, and water vanquishes fire, and the two can never truly meet."

"They can. I've invented underwater fire."

"That's impossible." She said it not in a conflagratory tone but in the way she would counter someone telling her the earth was square.

"I assure you—"

A net fell over him.

Again.

His tail lashed like a sword within the net, but he only succeeded in entangling himself further. It was a different net than yesterday's, not the lightweight one he'd invented but a net of thick, strong twine. Izar had designed his lightweight fishnet to capture schools of small fish; this more old-fashioned net was intended to capture large, powerful creatures like Pavonis. Attached to a beam of a rod like those used for construction cranes, it worked by means of lifting its prisoner into the air and letting him suffocate there.

Suddenly, Izar found himself wrenched out over the waves and suspended in air, curled within the net like a fetus in a womb. Because it was a cloudy day and the glare of the sun was less pronounced, his eyes adjusted more quickly than they had yesterday. Serpens was staring at him from the bow of the Silk-fleet Ocean Dominion ship, Izar saw, his eyes glittering cheerfully above his red beard. He could easily shoot Izar with the gun in his hands, but Izar knew he wouldn't—he would instead watch him suffocate slowly, painfully, to death.

Coralline stared up at Izar from just below the waves, her hand wrapped around her dagger. His body was thrashing spontaneously for oxygen, his gill slits flat against the sides of his neck, his scales bleaching one by one from indigo to a dead white. He dangled four feet above her, in the air, so she could not simply cut him out of the net as she had yesterday. She could do nothing for him, yet she could *not* do nothing—the quandary made itself felt as sharp pangs in her tail.

"We have to leave!" Pavonis said in a panicked voice. "We're so close to the surface that they'll attempt to catch us next."

"They won't," Coralline said. She surveyed the three men's faces through the screen of froth—they were laughing at Izar, especially the red-haired one. "Yesterday, I thought the attack was random, but now, I think they're targeting Izar specifically."

Izar became perfectly still, his head lolling in the cradle of the net. An idea fell into Coralline's mind as suddenly as a drop of rain upon the ocean: She could try something she'd never heard of anyone trying before. If it worked, Izar might live. If it didn't, she might die.

"Do me a favor, Pavonis," she called. "Lurch the ship."

"Lurch the ship! Are you out of your mind?"

"Please."

Her request was unfair, Coralline knew. Given his tremendous size, Pavonis was difficult to miss, easy to shoot. He recognized the danger, too, but, giving her a caustic look, positioned himself beneath the ship. At thirty feet long, he was almost the length of the ship itself. He became as still as a boulder—clenching his muscles and gathering his strength, Coralline knew—then he suddenly pushed himself up, his yellow-spotted back slamming against the base of the ship. The vessel rose askew over the waves and landed at an angle, the three men rolling over its platform like unmoored rocks.

It was exactly what Coralline had envisioned.

"Whatever you're planning to do, Coralline, don't!" Nacre cried from the satchel.

"Just *look* at Izar," Altair added. "He's already dead."

Every one of Izar's scales was bleached, Coralline observed with a small shock. But she'd seen him that way once before, she reminded herself. He'd returned to life then; he might again.

Smacking her tailfin right and left for propulsion, she cracked out of the water and into the air—first her hands, then her face, neck, torso, and much of her tail. The wind slapped her cheeks and flattened her gills against the sides of her neck. Her eyes started to bulge from the oxygen deficit, but her fingers managed to crook around the bottom of the fishnet and cling on.

Dangling by her arm, she raised her dagger and slashed through the weaves of the net, cutting through the side rather than the bottom in order to avoid gashing Izar's scales by accident.

A bullet whistled past her ear. "You're getting yourself killed for a dead man, sweetheart," yelled the red-haired man. A bullet roared past her hip, but she managed to slash the fishnet one final time. Izar tumbled down through the gap, and they fell together into the froth.

Extending one arm in front of her, clasping Izar's shoulders with her other arm, Coralline fled straight down. Pavonis dove in front of her, creating a well that helped reduce water resistance, for Coralline was fighting water resistance for both herself and Izar.

When they reached the seabed, she tried to flap Izar's gills open with her fingers, but it was like trying to massage a heart into beating with one's hands.

"He's dead," Altair said solemnly. Coralline glanced up to find that the seahorse had turned practically white himself, as though to pay his respects by trying to match Izar's bleached condition.

"Look!" Nacre said, tentacles waggling in the direction of Izar's tailfin.

His tailfin was twitching. It had to be a post-mortem spasm, Coralline thought, even though, in all her medical textbooks, she'd never come across such a spasm before. But then Izar gasped, and his eyes flew open.

18

The Chip

He had died. He had felt his heart squelch out its last pulse. Yet he remained alive. *How*, he did not know.

Coralline was staring at him with the attention of a doctor. Her expression made him think of the other doctor he knew, Doctor Navi, who had inserted the platinum chip in his wrist three years ago—that had to be it! That had to be how Serpens had found him! The platinum chip Doctor Navi had inserted in his wrist must be a tracking device.

Frowning at the waters above, Izar thought back to that day three years ago: In addition to Antares, Zaurak had visited Izar just before the chip-implant procedure. Doctor Navi and Zaurak had conversed at length in a corner of the room, out of Izar's earshot. They had developed a rapport since the time of Zaurak's leg accident twenty-seven years ago, and Izar had assumed they were simply catching up. But no, Zaurak must have been telling Doctor Navi to insert a tracking device in Izar. He must have paid him well for it, too. Doctor Navi had shifty eyes that scurred right and left like a rat's—Izar could not imagine him as being difficult to persuade.

But this meant that Zaurak had wanted to kill Izar for at least the last three years, since the time of the chip implant. *Why*, Izar still couldn't fathom.

Anyhow, the chip had enabled Zaurak to track Izar's every movement, as by satellite. No wonder the derrick had fallen on *Dominion Drill I* precisely where Izar had been standing. Also, after Alshain had hurled Izar overboard, he must have spoken to Zaurak, but even had the giant not done so, Zaurak would have known Izar remained alive simply through the platinum chip. And so Zaurak had dispatched Serpens to the Atlantic Ocean to kill him. Because of the chip, Serpens had located Izar and hurled nets over him with precision.

Izar considered today's ship attack from Serpens and Zaurak's perspective: Izar had died in the fishnet, and so Serpens must believe he'd succeeded in killing him. Serpens had then seen Coralline bringing him down into the water—thus, the downward movement of the platinum chip would have been accounted for by her. But if Izar budged at all from his current position, Zaurak and Serpens would know he remained alive—because of the movement of his platinum chip—and they would hunt him again. If he swam deep, they wouldn't be able to find him for a time, but, eventually, whenever he found the elixir, transformed, and approached shore, they would catch him like a homing pigeon. They wouldn't let him reach Menkar alive.

In order to live, Izar would have to remove the platinum chip. It would be best to do it immediately, so that Serpens and Zaurak continued to believe him dead.

A shadow fell over him. Coralline reached a hand up and patted Pavonis's endless white belly.

"Get out of the way, Coralline," he said in a low, ominous voice.

Coralline opened her mouth as though to argue, but her lips snapped shut—even Izar could tell there would be no arguing with Pavonis in his present state, quivering with anger.

Previously, outside Bristled Bed and Breakfast, Pavonis had tossed Izar up and down until Izar's stomach had churned; now, Pavonis's stomach came down upon him, flattening him against the pebbles. Izar tried to push up against the whale shark, but it was like trying to dislodge a tractor. He felt like a balloon on the verge of popping.

"What are you trying to do, Pavonis?" Coralline cried. From underneath Pavonis, Izar turned his head to find Coralline's bronze tailfin at his eye level, flicking worriedly.

"I'm going to squash the lies out of him. I'm not going to stop until he's dead or every last lie is out, whichever comes first. Now, human," Pavonis said, pressing down until Izar's ribs creaked, "do you realize you've endangered us, not once but twice?"

"Yes," Izar squeaked, his voice high-pitched, for even his throat was constricted by Pavonis's weight. "And I'm sorry for it."

"Sorry? Is that all you have to say? Did you know that your friends were shooting at Coralline? Did you know that she could be dead right now, at this moment?"

Izar must have died in the fishnet before the gunshots, so he had not heard them. He looked at Coralline's tailfin again, still at his eye level—translucent at the edges, it was as delicate as a handkerchief. He imagined her bleeding to death, her scales turning white. A shudder ran through him.

"I'm sorry," he repeated weakly.

"Now, human," said the shark, his belly pressing down farther, until Izar's shoulder blades were scratched against the pebbles beneath, "I need you to tell me the truth. What did those men want with you? And who are you, really?"

"He's already told us, Pavonis, remember?" Coralline said.

"I don't remember."

"He works at Ocean Protection, and Ocean Dominion is his enemy. That must be why they attacked him today."

"Must it? *Say* it, human."

Izar swallowed hard. Under no circumstances could he reveal to them that he belonged to Ocean Dominion. They would not forgive him; they would not accept him. He could not tell them the truth, yet he could not continue to lie either. Or could he? If Coralline removed the platinum chip from his wrist, a ship could not possibly attack them again. As such, although Izar had twice exposed them to danger by his presence, he would no longer be doing so if the chip was removed. He wanted to burn out his own tongue, but he repeated Coralline's words in his high-pitched voice.

"How did they find you?" Pavonis demanded, doing a sort of jiggle above Izar, leading his scalp to scrape against the pebbles.

"I was just about to get to that," Izar groaned. "On that note, I have a favor to ask."

"Do you really think you're in a position to ask favors?"

"Let him ask it, Pavonis!" Coralline said. "And let him rise."

Pavonis jiggled some more, quite fervently, before reluctantly moving away with a swing of his tail. Izar lay there, rubbing his ribs. When he could speak again, and his voice was almost normal, he said, "There's a platinum chip in my wrist that's a tracker. That's how they found me, and that's how they'll find me again—and kill me, unless you extract it, Coralline."

Coralline plopped down next to Izar on the pebbles, her tail extended in front of her. She pressed the skin of his wrist with her thumb, first gently, then hard. Her eyes widened as she felt the small slab of metal. "I would help you if I could," she said, "but the chip appears to be a part of your bone itself. Its extraction would require slitting your veins, which would, quite possibly, kill you."

"I'd rather die at your hands than theirs."

"I'd rather you didn't."

"I believe in your skills."

"You shouldn't. I don't have a medical badge."

"Are you afraid you'll get in trouble legally?"

"No. You don't have any underwater records, so, even if you die, a murder charge cannot arise against me."

"That makes me feel better!" He smiled, hoping to tug a smile to her lips as well, but the set of her mouth remained somber. "You're clearly competent at what you do, Coralline," he persisted. "You helped both my shoulder and my hand with your salves."

"You don't understand. Surgeries are performed in clinics, not open water. At present, I have only my apothecary arsenal with me, which contains only a limited number of implements. Also, surgeries are performed only by apothecaries who are at the level of manager or master. I've never operated on anyone before. I was a lowly apprentice, and even in that role, I managed to get fired."

"Why were you fired?"

"My boss, Rhodomela Ranularia, said I wasn't thinking for myself. She said I was relying too much on my medical textbooks. On this note, I don't have any of my textbooks with me at present. For a procedure as delicate as this, I would have liked to consult *Smooth Scalpels* as well as *Snip and Stitch*."

"Well, if your boss thinks you don't need textbooks, I'm sure you don't."

"That wasn't the only reason I was fired," Coralline said, her cheeks reddening. "I have a flaw considered fatal in my profession."

"You enjoy killing patients?"

"No."

"Torturing them, when no one's looking?"

"No. This isn't a joke, Izar. I'm afraid of blood. It acts as a sort of tranquilizer for me. As soon as it enters my nostrils, I feel dizzy. It's possible I'll faint during your procedure."

"If you don't extract the chip, I will certainly die," Izar said quietly. "If you do, I may live. My fate is in your hands."

"What do the three of you think?" Coralline asked. She looked from Pavonis to Altair, his tail wrapped around her pinky finger, to Nacre, on her right shoulder. The four of them had left Izar twenty feet below on the seabed, but Coralline still spoke softly, in case he could hear. "Should I help Izar by removing the chip?"

"You've already helped that ingrate more than enough," Pavonis rumbled. "You have an instinctive desire to save everyone you encounter, and while this instinct might be helpful to you in your career, you need to remember that your role now is *not* that of an apothecary. You need to be single-minded on your elixir quest if you want to save your brother. Yes, we are not at the Ball of Blue Bottle yet, but still, sometimes I look at you and get the sense that you've forgotten why we're out here anyway. The elixir and its attainment must be foremost in your mind at *all* times. Whether the human lives or dies is not your concern."

"I would like to offer another angle," Nacre said. "We could use all the help we can get on this Elixir Expedition. You seem to be assuming the Ball of Blue Bottle will mark the end of your quest, Coralline, but I believe the Ball will form the gateway to the greatest test of your life. And I think Izar will help you triumph in that test. As such, my vote is that we keep him alive."

Coralline glanced at Altair.

"I'm simpler in my views," said the seahorse. "To me, it seems wrong to let him just die, human or not. If you can help him live, I think you should."

"I think so, too," Coralline said.

"Well, I hope the surgery kills him!" Pavonis huffed.

Coralline patted his side, then swam down to Izar. "I'll do my best to remove your chip," she said, "but I can't promise you'll live."

He grinned at her. She did not smile back. To increase her chances of success, she would pretend she was Rhodomela. The first thing Rhodomela would have noted, were she here, was that the arrangement was unprofessional. Had there been a surgical bed, even if a makeshift one, Coralline would have hovered vertically next to Izar. Now, in the absence of a bed, Izar was sprawled over the pebbles, and she had no choice but to hover over him horizontally.

She opened her apothecary arsenal next to him. She pressed his wrist again and, with her pen, drew a black rectangle over it to mark the boundaries of the chip. Then she extracted a vial of anesthetic from her case and emptied it into his mouth. He winced as he swallowed it, but, in a matter of moments, his eyes closed.

Drawing a deep breath, as though she was about to slit her own wrists, Coralline extracted her scalpel from her case and made an incision over one side of the rectangle she'd drawn. Blood oozed out. Her fingers trembled. *Focus*, she told herself sternly. She cut along a second side of the rectangle, then a third. His blood flowed now like the ink of an octopus—it invaded her nostrils.

Coralline forced a tiny pair of clippers through the hole she'd made in his skin. The clippers soon encountered the chip and grasped its edge, but it was as embedded in his bone as olivine stones in her hair comb. She loosened the chip's edges painstakingly with her clippers, then tugged again, and again. The chip released its hold on him abruptly. Breathing a sigh of relief, Coralline dropped both the bloodied chip and the clippers onto the pebbles.

"This is the perfect opportunity to kill him," Pavonis said from above, speaking softly, as though to convince her the voice was coming out of her own subconscious.

Coralline extracted needle and thread from her arsenal and turned back to Izar's wrist. The five fingers of his hand suddenly swelled to ten. She blinked; the ten became five again. She shook her head—it felt as light and loose as a jellyfish. She felt herself drifting downward, such that she was almost lying atop Izar, scale to scale, shoulder to shoulder. No longer possessing the strength to hover horizontally over him, she sat down on the pebbles next to him, her back slumping, her tail extended in front of her.

She was not just faint-headed; she would soon faint, she recognized. From the numerous occasions on which she'd fainted before, she knew she had only minutes before her mind would force a shut-down—minutes in which to stitch, salve, bandage, and anti-infect, tasks that would otherwise consume the better part of an hour.

"Skin is just a fabric," Nacre said encouragingly. "Pretend you're a seamstress, like your mother."

Coralline thrust her needle into Izar's skin. Stitch upon stitch she made, concentrating on each tiny cross as though it were a universe in and of itself. When it was all complete, she sat back and surveyed her crosshatching. The sutures were messy and crooked, but they were serving their purpose: They stopped the bleeding. At least he would not die of blood loss.

Blinking heavily, Coralline unlidded her vial of toothed wrack salve and dabbed the balm onto his wrist. She then sheared strips of pyropia with her snippers, wrapped the gauzy swaths tightly over his wrist, and tied it all in place with two strands of spiny straggle.

Her vision blurred into overlapping circles. She pinched her hand to remain conscious for the final step, anti-infective. She dumped the contents of her vials of sea oak, golden-brown in color, and dabberlocks, olive-brown, into a flask, and clamped a stopper atop the flask. The two algae sputtered and spewed upon contact—they sounded like they were shrieking at the top of their voices. She had once prepared precisely this anti-infective before, but the reaction had been far milder then, more of a simper than a screech.

She must be hallucinating, her mind exaggerating the reaction.

"Kill him, Coralline," Pavonis whispered from above.

Coralline cradled Izar's head with one hand and emptied the contents of the flask into his mouth with the other.

At last the operation was complete, she thought, sitting back dizzily, her hands to either side of her on the pebbles to prevent her from collapsing flat on her back. Though she was disbarred, she had now reached a new level as an apothecary—she had performed her first surgery. Rhodomela would be proud—

Izar's arms shuddered and his tail quaked, his body writhing as though in the midst of an internal attack. Such writhing was known to occur only after consuming desmarestia. But Coralline hadn't given Izar the acid kelp.

Her head jerked down to the row of vials in her apothecary arsenal. There was the vial of desmarestia, untouched. Picking it up, she looked at it until her eyes crossed, and the tip of her nose almost touched the vial. She gasped.

She hadn't labeled the vials earlier and, in her faintness now, had mistaken dabberlocks for desmarestia, both of them olive-brown in color. No wonder she hadn't recognized the screeching reaction in the flask.

She looked at Izar again. His back was rattling against the pebbles, which were rattling against one another, creating a discordant cacophony. He wasn't dead yet, but he soon would be. Coralline had saved him from the fishnet, then poisoned him herself.

"I knew you could do it, Coralline!" Pavonis roared.

"You're wilier and trickier than I ever imagined," Nacre said.

"Let me warn you," Altair whispered, "murder does not sit easy on the conscience."

Coralline's head swiveled, and she folded into unconsciousness, her cheek landing gently against Izar's chest.

Coralline swam out the lobby of Big Blue Bed and Breakfast. Named and shaped after the big blue octopus, each of its eight arms formed a twirling, three-story tower, with the lobby of the hotel serving as the head of the octopus. It was the sixth hotel Coralline had tried in Blue Bottle. The concierge had just told her what they all had: With the Ball of Blue Bottle tomorrow night, there were no accommodations to be had anywhere in the capital.

Coralline looked at the buildings rising from the seabed all around her, the tallest among them more than twenty stories. Apartments, a novelty to her, were rather like shelves, she thought, except that instead of books, they housed people. Another intriguing aspect of Blue Bottle was its luciferin lampposts, which Coralline had never seen before. Luciferin lampposts were just like luciferin lanterns, except that their rods were long—at least twice her own length—and several large orbs dangled in clusters from each rod. Luciferin lampposts rendered the city bright despite the late hour.

Coralline swerved around a building called Needle-to-the-Sky, shaped like a column of beads, and she swam into the clearing where she had left Izar, Pavonis, Altair, and Nacre. Izar lay unconscious on the seabed, his face gray and his jaw taut, suggesting that he continued to suffer within even while he remained still without. His scales were neither indigo nor bleached, but, strangely, a shade in between—lilac—as though he was lingering mercilessly between life and death. Coralline pressed two fingers to the side of his throat; his pulse was so low, she had to close her eyes to hear it.

"Do you think he's going to die?" Pavonis asked in an exuberant voice.

"Yes," Coralline said, with a twinge of sadness. "I actually can't understand why he's not already dead, given that I accidentally gave him desmarestia."

When she had risen from her faint, she had buried his platinum chip among the pebbles. Pavonis had suggested burying Izar with his chip, but Coralline had grasped Izar's hand and dragged him to Blue Bottle with her. She didn't want him to die alone.

"There's no vacancy in any hotel," Coralline told Pavonis now. "I'll have to sleep here with all of you."

"You're reduced to homelessness!" Altair gasped, from somewhere in Pavonis's shadow. His voice shrinking to a moan, he continued, "How I will ever face your father again, I can't imagine."

"Don't worry," Pavonis said. "I'll remain awake all night."

Coralline had disliked Bristled Bed and Breakfast, but at least it had provided a roof over her head. Now she felt a little like a lobster as she tried to settle among the rocks. She found solace in the luciferin lamppost directly above her, yet it also seemed to be spotlighting her homeless condition. In Blue Bottle, there were few loiterers—in contrast to the many she'd seen in Hog's Bristle—but there seemed an abundance of constables. They were easily recognizable, wearing deep-purple waistcoats with the circular black seal of the Under-Ministry of Crime and Murder. She'd passed three constables already.

Turning her face away, she had rushed past each of them. The Constables Department of Blue Bottle might already have her details, including her portrait, from the Constables Department of Hog's Bristle. They might already be on high alert for her.

Coralline could not afford to sleep; no, she'd better be prepared to dash away at a moment's notice. She would remain awake all night, vigilant, alongside Pavonis, she decided. She fixed her attention on the luciferin lamppost above her, with its half-dozen immense orbs. Her gaze swung from one orb to the other, then back again, as over stars in a constellation.

As long as she stared at them, she could stay awake. She tried to recall passages from Venant Veritate's *The Universe Demystified*; that would help her remain awake. . . .

"Coralline!"

Her eyes snapped open. The voice was Pavonis's. She followed the direction of his eye.

A merman hovered at the outskirts of the clearing. He had a gray tail, towering shape, and bulbous nose. His waistcoat was a deep-purple color. He was a constable, here to capture her! Coralline bolted upright, her hands over her heart. But as she continued to look at him, she saw that his waistcoat was not deep purple but a glistening navy blue—the kind of waistcoat a merman might wear to supper at a nice restaurant.

An aquamarine-tailed mermaid hovered next to him. She was dressed like Coralline had been at her engagement party—in a high-necked bodice shimmering with sequins, except that hers were red and green rather than the orange and purple Coralline had worn. Abalone had said she'd designed the bodice after the latest fashion in Blue Bottle—it seemed true.

"My name is Limpet Laminaria," began the merman, "and this is my wife, Linatella." His voice was aloof, formal, a voice of obligation rather than warmth. "We live just here." His hand beckoned to the building Needle-to-the-Sky. "Are you in need of a place to stay the night?"

"Yes."

"You're welcome to stay with us, in that case," said Linatella.

"Thank you!" Coralline beamed.

Deneb Delphinus read the press release yet again, but he still could not make sense of it.

> Izar Eridan, co-president of Ocean Dominion, has died. Saiph Eridan will be the sole president of Ocean Dominion from this date forward.
>
> "I am more saddened by my brother's loss than anyone can ever know," Saiph Eridan has stated. "We are still uncovering the details of Izar's death. They will be shared as soon as they are available. . . ."

Deneb himself had saved Izar twice—yanking him out of the path of the falling derrick on *Dominion Drill I* and grabbing his arms the next day to prevent him from plummeting through the borehole. How could Izar have died?

Shaking his head, Deneb dropped the press release into the bulletproof tank of water below the platform under his feet, as though drowning the announcement would make it disappear. The paper floated away from Castor.

Deneb found the robot terrifying—the most lethal thing he had ever laid eyes on. His hands were clammy to even stand above Castor, for he had the sense that he was standing above a time bomb. No one had told Deneb this Invention Chamber belonged to Izar, but he had known it from the scar along Castor's jaw, matching Izar's own.

Why me? Deneb asked himself. *Why do I have to be here?*

He had not been given a reason. He had been summoned to a manager's office, handed a new identification card, and told to guard the contents of the room on the floor B2. As soon as he'd entered the room, he'd understood why it needed guarding—not just because of Castor but because the room was highly flammable, with hundreds of flasks of combustible chemicals lining the walls. The place was an underground explosive device, a dynamite bomb of sorts. If it fell into the wrong hands, Ocean Dominion could burn to the ground.

And so Deneb found it ironic that he'd been told to guard it, for his were the wrong hands.

He traced a finger over the mermaid tattoo across his forearm. He had gotten the tattoo because he thought mermaids were beautiful. And he'd joined Ocean Dominion because he wanted to see a mermaid. But, despite all his trips on the waters, despite perching like a gull on the rails for long hours, he hadn't yet seen a single mermaid in his two months at the company. They dove down at the sight of ships—they considered humans the enemy. And his fellow crewmen considered him a fool, mocking him for his tattoo.

Deneb descended the ladder to the side of the tank of water. Earlier, it had been difficult for him to even walk in this Invention Chamber, with all the landmine-like tripping hazards everywhere—rounds of bullets, ores of iron, sheets of magnesium. He had tidied the place up, feeling rather like a laboratory assistant. Now, in the cleared space, he strode to the shelves of combustible chemicals.

On the day of the oil spill, Izar had told Deneb that mermaids would not exist much longer. Deneb had not understood Izar's words then, but he understood them now. From having read Izar's crimson-covered journal, its yellowed pages spilling with notes and formulae, he had come to learn that Izar called this room his Invention Chamber, and that, in this Chamber, Izar planned to produce an army of Castors that would plunder the ocean floor for gold and diamonds—meanwhile extinguishing the civilization of merpeople.

Deneb could prevent it all, if he chose. He could save the mermaids he so adored. All he would have to do would be to light a match and throw the flame upon some combustible chemicals. Then Castor, the crimson-covered journal, this Invention Chamber, the thirty-floor bronze-glass building itself, would all blaze like a bonfire.

A clanging noise made him jump. He glanced at the floor, for the sound seemed to have come from just below his feet. It had sounded like someone was trying to rattle a door open. But the floor below this, B3, was accessible only to the president of Ocean Dominion—Saiph, at present—and was known to be empty. No, Deneb must be mistaken. His long hours alone in the Invention Chamber must be playing tricks with his mind. The clang must have issued from the maze of pipes in the ceiling, for they burped and gurgled constantly, to his irritation.

Turning his attention back to the flammable liquids and powders, Deneb pulled a set of matches out of his pocket.

19

Enmity

T he rug to his side of the bed was white pile. The windows were shuttered, but the blinds were pink rather than the usual shades of gray he'd seen so far. An ornate copper dresser stood along the wall, scattered with miscellaneous hair combs and ropes like the kind Coralline used to tie her hair, along with a bowl of little pewter-colored shells. Two books were stacked to one side of the dresser: *A Hair Dresser's Collection of Ultimate Updos* and *Egregious Egregia: A Novel*.

The room was cloyingly feminine but cozy. Last Izar remembered, he'd been lying on the pebbles, swallowing the anesthetic Coralline put to his lips—

Coralline. She lay wrapped over the right side of his body, he saw, her head tucked into the hollow of his shoulder. Her arm lay over his chest, and her hair cloaked both of them over the blanket.

A confused smile spread on Izar's lips. Their first night, in Hog's Bristle, they'd taken separate rooms; their second night, in Rainbow Wrack, they'd shared a room, but he'd slept on the floor; now, at the culmination of their third night, here, wherever it was, they were sharing a bed, and she was in his arms. He seemed to have done himself a great service by being unconscious.

Izar glanced at his wrist. It was covered in some sort of gauze and tied with red strings.

He lifted his hand from the blanket with caution. Pain did not prickle through his nerves, even when he slowly, experimentally, started to flop his hand about and angle it. Coralline was clearly good at her job, despite her low confidence about it.

She stirred. Her head rose from his chest, and her gaze struck him with the force of a collision. She sat up, declaring, "You're alive!" She was wearing an ivory chemise with short, slit sleeves that fluttered about her shoulders. She threw the blanket off both of them. Looking down at himself, Izar saw with a small shock that she had unbuttoned his waistcoat before putting him to bed.

Was it possible something had happened between them that he could not remember?

Coralline shifted to hover horizontally over him. She looked as though she were levitating above him, held up by invisible strings from the ceiling. Her eyes roved over him as though he was an object—he did not mind being an object, he found. Like a slippery fish, she was entirely unpredictable, Coralline.

Through his undone buttons, she pressed her hand flat against his heart, her long locks falling upon his face. Even the ends of her hair were soft and supple, and there was a particular, sweet scent to them as they tantalized his nostrils. His hand rose to twirl a strand of hair around his finger, but she shifted to the side.

Her eyes darted from his wrist to his face; their blue-green color made him think of water swirling at the base of a teacup. "I've made a major medical breakthrough," she whispered.

His stitches had faded well into his skin, and the skin around them was not even puckered, as though the chip-extraction had occurred not a day, but months, ago. His wrist had fully recovered.

Coralline tried to delineate the mechanism of her medication. Desmarestia was acidic, and sea oak was saline; the latter must have neutralized the acids of the former. Desmarestia was the pivotal ingredient in the reaction, but its potency and power made it poisonous when swallowed by itself. The acid kelp was so universally reviled that no apothecary had ever experimented with it before, not even someone as unconventional as Rhodomela.

What would Rhodomela say when Coralline told her she'd invented an unparalleled healer, a miracle medication? Rhodomela would apologize for having fired Coralline; she would plead for her to return. Coralline would demur at first, just to make the master apothecary squirm, then she would accept, on two conditions. First, she would request to skip a rung in her career, to travel straight from apprentice apothecary to senior apothecary, without the intermediate title of associate. Then, she would request a tripling—no, *quad*rupling—of her wages, from fifty carapace per week to two hundred carapace.

Coralline's tailfin quivered with anticipation; she could not wait to make a dramatic comeback at The Irregular Remedy.

"As a result of having treated you with desmarestia, a poisonous algae," she gushed to Izar, "I'll be able to get my job back—with a raise and promotion. Thank you!"

"Thank *you*," he said huskily.

Following the direction of his gaze, she glanced down to see that she was clad only in her chemise; she'd been so stunned at his being alive that she hadn't paid any attention to propriety. Now, she bolted under the blanket. When she'd entered this guest bedroom last night, dragging Izar by a hand, it had seemed cruel to make him spend the last night of his life on the floor. So she had deposited him in bed and had unbuttoned his waistcoat to check his heartbeat. Modesty hardly mattered where a dead male was concerned, and she'd been unable to resist changing into her chemise for her comfort.

"Don't look at me as I change," she warned Izar now as she sprang out of bed. Full of zest, she slapped her tailfin to her backside, feeling herself shrouded in a brilliant, invisible glow in the wake of her medical discovery.

The day called for celebratory color, and she browsed her satchel with twittering fingers. But there were only two corsets she hadn't yet worn on the Elixir Expedition, and the more vibrant of the two was hardly vibrant at all: It was a sleeveless honeydew with tawny strings.

Once she was ready and had turned around to face Izar, he rolled out of bed. He shrugged off his waistcoat and swung his arms through another he found in his satchel, a stiff sable piece with spirula shells for buttons. "Could you help me do up the buttons?" he asked Coralline, holding his wrist out as explanation.

Coralline frowned. As far as she could tell, the joint was fully healed, but perhaps Izar feared overextending it. Flitting over to him from across the bed, commencing with his lowest buttons, in order to align the two halves of the waistcoat, Coralline inserted the tiny white shells through the slits. By the time she'd slid the last spirula into its buttonhole, at his collar, her cheeks were flushed, as they had been when she'd unbuttoned his waistcoat in Rainbow Wrack.

"After you," Izar said, opening the bedroom door with a flourish. Coralline slipped into the living room, trailed by him.

"Glad to see you're feeling better!" came Linatella's voice from the kitchen.

Coralline had liked Linatella and Limpet's apartment at night, and she found that she liked it even more during the day. It was a home rather than a hotel, for one; in that sense, though they shared little direct similarity, the apartment made her think of her own home in Urchin Grove. Second, it was brightly lit: Dozens of windows, the size of supper plates, were carved into the walls, offering a tenth-story view over the capital. Third, placards with inspirational proverbs dangled on the walls: *Scratch the surface of your dreams*; *like a whale, you were born to make a splash*.

Even had the apartment been a hovel, Coralline would have been happy in it, because if constables in Blue Bottle were searching for her, they would be looking in hotels, not homes. Linatella and Limpet Laminaria were, without their knowledge, harboring a fugitive from the law. A part of Coralline felt guilty to be putting them in such a position, but another part felt relieved—they would come to no harm from harboring her, and she would benefit.

"Limpet's gone to work," Linatella bubbled, "but I have some breakfast ready for you."

"Thank you!" Coralline smiled.

She and Izar swam to the dining table and took seats across from Linatella. It had been difficult to tell at night, but Coralline saw now that Linatella was buxom and pretty, perhaps in her mid-thirties, with waist-length white-gold hair and a somewhat maternal manner, such that Coralline felt as though she was in the home not of a stranger but of an older cousin.

Linatella piled heaps of felty fingers onto Coralline's and Izar's plates. She then stared as they devoured the slender green fronds. Neither of them had had a bite to eat since a rushed breakfast in Rainbow Wrack yesterday, and they ate voraciously. Linatella herself ate ulva, and she offered the sea lettuce to Coralline. Coralline shook her head vehemently at the diet food. She would probably be eating big bowls of ulva soon, though, she thought with a gulp—her mother would give her nothing but ulva in the days before her wedding.

"What brings you two to Blue Bottle?" Linatella asked.

"The Ball of Blue Bottle tonight," Coralline replied.

Linatella's stone-sticks clattered against her plate. "It's an event for the most illustrious and successful people in Meristem, most of them twice to thrice your age. How ever did you two manage to get an invitation?"

"We were just lucky, I suppose." Coralline didn't want to mention Tang Tarpon to Linatella, given that she was the principal suspect in his murder.

"Attending the Ball of Blue Bottle would be a dream come true for me," Linatella said. "I adore fashion, and the Ball is considered the very height of fashion. What are you wearing to it?"

When Coralline had packed her satchel for the elixir quest in her bedroom, she had not planned on attending any parties, let alone the Ball of Blue Bottle. The prettiest corset she'd brought with her had been the sky-blue one that Ecklon had liked, which now lay in tatters at the bottom of her satchel.

"I have nothing to wear," Coralline said, somewhat worried.

"I don't know my origin," Izar said. "I was adopted by a benevolent businessman, Antares, whom I consider my father and whose son, Saiph, I consider my brother. . . . I've always been passionate about inventing things. . . . I suppose what drives me is the idea of connecting two things no one has connected before—it's similar to your medical breakthrough this morning, the thrill you got from connecting two kinds of algae no one has connected before. . . ."

Izar listened to his own words with some incredulity, for though they were true, they sounded foreign—he had never spoken much about himself to anyone, not even Ascella. Now, as he chatted with Coralline, the darkness of his childhood, the desperate loneliness of it, seemed a lifetime away—like glass that had shattered at a distance, unable to draw blood.

The Ball was to take place in the evening, and he and Coralline had had nothing to occupy them after breakfast with Linatella, so they'd set out to explore Blue Bottle. As she swam next to him, Coralline's hair formed a swaying rope over her shoulders, and her scales shimmered like panes of tiny mirrors, her tailfin fluttering like a silk fan.

Of all the settlements Izar had seen so far in Meristem, Blue Bottle, with its tall buildings, most resembled his hometown of Menkar. Buildings underwater were similar to buildings on land, he saw, except for their frequently bizarre shapes. The building in front of him resembled a prickly cactus, and the one to his left looked like a snake slithering upward.

"I've never seen this algae before!" Coralline exclaimed. Hovering horizontally, she fingered something that Izar thought looked like a cross between a wrinkled gnome and a head of broccoli. Though she was not looking at him, he could not help but smile at her state of rapture—she was as passionate about algae as Ascella was about jewelry.

Turning vertical again, Coralline grabbed his hand and peered at his wrist. There was nothing to see there anymore, not even a scar to mark the procedure. "Any pain?" she asked, flopping his wrist back and forth then right and left, such that he appeared to be waving.

Izar shook his head, finding himself speechless. Coralline placed two fingers to the side of his neck beneath his earlobe. "Your heart is beating fast," she observed in a dispassionate voice. "Perhaps after the procedure yesterday, even the moderate pace of our swim through town today is too fast for you." And then, just like that, she turned and started swimming again—at a slower pace, for his sake—her tail a carpet of traveling coins.

Her effect on him was heady; he felt like he was an adolescent spending the day with his first crush. Catching his breath, he caught up with her. "There's something I've been meaning to ask you," he said, tracing the line of the scar along his jaw. "Do merpeople ever drown boats?"

"No. I've never heard of that before."

So, if merpeople had not drowned his biological parents' fishing dinghy, how had his parents died? Could someone—a man rather than a merman—have bludgeoned them, as their neighbor Rigel Nihal had insisted on the island of Mira? If so, who could the man have been?

"I've told you a little about my life," Izar said softly. "Will you tell me about yours?"

"Sure," Coralline began with a smile. "I'm from a little village called Urchin Grove. I have an eight-year-old brother, my mother is a seamstress, and my father is—or *was*—a coral connoisseur. As I focus on merpeople anatomy, my father used to focus on coral reef anatomy, studying reefs and trying to heal them—because of human activities, reefs have really been suffering. But my father's hand was blown off in a coral reef dynamite blast seven months ago."

A coral reef dynamite blast . . . a hand . . . Izar thought it should mean something to him, but he could not imagine what.

Coralline stopped and looked at him, her eyes more serious than he had yet seen them. "There's something I've been meaning to ask you as well," she said quietly. "Do you know a man named Zaurak Alphard?"

"What?" Izar said, his face blanching.

"I found a pen in the midst of the black poison spill in my village." Coralline rummaged through her satchel and handed Izar the pen he recognized well, engraved with Zaurak's name in block letters and the bronze-and-black insignia of Ocean Dominion. As Izar clasped the pen, he felt as though he was holding Zaurak's face in his hands.

His mind churning, Izar thought of telling Coralline that he didn't know Zaurak. But she was looking directly at him and would know he was lying. "Yes, I know Zaurak," he said, avoiding her eyes. "I consider him an enemy." It was true, unfortunately. "But why were you there, in the oil spill?"

"Oil? Do you mean black poison?"

"Yes, I suppose."

"I was there to find my brother, Naiadum. Black poison is what made him terminally ill and led me to embark on this Elixir Expedition to find a way to save him. I've never wanted to murder anyone before, but I would like nothing more than to strangle this man Zaurak with my own hands."

Sick to his stomach, Izar regretted all the felty fingers he'd gobbled up for breakfast. Coralline had mentioned the term *black poison* to him during their first conversation, when he'd asked her why she was looking for the elixir, but he hadn't understood the term until now. He had assumed from the word *poison* that her brother must have gotten sick from what he'd eaten. But it was Izar's oil spill that had sickened him; it was Izar who had obligated Coralline to leave her home and confront all manner of danger in an effort to save him.

The oil spill had been in Zone Ten, which meant that Urchin Grove fell under Zone Ten in Ocean Dominion's map of the Atlantic Ocean. There were no names of merpeople settlements on the Ocean Dominion map, only neat little squares dividing the Atlantic from North to South Pole. Now that Izar thought about it, the map was the sort that colonialists might once have drawn, with arbitrary lines dividing people into countries. Well, at least Zone Ten was relatively under-exploited, Izar consoled himself. Other than the oil spill, Ocean Dominion had done little in Zone Ten in recent years except for a coral reef dynamite blast about seven months ago—in which they'd caught few fish, but a merman's hand.

Her father's hand.

Coralline continued to swim, but Izar stopped, his tailfin appearing to have turned to stone. He had lulled himself into a sense of peace and security with Coralline, but there could be no peace or security between them. There was an enmity between their worlds, there always had been. As a leader of Ocean Dominion, Izar was at the forefront of that enmity. He had temporarily crossed over to the other side and seemed to have forgotten the sharp divisions that existed between their two worlds.

He looked at the city all around him, the city that reminded him of his hometown. He imagined the buildings around him as a pile of fragments; he imagined Needle-to-the-Sky, where he and Coralline were staying, as a heap of rubble.

He had never seen Coralline's home, but given that she lived in a village—and extrapolating from the Purple Claw village they'd visited—he imagined her home as a semicircular mound, like half of a bubble. His army of Castors would trample it and burn it, destroying her books, her desk, her bed. She would have nowhere to live, nowhere to sleep, nothing to eat. For a while, perhaps weeks or months, she and her family would find other places to stay, but, eventually, all settlements in Meristem would lie in ruins, and there would be nowhere else for them to go.

At that stage, Coralline, like all other merpeople, would die. Izar would have killed her as surely as though he'd stabbed her with a knife. But how could he bring himself to stab her with a knife, given that she'd saved his life not once, not twice, but thrice—cutting him out of a net on two occasions, then extracting his platinum chip.

"What's the matter, Izar?" Coralline asked. Hovering vertically ahead, she waited for him, tailfin flicking.

He turned and swam away.

Jellyfish floated above Coralline like watchful ghosts, translucent, effervescent. Below her, garden eels bobbed in the sediment, their heads poking out of their burrows while the rest of their bodies remained hidden.

"Oh, look at that hammerhead!" Nacre commented from her perch on Coralline's shoulder. Her tentacles waggled in the direction of a fifteen-foot-long shark with a wide, flattened head resembling a hammer. "How hideous. Thank goodness I was born a beautiful snail rather than a mis-shapen beast. Oh wait, is that monstrosity actually a mermaid's muse? And I thought your Ogre was bad!"

Coralline saw that the hammerhead shark was accompanied by a young mermaid, whom she hadn't noticed at first because the mermaid was swimming to the shark's other side. The sight of the two of them made her smile—it was the first time she'd seen a mermaid other than herself mused by a shark. Her smile widened to spot another mermaid, farther ahead, swimming out an apartment window. Coralline's mother always reprimanded her for swimming in and out windows rather than doors, but in Blue Bottle, there seemed to be no such rules for female social etiquette. Coralline was liking the capital more and more as the day passed.

"That corset is so fashionable!" Nacre commented, her tentacles pointing at a mermaid wearing a bodice shimmering with black-and-white sequins. "I know your mother would just love it. Don't you think so? . . . Can you believe the Pole Dancer—Altair, I mean—will give birth in just a week and a half to hundreds of little nuisances? In fact, if I'm not mistaken, I think his delivery date is your wedding date. . . ."

Coralline sighed, trying to block out Nacre's voice. Snails were often private and quiet, spending much of their time inside their carapace, but not Nacre. Coralline had been exploring Blue Bottle alone, perfectly happy, when she'd happened to pass Needle-to-the-Sky. Nacre had called to her from the wall of the building, crawled up her arm, settled on her right shoulder, and ordered: "Show me the capital." Coralline would much rather have explored the city with Pavonis, but he'd left early in the morning, saying: "There's so much to see, and such little time—I'm going to make the most of my day." He'd said he'd be back late at night and would meet her and Izar at the Laminaria apartment after the Ball of Blue Bottle. As for Altair, he was spending the day alone in a square of paddle-grass close to Needle-to-the-Sky, trying to regain his "moral compass."

"Where is Izar?" Nacre asked.

"We were swimming together, then he left quite suddenly. I can't imagine why."

"I can. It's because he has feelings for you and is conflicted about them."

"Don't be ridiculous," Coralline scoffed, her eyes crossing to look at Nacre.

"I have an eye for such things. I've often kept my tentacles trained on him during our swims. I've noticed how often he looks at you when he thinks no one's looking. This is an advantageous position for you."

"How so?"

"If he thinks you return his feelings, he might give the elixir to you, if or when the two of you find it. Do you return his feelings?"

"I'm engaged to Ecklon, Nacre. What do you think?"

"Be honest, Coralline."

"I *am* being honest!"

"I think you might feel more for Izar than you're letting on—even to yourself."

"If you say so." Nacre was light in weight but heavy in every other way, and Coralline would rather have carried three satchels than this one snail.

"Oh, what's that?" Nacre exclaimed.

Among the buildings, one structure stood out, for it was not tall; it was stout, a house rather than an apartment. Specifically, a house shaped like a snail. The snail's flesh was fashioned of light-brown shale, and its carapace of blush-pink shale, set in the shape of a series of whorls ending in a spire. A tall cylinder marked the front of the home, culminating in two long windows meant to resemble snail tentacles.

"Does a sage live inside?" Nacre asked Coralline in an awed voice.

"How would I know?"

"Read the placard!"

Following the direction of Nacre's tentacles, whose tips had joined and were pointing as one, Coralline saw a small placard tucked in the garden surrounding the snail. "*For one carapace, let Sage Dahlia Delaisi tell you about yourself!*" Coralline read out loud. "How did you know, Nacre?"

"Call it my sixth sense. Now, we must go in!"

"Don't be silly. How can a sage tell me anything about me, without ever having met me before? The more accurate term for a sage is fortune teller, and fortune tellers are all shams."

"I've accompanied you all over Meristem during your Elixir Expedition," Nacre said in a hurt voice. "Visiting with this sage is the one thing I ask of you, for your own good. Is it so much to ask?"

"I guess not." Coralline sighed, thinking that Nacre's emotional manipulation was similar to Abalone's. "If you're so interested in hearing the sage tell me about myself, who am I to stop you?"

Coralline rapped her knuckles on the door.

"Use your head, and use the window to the side of the door!" barked a shrill voice.

Coralline shifted to the window and looked in.

Sitting upon a settee, Sage Dahlia Delaisi was as orange as a clown anemonefish. Everything about her was orange, from her thick lips to her low-cut corset revealing plump, wrinkled cleavage. Each of her fingers was studded with a ring, such that they were splayed by necessity. Coralline wished she'd had the foresight to peek through the window before knocking—Sage Dahlia's sight would surely have dissuaded her.

A large true tulip snail perched on Sage Dahlia's shoulder—her right shoulder. His brown-and-white shell was twice the size of Nacre's but half as pretty. "Well, hello," he said, waggling his tentacles in Nacre's direction.

Nacre waggled back enthusiastically. "Not only does Sage Dahlia live in a house shaped like a snail," she whispered to Coralline, "but she also has a snail for a muse. I'm sensing excellent judgment and gratuitous wisdom here."

Coralline rolled her eyes at Nacre, then extracted from her satchel a one-carapace moon snail shell (which she'd borrowed from Izar), and added it to the carapace crock on the windowsill. She then swam into the living room.

"Get in there," the sage ordered, pointing an index finger at a large ampoule with a narrow neck and wide base, filled one-quarter of the way with pearl-white sand. "Swish your tailfin around in the ampoule."

Coralline did as she was told, feeling rather idiotic.

"That's enough!" Sage Dahlia called eventually.

"No more!" screeched Nacre, as though Coralline might not have heard the sage.

Coralline slipped out of the ampoule.

221

In all her clownfish-like glory, Sage Dahlia approached the ampoule and surveyed the sands at its bottom. There were now some streaks in the sands—a pattern of jagged lines not more sophisticated than Naiadum's drawings.

"You don't trust me," Sage Dahlia pronounced. She was frowning at the sands as though she'd gleaned this particular tidbit there rather than in Coralline's expression. "Very well. I shall tell you a few things about you, in order to get you to trust me."

"Go ahead."

"You're an apothecary."

Coralline looked down at herself—her satchel, her honeydew corset, Nacre; nothing about her appearance should have indicated her profession.

"You're no *longer* an apothecary," Sage Dahlia continued. "At least not in terms of official employment."

Coralline swallowed hard. How could the sage have known?

"You're searching for the elixir for your brother," Sage Dahlia persisted, her gaze unveering from the sands. "Your brother is young in age . . . *eight*, if I'm not mistaken."

"Yes," Coralline sputtered. Nacre gave her an I-told-you-so look.

"Am I right about everything?" Sage Dahlia said, now looking up from the sands to Coralline. Her eyes were squinted and tired, as though deciphering the sands had been draining.

"Yes, but how did you know—"

"Never mind that. Do you trust me now? Do you trust me *wholly*, with both your heart and mind?"

"I guess so," Coralline replied quietly.

"Do you want me to tell you something the streaks in the sands are telling me about you, something that you don't already know?"

"Yes," Coralline said, curious now despite herself.

"Fine. You are being betrayed by your love."

The words struck Coralline in slow motion, like repeated clobbers to her head. She slid away numbly from the ampoule, feeling as though the walls were closing in on her. The back of her tail bumped into the sage's settee, and she fell upon it in a daze, her blood pumping thinly through her veins.

Ecklon was betraying her. While Coralline was away on a mission to save her brother's life, Ecklon was betraying her. Coralline imagined Rosette's long red hair draping his chest, their scales shimmering together, silver and crimson. Perhaps at this very moment, they were lying together in the Mansion.

You've loved Ecklon six months, Rosette had said to Coralline. *I've loved him since I was six years old. I'll steal him away from you before your wedding, mark my words! And I promise I'll ruin you.*

Could Sage Dahlia be wrong? Coralline wondered. No, she couldn't; she'd been right about everything else.

Ecklon was betraying her.

20

Immoral and Immortal

"W ow!" Coralline gasped.

The Ball was in an auditorium-like building called The Cupola. It had a dome-shaped ceiling and windows in the shape of half-moons, each half-moon facing its counterpart to form a full. Hundreds of luciferin orbs traversed the ceiling, like constellations in a bustling galaxy, and they dangled also in threaded clusters over pillars, making Izar think of bunches of grapes. Most mermaids wore sequined corsets that reflected and amplified the light of the luciferin orbs, creating a kaleidoscopic effect throughout The Cupola. Izar had the sense of having swum into a swirling disco ball.

From the corner of his eye, he admired Coralline in profile: Her corset shimmered with silver sequins like droplets of starlight. At breakfast, when Coralline had told Linatella she had nothing to wear to the Ball, Izar had decided to get her a corset. The one he'd chosen for her fit like a glove, its single strap emphasizing the slender line of her shoulders and the hourglass curve of her waist. He had purchased it at a little shop called Bravura and had presented it to Coralline just before the Ball. He had never given a woman, let alone a mermaid, clothing before, and had been nervous at the gift, but Coralline's eyes had sparkled, and she'd beamed and hugged him, appearing more pleased by the thirty-carapace corset than Ascella had been by the thirty-thousand-dollar bracelet he'd given her on her birthday. But as soon as Coralline had clutched the fabric in her hands, Izar had regretted his choice—in both its silver color and single strap, the bodice very much resembled the gown Ascella had worn during his last dinner with her at Yacht.

While Izar had waited in the living room, Linatella, a hair dresser by profession, had helped Coralline get ready for the Ball, twirling her hair elaborately over one shoulder and embedding little pewter shells throughout its length like stardust.

Izar straightened the lapel of his own waistcoat, which, come to think of it, looked like a spaceship tuxedo. He'd never dressed to match a date before and would generally have laughed at such foppishness, but he'd gotten himself a waistcoat with a silver-sequined lapel to match Coralline's corset.

He had pondered it all afternoon, but he'd been unable to figure out what to make of the past between him and Coralline—the oil spill and reef blast—and the future—which would feature Castor. Giving up, he'd decided to think about it another time.

Next to him in The Cupola, Coralline absentmindedly fingered the pale-pink shell at her throat. "Why do you always wear that shell?" Izar asked.

"Oh, this?" Her hand dropped to her side. "It was a present."

"Anyone special?"

Coralline was silent.

The corner of Izar's tailfin knocked a decanter out of a merman's hand. Izar stopped to apologize, then he and Coralline continued to flit about The Cupola side by side. About equidistant between the floor and ceiling, they formed part of a middle layer of minglers. On land, people moved in a single layer about the floor, like ants; in the water, people moved above, they moved below, they formed numerous layers—which meant that any part of one's body could bump into any part of anyone else's at any time. In thronged spaces like The Cupola, people moved slowly, vertically, in order to avoid collisions, their tailfins generating no more than the gentlest of currents. But despite his deliberate slowness, Izar found himself having trouble not bumping into others. Mingling underwater seemed a sort of delicate dance.

Izar picked up two decanters of parasol wine from the tray of a passing waiter and handed one to Coralline. He liked the dark-green wine more this second time he drank it—it stung his throat less and tasted sweeter.

Music started abruptly, emanating from a pod carved into the wall, where half a dozen musicians clutched instruments resembling violas, their fingers pressing into the strings until their nails whitened. Izar did not know how to dance on land, let alone in the water, but the wine started singing through his veins, making his tailfin flick automatically.

The first song was called "The Undulating Jellyfish," Coralline told him. She and he began fluttering up and down along with everyone else, their arms rising and falling like the tentacles of a jellyfish—but Izar's hand smacked someone in the chin. After "The Undulating Jellyfish" came "The Anemone Dance," which involved swaying loosely side to side, arms swinging right and left. The motions resembled those of a homeless man on drugs Izar had once seen, but he enjoyed performing the dance with Coralline. The third song was tender and tragic, of longing and separation, of love that would remain unrequited. Unlike the previous two numbers, this dance, "The Seahorse Sprance," was a precise duo—Izar and Coralline twirled tautly up and down, arm in arm, as around an invisible pole.

Then, before Izar could stop himself, he leaned forward and kissed Coralline.

The lips that pressed themselves against hers were tender but insistent, pleading but punishing. Fingers rested like a whisper along her tailbone, then skipped up to the nape of her neck, creating pockets of tingles along the line of her spine. She leaned into the kiss. If Ecklon was betraying her, why should she not betray him?

"Cora," Izar said softly.

"*Coralline*—" she corrected emphatically, pulling away. Only Ecklon ever called her Cora.

Her hand curled around the rose petal tellin at her throat. The shell's smoothness, its gentle ridges, felt foreign under her fingers. Ecklon was betraying her—not for one moment had she stopped thinking about it since Sage Dahlia Delaisi had told her—but, still, that did not justify her betraying him.

What was she even doing here, at this Ball? *Meet me at the center of The Cupola when the music ends*, the back of the invitation to the Ball had stated. The Cupola was dome-shaped, and so its center was easy to pinpoint—and the floor was anyhow marked with a cross at the center—but who were they to meet at the center? Also, whoever it was, he would be looking for Tang Tarpon, not them. He would have no way of identifying Coralline and Izar, just as they had no way of identifying him. In fact, perhaps he'd heard of Tang's death and decided to skip the Ball altogether.

"What's wrong?" Izar asked her.

Coralline was too distraught to reply. She, who'd never had a tantrum before, felt like shouting with frustration. But then the music ended, and she busied herself with casting a frantic glance about The Cupola—for whom, she did not know. A face close to the ceiling caught her eye, belonging to a gangly, topaz-tailed merman wearing an off-white waistcoat. The merman's hair formed disheveled, white-gray streaks, and his eyes looked feverish and brooding. His complexion made Coralline think of a green moray eel. She recognized him—she'd never met him, but, somehow, felt certain she knew him.

His eyes were scanning the crowds, just like hers. Appearing to not have found the person he was looking for, he turned on his tail and started cutting a path toward the doors of The Cupola.

"Let's follow him!" Coralline called to Izar.

Colliding into heads and tails, Coralline and Izar hurtled upward diagonally through The Cupola in the merman's direction. But he was almost at the doors, just about to disappear into the darkness outside—in which case he would be practically impossible to find. Swerving around people, apologizing over her shoulder for knocking decanters out of hands, Coralline reached the merman just in time. Huffing for breath, she tapped his shoulder from behind. He turned around, but Izar, coming to a sudden stop behind her, collided into her, such that she collided into the merman. The decanter of bell sea wine in the merman's hand spilled upon his waistcoat, splotching the off-white fabric with green. He contemplated her with ill-concealed irritation from beneath ice-white eyebrows.

At close range, his face was unmistakable: She had seen it in the inside-jacket cover of *The Universe Demystified*. "Are you Venant Veritate?"

"Yes."

Beaming, Coralline introduced herself and Izar. She felt aflush with excitement at meeting her favorite author, but she tried to keep the giggle out of her voice and the idolism out of her eyes. "Are you looking for Tang Tarpon?" she asked. "And did you write the note on the back of Tang's invitation to the Ball, requesting him to meet you when the music ends?"

"Yes," Venant said, looking from her to Izar in surprise. "Tang is a good friend of mine."

But of course: The only volume on Tang's bookshelf other than the books he'd written himself had been *The Universe Demystified*. And of course Venant would be invited to the Ball of Blue Bottle, given his status as an esteemed stargazer. The murky anxiety that had just moments ago shrouded Coralline vanished—Venant was the most brilliant merman in Meristem, in her opinion. If anyone could help her find the elixir, it was he.

"Where is Tang?" Venant asked.

"Sadly, Tang has died. . . ." Coralline let her voice trail off.

"I didn't know that," Venant said, his face turning a dull gray. "How did he die?"

"He was murdered."

"By whom?"

Coralline glanced at Izar before turning back to Venant and muttering, "We're not sure."

"Is there a principal suspect at least?"

"No," she lied, swallowing her guilt. It would not do to inform Venant that she was the principal suspect in his friend's murder. In addition to refusing to help her, he might well turn her in to the Constables Department of Blue Bottle. "We're looking for the elixir," she said. "Tang suggested that the merman who wrote the note on the invitation—you—might be able to help us find the elixir, just as you helped him, thirty years ago. Would you know where we can find the elixir?"

Venant pointed a long forefinger toward the ceiling. Coralline glanced up at the luciferin orbs roving over it, then turned back to Venant quizzically.

"Eons ago, a star exploded in one of them," he said.

"One of what?" she asked.

"The constellations, of course."

"What do the constellations have to do with the elixir?" Izar asked.

"Everything, given that the elixir is made of starlight."

"Hmm . . ." Coralline said. "But do you know where the elixir can be found?"

"The deep sea."

But less was known about the deep sea than was known about the moon; was Venant the only person who did not know that? Had his studies of the universe led him to forget the basic tenets of life on earth? "The deep sea lies five thousand feet below the surface," Coralline said, trying to keep the impatience out of her voice. "It's a pitch-black abyss considered inaccessible to merpeople. Entering the deep sea is known to be a suicide mission. Wouldn't we die if we were to go there?"

"It's possible," Venant agreed.

A throng was starting to form around them—people were beginning to recognize Venant. He squirmed visibly, wringing his hands.

"If we were to enter the deep sea," Izar said, "how would we proceed once there?"

"I'll tell you what I told Tang: Seek the light."

"But isn't that an oxymoron," Coralline countered, "given that not one iota of light penetrates the deep sea?"

"If you require any further assistance," Venant continued, as though Coralline had not spoken, "you may find me at my Telescope Tower. It's a solitary place a short distance precisely southwest of Blue Bottle, about a half-hour's swim from here."

"Any further assistance!" Coralline cried. "But you haven't helped us at all. I can't imagine how I ever admired you!"

Venant's lips pressed together, and he looked at her grimly. Then, with a swish of his tailfin, he swam out the doors.

"Let's leave!" Coralline fumed to Izar.

She sliced a path through the throng toward the alcove where they'd deposited their satchels with a guard. They could have left their possessions in the Laminaria apartment, but Coralline's satchel had been on her person so consistently over the last days that she now considered it almost a part of her—like a turtle shell—and had decided to bring it along with her to the Ball. Izar had done the same.

On their way back to the Laminaria apartment, Coralline and Izar swam just over the seabed, because it was brightly lit by luciferin lampposts. Coralline knew it was farfetched, but she had hoped she would be leaving the Ball of Blue Bottle with the elixir in hand—she had even gone so far as to envision that, early tomorrow morning, she would start on her way home to Urchin Grove. Instead, at present, she did not even possess a reasonable *path* to the elixir, let alone the elixir itself.

"What's the matter, Cora?" Izar asked.

"Everything's the matter," she snapped. "And how many times do I need to tell you—it's *Coralline!*"

He scrutinized her but did not say anything.

Soon, Coralline saw the string-of-beads shape of the building Needle-to-the-Sky. Swinging her tailfin, she ascended from the seabed to the tenth-floor apartment, alongside Izar. But just as she reached the door, the waters above swirled as sharply as though clouds were plopping down into the ocean from the sky. The ripples were so thick and heavy that Coralline could see nothing through them, but she did not need to see to know who it was—Pavonis. The ripples were an alarm signal that something was wrong.

"Don't!" she whispered to Izar, but it was too late—he knocked on the door.

It flew open immediately. Limpet stood there, accompanied not by Linatella but by two mermen. All three of them wore deep-purple waistcoats with the black seal of the Under-Ministry of Crime and Murder. Limpet was a constable, Coralline realized with a jolt. She'd been pleased about staying with Limpet and Linatella because she'd thought constables would not search for her in a home—she'd never imagined that her host himself might be a constable. No, that was not true—she *had* imagined it, just briefly; when she'd first seen Limpet at the outskirts of the clearing around the corner, she had thought of a constable.

Now, his nostrils flared, and his brow furrowed dangerously—by sheltering someone beneath the law, he had, even if unintentionally, broken the law, probably for the first time in his life.

"Hands up, Coralline!" he said. "Not a flick of your tailfin!"

Coralline could not move even had she tried. In Limpet's scowl, she saw the Wrongdoers' Refinery; in his narrowed eyes, she saw a prison cell, with five bars across the windows, like gill slits. Her own gill slits no longer seemed to be functioning; she could not breathe.

Limpet extended a hand through the doorway to grasp her arm, but his hand was blocked: Pavonis descended vertically in front of the door, a pillar of muscle. His thirty-foot-long body trapped Limpet and the two other constables indoors. The supper-plate-sized windows of the apartment were too small to fit through, and this door formed the only way in and out of the apartment—unlike houses, apartments did not have back doors. In order to get out, Limpet and the two other constables would have to push Pavonis away from the door.

They started to thump his flesh, to push it with all their strength—Coralline could hear their efforts from Pavonis's other side. "Go, Coralline, go!" Pavonis said, in a voice muffled with pain.

"I'm not leaving without you," she cried, wrapping her arms around as much of him as she could.

"Stop being a fool, Coralline!" said a shrill voice.

Nacre. Coralline raised her head and looked about, discovering the snail on Pavonis's head, forming a small, bumpy shape like a wart.

"I'll follow you, Coralline," Pavonis muttered. "But I want you to get a head start on the constables."

"How will you follow me? How will you know where to find me? If we don't leave here together, we may lose one another."

"We can meet Pavonis at the Telescope Tower," Izar suggested hurriedly. "Venant said it's just a half-hour's swim precisely southwest of here."

"I'll find you there," Pavonis agreed, but with a grimace, as the wallops on the other side seemed to turn to thuds. "Now, *go!*"

"I won't leave you." Coralline curled around Pavonis such that her tail and torso together formed a C-shape around his length.

"Make yourself useful, human, and take her away!" Pavonis growled.

Izar's arm wrapped around Coralline's waist, and, in a single swipe, wrenched her away from Pavonis.

Abalone looked at Naiadum. His face was yellow and waxen, and his hands were folded over his chest as though he was already dead. Abalone wished she could leave his bedside, she wished she could change out of the mourning-black corset she'd been wearing for the last four days, but it would make her a bad mother. A good mother was supposed to sit by her son's bedside and watch him die.

"I hope Coralline returns with the elixir," Trochid said. He was sitting on a chair to the other side of Naiadum's bed, wearing a mourning-black waistcoat. "I wish she'd taken my dagger."

"I'm glad she didn't," Abalone rejoined. "Well-mannered mermaids don't wield daggers."

"Manners will not help her on her elixir quest."

"Well, they will help her get married. And goodness knows she could use help in that department. I can't even sleep anymore—that's how worried I am that Ecklon will cancel his wedding to her. Did you know, Rosette has been spreading rumors that Coralline left Urchin Grove for a lover?"

"We can't pay attention to rumors, Abalone."

"Well, everyone else does—Ecklon's mother, Epaulette, in particular. She's never liked us to begin with, and now she's adamant that Ecklon should cancel his wedding to Coralline. Sepia told me that our neighbors are laying bets on whether or not Ecklon will ditch Coralline. Most are betting that he will."

Abalone knew and followed gossip with the same passion and precision with which Trochid knew and followed science. She had not been surprised at Rosette's rumors; she had spread similar rumors herself twenty-five years ago, in order to ensure that it was she who married Trochid. There was a particular art and subtlety to the propagation of rumors; they were like the loose hair buns she often wore, appearing effortless and natural from outside but tightly pinned underneath, so as not to unravel.

"Don't worry," Trochid said. "Ecklon loves Coralline, and she loves him. It's as simple as that."

But it was never as simple as that, Abalone knew. Trochid did not know the lengths to which mermaids such as Rosette, and Abalone herself, went to secure good marriages.

Abalone found herself wishing, as she had repeatedly over the years, that Coralline were more like her. She wished Coralline had inherited her golden locks rather than having infernally black hair—hair that looked just like Rhodomela's. She wished Coralline paid more attention to edible algae than remedial—on feeding a merman's stomach rather than healing it. She wished Coralline took an interest in corsets, hair arrangements, homemaking. She wished Coralline were clever rather than intelligent, wily rather than kind.

Ever since Coralline was a young mergirl, Abalone had tried to influence and change her, and she would continue to try until the day she died, but she sometimes fretted that it was hopeless. After all, it was not easy to change people. If her marriage had taught her anything, it was that.

Glancing at Trochid, Abalone asked herself: After twenty-five years of marriage, how could it be that she and he felt differently about everything under the sun, including their children? (Everything that she considered to be a vice in Coralline, he considered a virtue.) Were they a happy couple? Would Trochid have been happier with the mermaid he was supposed to have married, twenty-five years ago? Had Abalone done the wrong thing by stealing him away, as Rosette was now trying to steal Ecklon away?

Coralline peeked out from around the wall of the Telescope Tower, a solitary structure that stuck straight out of the sand like a pen. She and Izar had found it easily—it was precisely southwest of Blue Bottle, as Venant had said.

"Where is Pavonis?" she whispered. "We've been here awhile, and he should have arrived here soon after us. Do you think Limpet and the two other constables injured him so much that he can't swim?"

"I hope not," Izar said.

If anything happened to Pavonis, she would never forgive herself. Life without him greeting her at the window and making sarcastic jokes was a life she could not bear to imagine. Could it be that he wasn't here because he was dead—just as his best friend, Mako, was dead? Coralline collapsed against the wall, limp as a starfish at the thought.

"Look, Coralline!" Izar cried.

She jerked her head up. She held her luciferin lantern over her head, but in the darkness of night, she could see close to nothing. She could *feel,* though, what Izar must also be feeling—a rising swell of water. It was a swell she knew, but it did not shove her away by its power, as it usually did—instead, it nudged her weakly. It was Pavonis, but Pavonis debilitated.

No sooner had Pavonis's snout come to a stop than Coralline threw herself at him, wrapping herself around him as tightly as a bandage of pyropia. "I'm so glad you're alive, Pavonis!"

There was a stiffness to his flesh. Coralline recognized it as surely as she would recognize a change in a mattress upon which she'd lain all her life. "How are you?" she whispered.

"Fine."

"He's not fine!" said a low, tremulous voice. Coralline held her luciferin lantern toward the line of Pavonis's mouth. Altair was slipping out from

233

within, a flame of orange. "I'm shaking myself, and I was safe and sheltered in his mouth throughout the altercation. He stayed there blocking the door for long, very long, to ensure you got a head start, Coralline. When he eventually removed himself from the door, the constables followed him, but he swam fast enough to lose them."

"The Ogre is a hero!" Nacre said, her twittering tentacles creating shifting shadows over Pavonis's head, "and I am a heroine, for having orchestrated the escape. The Pole Dancer may wear a coronet, but I'm a Queen. While he was shuddering in the Ogre's mouth, I was riding atop the Ogre's head—"

"Stop calling Pavonis an Ogre and Altair a Pole Dancer!" Coralline snapped. "And this is not the right time to be drowning yourself in praise."

"In her defense," Altair said with a sigh, "much as I hate to admit it, Nacre did play a crucial role in the escape tonight. If not for her skillful snooping, you would be at the Wrongdoers' Refinery at this moment, Coralline, awaiting trial for the murder of Tang Tarpon."

"Yes indeed!" Nacre huffed. "The least you can do is give me a little credit, Coralline, and learn how I did it all. I was lounging in the Laminaria guest bedroom and was just about to do my second-favorite thing in the world, snoozing, when I was called upon by fate to do my first-favorite thing, snooping. I heard Limpet return home and tell Linatella that he'd come to learn you were wanted for murder, Coralline, according to a scroll the Constables Department of Blue Bottle had just received from the Constables Department of Hog's Bristle. Limpet and his fellow constables decided to await you at the door and to arrest you upon your return from the Ball of Blue Bottle. When the Ogre—Pavonis, I mean—returned from his day-long excursion around the city, I attracted his attention by waggling my tentacles from the guest bedroom's windowsill. He approached me, I clambered onto his head, and we swooped down to the rocks to gather the Pole Dancer—Altair, I mean. Like the three constables, the three of us awaited the two of you."

"Thank you, Nacre," Coralline said, feeling guilty for how she'd spoken to her. "And thank you also, Altair." Turning back to Pavonis, Coralline stroked his side and asked, "Where exactly are you hurting?"

"In my inner ear."

"What?"

"I'm hurting from this conversation."

"This is not a time for jokes, Pavonis. You should not have taken a beating for me. Oh, how I wish I were an animal apothecary, so I could help you!"

"You can help me by going inside the Telescope Tower. I think we lost the constables, but it's possible they're still out and about, searching. I don't want my efforts to have been in vain."

Nodding, patting him once more, Coralline turned to the door of the Telescope Tower. Drawing a deep breath, feeling quite beggarly, she knocked on the door.

"Well, hello," said Venant, holding the door open for Coralline and Izar to enter, as though he'd been expecting them.

His living room was small and cluttered, with two old, low settees scattered with books, pens lying idly in the curve of their spines. "We are each grains of sand in the billowing vastness of the universe," stated a placard on the wall; Coralline recognized the sentence as belonging to *The Universe Demystified*. A large map of Meristem hung next to the placard, settlements marked on it as bubbles. Coralline found it ironic that Venant, who'd helped map the Milky Way galaxy, lived in a place that was not even on the map of Meristem—how strange that an explorer of the universe should have such a narrow personal universe.

Venant shuffled aside some books to make room on the settees, and Coralline and Izar took a seat across from him.

"I'm sorry for how I spoke to you at the Ball," Coralline said, her cheeks flushing. "I will always admire you and your work. I didn't mean what I said."

"Think nothing of it." Venant's slight smile reminded Coralline of her father's.

"I also lied to you." Ignoring Izar's warning look, she continued, "*I* am the principal suspect in Tang Tarpon's murder. He was stabbed by a dagger. I was about to pull out the dagger, but a loiterer saw my hands wrapped around the hilt and assumed that it was I who had stabbed him."

Coralline had not told Limpet about Tang's murder and had been chased away by him; if Venant wished them to leave, she would rather leave now.

Venant frowned at her for a long, unblinking moment. "I can't imagine your having done it—" he began, but his words were interrupted by a cough that racked through his chest, juddering through each of his ribs. "Excuse me . . . I'm not well," he spouted out from between hacks.

The reason Coralline had thought of a green moray eel when she'd first seen Venant was that there was a greenish hue to his complexion, she realized now. She almost rose to examine him, but she pressed her tail down onto the settee with her hands, in order to remain where she was. Just as she could not treat Pavonis, given that she was not an animal apothecary, she could not treat Venant, given that she was a fired apprentice apothecary.

"Please help us find the elixir," Coralline said, when Venant's cough had settled.

"I know the deep sea seems terrifying, and I confess I've never ventured to it for that reason myself, but it is there that you will find the elixir—so long as you seek the light."

"What stretch of deep sea do you recommend?" Izar asked.

"Swim straight that way," Venant said, his hand pointing out the window behind Coralline. Noticing the luciferin lantern sticking out of her satchel, he continued, "Feel free to take an extra lantern with you, that one on the side table there. Also, I should warn you: Constables do occasionally visit my home when searching for suspects, so I suggest you start your voyage to the deep sea early in the morning." After a vigorous cough, he sputtered, "Now, I'm afraid I must retire."

Rising from the settees, Coralline and Izar followed Venant out the living room window. Venant's bedroom was directly above the living room, and he entered his bedroom through its window, calling over his shoulder that the guest bedroom was directly above his.

Izar entered the guest bedroom first, followed by Coralline. The Telescope Tower narrowed as it ascended, which meant that the guest bedroom was even smaller than the living room. It contained a dilapidated desk, a worn chair, and a bed adorned with a ragged blanket. Coralline would have liked to ask Izar to sleep on the floor, or anywhere but the bed, but the room was so tiny, there was no space on the floor. As she wavered next to the bed, Izar collapsed on the blanket on his stomach. He turned his face to one side, closed his eyes, and, in a matter of moments, started making a series of repetitive noises, like the snorts of a grunt sculpin.

Perhaps he was unwell, too, Coralline thought, as everyone else seemed to be—Venant, Pavonis. She came to hover horizontally over him, and, smoothing his chestnut curls back from his forehead, touched his brow with the back of her hand. He did not have a fever, at least. And yet he continued to rumble rhythmically, monotonously. Perhaps these were sounds humans made as they slept, she thought.

As she looked down at his face, she wondered whether it could be true, whether he had feelings for her, as Nacre had asserted. Was that why he'd kissed her at the Ball? Why had she kissed him back, though? . . . Because she'd had a momentary desire to betray Ecklon, as Ecklon was betraying her. Yes, that had to be it.

She did not have the heart to nudge Izar awake and ask him to find alternate accommodations. She started to drift to her side of the bed, eager to rest her head on the pillow—but she jumped along the way: An eye was watching her through the window.

"We need to talk," Pavonis said coldly.

"Are the two of you sharing a bed tonight?" Altair asked Coralline.

"Yes, but—"

"Did the two of you share a bed last night?" Altair persisted, in an interrogative tone that reminded Coralline of Ecklon.

"Yes, but nothing happened." Coralline dangled her lantern over the smattering of stones from which Altair's voice was emerging, but he had camouflaged himself so thoroughly that she could not locate him. His voice seemed to be spewing out of a vacuum.

It was Altair's extremities that turned orange first—his star-shaped coronet and the tip of his tail—and then the rest of him blazed to life, forming a contorted, glowing arrow the size of Coralline's hand. "Will you be journeying into the deep sea with Izar?"

"*Yes.*" The vehemence of her reply told Coralline that her decision was made—she would be exploring the deep sea, even if it killed her.

"What about Ecklon?" Altair asked.

"What about him?" Coralline said impatiently.

"What about him! You are to marry Ecklon in just ten days, and yet you are cavorting with a human, spending not only your days but also your nights with him. Do you even realize that you're at the center of a lurid love triangle?"

"No."

"I knew it was a bad idea to leave on this Elixir Expedition without Ecklon," Altair continued, somewhat hysterically. "I knew—"

"Izar and I haven't *done* anything," Coralline snapped, though she supposed it wasn't quite true: Her lips were still tingling from their kiss at the Ball.

"Infidelity is not an act," Altair countered quietly, "but a feeling."

"Well, Ecklon need be none the wiser about anything," Nacre quipped. "Also, Coralline and I have it on good authority that Ecklon is betraying her."

"What authority?" Pavonis said.

"A sage," Nacre said conspirationally.

"A *sage*!" Altair sputtered. "A fortune teller! You're making life decisions now based on a fortune teller, Coralline? Is that how bad things have gotten?"

"I know what you mean," Coralline said, "and I felt similarly at first, but the sage was uncannily right about everything else about me. I don't see how she could be wrong about this. Either way, what do you want from me?"

"I want you to understand," began Altair, "that entering the deep sea with Izar—relying on him wholly for survival, as he will rely on you—will forge an unbreakable bond between the two of you. For that reason, and for the reason that a mission to the deep sea is known to be suicidal—I suggest we turn back now and return home. You may be immoral these days, but do not fool yourself into thinking you are immortal. If you return home now, you will not save your brother, but you will at least save your relationship with Ecklon. If you enter the deep sea with Izar, you risk losing not only your brother, but also your own life, and the life you are soon to share with Ecklon."

Coralline trembled, offended by Altair but unable to deny his logic.

"Stop preaching, Pole Dancer!" Nacre's tentacles waggled at the greatest speed Coralline had yet seen. "Coralline is not going to turn back now, not when she's so close to the elixir. You just want to go home because you've been useless throughout the Elixir Expedition. Pavonis has led and navigated; I have eavesdropped and orchestrated. What have *you* contributed to this Elixir Expedition, besides your unsolicited sermons? Nothing, that's what. Coralline may be too blind to see through your veneer, but I'm not: You just want to return home so you can continue to live your boring little life in your boring little reef, where you can start your boring little family!"

"How dare you, you unbearable wretch!" Altair said, in a voice like a cracking urn. "Coralline may be unable to see through *your* veneer—your desire to manipulate and control her, just like her mother!"

Coralline shivered. She had heard Nacre rant before—and Pavonis as well—but Altair losing his temper was as unprecedented as her father shouting in anger.

"What do you think, Pavonis, about the idea of my entering the deep sea?" Coralline asked, drawing the lantern toward the line of his mouth.

"I'll accompany you. Nacre and Altair will not be joining us, thankfully, given their inability to withstand the pressures of the deep—pressures both internal and external. I myself have always dreamt of venturing into the heart of darkness. It will be the height—or rather, the depth—of adventure."

"You can't enter the deep sea with me. You're injured."

"I'll be fine by morning."

"You won't. I can't examine you now, in the dark, but I don't need to be an animal apothecary to know that you must be severely bruised—if not worse. It'll take at least a few days for the pain to go away, and then at least a couple of weeks after that for a complete recovery."

"Don't you understand?" Pavonis said. "Even in the best of circumstances, you can never trust a human. In *this* human's case, in particular, I'm willing to bet my snout he's keeping a secret from us—a secret that would change everything. In the deep sea, if the two of you do find the elixir, he might well kill you for it. He might well take the elixir, transform to a human, and return to land, without anyone being any the wiser. I can protect you, Coralline, as I always have."

"You have always protected me, it's true, and I am grateful for it, but I don't need protection anymore." Coralline paused, as her statement sank in.

"Stop with the bravado!" Pavonis said. "You do need protection."

Just a short while ago, the sight of Pavonis arriving at the Telescope Tower had filled Coralline with relief; now, she clenched her hands at her sides and quivered, hurt by his words.

"Let's all go home, Coralline—" Altair began.

"We will not go home—" Nacre interrupted.

"Stop telling me what to do with my life, all of you!" Coralline bellowed. "I'll make my own decisions. I wish I hadn't embarked on this Elixir Expedition with all of you. I'm glad you won't be with me in the deep sea. Good riddance!"

Holding her lantern high above her head, she rose rapidly up to the guest bedroom, knowing that three sets of eyes stared after her.

21

Abyss

Coralline took her own lantern, and Izar took Venant's lantern from the side table in the living room. They swept out the window just as rays of dawn were starting to lacerate the waters.

"Do you see them?" Coralline asked.

"Who?"

"Pavonis, Altair, and Nacre."

Izar cast a glance about the vicinity of the Tower—Pavonis was as difficult to miss as a helicopter; as for the other two, they were, in general, too small for him to notice. Coralline's eyes scanned the waters thoroughly, her face falling when she failed to locate them.

"I was mean to them last night," she confessed. "I think they've disappeared because they're upset. I would have liked to apologize to them before leaving, but I can tell they don't want to talk to me."

"How can you tell?"

"Altair and Nacre can't go far alone, given their species. They're probably watching us as we speak, Altair camouflaged, Nacre hidden in some crevice. Pavonis is probably not far from here either. . . . I don't know what's gotten into me. I was awful to Venant; I was awful to them."

"Don't be hard on yourself. You're under a lot of pressure."

"That doesn't justify anything."

"We don't have to enter the deep sea, you know."

"Venant said the elixir is in the deep sea," Coralline said in a mechanical voice. "I must get it to save my brother."

Izar swallowed his guilt—if not for his oil spill, she would not be in this situation to begin with. When he had awoken this morning, he had found Coralline curled to the other side of the bed like a partially coiled snake. The line of her shoulders, the narrowness of her wrists, even the slant of her chin—everything about her had looked as fragile as china, and he had been loath to wake her up, let alone urge a trek into the darkness. But she'd awoken on her own soon after him and had said they must hurry. Facing away from each other, they had changed under the shifting glow of the luciferin orbs traveling the ceiling. They had turned around to discover that they were both wearing gray—dull attire to match their dull mood.

Now, they proceeded in the direction indicated by Venant last night. They traveled just over the seabed, which sloped downward, then started to plummet as precipitously as a cliff. The level of light began to dissipate abruptly, such that Izar had the sense he was voyaging through angry storm clouds. Having assumed the darkness would commence slowly, he felt thwarted by its rapid approach, as though he was being subject to a sudden burn when he'd registered for a slow flame.

But the burn kept intensifying.

Sheets of blackness folded in all around them. The darkness of the deep sea was not of night but of eternal night, Izar saw, and so it was constituted of a different fabric, like air from a different planet. It was torturous—Izar felt as though he'd blindfolded himself, and, with every flick of his tailfin, the blindfold was growing tighter.

He turned his head toward Coralline. Though he could feel her presence by his side in the ripples of water, he could not see her until he held his luciferin lantern in her direction. He extended his hand toward her, and she extended her hand toward him simultaneously. Their fingers intertwined, and a shiver tingled down his back. He asked himself why he'd kissed her at the Ball. He could think of no answer.

Lights appeared and disappeared all around them like fireflies in a forest. Unlike fireflies, though, these glimmers approached him and Coralline, brushing past their skin and scales. In the darkness, it was impossible to make out the colors and patterns of the animals—only their sparks and silhouettes were visible.

"Why are they approaching us?" Izar asked Coralline.

"Because they've never seen people before."

"I wish they'd leave us alone. What kinds of animals are they?"

"I'm not sure. Even if I could see them, I wouldn't recognize them, because I've never seen them before. The deep sea is almost as different from the open ocean as the open ocean is from land."

Izar shuddered as a creature several times his length, with the silhouette of a squid—could it be a giant squid?—grazed past his shoulder. "Venant told us to seek the light," he said, trying to focus. "What do you think he meant by that?"

"I can't imagine."

"You said you're the detective investigating the murder of Tang Tarpon?" Limpet clarified.

"Yes," Ecklon replied. "As you know, Coralline Costaria is, at this stage, the principal suspect in Tang Tarpon's murder."

"Yes, but how did you come to find us?" Limpet asked suspiciously.

"The Constables Department of Hog's Bristle informed me. They received a memo from the Constables Department of Blue Bottle stating that Coralline Costaria was last sighted here, in your home."

Limpet nodded, his brows scrunching over his bulbous nose. Ecklon imagined it didn't bode well for Limpet's career that a murder suspect had slipped out through his fingers.

"We felt sorry for Coralline and her companion Izar," Linatella said, toying with her white-gold hair, "and invited them to stay in our home. They accepted."

"I see," Ecklon said, trying to keep the drowsiness out of his eyes, the sleeplessness out of his voice. He had swum straight through the night in order to arrive in Blue Bottle this morning. His head was pounding, and he longed to press his thumbs to his temples, but in an effort to be professional, he continued to sit straight on the settee and look at Limpet and Linatella evenly.

"What did the relationship between Coralline and Izar appear to be?" Ecklon asked in a deliberately nonchalant voice. As a detective, he was trained to pose questions casually, in order to ensnare others into betraying information casually, but now, his sole goal was to try to not betray his personal stake in the case. If the Laminarias learned he was Coralline's fiancé, it would affect what they shared with him.

"Coralline and Izar were a couple, of course," Linatella replied.

"What leads you to say so?" Ecklon inquired, more sharply than he'd intended.

"It was obvious," Linatella said, "in the way Coralline cared for him when he was ill, in the way Izar looked at her during breakfast, in the rose petal tellin shell at her throat, in the beautiful corset he got her for the Ball."

Forgetting himself, Ecklon dropped his head into his hands and massaged his temples. He had planned to get Coralline plenty of corsets when they were married, but he had never gotten her one before. It was such a personal present, something ordinary but intimate, worn directly on the skin.

"Coralline and Izar shared that guest bedroom there behind you," Limpet said.

Swiveling from the waist, Ecklon stared into the guest bedroom through its open door. Limpet and Linatella would assume he was trying to memorize the details of the room, but all he noticed was its bed—the narrowness of it. The loiterer Wentle Varice in Hog's Bristle had mentioned that he had seen Coralline with a merman in Tang's home. Ecklon had not thought much of it then, but he could not avoid thinking of it now. He also could not avoid thinking of the rumor he'd heard in Urchin Grove—that Coralline had left home not to save her brother but for a lover.

Now that he was turned away from the Laminarias, he permitted his face to crumble, his eyes to fall half closed, his cheeks to sag. But when he turned back to Limpet and Linatella, his face was again a closed mask.

"Do you think Coralline will get caught?" Limpet asked.

"If she's guilty, yes."

A rumble sounded. Coralline could not tell whether it had issued from her stomach or Izar's.

"Are you hungry?" Izar asked.

"Famished. And you?"

"Same. How long do you think we've been in the deep sea?"

"I'm very sleepy," Coralline said, "which leads me to think we've been here at least a day, and likely closer to two days."

Time and space were anchors of life, but in the deep sea, Coralline had no measure of either. The loss of both anchors was, for her mind, equivalent to what the loss of her arms would be for her body. She was flailing, drifting, unmoored, unbalanced. As she looked about her into the impenetrable darkness, she had the sense of wandering through a black hole in space.

She, of all merpeople, was particularly unaccustomed to darkness, being among the few adults she knew who kept all her luciferin orbs bright all through the night. If ordinary darkness could be compared to a scratch on the skin—causing temporary discomfort—the darkness of the deep sea could be compared to a malignant tumor, fast spreading through the organs, she saw now. Last night, her challenge had been to lose the constables; this eternal night, her challenge was to not lose herself. People died in the deep sea not of the darkness outside but of the darkness within.

Izar tugged at her hand. Her eyes opened; only then did she realize that they had closed. Her eyes were redundant in the deep sea—it did not matter whether they were open or closed, for she could not see regardless. Izar also could not see, but he must have sensed her semiconscious state in the looseness of her hand. "Stay with me, Coralline," he said gently. "Let's seek the light, as Venant instructed."

Her eyes closed again, as heavily as though stones had settled upon the lids. There was a strain on her shoulder socket, and she had the sensation of lying upon a mattress of shifting ripples; it meant that Izar was dragging her along by a hand.

"What's that, Coralline?" he said, juddering her arm.

Her eyes opened lethargically, then widened. In the distance stood what looked to be an immense luciferin orb, blindingly bright, many times larger than The Cupola.

"This has to be the light Venant was referring to!" Izar cried.

Tails swinging, they swam to the light—then entered the light itself. Coralline reached out a hand; the particles of light danced away from her, as though they had a life of their own.

The seabed below the particles looked like a fragmented plate of rocks; through the cracks, she could discern more light below, as though a slice of the sun were hiding there, at the bottom of the ocean.

A rock-face flew open. A column of light erupted—magnetic, irresistible. The light yanked Coralline and Izar down through the rock-face like a rope to the navel.

Izar found himself in a vast bottomless cavern, shimmering with thousands of silver particles like stars in the night sky. The particles' energy filtered through his muscles, replacing sleep and sustenance. Previously exhausted, though he'd tried to hide it from Coralline, he suddenly felt exhilarated.

"Many have tried to find me but failed. You succeeded."

It was a voice that could not be detected by the ears, a voice that went straight to the heart. It did not belong to the ocean; it did not belong to earth. Izar and Coralline cast a glance about the cavern to discover its source, then turned back to each other, puzzled.

"I am everywhere, and I am nowhere."

The voice seemed to be coming from each silver particle, and yet no particle.

"One must experience true darkness in order to know true light. You did, and so I let you into my universe."

"Who are you?" Izar asked.

"Mintaka."

"*What* are you?" Coralline whispered.

"A fragment of a star."

Izar looked at Coralline, then turned back to the stardust.

"When I was a whole star," Mintaka continued, "I yearned to nourish planets with my energy. My desire to nurture life outside of my own was the desire to become a mother, in essence. But I could not be a mother—unlike most stars, I was not blessed with a family of planets. One day, my despondence reached such an abyss that, I'm ashamed to say, I exploded. I had hoped to die, but I learned that stars don't easily die—our energy is boundless, practically immortal.

"Shattered, I floated about the universe, trying to decide where I wished to settle. After thousands of years of wandering, I happened to pass the earth. I saw that it harbored life. Life was what I most cherished, what I'd most wanted to birth, and here, I saw that it existed in absurdly lush abundance. I glided down to earth. Once here, I decided to settle in the deep sea because it most resembles the universe, with its darkness broken by sparks of light. In this hidden universe I created my own hidden universe. The particles all around you possess the power to heal, because every particle of a star creates light in darkness, something in nothing."

Numerous particles coalesced in front of Izar and Coralline, forming a silver ball with the diameter of a quarter. They extended their clasped hands toward the ball, but it shifted out of their reach. They tried again; the ball moved farther away.

"The elixir is a blessing that comes accompanied by a curse," Mintaka said. "Would you still like to have it?"

"Yes," Izar and Coralline said simultaneously.

"Very well. I will tell each of your curses to you alone. Only you will know it, not the other."

The celebration will be a funeral, Izar heard.

What could it mean? he wondered. What celebration? Whose funeral? Would it be his own celebration or his own funeral—or both? There was no celebration he was anticipating in the near future. It did not have to be the near future, though, he reminded himself: Tang Tarpon's curse—*Beware of the serpent*—had materialized thirty years after Mintaka's pronouncement of it. There was no reason for Izar to assume that the celebration and funeral in his own future would occur in a matter of days rather than decades. The thought brought him relief.

He turned to Coralline. Her lips were dejected, her eyes drooping. Whatever Mintaka had told her, it seemed more serious than what she had told him.

Izar looked at the elixir dangling in front of them. It was so light yet so heavy, life-saving but potentially also life-taking. He and Coralline reached for it together with their joined hands. Izar's hand was over Coralline's, and so it was the palm of her hand that wrapped around the elixir, but energy from the elixir transmitted through to his own fingers—he felt stronger even just holding the elixir.

"Thank you, Mintaka," he and Coralline said.

Together, they ascended through the cavern and slipped out of the blinding light into the blinding darkness. They continued to rise steadily up, the elixir acting as a tiny but powerful torch illuminating their path.

22

Healer

To Coralline, the sight of the Telescope Tower was not just the sight of the Telescope Tower—it was the sight of reality. The voyage into the deep sea had started off a nightmare, and then, in Mintaka's cavern, had turned into a dream. The only evidence that it had all actually happened was the elixir in her hand.

"Well, finally," drawled a voice. "I thought my tail might lob off while I waited."

Coralline looked up to see Pavonis's great white belly swooping down, generating a ripple that pushed her back. His snout arrived before her, and she patted it eagerly, resting her cheek against it for a moment. "I missed you!" she said. "I'm sorry for what I said to you before I left. I didn't mean a word of it."

"I'm sorry, too. You're right—you don't need my protection. Your return from the deep sea proves it."

Coralline cringed to see a dark bruise almost as long as her on his side, a souvenir from the constable altercation at the Laminaria apartment. She pressed her fingers into the bruise—his muscles tensed. "Does it hurt?" she asked.

"Only when you prod it."

"You're back!"

Nacre. Turning away from Pavonis, Coralline located the snail's red-and-white carapace not next to a window, where she would have expected it, for ease of snooping, but in a spot of short, stubbly grass.

Altair favored grass, Coralline knew, because he could wrap his tail around a strand and thus anchor himself against the currents. As such, Coralline sought him in the same patch, for it was the only patch of grass in the vicinity of the Telescope Tower. He materialized momentarily, glowing orange.

"I owe the two of you an apology as well," Coralline said, looking from the snail to the seahorse.

They didn't seem to be listening—they were staring at Coralline's and Izar's clasped hands. Nacre's tentacles fell perfectly still. Altair paled, as though by being unseen, he could unsee. Pavonis swerved his enormous head to study their joined hands with his second eye, as though to ensure the first eye had not become defunct.

Coralline became aware of the location and angle of each of her fingers as they lay intertwined with Izar's. What were the two of them doing holding hands? And why did it feel so natural that she had not stopped to think about it before now?

"Do you have the elixir?" Nacre demanded.

"Yes!" With a smile that flooded her whole being, Coralline jutted her and Izar's clasped hands forward. Both sets of fingers opened in unison, and there it glimmered, as dazzling as a spot of sunlight.

"Victory is ours at last!" Pavonis yelled, his tailfin thumping against the shale of the Tower.

"Careful!" Nacre said. "You'll wake Venant up."

"Why is Venant sleeping at this hour?" Coralline asked. "It's not even dark yet."

"He's sick," Altair replied.

Continuing to clutch Izar's hand, Coralline peered through Venant's bedroom window. The stargazer lay curled and slumped in bed, his fingers clasping the edge of his blanket. His complexion was pastier than before and made Coralline think not of a green moray eel anymore, but a wrinkled turtle. He coughed in his sleep, so hard that the entire bed frame rattled. She should have examined him before she'd left; had she done so, maybe he would not be so sick now.

"I'll check on him," Coralline said, turning her head to look at Izar.

He nodded at her and started to disentangle his fingers from hers. It was necessary, for she would be unable to check on Venant while holding hands with Izar, but they had held hands for so long—they'd been in the deep sea for the better part of two days—that their fingers seemed to have molded around each other's. As their hands separated, Coralline cringed first with pain, then with anxiety. As long as they'd both held the elixir, it had belonged to both of them. Now, would it belong to him or to her?

An argument could be made that it should belong to him, for she had been useless in the deep sea, flopping about limply. Nacre had been right in what she'd said earlier: The Ball of Blue Bottle had served as the gateway to the greatest test of Coralline's life—the deep sea. Nacre had also been right about the crucial role Izar had played in the test—Coralline would have been unable to voyage through the deep sea without him. In the environment of starvation and sleep deprivation, he had formed her sole sustenance—his hand in hers had served as her only reminder that there existed consciousness outside of herself. He could have abandoned her at any point; exhausted, faint-headed, she would quite possibly not have had the strength to find her way out of the deep sea and would have died there, in the dark.

Izar's hand reached toward the elixir on the palm of her hand. Coralline feared he would snatch it away, but instead, he closed each of her fingers around it.

Should I become human again, Izar asked himself in the guest bedroom, *or should I remain a merman? In other words, should I return to the helm of Ocean Dominion or remain with Coralline?*

Sitting at the foot of the bed, Izar examined his identification card. His name was written in small letters below the company name, as though Ocean Dominion were his primary identity and his name a secondary one.

The night of the press conference, Izar had been shattered at the thought of being forced out of Ocean Dominion. Now, when he was co-president, could he truly leave it all behind? All those long nights in his Invention Chamber, all those long days in his office and aboard ships—were they all to amount to nothing? To not lead Ocean Dominion to new heights, to not plunder the ocean floor to new depths, to not see the things Castor was capable of—would that not be as good as death? Could Izar give up everything he'd ever worked for—and that, too, for a mermaid?

No. He'd told Coralline he belonged to Ocean Protection, and he seemed to have come to believe it. His time in the water had muddled him—

The doorknob turned. The identification card in his hand slipped from his fingers. Catching it, he lurched off the foot of the bed and extended his arm toward his satchel on the desk chair, dropping the card just above the satchel—it would waft down into the satchel on its own, as everything lilted and wafted in the water. Coralline slipped into the room just as he plopped down again on the foot of the bed.

"Venant has the flu," she said, speaking more to herself than him. "It's severe, but not life-threatening. The waters are getting dark now, and it's hard for me to tell fronds apart at night, but I'll prepare a remedy for him first thing in the morning. Probably Virus Vanquisher or Flu Fighter. . . ."

Izar thought of their times together: The moment he'd first seen her, staring at him with her big blue-green eyes; the turbulent morning in Bristled Bed and Breakfast, when he'd saved her from the lecherous brothers; the nervous concentration in her face as she'd prodded his wrist before agreeing to extract the platinum chip; her arm draping his chest when he'd awoken in the Laminaria guest bedroom; the shimmer of her silver-sequined corset at the Ball.

Since the Ball, he'd wondered why he'd kissed her. Now, his mind began to create a list of attributes to describe her—kind, fair, intelligent—but his heart told him that such a list was pointless. His feeling for her could not be reduced to a formula; it was more like a fragrance—impossible to disassemble into constituents. She was a healer, and, somehow, she had healed him. Through her presence, she could continue to heal him.

He would return to Menkar to see his brother and father, he decided, to tell them he was still alive. It would be risky to return to land—Zaurak and Serpens might well try to kill him—but Antares and Saiph must be worried sick about him, and he did not want them to spend the rest of their lives searching for him. He would tell them that he'd met a mermaid and wanted to see if they could have a future together. It went without saying that he would no longer be able to work for Ocean Dominion.

It also went without saying that he would have to destroy Castor.

But the thought of destroying Castor was like stabbing one's own son, for he'd spent six years developing Castor. He had no other choice, though—it was either Coralline or Castor, and it had to be Coralline. She would never come to know it, but, because of her, merpeople would be saved; they would continue to live.

Upon his return from Menkar to Meristem, Izar would tell Coralline the truth about everything. He would tell her that he had worked not at Ocean Protection but Ocean Dominion, and that he was responsible for the oil spill that had sickened her brother and the dynamite blast that had severed her father's hand. It was possible she would not forgive him, and, by then, he would already have detached himself from Ocean Dominion. Her refusal would leave him hopelessly adrift, like a log of wood on the waves, belonging neither to land nor to water, but it was a chance he was willing to take.

Coralline approached him, hovering just before him at the foot of the bed. "What shall we do about the elixir?" she asked quietly, her hand unfurling. The elixir's light broke through the room, making her eyes glitter like liquid crystals.

"The elixir is yours," Izar said, "for your brother."

"But how will you become a human again?"

"I think I can transform without the elixir, actually."

"What? But how?"

"I've been thinking about it. When that Ocean Dominion ship strung me up in the air in a fishnet, my gills prickled, and my tail hurt as though a saw was cleaving it into two. I believe it's because I was about to transform into a human again. When you slashed me out of the net and took me into the water, the merman-human transformation was thwarted, and so I ended up remaining a merman. It's just as well, because the men would have shot me if they'd seen me come back to life in the net. In the air, my body seems to automatically become human, and, in the water, it automatically becomes merman."

"How can that be?"

"I can't imagine."

"Did you realize this before the deep sea or after?"

"Hmm . . . Before, I suppose. Why?"

"Because if you didn't need the elixir, I don't understand why you would enter the deep sea with me and risk your life to look for it."

Izar chuckled. His contemplation moments ago had clearly been an exercise in mental circles, for his actions suggested that his decision was made—he chose Coralline over Ocean Dominion. "I love you," he said softly.

Coralline's heart fluttered.

As a healer, she had always cared for others. No one had ever cared for her as Izar had in the deep sea. In Mintaka's cavern, when she'd looked at Izar's face, in that true light, she had felt as though she were glimpsing his true self. She had felt as one with him, and it was that oneness that she'd wanted to preserve, she realized now, when she'd refused to leave his hand in front of Pavonis, Altair, and Nacre.

"I think I love you, too," Coralline whispered.

23

Hummer

Half a dozen luciferin orbs traveled above Izar and Coralline, but their glow was beginning to dull, for rays of dawn had started to lash the waters outside. It was an ingenuity of nature, Izar thought, that the bacteria inside the glassy spheres glowed automatically in the dark and faded automatically in the light; it was equivalent to lightbulbs switching themselves on and off and also moderating their own intensity.

Izar turned his head to look at Coralline, next to him in bed. Though one hand of hers was clasped with his, her other hand was tracing circles over the pale-pink shell at her throat.

"What's wrong?" he asked.

"Nothing," she said, but she did not meet his eyes.

Izar slipped out of bed and fumbled through his satchel on the desk chair. He extracted the amber scroll from his gray tin, then slipped back under the blanket. Unrolling the scroll, he perused the single line scribbled on it: *Find Tang Tarpon. He will guide you to the elixir.* Below the line, at the bottom-right corner of the parchment, only the letter *O* remained in the name of the author; the rest of the name had been erased when Izar had held the parchment under the faucet at Ocean Dominion. Izar turned the note over and ran his thumb over the embossed P&P logo Tang had noticed in its top-left corner.

"When we were in Tang's house," Izar said, looking at Coralline, "he said that this logo is of a stationery shop called Printer & Parchment, located in Velvet Horn. I'd like to trace this note back to that stationery shop and locate this person whose name starts with the letter *O*. According to the map of Meristem in Venant's living room, Velvet Horn is just a short distance away from here. It should be a swim of about an hour or so, I think."

"But why do you want to trace the note?"

Because Izar wanted—rather, needed—to know: How had he come to possess the note? What was he even doing in the ocean? How could he transform automatically between human and merman? There was a chance he would find the answers to these questions by tracing the note to its source. But he could not find the words to explain any of this to Coralline. It was, more than anything else, a hunch.

"You can consider it a personal errand," he said. "I'll explain when I'm back. In the meantime, I'm sorry to ask this—I know you want to return home with the elixir as soon as possible for your brother—but would you give me just this morning to see if I can trace this note? Maybe you can prepare a remedy for Venant while I'm gone? I promise I'll be back to you no later than noon. Then I'd like to accompany you to Urchin Grove."

"What? Why?"

Izar had been hoping for enthusiasm, but he could understand her alarm—things were moving at lightning-speed between them. "Don't worry, I won't enter your home or meet your family," he clarified. "I just want to see you home safe. After that, I'd like to return to land, tend to some unfinished business, then return to you as soon as possible in Urchin Grove."

"What then?"

"Then I'd like to give us a chance. A real chance. I'd like to move to Urchin Grove to be with you."

Coralline's eyes widened, then blinked so rapidly that her eyelashes made Izar think of windshield wipers.

"We can discuss the details later, but may I accompany you to Urchin Grove before I leave for land?"

Coralline nodded slightly. Then she swiveled away from him, reached a hand into her satchel on the floor, and turned to face him again. The room was suddenly lit by the elixir, which she placed on the palm of his hand. He raised a quizzical eyebrow at her.

"Venant warned me that constables were here just yesterday, looking for me," Coralline explained. "He told them he's never seen me before, but he said they seemed dubious, because they had heard he'd been seen talking to me at the Ball. He thinks they may return this morning. In case they do, I'd like to ask you to carry the elixir with you. If they catch me, I'd like you to take the elixir to my brother. If they don't, I'll take the elixir from you when you return from Velvet Horn."

Izar curled his fingers around the silver sphere; the light disappeared in his fist like a smothered flame. He buried the elixir in an under-compartment of his satchel, in order to hide its light.

Coralline whirled away from him and dug again through her satchel. When she turned to face him again, she handed him a pen and a notepad embossed with algae. "You can use these in case you need to write directions or anything else while tracing your elixir note," she said.

Izar smiled at her, and she smiled back, but the smile did not reach her eyes.

"You said we'd leave for Urchin Grove when morning turned to afternoon," Pavonis said through the window. "It's afternoon now."

"Yes," Coralline agreed, from her perch on the windowsill, her gaze roving the waters for a sign of Izar's indigo tail.

"I, too, don't understand why we're still here if you have the elixir, Coralline," Altair grumbled. Rising from the seabed, he arrived at her elbow at the windowsill, his dorsal fin beating so fast that it was transparent. "You prepared a remedy for Venant, and he's feeling better, yet we're still here."

"Yes," Coralline said absentmindedly.

She'd had second thoughts about Izar when they'd lain together in bed. She should have told him she was engaged, but she hadn't because she was planning to end her relationship with Ecklon immediately upon returning to Urchin Grove, given that he was betraying her. She would tell Izar about Ecklon later, when Izar returned to her from land, by which time Ecklon would be a part of her past, not her present. When Izar returned to her, she and he would begin a relationship built on a foundation of honesty.

"Where is the elixir?" Nacre asked, appearing over the top of the windowsill, her tentacles dangling downward above Coralline's head.

"It's with Izar."

The three animals cried out in unison.

"The elixir is for Naiadum," Coralline clarified, "but Izar is carrying it for now. Don't worry: It was my idea. He'll give the elixir back to me as soon as he gets back."

"From where?" Pavonis demanded.

"A personal errand."

"A personal errand . . ." Altair repeated sickly.

"You young fool!" Nacre screeched, her tentacles jerking wildly. "You lost the elixir just when you had it!"

"Izar won't return," Pavonis growled. "He's probably on his way back to land as we speak, where he'll soon begin prancing about on his ugly legs. I was right about him—we should never have trusted a human. And I was wrong about you, Coralline—I thought you were smarter than this."

"You're wrong, all of you!" Coralline cried. "You don't know Izar like I do." She glared at each of them in turn, then sprang off the windowsill to create distance from them.

"What's that, there?" Nacre called, her tentacles waggling in the direction of the desk chair.

A flat, soft-edged rectangle lay on the floor next to the chair, Coralline saw. Picking it up, she turned it over. The face stamped upon it was Izar's, but, with the aloof eyes, callous lips, and terse forehead, it was a face she hardly recognized. *Ocean Dominion*, stated the top of the card.

The directions Izar had scribbled on the notepad turned out to be accurate. *Printer & Parchment*, announced the placard outside the hole-in-the-wall shop. "I'm Chiton," said an elderly merman from behind the counter in introduction, his face like a withered pear.

Izar caught his breath, placing his hand on the counter. It was not easy to navigate underwater, without any landmarks, a fact that led him to newly appreciate Coralline's shark. After much meandering, after requesting directions of a merman he'd passed, Izar had finally managed to make it to Velvet Horn.

There was no sand-clock in Printer & Parchment, but it had taken him well over the hour he'd estimated to arrive here. He would have to rush in order to return to Coralline in time.

"Is this paper—parchment, rather—from your shop?" Izar asked hurriedly, unrolling the amber scroll and handing it to Chiton.

Chiton turned it over, thumbed the embossed logo, and nodded.

"Do you know who wrote the note?" Izar pursued.

Chiton produced a microscope from underneath his counter. Placing the parchment on the counter, he bent his head over it, closing one eye and positioning the other just above his microscope, muttering to himself as he read the single line.

"I believe this note was written by one of my long-standing customers, Osmundea Ranularia," Chiton said, looking up at Izar. "I recognize her handwriting, because I've printed lots for her over the years."

The old merman offered Izar directions to Osmundea's home. Izar wrote them down carefully in Coralline's notepad. Upon following the directions, he found himself knocking on the door of a small, rounded house at the end of a row, hemmed with a little garden. As he waited at the door, he started to return the notepad to his satchel, but a little square drifted out from within. It started to float away, but Izar caught it and turned it over. It was a portrait of a merman, a handsome fellow with a vertical cleft in his chin and traces of dimples in his cheeks. Who was he? Izar wondered. And what was his portrait doing in Coralline's notepad?

The door opened.

The mermaid who hovered before Izar had indigo eyes and scales, just like his own. There was a one-inch-long horizontal scar along the side of her mouth, appearing a direct extension of his own. "You found me," she said in a breathless whisper.

Her voice was soft in the center and frayed about the edges—he *knew* this voice, from a long, long time ago, and his face almost crumpled to hear it. She held the door open, and Izar slipped inside her living room, his mind buzzing with questions. Who was she? How could he so resemble her? How could he recognize her voice? He wanted to ask her, but he could not unglue his tongue from the roof of his mouth. He took a seat on the settee across from her.

"Will you let me tell you a story?" Osmundea asked, her eyes as gentle as cotton swabs.

Izar felt himself give the slightest nod.

"There was once a young mermaid in Urchin Grove who lived with her parents and sister. She taught a class called *Legend and Lore* at Urchin Liberal Arts Academy. She focused on two areas of legend and lore: the elixir and hummers. Do you already know about the elixir?" Upon his nod, she continued, "In that case, let me tell you about hummers. The word *hummer* derives from half-*hum*an, half-*mer*person. Hummers are a unique breed of people—people who have one human parent and one merperson parent. Any sort of interaction between humans and merpeople is exceptionally rare, let alone any children—so you can imagine how rare hummers are. They are, in fact, so rare as to fall in the category of lore.

"At a biological level, hummers have both gills and lungs, the gills from the merperson parent and the lungs from the human parent. It's a little-known fact that, because they belong equally to both land and water, hummers transform automatically based on their environment. When they are in the water, hummers have a merperson form; when they are on land, they have a human form. When they move from one environment to the other—land to water, or water to land—their body dies and then returns to life in its new form. At an intellectual level, because hummers belong to all of the earth, they are capable of forming connections between things that others cannot even conceive of. As such, they are particularly inventive people, the most inventive on earth.

"One day, the mermaid noticed a new merman in her *Legend and Lore* class. He approached her after the class and asked her to help him find the elixir. She gave him a slip of parchment with the name of someone who could assist him in his quest. But he had a mistaken impression about the elixir; he thought that it could make him immortal. She told him that it could save his life, or someone else's, were death imminent, but it did not have the power to bestow immortality—nothing did. The elixir saved life once, and that was it. The mermaid also asked the merman why he would wish to be immortal. He said it was because there was something he wanted to invent, and he worried he wouldn't find a way to invent it in his lifetime. On the topic of invention, she told him about hummers and their inventive qualities. He seemed enthralled by the idea of hummers.

"There was something very different about this merman, and the mermaid found herself falling headlong in love with him, just as he seemed to be falling headlong in love with her. One day, she told him she was expecting. Clasping her hands, he promised her they would marry soon. She broke in half a large shell—a lion's paw scallop. She retained half and handed him the other half—symbolizing that they each now carried the heart of the other and the power to break it.

"But after that day, the merman vanished without a trace. She assumed he'd died on his quest for the elixir, and she blamed herself for having played a role in his quest. Nine months later, their child was born. The mermaid's parents helped raise him, as did her younger sister. The child was precocious: Before he turned three, he could speak, read, and write.

"One day, when the mermaid was out on an errand with him, an orca dived down and asked her, *How old is your hummer?* The whale could detect his lungs through echolocation, a process of sending out sound beams and using the echoes from those sounds to identify objects; echolocation gives whales the ability to see through things. The mermaid was shocked. She realized then that the father of her son was not a merman but a human. He had transformed somehow from a human to a merman, perhaps through some magic potion. He had deceived her by letting her believe him to be a merman. He had used her in order to create a hummer who would invent what he wished. He had likely not died on an elixir quest, as she had first assumed; instead, he must have left the ocean and transformed back to a human.

"Now at least the mermaid understood their child's precociousness—it was because he was a hummer. She guarded him vigilantly, worried that his father would return to kidnap him. Her nightmare soon materialized. The villain burst through the door of her home on the night of the child's third birthday. The ruckus awoke the mermaid's parents in the next room, and they emerged into the living room. The villain clubbed them to death. Then, grabbing the child, he rushed to the surface. The mermaid followed him up to the waves and managed to wrest the child back. The villain tried to slash her throat with the half-shell she'd given him, wielding it as a dagger. But his aim was inaccurate in the dark. He ended up slashing the child's cheek, starting at his earlobe, and a part of her face, culminating at the lip. Then he knocked her unconscious and escaped with the child."

Osmundea slipped out of the living room, and Izar was glad, for it was all too much—he keeled over, his head in his hands. His scar prickled as though an electric wire were sparking to life beneath it. Osmundea returned soon with a large half-shell with long, flaunting beige ridges and dark-pink fan-like ribs. Izar's fingers quivered as he extracted the half-shell from his own satchel and held it against hers. The two halves fit perfectly, crease against crease, forming two parts of a broken heart.

"Tang Tarpon found the elixir thirty years ago," Osmundea said quietly. "I interviewed him as part of my research on the elixir. Then, twenty-nine years ago, Antares Eridan approached me after my *Legend and Lore* class, requesting assistance in finding the elixir. To help him, I wrote on a piece of parchment: *Find Tang Tarpon. He will guide you to the elixir.* Soon after, upon finding myself expecting, I gave Antares the half-shell you are now holding in your hands. I've waited twenty-five years for you to find me, son, for you to return home to me."

Izar's jaw clenched. How dare Osmundea accuse Antares? Yes, she knew both Antares's name and Tang's; yes, her name started with *O*, as did that of the author of the elixir note in his satchel; yes, the single line on the parchment precisely matched the words she'd just spoken; yes, the two halves of the shell fit together like the two halves of a coin; yes, her scar was a direct extension of his own; yes, Izar's being a hummer would explain his transformation from a human to a merman; yes, Izar's resemblance to her was uncanny, with the indigo eyes and tail; yes, the dates she mentioned aligned with his own, but she could not possibly be his mother, for the man she described—a murderer, an abductor—could not possibly be his father.

Izar rose abruptly and started to shift to the door, but he found himself so disoriented by the conversation that he stopped to lean against the mantel. A pretty piece of ivory parchment with cursive gold writing caught his eye. He read it absentmindedly:

The Elnaths and the Costarias request the pleasure of your presence,
along with your family,
at the engagement party of Ecklon Elnath and Coralline Costaria,
at noon on the fifteenth of July in the garden of the Elnath Mansion;
and, pursuant, their wedding two weeks after,
at noon on the twenty-ninth of July at Kelp Cove;
please confirm your attendance as soon as possible,
by scroll to either the Elnath or Costaria home in Urchin Grove.

Coralline Costaria, in Urchin Grove; it could not be his Coralline, could it? He tried to ask Osmundea, but he could not speak: His tongue flopped helplessly against the roof of his mouth, as loose as jelly.

"My sister, Rhodomela, invited me to Coralline's engagement party and wedding," Osmundea explained.

Rhodomela, Coralline's former boss. That meant this wedding invitation *was* for his Coralline. Izar's hands shook so violently that it took him long minutes to extract the merman's portrait from within Coralline's notepad. He handed it to Osmundea without a word.

"Yes, this is the merman she will wed—Ecklon," she said, startled. "But how do you have this?"

The twenty-ninth of July was a week away. Coralline was going to marry Ecklon then. His Coralline was going to marry someone else.

A small sand-clock stood on the mantel, white sand trickling from its upper to lower ampoule through a narrow neck. Izar bent his head to read the horizontal lines engraved into the hourglass. His eyes widened. The time was almost two; he'd promised Coralline he'd return to her before noon. He bolted out the door.

When her sobs dwindled to hiccups, when her face became squashed in her pillow—only then did Coralline turn over onto her back. She stared unseeingly at the ceiling.

The men on the ship the day of the black poison spill—Izar must have been one of them. And she hadn't stopped to think about it before now, but Izar had blanched when she'd shown him the pen engraved with the name Zaurak Alphard—he must know the man.

As a human, Izar was the enemy generally; what the card in her hand showed was that he was also the enemy specifically. It was because of him that her father's hand was severed, and her brother lay on his deathbed.

All along, Izar had played a game with her in order to trick her for the elixir. Everything he'd done—rescuing her from the two brothers in Bristled Bed and Breakfast, dancing with her at the Ball, accompanying her into the darkness of the deep sea—was so that he could obtain the elixir. Last night, when he'd told her that he wanted her to have the elixir, it was so that she would loosen her guard about it, perhaps also so that she would sleep with him—as she had. He had probably planned to steal the elixir from her this morning, but he hadn't needed to—she had placed it in the palm of his hand.

Coralline glanced at the sand-clock. The time was half past two in the afternoon. He would not return.

She turned to Pavonis, Altair, and Nacre, lingering together at the window, watching her. "I'm sorry to have let you down," she said, "especially after all of you risked your lives to accompany me on this Elixir Expedition."

"It's not your fault you have no sense," Nacre said with a sigh.

"If I ever see that despicable specimen again," Pavonis growled, "no force on earth will prevent me from crushing him against the seabed!"

"I'm just glad we're going home," Altair said. "I can't wait to return to my Kuda."

How wonderfully simple it was between Altair and Kuda, Coralline thought. They would remain a pair until the day they died. Not for a moment before would either falter. And if one of them died before the other, the survivor would not seek a new mate. The word *betrayal* did not exist for seahorses.

A knock sounded at the front door, to the other side of the Telescope Tower.

"I'll see who's at the door," Pavonis said. "If it's constables, I'll make a lot of noise, both to alert you and distract them. Once you hear me, escape out the window with Altair and Nacre, and I'll come find you later. Understand?"

Coralline nodded, and Pavonis left. She crept out of bed and shifted to the window, her fingers grasping the windowsill nervously. "Coralline!" Pavonis called, from the front of the Telescope Tower. "You'll never guess who it is."

Her eyes widened. Izar, it had to be. He was late, but he had returned to her—with the elixir she'd given him for safe-keeping! She darted out her window, in through the living room window two stories below, and pulled the front door open.

The merman at the door had a silver tail, and his hair was the shade of pebbled sand. Dimples carved sudden triangles into his cheeks. Ecklon.

She did not know who moved first, but before she could draw her next breath, they were in each other's arms, and he was twirling her in circle upon circle. They held each other so tightly that she thought her ribs might crack, but she didn't care—Ecklon had come for her; halfway across Meristem, he had found her.

When they stopped twirling, Coralline peered into his silver-gray eyes. She had been upset with him about something in the last few days; what was it? . . . It came to her with such force that her voice turned harsh: "Are you betraying me with Rosette?"

"Of course not. What would give you such a ridiculous idea?"

He was telling the truth, Coralline knew, because he was looking directly in her eyes. Her stomach dropped to the level of her tailfin, and she suddenly felt as sick as though she'd caught Venant's flu. She sagged against his chest, in part from weakness and in part so that he could not see her face.

Sage Dahlia Delaisi had been wrong. Ecklon was not betraying her. But Coralline had betrayed him.

Her head lifted cautiously from his chest. His silver-gray eyes were not looking at her, but were staring past her into the living room of the Telescope Tower, through the door Coralline had left open. "Where is he?" Ecklon demanded, a hard rim to his pupils.

"Who?" Coralline asked in a small voice.

"Venant Veritate," he said, his gaze returning to her. "This is his home, is it not? I'd like to meet him."

Of course. Ecklon admired Venant's work just as much as she, having memorized whole passages from *The Universe Demystified*.

"He's ill," Coralline said, "*and* contagious." It was true, at least, she consoled herself, but the real reason she did not want Ecklon to meet Venant was that Venant had assumed she and Izar were a couple. He would be surprised to see her in Ecklon's arms and may ask where Izar was. "I know you'd like to meet Venant, but he's . . . napping." Venant *was* likely napping, she thought, for he would otherwise have emerged from his bedroom at the commotion outside his home. One of the three algae in the Virus Vanquisher solution she'd prepared for him this morning had happened to be sleep inducing. Coralline had never before been so grateful for someone's sleep. "We should speak softly for the sake of his recovery," she suggested, in a voice just above a whisper. "How did you know to find me here?"

"It was a hunch. I thought that if you were in the Blue Bottle area, you might try to meet our favorite author before leaving. And I already knew his address, because I'd gotten it from the Under-Ministry of Residential Affairs before your birthday, in order to send him a copy of *The Universe Demystified* to autograph for you."

It hadn't been quite how Coralline had come across Venant, but it could just as well have been. Touched by Ecklon's explanation, she tousled his hair, finding the strands to be just as sleek as she remembered. "How did you know I was in the Blue Bottle area?" she asked.

"I've been following your movements. I'm the detective on Tang Tarpon's murder case."

"What? How?"

"I took the case to clear your name, of course."

To clear her name . . . Ecklon was clearing her name. . . . His boss, Sinistrum Scomber, would not have wanted him to take the case, because the personal nature of it would raise questions of credibility. But Ecklon had taken the case regardless in order to defend her. Here he was, far from home, fighting for her freedom, while she was cavorting with someone else—the enemy, no less.

"Is there anything you wish to tell me?" Ecklon asked.

It was a question he'd never asked her before, and in a way he'd never asked her before. Could it be that he'd learned about Izar over the course of following her movements to this Telescope Tower? Could he have spoken with Limpet and Linatella Laminaria, perchance?

No. If he had learned about Izar, Ecklon would not be here.

"There's nothing I wish to tell you," Coralline said.

This is the merman she will wed—Ecklon, Osmundea had said. The sentence looped through Izar's mind in circles, such that even though he was swimming straight, hurtling toward the Telescope Tower at the highest speed he was capable of, he had the impression he was chasing his own tail.

He should give her the benefit of the doubt, he told himself, for he was also guilty of keeping secrets from her. Perhaps she was planning to leave Ecklon for him, just as Izar was planning to leave Ocean Dominion for her. And perhaps she was planning to tell him about Ecklon after ending her relationship with Ecklon, just as Izar was planning to tell her about Ocean Dominion after ending his relationship with Ocean Dominion.

Finally, there it was, farther ahead, the Telescope Tower, looking like a drowned lighthouse on the seabed. A small kelp forest sprouted between Izar and the Tower, and Izar started to cross the long flaps of bright-green leaves, but he stopped suddenly at the sight in front of the Tower.

Her bronze scales shimmering, her long black hair glistening down her back, Coralline hovered in the arms of a merman. Turning her neck up as gracefully as a swan, she kissed him.

Coralline's fist thudded on the door to the snail-shaped house.

"Use your head, and use the window to the side of the door!" barked a shrill voice.

Coralline burst in through the window and bolted to Sage Dahlia, who was sitting plumply on the settee. With her hands on her hips, she stared down at the sage. Coralline had a murder charge to her name; she might as well earn it. Just as there were multiple ways to save someone, there were multiple ways to murder someone. She could wrap her hands around the sage's gills, but the thickness of the neck would make it difficult for the sage to suffocate. She could stab the sage in the heart with a dagger, but the dagger was in Coralline's satchel, and she had given her satchel to Ecklon to hold.

He was waiting for her in the shadow of a building around the bend, accompanied by Pavonis, Altair, Nacre, and Menziesii. It was risky for Coralline to be in Blue Bottle, Ecklon had repeatedly warned her on the way here—a whole squad of constables must be searching for her—but Coralline's desire to kill Sage Dahlia had overpowered her sense of reason.

"How may I help you?" Sage Dahlia asked in a polite, placid voice.

Coralline had treated the sage's statement as a prophecy, but this orange clown did not even remember her. "You were wrong!" Coralline bellowed.

"Was I, now?" she said, in the over-calm tone of addressing a child having a tantrum.

"You told me I was being betrayed by my love!"

Now Sage Dahlia sat up straight, her eyes blinking with recognition.

"I am *not* being betrayed by my love," Coralline said hotly. "Far from betraying me, my love is waiting for me outside."

"Show me."

The voluminous form pushed past Coralline at surprising speed. Trailing Sage Dahlia to the window, Coralline gestured toward Ecklon with her hand.

"Oh, him," Sage Dahlia said, turning back to Coralline. Pity reigned in her watery eyes, reminding Coralline of Rhodomela's gaze whenever Rhodomela was about to impart a tragic diagnosis to a patient. "He is not your love."

Coralline reeled back. If Ecklon was not her love, it meant Izar was her love. And so the sage's statement—*You are being betrayed by your love*—was true after all, for Izar had been betraying her every moment, belonging as he did to Ocean Dominion.

White dots flashed before Coralline's eyes, and she fainted.

ZONE III

Midnight

24

Home

Throughout the Elixir Expedition, Coralline had wondered how it would feel to return home. Which of her parents would open the door, and what would she say to them after having left in the middle of the night?

But now that she stood outside the door, there was no time to feel anything, nor even to knock. She swept in through the tall, arched living room window and darted past the settees toward Naiadum's bedroom. Hovering silently in the doorway, she peered in.

Had she not known he would be in bed, she would have thought the bed empty—previously pudgy, Naiadum formed a skeleton under the blanket now, his cheeks concave and yellow. Abalone and Trochid sat on chairs to either side of his bed.

Trochid spotted Coralline in the doorway first. He looked in her direction, but she had the sense he was looking not at her but through her—in

271

his grief, he seemed to have lost the power to perceive. Following his gaze, Abalone turned her head to the door. Her lips pressed together at Coralline's sight.

Swimming in slowly, Coralline perched on the precise place on Naiadum's bed where she'd sat every night, reading him a story. During storytime, he'd often been breathless with anticipation as she'd cackled and giggled while playing characters. Now, the gills along the sides of his neck lay still—he was barely even breathing. Coralline considered pressing two fingers to his wrist to measure his pulse, she considered opening his eyes to check their whites, but she would be pretending—from one look at him, she knew he would be dead before the end of the night.

"Do you have the elixir?" Abalone demanded.

"No, Mother."

"Naiadum is dying because of you. You abandoned us in the most difficult week of our lives, and now you've returned empty-handed. Don't you have any shame?"

Abalone snapped out of her chair and hovered before Coralline. Perhaps it was because she was wearing the black of mourning, but Coralline had the sense that it was not her mother, but her mother's ghost, in front of her. The feeling evaporated when her mother's hands landed on her shoulders and shook her until her teeth rattled—

"Stop it, Abalone!" Trochid said, as he arrived between them and wrenched them apart. "It's not Coralline's fault she couldn't find the elixir. She did everything she could."

"It's all right, Father. It is my fault. I found the elixir, but I lost it. I'm sorry."

With a sob, Coralline darted out of Naiadum's bedroom, then out the living room window. "*Coralline!*" her father called after her, but she did not look back.

She swam aimlessly through Urchin Grove, aware only dimly that Pavonis was swimming above her. She did not stop to notice the shops she passed, the houses, the lanes through which she'd swum countless times over the years. She did not stop to talk to anyone, not even people she recognized. They didn't seem keen to talk to her either—whispering behind cupped hands, they refused to meet her eyes.

Coralline stopped only when she found herself at the door of The Irregular Remedy. It had previously formed her whole world; now, she saw that it looked no different than any other place in Urchin Grove: It was a low mound of gray shale rising from the seabed. Previously, the distance between her home and the clinic had seemed substantial; now, after her endless swimming over the course of the Elixir Expedition, Coralline felt as though The Irregular Remedy was practically next door to her home.

But there was no place for her at The Irregular Remedy anymore, she remembered—it was simply habit that had brought her here. Turning away, she found herself facing a patch of desmarestia that sprouted close to the clinic. She was about to swim over the side of it, in order to avoid the Doom of Desmarestia said to come from crossing over it, but Pavonis said, "You know better now than to follow senseless misconceptions!" Nodding up at him, Coralline started to traverse the olive-brown fronds, but she stopped with a gasp.

Her desmarestia-sea-oak solution had healed Izar's wrist completely, almost miraculously. What if desmarestia's use was not limited to healing external wounds? Could desmarestia's toxins, when reversed, heal all manner of things? Specifically, could desmarestia, in combination with sea oak, cleanse contaminated blood?

It was possible, but it would be risky, more for her than Naiadum. Without the solution, he would certainly die; with it, there was a sliver of a chance he would live. But Coralline would suffer whether he lived or died. If he lived, she would be condemned under the Medical Malpractice Act for having practiced without a badge—in which case she would be barred for life from practice again. If he died, a second murder charge would be added to her name—Naiadum Costaria in addition to Tang Tarpon—and she would be imprisoned for life in the Wrongdoers' Refinery.

Was she willing to take these risks? Yes, she decided, if there was a possibility to save him.

Coralline rushed through the door of The Irregular Remedy. Rhodomela was not there, to her relief. She must be visiting a patient at home, likely someone sickened by the black poison Izar had spewed all over Urchin Grove.

Coralline's gaze fell on the white-gray limestone urns on her shelves: Swelling Softener, Rash Relief, Gill Gush, Cough Cure. . . . The urns had meant everything to her when she'd worked here, the medication in each prepared painstakingly by her own hand, but she found they meant nothing to her now—she could just as well be looking at another healer's work. Why had Rhodomela not disposed of her urns? Coralline wondered, before leaping into action.

Grabbing her snippers, she swam out the window into the remedial garden. She sheared straggly golden-brown strands of sea oak, then moved outward to the patch of desmarestia and snipped several fronds. Stuffing the two algae in separate vials, she rushed back inside The Irregular Remedy and ground sea oak and desmarestia one after the other in her mortar and pestle. She returned the two algae to the vials and lidded the vials. When she looked up, a face was staring at her from the window.

It was not Rhodomela but a mermaid Coralline wished to see even less: Rosette. "Who are you trying to poison?" Rosette demanded, eyeing the vial of desmarestia.

"That's none of your business."

"How was your lover?"

Coralline looked at her in stunned silence.

"I told everyone you left Urchin Grove for a lover," Rosette said slyly.

Now Coralline understood why the people she'd passed on her way to The Irregular Remedy had whispered behind cupped hands and refused to meet her eyes.

"My rumor became reality, didn't it? I can see it in your eyes!"

Coralline placed the vials of desmarestia and sea oak in her satchel, along with an empty flask, then she pushed past Rosette out the window. Her swim home was a blur—she was aware of nothing, not even Pavonis, above her. Her senses returned only when she was sitting again at Naiadum's bedside and extracting the two vials and the flask from her satchel. She emptied the vials into the flask. The two algae started to sputter and spew and screech, like people shrieking at the top of their voices. The shriek was disturbing but also reassuring—the reaction was exactly as it had been in Izar's case. Coralline placed the flask to Naiadum's lips, but a hand snaked around her wrist.

"What's this?" Abalone asked.

"A solution that may save Naiadum." Coralline tried to wring her hand free, but her mother's grasp tightened.

"If something could save Naiadum, Rhodomela would have told us. What, precisely, is in the flask you're putting to my son's lips?"

"Sea oak and desmarestia."

"*Desmarestia?* You're poisoning Naiadum? Is he not dying quick enough for you?"

"I believe sea oak can reverse desmarestia's toxins, Mother. I tried it once before, and it worked."

"Nothing can reverse desmarestia's toxins. If anything could reverse them, someone smarter and more experienced than you would have figured it out before now. You can give this so-called solution to him only if you also take it yourself."

"Don't be absurd, Abalone!" Trochid interjected.

"I insist," she yelled. "It's Coralline's fault he's in this condition; I want to be sure she isn't trying to poison him."

Coralline bit back her tears. It would not do to cry now, even though her mother's words felt like pinpricks all across her body. It would be dangerous for Coralline to take such a strong dose, given that she wasn't sick, but she could see no other choice: The reaction was starting to fizz, the flask in her hand no longer rattling. It was losing potency by the second. There was no time to argue with her mother or explain to her the medical risks of what she was proposing. Coralline would have to act now, or it would be too late. "All right. I'll drink the solution, too."

Abalone released Coralline's hand.

Coralline tilted the flask at Naiadum's lips. Just as soon as half of it was empty, she tilted her own head back and swallowed the rest.

The potion burned a twisting path down her throat. The sun itself seemed to be licking her to flames from the inside. She started to writhe, every muscle in her body shaking, as though attempting to escape the burn. Naiadum thrashed as well, so hard that his bed frame thudded against the wall.

She'd made a huge mistake. They were both going to die. Coralline's eyes closed, and she folded to the floor.

Izar rummaged through his satchel for his identification card. It must be in some under-compartment, he thought. Giving up on finding it, he knocked on the glass door to Saiph's office.

Saiph glanced up. The pen fell from his hand, and he blinked at Izar repeatedly, as though he was looking at a spirit returned from the dead. Then Saiph pressed a button under his desk; the door buzzed, and Izar walked in.

The sight of Saiph in the same room as him filled Izar with a sense of such relief and safety that he paused midstride over the cream carpet. Izar had transformed physically on shore, but not until this moment, when he was looking into Saiph's charred-kale eyes, did he transform psychologically: He became Izar Eridan, co-president of Ocean Dominion.

He wanted to hug Saiph, but it would require taking two extra steps into the office, and he could not conjure the strength. He collapsed in the chair across from Saiph's mahogany desk.

"Father and I thought you were dead," Saiph said in an accusatory tone. "What happened?"

"I was thrown overboard and transformed into a merman."

The transformation to a human had been much more difficult than that to a merman. Izar had swum for a day straight to reach the shores of Menkar, stopping not even for the night, so eager had he been to leave Coralline and her world behind. From the sea, he'd recognized his city by its skyline of skyscrapers, standing straight and parallel like pushpins. He'd dragged himself out of the waves onto a secluded cranny of the coast, separated from the rest of the beach by rocks to either side. There, he'd died a most tormented death, his gills closing, his tail throbbing like it was being sawed down the middle.

When he'd awoken, he'd discovered that he had legs again and that his chest was rising and falling—his lungs were again functioning. The transformation was complete—or so he'd thought. He'd attempted to stand, but he had felt as though he was trying to support himself on cotton balls—his bones had been as soft and malleable as a baby's. Crawling on his belly to the froth, he'd dipped himself in to remove the residual slime from his legs. He had shivered, the water frigid against his skin; he was warm-blooded again. He had thought to crawl back to the rocks, but his strength was depleted. He'd lain his head down on the sand and slept.

When he'd awoken, the droplets of salt water on his skin had transformed to a sheen of perspiration, as a result of the sizzling heat. He'd risen slowly and, after falling numerous times, had taught himself to walk again. Every step had felt like nails were being hammered into the soles of his feet. The adjustment to being a merman had been much easier than that to being a human, perhaps because in the water one always hovered—the lack of contact with the floor meant there was little impact on newly shaped bones.

His limping had eventually turned to strolling, and he'd ambled about on the beach in search of scraps of clothing, just as a scavenger might seek carcasses. He'd eventually discovered a smudged cotton shirt and khaki shorts. He'd then walked barefoot to the bronze glass arrow that was

Ocean Dominion. Along the way, he had found himself looking at Menkar not through the eyes of the man he had been but through the eyes of the merman he had become—and through the eyes of the mermaid with whom he had been.

What he'd always assumed to be a wisp of clouds over the city was actually, he'd seen, a layer of smog. And there was something stifling about all the glass buildings, about their concentration—he'd had the impression he was trodding among shards of glass. The tinted windows rising from the ground to the sky had made him think of coffins stacked one upon another unto infinite. Was this the city he'd loved? What had he loved about it?

"How did you transform?" Saiph asked.

"I'm still figuring that out." According to Osmundea, he'd transformed because he was a hummer.

"How was life in the ocean?"

"I fell in love with a mermaid, Coralline," Izar said in a harsh, self-condemning voice, "but she turned out to be engaged to someone else. She's getting married on the twenty-ninth of July in a place called Kelp Cove, in her village of Urchin Grove—Zone Ten, to us, the site of the oil spill. . . . Oh, Saiph, I've been betrayed twice in as many weeks, first by Ascella—whom I discovered cheating on me—then by Coralline."

"I'm sorry, brother," Saiph said softly. "Will you excuse me for a minute?"

Izar nodded. Saiph strode across the cream carpet and out the door.

25

Murder

Coralline's eyes opened groggily. She was not in her own room but
Naiadum's, her tailfin dangling over the end of his bed because of
its small size. But where was her little brother?

She turned her head to the door and cringed to see her flask in the
doorway. Sea oak and desmarestia: that was what she'd poured down his
throat. It must have killed him—that was why he was not here. Her parents were likely burying him at this moment, without waiting for her. She
couldn't blame them.

"Coralline!"

A tawny tail materialized in the doorway. Coralline rubbed her eyes; no,
she was not imagining it. She hardly recognized him because of the hollow
pits under his eyes and his skinny frame, but it was Naiadum. She bolted
upright, and he darted over to her, wrapping his arms around her neck.
She felt his arms up and down; they were real—not the pudgy arms she
recognized, but still, they were his arms.

She had saved him, she realized dazedly. The elixir had not saved him—she had, with her own mind and skills. Halfway across Meristem, she had traveled to find the elixir, but the solution had been right here in Urchin Grove all along—the solution had been her. She would not have known it, though, had she not left on the elixir quest.

Trochid and Abalone swam into the room and, beaming, joined Coralline and Naiadum in their embrace.

"I knew it!" Trochid said. "You're the best apothecary in the world."

A gentle, wistful smile lighting her face, Abalone stroked Coralline's hair. "I'm so very proud of you," she said. "I'm sorry I doubted your solution."

Coralline looked at her mother with surprise, for her mother had never once apologized to her before. Coralline wished she could remain in this moment forever—her mother's hand on her hair was the most soothing sensation she'd ever experienced—but a knock sounded at the front door.

"I'll get it." She sighed, rising reluctantly from Naiadum's bed. "It's probably Ecklon."

Naiadum collapsed on his now-vacated bed, and, in the time it took Coralline to blink, he fell fast asleep. After the week he'd spent comatose, his bones and muscles would require time to rebuild their strength, Coralline knew. She tousled his hair, then swept into the living room, trailed by her parents. She pulled the door open.

The merman had a long, lanky frame, as though someone had stretched him end to end. His features seemed at war with one another—he looked equally pleased and disappointed to see Coralline, as though a part of him had been hoping no one would answer the door. He was attired in a deep-purple waistcoat with a circular black seal of the Under-Ministry of Crime and Murder stitched upon the breast pocket—he was a constable.

"I'm Pericarp Plicata," he said nervously, pulling handcuffs out of his satchel. "Coralline Costaria, I pronounce you under arrest. Place your hands behind your back . . . please."

The Constables Department of Urchin Grove must have been on alert for her, Coralline thought, waiting for her to return home, knowing that she would eventually.

A crowd started to form behind Pericarp, people gathering in thin, whispering strings. Coralline recognized some faces and not others, but she had a difficult time telling them apart—they all wore identical expressions of gleeful nosiness.

"On what charge are you trying to arrest my daughter?" Trochid bellowed. Arms crossed over his chest, he slipped between Coralline and Pericarp, his dark-brown eyes bulging.

"Father, it's all right," Coralline said hurriedly. She did not want her parents to know about her murder charge, not like this, with the whole neighborhood watching.

"Coralline Costaria is under arrest for the murder of Tang Tarpon in Hog's Bristle," Pericarp replied.

"*Murder!*" voices repeated. Neighbors beckoned passersby over to watch, such that the crowd behind Pericarp swelled to around the same size as that of her engagement party—a hundred or so people. For the first time, Coralline understood Pavonis's aversion to Urchin Grove.

"You're mistaken," Trochid said, glowering at Pericarp. "Far from being a murderess, my daughter is a savior. Just before your unceremonious arrival, she saved her brother Naiadum's life in a most revolutionary way."

Coralline placed a warning hand on her father's elbow. He did not know that a second criminal charge could easily be added to her name, on account of her defiance of the Medical Malpractice Act.

"This is not a time for humility, Coralline," Trochid continued loudly. "Everyone should know you're a genius, the most brilliant mind this village has ever seen. Yes," he boomed to the crowd, "Coralline gave Naiadum a solution of desmarestia and—"

An uproar erupted, drowning out the rest of his words like a breathless, out-of-tune orchestra.

Coralline whirled around to look at her mother. Abalone had been in the doorway earlier, but she'd retreated to the middle of the living room now, distancing herself from Coralline. When their eyes met, she looked at Coralline like she did not know her. Blinking back her tears, Coralline turned back to her father and Pericarp.

They were glaring at each other, as though the first to break eye contact would be the one to lose the battle for mental domination.

The waters swelled, and Pavonis swooped down suddenly, the gush of water from his descent pushing Pericarp into Trochid's arms. The constable looked up at Pavonis's gargantuan white belly, then, disentangling himself from Trochid, dashed through the door of the Costaria home. Coralline followed him in, as did Trochid, muttering under his breath. Pericarp slammed the door and leaned against it, his shoulders slackening with relief at having escaped Pavonis. But Pavonis's head materialized in the window, his dark orb of an eye staring steadfastly at Pericarp. The constable gulped.

"I'll show you my son," Trochid said, "back from the grave, thanks to Coralline."

Coralline trailed Pericarp and Trochid to Naiadum's bedroom. Pericarp stopped in Naiadum's doorway, his face blanching. Coralline considered the scene in the room from his perspective: a pale, emaciated merboy, passed out in the middle of the day. Pericarp bent to the floor and, with a long, shaking hand, collected the empty flask next to the door, his fingers clasping it gingerly at the neck. He placed it carefully in his satchel; it would serve as evidence, Coralline knew.

"Show me your medical badge, please," he said.

Coralline could pretend to search for the sand-dollar shell, she could pretend to have misplaced it, but what would be the point of prolonging the inevitable? A part of her was relieved it was over, relieved she would no longer have to look over her shoulder to see if a constable was following. "I don't have a badge," she said.

Pericarp looked at her apprehensively, then at Trochid, whose gaze had a manic quality. Appearing to deem himself safer outdoors than indoors, Pericarp swam out the front door. Coralline and Trochid followed him. The mob of neighbors slipped back just enough to create a wedge of space for the three of them to emerge.

Coralline turned away from Pericarp, her hands behind her back, her wrists together. Her father started to protest, but she stopped him with a shake of her head.

"Coralline Costaria," squeaked Pericarp, "I pronounce you under arrest for the murder of Tang Tarpon and for defiance of the Medical Malpractice Act."

The clang of handcuffs around her wrists made Coralline think of the two ampoules of a sand-clock, neatly dividing the past and future. So excited had she been in Blue Bottle about her desmarestia discovery, about how it would change the future of healing, but none of it meant anything anymore. Naiadum was to be her last patient.

"What's going on here?" a voice demanded.

"Ecklon!" Coralline said, as his silver tail arrived next to her and Pericarp.

"Answer me, Pericarp," Ecklon said.

"Coralline Costaria has committed two crimes—" the constable stuttered.

Ecklon held up a hand. Pericarp's lips closed immediately. "A word, please," Ecklon said. Before the constable could reply, Ecklon grabbed both Coralline and Pericarp by the elbow and, ushering them in through the doorway of the Costaria home, slamming the door in the faces of onlookers.

"How long have you known me?" he demanded of Pericarp.

Coralline had never seen Ecklon at work before. He had often seen her at work at The Irregular Remedy, when he'd collected her there for supper, but his work was necessarily of a more discreet nature. There was a natural command to him, she saw now, a clear authority—he did not raise his voice because he did not have to.

"Hmm . . ." Pericarp glanced up at the ceiling, as though trying to not get distracted while he counted the years. "About six years, I suppose," he stated eventually.

"Precisely." Ecklon nodded. "That's how long I've been at Urchin Interrogations. In that time, I've apprehended plenty of criminals for you and your fellow constables. I have not merely directed you to them, but have brought them to the Wrongdoers' Refinery in handcuffs. As such, I've done your job, or aided you with it, time and again. And I am the detective on Miss Costaria's case."

He was using her last name, Coralline knew, so Pericarp would not detect they knew each other personally.

"I intend to prove that the allegations against Miss Costaria are mistaken. I've never asked the constables of Urchin Grove for anything, but I ask you now to give me a week to solve Miss Costaria's case. In this week, leave her on house arrest here instead of detaining her for trial at the Wrongdoers' Refinery. If I am unable to prove her innocence by the end of this week, you can arrest her then."

It was not a coincidence Ecklon was requesting a week, for their wedding was in a week. If he could not prove her innocence by then, they could not marry.

"When allowances such as house arrests are made," Pericarp said, "guarantees are usually offered. What is your guarantee?"

"If I cannot prove Coralline's innocence, I will resign from my tenured post at Urchin Interrogations."

"*No!*" Coralline protested. Her own career was over; she couldn't bear the thought of ruining his as well.

"That is my guarantee," Ecklon insisted, giving her a sharp look before turning back to Pericarp.

"I accept your guarantee on behalf of the Constables Department of Urchin Grove," Pericarp said. "I only hope you don't come to regret it."

Izar looked out the window of Saiph's office. Ocean Dominion ships stood anchored to shore far below. Even from the thirtieth floor, Izar could recognize each and every vessel—its make, manufacture, age, purpose. They were his stable of stallions, ready to gallop upon the waters at his orders, and he knew them better than he knew his men, for he had led their design and acquisition.

Izar turned to Saiph's desk, littered with papers and folders. He knew he shouldn't pry, but he was co-president, and browsing the papers would help him catch up on what he'd missed in the only week he'd ever been away from Ocean Dominion. He opened a thick folder on the corner of the desk. Each page in it featured a map with a dot, along with a time, date, and coordinates of latitude and longitude. The most recent of them was from five days ago. But who was Saiph tracking? Izar wondered.

His eye caught on a glint of red underneath a stack of papers. Shuffling the papers aside, he discovered a crimson-covered notebook. It was the journal recording his Castor experiments—the journal that made Castor replicable. The numbers and formulae on its yellowed pages were more personal to Izar than the contents of any diary he could have kept, for he had written each after painstaking trial and error. To discover his Castor journal so casually on Saiph's desk made him nervous.

The door opened.

Saiph entered, trailed by three men clad in black. One of them had earlobes pierced by spears and was grinning through a shaggy red beard—Serpens. The other two had over-muscled arms and large, shaved heads—they were the men who'd accompanied Serpens on the waters, during Serpens's attempts to kill Izar.

The journal slipped from Izar's fingers.

"Hold him!" Saiph commanded.

Serpens and the two lackeys approached Izar as one, while Saiph remained back, a small smile on his face. Drawing his fist back, Izar landed a punch on the ribs of one of the two bulldozers—it was like hitting a wall. Serpens's arm darted forward, his fist landing on Izar's stomach with the force of a sledgehammer. Izar gasped; each of the two lackeys clasped one of his arms. Something cold pressed between his eyebrows—he looked up to discover it was a pistol. Saiph cocked the trigger.

"You know," Saiph said, smiling, "I've been waiting to kill you ever since that first day Father brought you home, twenty-five years ago. I detested you from that very first day. I resented your presence in my home. I hated sharing Father with you. But you were brilliant, and Father felt convinced that you, and you alone, could invent underwater fire—and thus mine gold and diamonds from the bottom of the ocean—a breakthrough that would make us wealthy beyond measure. So, patiently, day after day, year after year, I waited until you invented your Castor. And then, just two weeks ago, you did."

Cold trails of sweat ran down Izar's back.

"Immediately, I commenced on my plan to kill you, working with Serpens. It was he who loosened the tower on your drillship. It fell during the drillship check precisely where you were standing, because the platinum chip in your wrist made such precision possible. Had you been crushed that day, as I'd planned, it would simply have been treated as an accident. But you survived. The very next day, I orchestrated my second murder attempt: Serpens switched out a blowout preventer, in order to sink your drillship. But even that you managed to survive."

"You were willing to kill innocent men in order to kill me," Izar said quietly. "And you were willing to kill Ocean Dominion's reputation as well, through the oil spill."

"I wouldn't hesitate to kill the whole world in order to kill you," Saiph said cheerfully, his eyes glinting like burnt grass. "But anyhow, after the two failed murder attempts, I knew I would have to be careful, so that no one should suspect me of anything. I decided to make you co-president, in order to show the world that we were aligned both personally and professionally."

How readily Izar had believed everything when he and Saiph had last spoken in this very office—Saiph's apology for never having accepted Izar, for having made his life miserable, Saiph's claims to want to be a true brother. Izar had even asked Saiph to serve as his best man at his wedding to Ascella.

"If you had managed to kill me," Izar said, "people might still have suspected you, in the form of Castor. They might have deduced that you did not want to share with me the wealth that I created."

"No one would have suspected me of anything. The patent for Castor is under my name, not yours. The world would simply have believed I invented him, not you."

Dazed, Izar looked down at the crimson-covered journal at his feet. The patent was the only area of Castor's life in which Izar had played no role, because Antares had assigned the matter to Saiph from the beginning. Izar had always assumed the patent would be under his own name, for he was the inventor.

"For my third murder attempt, I decided you should be killed in the water. That way, everyone in Menkar would think you'd simply disappeared. These two buffoons holding you placed that tin on your desk, leading you to the trawler of Alshain Ankaa. I paid that giant to hurl you overboard, which he did, but instead of drowning, you transformed."

The maps Izar had just seen on Saiph's desk—it was Izar whom Saiph had been tracking.

"Only later did I learn that Alshain was not only a contract-hire murderer," Saiph continued, "but also a magician of sorts. He creates potions that enable human-merpeople transformations, as well as potions that create memory lapses during these transformations. For whatever reason, he must have decided to save you instead of killing you. He must have assumed the ocean would offer you refuge from your enemies on land, and he must have given you a potion to transform you."

"He didn't give me a potion."

"If you insist." Saiph shrugged. "Nevertheless, Alshain did not know about your platinum chip. I knew you hadn't drowned because I was tracking the chip in your wrist, and I could see its movement. I decided I would simply kill you in your merman form. It should have been straightforward enough, but it wasn't, because of your mermaid companion—Coralline, isn't that the name you just told me?"

Izar swallowed hard.

"The first time Serpens caught you, Coralline cut you out of the fishnet. The second time, when Serpens pulled you out over the waves, she actually leapt out of the water to slice you out of the net. But you'd already died by then, Serpens was certain. Evidence seemed to indicate it as well—for your platinum chip fell still. But, it seems now, you figured out that you were being tracked, and you managed to find a way to extract the chip without killing yourself in the process. I wouldn't be surprised if Coralline helped you with that as well."

Coralline. Ever since Izar had seen her in the arms of her fiancé outside the Telescope Tower, it was as though a sheet of mist had fallen before his eyes, blinding him. It evaporated now at Saiph's words, as under the glare of headlights. At risk to her own life, Coralline had repeatedly saved him. Izar should not have left Meristem without speaking to her—there must be an explanation for the scene he'd witnessed outside the Telescope Tower. He would return to her, he decided now—if he lived. He would fight for her; he would cast aside his pride and beg her to choose him over Ecklon.

The door opened. A figure with pale-gold hair entered, wearing a tailored, cream-white dress and cream-white stilettos. A band of light blazed from her wrist, flashing sparkles across the room—the diamond bracelet Izar had given her on her twenty-seventh birthday. "Why did you ask me to come here, Saiph?" Ascella asked nervously, looking from Saiph to Izar.

Saiph did not turn around to look at her. Instead, he smiled at Izar. "The man in her shower that night was not Tarazed but me." Removing the pistol from Izar's forehead, he drew back his other arm and punched Izar in the gut. Izar would have doubled over, but the two lackeys were clasping his arms so tightly that his back remained as straight as an ironing board. His head, however, hung, his gaze coming to rest on the heels of Ascella's stilettoes, each like the needle of a clock. The needles moved, as she came to stand directly behind Saiph.

"Don't hurt him!" she cried. Izar's gaze rose slowly to hers. "I'm sorry, Izar," she said, her frost-blue eyes imploring.

It's not your fault, Izar wanted to say, but he could not speak because of the burning sensation in his gut. The same way Saiph had fooled Izar, he must have fooled Ascella. Izar wondered whether she wore the diamond bracelet he'd given her not because of its thirty-thousand-dollar value but because she still cared a little about him. "Leave, Ascella!" he managed to croak.

Her hand wrapped around the doorknob, her face ashen, but Saiph whirled around. He pointed the pistol at her forehead and pulled the trigger. The sound of the shot made Izar jump. A drop of blood fell onto her stilettoes, then she folded to the floor like a ragdoll, her eyes wide open, blood trickling down her face, such that she looked like a mannequin crying tears of blood.

Shaking, muttering to himself, Izar thought of Bumble, the teddy bear from his childhood. As Saiph had given Bumble to Izar twenty-five years ago, he had given Ascella to Izar a year ago, introducing him to her. Now, he'd killed Ascella, just as he'd killed Bumble then.

The pistol arrived again on Izar's forehead. Izar's arms stopped straining in the grasp of the lackeys, and all tension drained from him. He succumbed to death.

"Serpens got a good look at Coralline," Saiph said softly, "when she leapt out of the water to cut you out of the net. Black hair, bronze scales, turquoise eyes, young and pretty. I'll kill her at her wedding. Thank you for telling me, Izar, that she's getting married in a week at Kelp Cove in Urchin Grove. I'll find a way to get the precise coordinates for the venue and kill her there."

With every word Izar had uttered to Saiph about Coralline, he had cast a fishnet over her. If she died, it would be his fault. "I'll do anything you want," Izar pleaded. "You can keep Castor's patent—I won't fight you for it; I won't fight you for anything. I'll invent anything you want me to. Just don't hurt Coralline."

"I'm afraid that's not an option."

"Kill me, not her."

"I'll kill you both, brother. I'll kill her at her wedding through you—through your Castor. Then I'll hurl her dead body at your feet and watch as Castor torches you to death with that arm of his. You and Coralline will not be together in life, but you'll be together in death, in the form of your ashes."

Saiph laughed, his mirth echoing against the glass walls.

26

The Shadow of Death

W ill you read me a story?" Naiadum asked in his most persuasive voice.

He deposited *The Bizarre Tale of the Barred Hamlet* in the region of Coralline's stomach, atop her blanket. He then smiled at her like a young salesman and bounced eagerly in his chair as he waited for the story.

Coralline looked at him as an apothecary: Though his cheeks were not yet full, and he was not nearly as pudgy as he had been, his face had, in the last four days, regained a healthy measure of its color. He was recovering well.

"I'm sorry, Naiadum," Coralline said. "Not tonight. Maybe tomorrow."

She'd said the same yesterday, and the day before, and the day before that. Before the Elixir Expedition, she had swum into his room every night to read him a story; now, he came to her room every night begging for a story and always left without one.

"Are you sick?" Naiadum asked, his chin quivering.

"No. I'm just tired." Coralline tried to reassure him with a smile, but what appeared on her face was not so much a smile as the isolated movements of muscles near her mouth.

"Open the door!" a voice called. A slap sounded against the door, as though a tail was thumping against it.

Naiadum opened the door, and Trochid swam into the room. With a worried look at Coralline, Naiadum slipped outside, closing the door behind him.

Trochid was juggling four luciferin orbs in his arms, leading Coralline to think of a circus performer. Yesterday, he'd brought her three orbs; the day before, it had been two; and the day before that, it had been one. Like an apothecary increasing his daily dosage of medication for a patient, he might bring her five tomorrow, Coralline thought, though she could not imagine how he would carry five orbs in two arms, especially when one arm was missing a hand.

He released the white-blue spheres of light, and they floated up to the ceiling, bouncing against the others, turning her room even brighter. Coralline wanted to tell him she was practically squinting already, but it would hurt his feelings, for he was only trying to help, she knew, believing that the luciferin orbs would lift her spirits. Ordinarily, they would have, for they'd always made her think of traveling galaxies, but now she avoided looking at them because they reminded her of Mintaka's cavern and her companion in the cavern—Izar. She hoped her father would glean of his own accord that the constellations in the orbs would not help her stars align.

Trochid assumed a seat on the chair Naiadum had vacated at her bedside. Coralline could not remember whether it was her mother, father, or brother who'd placed her desk chair there, just next to her bed. During her first two days in bed, whoever had used the chair had slid it back under her desk before leaving her room, but in the last two days, they seemed to have reached an unspoken consensus to leave the chair there. She wished they hadn't, for the chair by the bedside made her room a sick room. She'd thought of returning the chair to its place, but she'd been unable to find the energy.

"My darling daughter, will you join me in the living room and read with me there, as we have on so many evenings?"

"Maybe tomorrow."

He frowned; she'd said the same over the last days. "You're on house arrest, dear," he said gently, "not room arrest."

Coralline wished she were on room arrest rather than house arrest, so her family would not expect her to leave her room. It would have been better still, in fact, if Ecklon had not fought for her house arrest, and she were awaiting trial at the Wrongdoers' Refinery. That way, at least her family would not have to suffer by watching her suffer. Her father's eyes were ringed with thick black circles at the moment; since his retirement, he'd often found it difficult to sleep, she knew, but his insomnia was exacerbated now because of her.

"I'm sorry, Father," Coralline said. "I'm just exhausted after the Elixir Expedition."

"I'm sure you also miss Ecklon, dear."

Ecklon had departed for Hog's Bristle immediately after Pericarp had left the Costaria home. There, he was working furiously to learn the identity of Tang Tarpon's murderer. Once Ecklon had an identity and a motive, Coralline's name would be cleared of the murder charge. But detective cases often took months to solve; Ecklon had very little time left—only two days remained to their wedding.

Trochid glanced once more at Coralline's crumpled condition, then rose and left abruptly, closing the door behind him. Coralline heard her father and mother speaking in hushed voices in the living room, and she knew they were talking about her, but she breathed a sigh of relief—finally, she was alone. Solitude was its own form of companionship, the only kind she wanted.

Her stomach growled. Coralline glanced perfunctorily at the covered bowl on her bedside table. She did not need to remove its lid to know that it contained the bland sea lettuce ulva. Every day, for breakfast, lunch, and supper, her mother gave her no more than ulva, so that she would become so slim by her wedding day that she would be "almost as transparent as a lobed comb jellyfish." Even if her mother had given her not ulva but the fragrant fronds of undaria, Coralline would have rejected them—although remnants of hunger persisted, her appetite had vanished since her return. Her sustenance now was not food but her secret, Izar—every thought of him seemed a morsel just for her. She slipped her hand under her pillow and extracted the card with his picture. She tried to imagine his life—what he was doing at this very moment—but she couldn't. It was like trying to imagine life on another planet; land was a foreign expanse to her.

She relived her moments with him. She'd done it so often in the last days that she'd begun to envision them with alternate endings. When she thought of the time she'd first seen him, hovering unconscious midway between the surface and the seabed, as though he were both human and merman—and she'd traced her finger over his scar, the line of the scar was gently curved in her memory, not sharp. When she thought of their night at Honeymooners Hotel in Rainbow Wrack, she imagined him sleeping not on the floor but next to her in bed. When she thought of their swims between settlements, she pictured herself and him swimming not at a distance of arm's length but hand in hand.

Every word he'd spoken to her, every glance he'd fixed on her, seemed imbued with a brilliant light, as though the sun were shining directly upon it. She often felt as though he were continuing to watch her even now, an omniscient god in the ceiling, his gaze caressing her shoulders like a blanket. But his gaze was most likely caressing someone else at this very moment. One day, standing on his stodgy legs, he would marry a human, like himself, and he would recall Coralline occasionally, if at all. The thought made Coralline want to die.

She thought of the curse Mintaka had pronounced to her: *You will die soon after the light dies*. In the cavern, Coralline had been dismayed by the curse, but now, she wanted to die.

She found it strange that she'd spent her life terrified of death. Death was, in its simplest form, non-existence, and the fact was that she no longer wanted to exist. As an apothecary, she'd considered early deaths tragic; now, she considered it a worse fate to linger on late. There was a time for everyone, and that time had, for her, come the moment she'd discovered Izar's Ocean Dominion card and realized he'd betrayed her. Since then, she was just lingering, unsettled as a ghost, like a planet confused about her orbit.

Suddenly, the luciferin orbs extinguished, their white-blue glow vanishing.

Coralline blinked—perhaps her mind was so muddled that she'd shut her eyes and confused internal darkness for external. But she blinked again, and again, and again—the darkness remained, just as dense as that of the deep sea. *You will die soon after the light dies*, Mintaka had said. The light had just died, which meant Coralline would soon die. *Thank you, Mintaka, thank you!* she whispered. She laughed for the first time since she'd returned home, and listened curiously to the ring of her laughter. She cherished the feel of water as it fluttered gently in and out of her gills, and she pressed her hand to her heart—her heart that would soon be still. Mintaka's curse was a blessing.

In a flash, the luciferin orbs sparked back to life, glowing as brightly as before. Coralline needed to talk to Pavonis; she needed to tell him she would die. Pavonis had tried to beckon her to her window often, even claiming his snout needed scratching, but she'd said she was too tired to move. He'd attempted all manners of humor to draw a laugh out of her: "The yellow spots on my back aren't contagious." "I know you're better than the lump you're pretending to be." "Getting enough sleep over there?" Coralline hadn't laughed at his words, but she'd smiled every time, if only to be polite.

Returning Izar's card carefully under her pillow, Coralline turned her head to the window, a black oval broken intermittently by sparks of bio-luminescence. Sitting up, she started extricating herself from the folds of the blanket. The process was like that of a snake moulting, for the fabric seemed to have become a second skin—she felt as much a part of the bed as the mattress. Dragging her tail over the side of the bed, she climbed out, almost crippled by the effort.

She looked down at herself. Her flesh was as soft and limp as the pillows upon which she lay all day. Her skin was tender all over, like a young, unmoving snail's. Her chemise was held up only by its straps, and she could discern the outline of each rib under the ivory fabric—she was fast disappearing inside herself. If someone were to press a hand into her, it would go straight through, as through empty space. Shifting to the window, she sagged against the windowsill, no longer having the strength to hover.

"Took you long enough," drawled a voice.

"Oh, Pavonis!" Coralline said, extending a hand into the darkness. His snout arrived neatly under her fingers.

"I missed you," he said.

He truly must have, for he would otherwise have derided such words as sentimental. "I missed you, too," Coralline said.

"There's something I have to tell you."

"Me, too. You start."

"Now that we've returned to Urchin Grove from the Elixir Expedition, I see that all the while I was trying to escape this horrible village, I was actually trying to escape my horrible self."

"You're not horrible, Pavonis!"

"But I am. And you'll think so, too, once you know the truth about Mako: He was killed by humans, yes, but he was also killed by me."

Coralline gasped.

"Soon after Mako and I left Urchin Grove for our North-to-South Expedition, an Ocean Dominion ship came upon us. The men ensnared Mako in a net. Instead of staying to try to free him, to try to distract the ship, I swam away as fast as I could, not looking back once at my best friend, who was crying out for me. My only friend in the world apart from you, and I left him to die a torturous death."

Coralline wished it were not dark, she wished she could look him in the eye, so that he could see she meant the words she said: "It's not your fault you were afraid, Pavonis. It's natural to be afraid. Forgive yourself."

He sighed; she did not hear it as much as feel it in the lilt of water. "Even if I forgive myself for Mako," he said, "I'll never forgive myself for you. I rescued you from a human fishnet when you were a baby, but I failed to rescue you from the human in our own midst during our elixir quest."

"I made my own mistakes, as far as the human in question is concerned."

"I know you love him, Coralline, but control your heart; don't let it control you."

"Oh, I wish I could!" Coralline's head dropped in her hands, and tears streamed down her cheeks in sticky trails. "But I can't help it!"

"In time, you'll forget all about him. Now, what did you want to tell me?"

"I wanted to tell you that there's no time. I'm about to die."

"There's no need to be dramatic!" Pavonis snapped.

"But I am about to die, I know it. In the cavern, Mintaka said that I would die soon after the light died. Just before you arrived, the light died, which means I'm going to die soon."

"You're usually quite humorless. Is this a convoluted attempt at a joke? If so, I must say it's pathetic."

"I'm not joking."

"Then why are you smiling?"

"Because I'm happy I'm dying."

She regretted the words as soon as she'd said them, for it sounded as though she did not care for him. "I'm sorry, I didn't mean it that way."

Whenever her mother had advised her to find herself another muse, Coralline had said she would consider it after Pavonis died, and she'd laughed inside, for whale sharks lived longer than merpeople. "I hope you find yourself another best friend after I die," she said tearfully, "someone who enjoys travel and adventure as much as you."

"How can you leave me alone in this world?" Pavonis cried. "You are my entire world."

His tail slammed against the wall, then the waters rippled, and he vanished.

The door opened. It was the taller of Serpens's two lackeys, Izar saw. Whistling a low tune to himself, the man bent down to place a tray on the floor. He then collected the old, empty tray and closed the door behind him, causing bundles of dust to liberate themselves from the doorjamb and sprinkle about the room.

The place was vast but dark, lit by no more than one naked, low-hanging yellow lightbulb of the kind Izar imagined in torture chambers, casting a jaundiced glow over a prisoner's head. It made a constant whirring racket, a steady drone that seemed to penetrate Izar's eardrums and grate against his brain. Another sound cracked through the whine of the bulb—a gurgle. Izar looked up at the ceiling, for he knew the gurgle spewed out of the pipes in the ceiling of his Invention Chamber, directly above this room. Imprisonment was a strange thing. His Invention Chamber on B2 held the precise proportions as this room and had the same untiled floor and unfinished walls, but Izar considered that room a haven and this room on B3 a dungeon.

Izar strode over to the tray the lackey had placed next to the door: two heaping bowls of soggy cereal—breakfast. Returning to the vicinity of the lightbulb, Izar squatted and carved a notch in the floor. The breakfast told him it was the start of a new day in his imprisonment, and the five earlier notches told him it was the sixth day. There were no windows on B3, three levels underground, and so it was not through sunrises but mealtimes that Izar gauged the passage of time.

There was just one day left to Coralline's wedding, and to his escape attempt.

The celebration will be a funeral, Mintaka had told him. It was possible that she'd been referring to Coralline's wedding. But she had not specified *whose* funeral it would be. Perhaps it would be Izar's own—he would prefer that to Coralline's.

He heard a rasp from the other side of the room. He collected the breakfast tray and marched in the direction of the sound. Zaurak Alphard sat hunched on the floor, leaning against the wall, his legs stretched out before him. Izar barely recognized his fifty-seven-year-old mentor, the director of operations, not only because his face was now bearded, but because his nose was broken, the nostrils encrusted with blood. The shin of his right leg was broken as well, a thick, angry red welt stretching diagonally across it. The leg had already been lame, but now, it was also injured and infected. A cloud of yellow pus circled it like growth in a petri dish, and flies buzzed around it, feeding, breeding. When the flies had first appeared, seemingly out of nowhere, Zaurak had twitched his leg at intervals to shoo them away, but he was too weak to do so anymore.

Izar plopped down cross-legged next to Zaurak's leg and swatted the flies away. If Coralline were here, he thought, she would know what to do. She could not bear to watch anyone suffer.

He passed a bowl of cereal to Zaurak and ate his own cereal absentmindedly.

"I'm not hungry," Zaurak said.

"We'll need the energy for our escape tomorrow."

Zaurak proceeded to take a few half-hearted mouthfuls of his cereal.

When Izar was done, he put his bowl down and said, "Let's practice walking. You'll need to be able to run tomorrow."

"Not now," Zaurak said, resting his head against the wall.

When they'd practiced walking yesterday, Izar had supported Zaurak with an arm around his shoulders, and Zaurak had hobbled about for a few minutes, then, crying out in pain, had collapsed.

Four days ago, when Serpens had shoved him through the door of this room, Izar had fallen flat on his chest. Closing his eyes, he'd rested his forehead on the floor—its coolness had reminded him of the ocean. A scuttle had sounded across the room. The place must be infested with rats, Izar had thought, but the scuttle had approached him steadily, an unevenness to its scurry. It had not been something, but some*one*, who was hobbling over to him, Izar had realized. He had risen to his knees and squinted at the man emerging from the shadows, his face like a rock with scraggly moss sprouted over it: Zaurak.

Over the last four days, Izar and Zaurak had shared with each other everything that they knew. After the derrick had fallen on *Dominion Drill I*, failing to crush Izar, Zaurak had spent the night double-checking parts of the drillship. He had marked off everything in his checklist and had placed it on Izar's desk. He had been about to leave for home when he'd noticed a flashlight on the drillship. He'd clambered back upon *Dominion Drill I* to investigate and had discovered Serpens there, switching out a blowout preventer. He'd tried to stop Serpens, but Serpens had broken his leg and knocked him unconscious. His pen had fallen out of his shirt pocket during the skirmish and gotten caught in the stopper of the borehole. When he'd awoken, hours later, he'd found himself locked in this room.

Zaurak's account complemented Izar's own. The night Izar had discovered the gray tin on his desk, he'd heard a series of sounds coming from below. He'd taken the private elevator down from B1 to B3, and had flashed his identification card before the scanner, but the elevator bars hadn't opened. Izar had assumed the sounds must be coming from the gassy pipes in his Invention Chamber on B2, but he knew now that Zaurak had been the source of the sounds, as he'd tried to escape.

Izar shifted such that he sat next to Zaurak, his back leaning against the wall, his legs stretched out before him. "I'm sorry," he whispered.

It was Izar's fault that Zaurak was trapped here, and in this condition. He had been double-checking the drillship to protect Izar, he had confronted Serpens to protect Izar. Serpens had imprisoned him here so that Zaurak couldn't interfere any more with further attacks on Izar's life. And yet, despite everything Zaurak had been doing for him, Izar had doubted Zaurak, believing him to have been responsible for the attempts on his life. His most loyal friend, he'd viewed as his most suspect.

"I don't know whether I'll survive our escape tomorrow," Zaurak said, "but—"

"Don't be ridiculous."

"Regardless of what happens tomorrow, there's something I have to tell you before I die."

"You're not going to die," Izar said crossly, "but, fine, tell me."

"It relates to Antares."

Izar stiffened. He had not told Zaurak what Osmundea had told him. He wanted to speak to Antares about it first. "What about Antares?" Izar said, turning his head to look at Zaurak.

Zaurak's eyes stared straight ahead, his pupils like circles of black ice. "Twenty-seven years ago, when my leg got caught in shark-skinning equipment and Antares paid for my medical care out of pocket, I felt deeply indebted to him and intensely loyal. I thought it was a sense of benevolence that had led him to help me. I did not know that he wanted something from me. Two years later, I finally came to understand.

"Antares phoned me late one night and ordered me to meet him at midnight. He asked me to bring with me my Worker Directory, a register containing the names and phone numbers of all the fishermen at Ocean Dominion. As director of operations, I alone had access to the Worker Directory. I also prided myself on knowing my fishermen by name. I did not ask Antares any questions but, trusting him, arrived at midnight upon the trawler he indicated. It belonged to a giant of a man named Alshain Ankaa."

Izar closed his eyes at the name.

"Antares, Alshain, and I set out into the night sea. Eventually, Alshain stopped the trawler and gave Antares a pearl-colored potion called moonmumble—made of liquid moonlight, he said—to transform him into a merman. I'd never heard of moonmumble or a human-merperson transformation before, and scoffed at the idea, but I was left with my tongue hanging out of my mouth when Antares dove overboard and disappeared under the waves. As Alshain and I waited for him to return, Alshain told me that Antares had transformed once before, almost four years before that day. His visit had had something to do with legend and lore underwater."

Legend and lore . . . Zaurak's voice mingled with Osmundea's in Izar's mind.

"Anyhow, Antares soon returned to the waves. But he was not alone; he was wrestling with a mermaid over a merboy. In the tussle, Antares tried to slash her throat with some sort of half-shell, but he ended up gashing the merboy's jaw."

Zaurak's gaze traced the hook-shaped scar on Izar's face. Izar thought of covering it with a hand, but found that his hands could not move.

"Antares knocked the mermaid unconscious and dragged the child onto the trawler. Alshain and I urged him to return the child to his mother, but Antares claimed the child was his son. He said the boy's mother was demented and he was rescuing the boy from her. I trusted Antares and believed every word he said. Alshain gave Antares a golden potion called sunsin—constituted of liquid sunlight—to turn him human again. Antares ordered Alshain to also give sunsin to the boy, as well as another potion—one that would lapse his memory of the water and enable him to have a 'fresh, happy start on land.'

"Upon drinking sunsin, Antares started convulsing on the trawler during his transformation from merman back to human. Alshain came to stand over the boy but did not give him sunsin. I held the boy in my arms. He was shaking so severely that the blood from his cut was splattering all over my shirt. When his body stilled, I saw that his tail had separated into legs and his chest was moving up and down, powered by lungs. Alshain strode up to me and said the boy's transformation proved the truth of Antares's words, that the boy was his son. The boy had to be half-human and half-merperson—a hummer, Alshain said—otherwise he could not have transformed without a potion. Alshain emptied a vial of a pale-blue potion at the boy's lips, to lapse his memory of the water."

That was why Izar remembered nothing of his life before that day.

"I hoped we would return to Menkar and the ghastly night would be over, but Antares asked me to phone a fisherman with a son of a similar age and appearance as the boy on deck. Looking at the boy, I thought immediately of an Ocean Dominion fisherman on the island of Mira, Heze Virgo, who'd had a son just about three years ago, a boy with curly brown hair, like the one I was holding in my arms. I found Heze's phone number in my Worker Directory. I called him and handed the phone to Antares, who ordered Heze to meet us in the waters near Mira with his wife and boy, otherwise his fisherman position with Ocean Dominion would be terminated. Heze hurried over to our trawler in his fishing dinghy, his wife Capella and their boy cowering behind him in the little boat. What Antares did next is something that has haunted me since."

Goosebumps crawled up Izar's arms. He thought of Rigel Nihal, the drunken neighbor of the Virgos, whom he'd encountered when he'd visited the Virgos' hovel.

"Antares bounded out of the trawler into the fishing dinghy and, before anyone could react, bludgeoned the family to death with a club. He hurled their bodies overboard. Soon after, the boy on the platform started to awaken, his memory wiped clean. By this time, I was so sick to my stomach that I had gone belowdecks—that's why you don't remember me from that night. . . . The next day, Antares told *Menkar Daily* that he'd happened to arrive while the fishing family was being drowned by merpeople. He told them that he'd managed to rescue the boy, and, most magnanimously, decided to adopt him."

Zaurak shook out his leg angrily on the floor, then, crying out in pain, grabbed his thigh with both hands. "I wish Antares hadn't saved my leg," he bellowed, "for it led me to feel indebted to him—which was why he'd saved it to begin with. I thought often of going to the Office of the Police Commissioner, but I was an accomplice to the killings—I had been on the trawler; I had dialed Heze Virgo. Plus, the chief police commissioner, that corrupt buzzard with his handlebar moustache, Canopus Corvus, has always been in Antares's pocket. Antares practically pays his whole salary, in the form of hefty donations to the Office of the Police Commissioner. As such, Antares can rely on Canopus's loyalty whenever he requires it."

Izar remembered his visit to Canopus that night, when the gash across his jaw had been bleeding a path down his face. Canopus had written everything Antares had said as though it was found in a history textbook. He had not questioned; he had not sought any other witnesses or alternate accounts. And when such an account had arrived—Rigel had discovered all three bodies—Canopus must have spoken to Antares about it directly. In the middle of the night, Antares had made the bodies disappear from the grave.

"Everything that you know about your past is a lie," Zaurak continued in a tortured voice, "and I've played my part in it. I'm sorry, Izar. I'll never forgive myself. . . ."

Zaurak's voice trailed off, but even if it hadn't, Izar no longer possessed the capacity to listen.

Why would Antares have gone to all this trouble to abduct him from the water? he wondered. Because Izar was a hummer, and hummers were inventive, and Antares needed something invented—underwater fire. Antares had tested Izar's intelligence that first day itself by asking him to construct a replica of his house. Izar had passed the test; had he failed, Antares might have thrown him back into the ocean. Antares had also kindled a fascination of underwater fire in Izar that first day by lighting a match and dropping it in a glass of water.

But why would Antares have killed the Virgos, Izar wondered, when he could easily have told the world a simpler story? He could have said, for instance, that he'd discovered Izar as a wandering orphan on shore and decided to adopt him. No, Antares had killed the Virgos to ensure that Izar grew up with a lifelong loathing of merpeople, believing they'd murdered his biological parents. Antares had wanted Izar to have no qualms about harming merpeople and their world.

Izar had thought Maia insane, with her allegations that he was the son of a mistress of Antares's, but she'd been right: Izar was born of Antares's liaison, except with a mermaid instead of a woman. But if Izar was Antares's biological son just as much as Saiph, why had Antares always loved Saiph but viewed Izar as a means to an end? Because Izar was partly merman, and thus, from Antares's perspective, he was beneath human—beneath Antares and Saiph—except in the realm of inventiveness.

When Maia's car had exploded on the way to a divorce lawyer, Izar had been blamed for it because he'd been tinkering with the hood of her car the night before. But nothing Izar had done should have caused an explosion. It must have been Antares who'd rigged Maia's car to explode, for she would have obtained half of his wealth in a divorce settlement. Pursuant to Maia's death, Antares had paid Canopus half a million dollars to get the charges against Izar removed. At the time, Izar had thought Antares had saved him from jail because of his love for him; now, he thought it must be because Antares had wanted Izar to be able to invent underwater fire, something impossible from a prison cell.

Izar touched his wrist where his platinum chip had been. When he had charred his wrist during his fire experimentation, he had gone to see Doctor Navi, and both Antares and Zaurak had visited him in Doctor Navi's office. In the ocean, Izar had assumed that Zaurak must have told Doctor Navi to plant the tracking device in him—now he knew it was Antares who must have done so. With the chip in him, Izar could be tracked and killed as soon as his purpose was served. And it was now served—Castor was ready—and Izar had transformed from an asset to a liability: Antares and Saiph did not want to share with him the wealth that he had created for them.

Antares and Saiph had to have been working together on the numerous murder attempts on his life. The contents of the gray tin that Izar had discovered on his desk, for instance—the amber scroll, the half-shell, and the card with coordinates—must have come from Antares.

Yer a pawn in a game, Rigel had said. Saiph, yes, but not Antares—Izar could never have imagined that Antares would want him dead—Antares, who had adopted him, cared for him, protected him against the world—Antares, for whom he would have given his life. Izar had been a puppet, Antares, the puppeteer.

"I'm sorry, Izar," Zaurak repeated.

"You've suffered plenty on my account," Izar said, looking at Zaurak's fly-swarmed leg. "I'm the one who should be sorry."

"No matter what happens to me tomorrow," Zaurak said gruffly, grasping the back of Izar's neck, "I want you to escape and live."

"You wouldn't leave me behind, and I'm not about to leave you behind. You're all I have left now."

On land, Zaurak was all Izar had left; in the ocean, there was a small chance he also had Coralline. He wondered what she was doing at this moment. She was probably busy with wedding preparations, he imagined, perhaps fussing over the lace of her bridal bodice or deciding how she would fashion her long hair. He did not know anything about weddings underwater, but there would be a bride and a groom, and Coralline would be the bride and Ecklon the groom. Unless, of course, she decided against marrying Ecklon. Unless she loved Izar, as Izar loved her.

He knew his thinking was wishful, but he could not help indulging in it, not only for his sake but also hers. If she decided against marrying Ecklon tomorrow, she would not be at the wedding venue, Kelp Cove, and Castor would find himself in an empty arena. If she did decide to marry Ecklon tomorrow, things would be very different. Assuming that his escape attempt worked, Izar was planning to reach her wedding in time to disable Castor, but he worried that the robot was practically invincible. With a chest full of bullets, Castor would shoot anyone who approached him or whom he deemed even a remote threat—Izar had programmed him with this self-defense instinct. And Castor's eyes were long-range, three-dimensional cameras, such that Saiph would be able to view Castor's underwater environment on a computer screen, and guide and focus his violence toward Coralline.

If Coralline married tomorrow, she would likely die tomorrow. If she didn't, she would live. Izar thought again of Mintaka's words: *The celebration will be a funeral.*

He needed to remember Coralline viscerally, the need just as stark as that for oxygen. Leaping to his feet, he rushed to his satchel below the jaundiced light-bulb. Made of treated algae, the sack was different on land than in it had been in the water—fully dry now, its folds were no longer malleable but starched and hard. The zip was also tighter, requiring more tugging. Izar opened it nonetheless and, reaching a hand inside, pulled out Coralline's notepad. The algae upon its cover looked like a shapeless smear, and many of the pages were stuck together, having lost their shape—but Izar cradled the little notepad as though it was her hand he caressed.

A glow emanated from within his satchel. Putting the notepad down on the floor, he rummaged inside the bag, shifting aside the stiff layers along its bottom, and gasped: There, in an under-compartment, shining as brightly as a torch, was the elixir intended for her brother.

Izar and Coralline had planned that Izar would give it to her upon his return to the Telescope Tower. But after his conversation with Osmundea, and then after he'd seen Coralline kissing Ecklon, he'd forgotten all about it.

"What's that light?" Zaurak called.

Izar could not speak, but he turned to look at Zaurak, so Zaurak would know he had heard him. An idea fell into his mind: He had forgotten to give the elixir to Coralline, but he could give it to Zaurak. It would heal Zaurak's leg, which would help them escape this room tomorrow, which would in turn help Izar get into the water and save Coralline from Castor.

Izar sprinted to Zaurak and knelt before him. Clasping the elixir between his thumb and forefinger, he held it before Zaurak's nose, such that its reflection shone as twin moons in Zaurak's eyes. "This is an elixir that will heal your leg and save your life. Take it."

"Save it for yourself," Zaurak said, "in case you need it tomorrow."

"No. Take it. I insist." Izar deposited the elixir in the palm of Zaurak's hand.

27

The Queen of Poison

You have a visitor," Abalone said, opening Coralline's door a wedge. Abalone slipped aside, and Rhodomela slithered in through the crack of the doorway, like an eel through a crevice. She was wearing a black bodice, and her black hair was wound in her signature, severe bun. She slammed the door in Abalone's face.

Rhodomela had never visited Coralline at home before. She must be here to collect an apology, Coralline thought. "I'm sorry. I should not have trespassed into The Irregular Remedy to prepare my desmarestia-sea-oak solution, and I should not have spoken to you as I did during my probationary review."

Rhodomela did not seem to be listening; instead, she was sniffing, her hooked nose twitching. Had the room started to smell? Coralline wondered. It might well have: When she had worked for Rhodomela, Coralline had once visited an elderly merman on his deathbed, and her nostrils had gotten a whiff of something as indescribable as it was discernible—intuitively, she had recognized it as the smell of death. Coralline's family had perhaps grown immune to her odor, because it would have grown steadily over the days; like a change in weight, it would be more noticeable to an outsider. Rhodomela knew death better than she knew life, and she'd detected it immediately. Coralline smiled—Rhodomela's reaction suggested that Coralline's death truly must be near.

Rhodomela arrived suddenly at Coralline's bedside. Coralline thought of inviting the master apothecary to sit on the desk chair next to her bed, but it would be far too close for comfort—yet it was equally intimidating to have Rhodomela hovering over her, forming a bony tower. Rhodomela handed her *The Annals of the Association of Apothecaries*. Coralline usually devoured the journal as soon as it arrived every month, reading it cover to cover in a single sitting from her perch at the living-room window, but the journal for this month was sitting unopened on her desk, deposited there by her mother earlier this morning.

Coralline saw a large portrait of herself on the front page of *The Annals*.

The Queen of Poison

From the village of Urchin Grove, twenty-year-old mermaid Coralline Costaria seems to have stumbled upon a shocking medical discovery.

Coralline worked as an apprentice apothecary for renowned, exacting Master Apothecary Rhodomela Ranularia, at Rhodomela's clinic, The Irregular Remedy. Coralline, the first person Rhodomela ever hired, was also the first person Rhodomela ever fired. Coralline worked for Rhodomela for six months before Rhodomela told her, "I'd rather die of blood contamination from black poison than see your hideously ugly face again," according to Rosette Delesse, an associate apothecary at The Conventional Cure next door.

Soon after Coralline's dismissal, a black poison spill lashed Urchin Grove, leaving Coralline's eight-year-old brother, Naiadum, terminally ill. Coralline decided to reject medicine in favor of magic to save her brother. Abandoning her family, she traveled far and wide through Meristem to find the legendary elixir of starlight. She returned empty-handed, but with a gruesome murder charge against her and an unsettlingly unconventional idea: that the reviled, poisonous acid kelp desmarestia, when combined with the alkaline algae sea oak, could be a healer of tremendous scope.

With her poison-based remedy, Coralline managed to rescue her brother from the brink of death. But a challenge unfolded: Without a medical badge from the Association of Apothecaries, she was in defiance of the Medical Malpractice Act. The punishment for such defiance? To be barred from practice for the rest of one's life.

Rhodomela arrived at Coralline's rescue. She said that Rosette was woefully mistaken and that she had never terminated Coralline's employment at The Irregular Remedy. As proof, she showed Coralline's apprentice apothecary badge to the Constables Department of Urchin Grove. Rhodomela said that Coralline had simply forgotten the sand-dollar shell at The Irregular Remedy, and thus had been unable to produce it when constable Pericarp Plicata had asked to see it at her home. Pericarp has dismissed the medical malpractice charge against Coralline.

Rhodomela visited next with the Association of Apothecaries, and presented a case to the Decision-Making Panel—consisting of three master apothecaries—that Coralline had invented an unprecedented, life-saving remedy, and should thus be awarded the title of master apothecary. The panel agreed unanimously.

With their decision, Coralline (whom Rosette has dubbed "Queen of Poison") becomes the youngest healer in the realm of Meristem to have achieved the title of master apothecary. (Rhodomela is the second-youngest healer to have achieved the title, at twenty-five years of age, when she invented the Black Poison Cleanser solution.)

But with the murder charge looming over Coralline, the question remains: Will the remainder of her healing occur at the Wrongdoers' Refinery?

"I don't understand," Coralline stammered, gawking at Rhodomela. "You fired me during my probationary review."

"Yes, but I realized soon after that I should not have. That's why I never mailed your badge to the Association of Apothecaries, as I was legally required to do. And that's why I never disposed of your urns of remedies.

With your desmarestia solution, you have now proven that you do know how to think irregularly."

"You lied to the Constables Department to save me," Coralline said incredulously. "Am I really a master apothecary now?"

"Yes."

"I can't believe it. It's a dream come true. . . . Thank you for getting the medical malpractice charge against me dismissed; thank you for convincing the Association of Apothecaries to award me the title of master. And I never thought I'd say it, but thank you also for firing me. Otherwise, I might have relied on my textbooks for the rest of my life, without bothering to think for myself."

"Think nothing of it," Rhodomela said. From her pinched expression, she seemed slightly embarrassed at Coralline's gratitude. "And here's your new badge."

She handed Coralline a sand-dollar shell. *Coralline Costaria, Master Apothecary* stated its smooth, round surface. Coralline read the words over and over, as though repetition would help with comprehension.

"Your remedy has the potential to change the future of healing. I am here today to invite you to join me at The Irregular Remedy not as an employee but as a partner. I would like for us to be two master apothecaries working side by side, together saving lives."

Rhodomela's tone was as flat as ever, but she'd just paid Coralline the greatest compliment of her career. Even in her most farfetched dreams, Coralline had never imagined she'd be a partner at The Irregular Remedy—an equal to Rhodomela! That meant more to Coralline than the title of master apothecary, for Rhodomela's approval was more difficult to achieve than that of the Decision-Making Panel. She envisioned a placard with the words *Coralline's Cures* dangling above her unit of shelves at The Irregular Remedy. She would not have her own clinic, but she would have her own practice at this clinic. Her logo would be a pink burst of coralline algae.

"Will you be my partner, Coralline?" The black eyes pierced Coralline, narrow but bright.

"I would love to," Coralline heard herself say, "but I can never heal again." She meant it for herself—if she could not heal herself, she could not heal others. And that was what Rhodomela had said to her during her probationary review: "In order to heal others, you have to first heal yourself." Even were Coralline not to die soon, she did not want to heal herself. There was an addictive element to her heartache for Izar, a beauty to her bitterness.

It hurt, but, with quivering fingers, Coralline handed the sand-dollar badge back to Rhodomela.

"Don't do this, Coralline," Rhodomela said, her face as stiff as a cloth wrung tightly through the hands. "You have too much talent and skill to waste."

"I'm sorry." Rhodomela had smelled Coralline's surroundings for herself, but Coralline did not want to explicitly tell Rhodomela that she lay on the verge of death; Rhodomela would see for herself soon enough. "You were right," Coralline said.

"What about?"

"Love. That it's a farce."

Coralline was about to blurt out more, to wail, to share her burden with someone—but, her eyes glittering, Rhodomela whirled around and departed. Coralline could not help but wonder whether Rhodomela was fleeing her own pain or Coralline's.

A knock sounded at the door.

"Come in," Coralline called.

Ecklon entered. His pebbled hair was swept off his forehead, and his broad frame was attired in a dark-ash waistcoat with buttercup lucine shells for buttons. His face, with the narrow line of his nose and the smooth set of his lips, was unbearably handsome, so much more so than Izar's, but Coralline felt as though she was regarding not the merman with whom she was supposed to spend the rest of her life but a beautiful stranger.

Ecklon squeezed into the desk chair at Coralline's bedside, but his frame was too tall and wide for it, such that his tailfin grazed the floor. Coralline herself sat not propped up against her pillows but with her tailfin over the side of the bed, next to his. At her mother's insistence, she had changed out of the mourning-black bodice she'd been wearing all week into a sun-orange corset with incongruously puffed sleeves. She found the bright color irritating—it seemed to be mocking her mood. She tried to keep her unsupported back straight, but her vertebrae could not stop from slumping.

"I just returned from Hog's Bristle," Ecklon said.

There was death in his manner, in the quietness of his voice. The case must have been negatively resolved, Coralline thought—he must have been unable to disprove the murder charge against her.

Ecklon reached into his waistcoat pocket and extracted a serpent-encrusted dagger. It hurtled Coralline back in time and space—she was hovering again over Tang Tarpon in Hog's Bristle, surrounded by his empty decanters of parasol wine, gasping as he bled to death.

"I interviewed a dozen dagger carvers in Hog's Bristle," Ecklon said, "and managed to locate the one who carved the serpent-hilt dagger that killed Tang. The dagger carver, an ancient, white-haired merman with weak eyes and steady hands, eventually remembered the purchaser of this dagger: a yellow-tailed merman named Sabre Sandeel. I obtained Sabre's information and portrait from the Under-Ministry of Residential Affairs. I went to the designated house and found Sabre there, as well as Charonia—Tang Tarpon's wife. Sabre tried to escape out the back door, but I managed to apprehend and handcuff him. Charonia, meanwhile, swallowed desmarestia, writhed, and died. Crying, Sabre confessed to Tang's murder and expressed his motive: He loved Charonia, and she loved him, but he feared she might return to her husband again one day, so he killed her husband to eliminate that possibility. Sabre is now awaiting trial at the Wrongdoers' Refinery for the murder of Tang Tarpon."

How selfish Charonia had been, Coralline thought. Tang had risked his own life to save hers—finding the elixir to cure her spinal tumor—but she'd fallen in love with someone else. By doing so, she'd ruined not only her own life but also the lives of both her husband and her lover. . . . But by judging Charonia, was Coralline not also judging herself? As Tang had saved Charonia, Ecklon was saving Coralline, risking his career for her. And as Charonia had chosen someone else—Sabre, capable of violence against others—Coralline had also chosen someone else—Izar, capable of violence against others. Charonia had killed herself upon learning her mistake; Coralline was, fortunately, going to die soon, based on Mintaka's curse.

She hoped death would find her before her wedding—even though only twenty-four hours remained to the event. She wanted to die not only because she could not be with Izar but also because she could not be with Ecklon—her betrayal of him was making her sicker by the day, like a dagger twisting deeper and deeper into her side. If she died before her wedding, she would not explicitly end her relationship with Ecklon—or tell him anything, she'd decided. She would not shatter him by her betrayal, as Izar had shattered her by his betrayal—his allegiance to Ocean Dominion. Coralline had other, more selfish reasons to keep Izar a secret from Ecklon: She did not have the courage to tell him about Izar, and she did not want his final memory of her to be polluted by her mistake.

"There is no more murder charge against you," Ecklon continued. "Your name is now clear. You are no longer under house arrest."

Even as he conveyed the good news, the manner of death remained in his voice. Given that it did not relate to the case—the case was positively resolved—could it relate to their relationship? Coralline wondered. Maybe he knew about Izar; maybe he was here to end things with her. She sat up straight and looked at him attentively, pining to hear him say that he no longer wanted to be with her.

"You are free to live," he said, "free to marry."

But she did not have long to live, and she did not want to marry.

"Is there anything you'd like to tell me?" he asked.

Was she imagining the emphasis in his voice, the new, rushed quality of it, the sense that he was punishing himself by his question?

"No," she said.

"Coralline," called a meek voice from the window.

Coralline felt her brow crinkle, but she couldn't tell whether she was awake or dreaming. She vacillated constantly between sleep and consciousness, falling as smoothly from one to the other as the trickle of sand in a sand-clock. Whenever she awoke, she doubted she had been asleep; whenever she slept, she doubted she had been awake.

"Coralline!" the voice called again.

She hoped it was Pavonis, but the voice did not have his authoritative tone—it was small and tremulous. She had not seen Pavonis since he'd stormed off after learning of her impending death. Maybe he'd returned now, she thought, maybe he was ready to forgive her for leaving him alone in the world after her death.

Her eyes opened slowly. A tiny orange form was suspended in the oval frame of her window—Altair. He was thick and shiny around the middle, due to give birth soon to hundreds of seahorses. The waters behind him held the gray hue of evening.

"I'm here, too!" piped another voice, from much closer, the corner of Coralline's pillow, in fact—Nacre.

"What's the matter?" Coralline asked, looking with little interest from the snail to the seahorse.

"Altair has something to tell you," Nacre said, turning slightly such that one of her tentacles faced him, and the other remained pointed at Coralline.

"I thought it my duty to let you know," he said, "that I was wrong."

"About what?" Coralline yawned.

"Before the Elixir Expedition, I believed in black-and-white clarity, in unerring monogamy. But I've been thinking about love ever since our return, and I've realized that being with the right partner enables one to glow brightly, while being with the wrong partner forces one to hide one's true self, to live camouflaged, in essence. I've been watching you since our return to Urchin Grove. With Izar by your side, you glowed brighter than ever; now, without him, you've become a shadow of your former self. You're so camouflaged, Coralline, you can hardly even see yourself anymore."

"What Altair is trying to say in his long-winded way," Nacre contributed, "is that when it comes to love, you should follow your heart, not your head. If you don't want to marry Ecklon, *don't*. But don't you dare tell your mother I said so!"

Her eyes closing, Coralline started drifting again into sleep. A clammy form arrived on her right shoulder and nestled in the hollow, tentacles patting her ear. Previously, when Coralline had been unaccustomed to Nacre, she'd found any movement of the snail's tentacles against her ear irritating, tickling, and she'd shrugged instinctively. Now, she found the movement of the tentacles soothing—they were Nacre's equivalents of pats on the head. "Poor darling," Nacre whispered.

Coralline nestled deeper in the bed. The bedsheets were Izar's arms, beckoning her closer and closer, and she sank keenly into their embrace. . . .

Izar stood with Zaurak next to the closed door, in the shadows, awaiting the two lackeys.

Zaurak was leaning against the wall, the foot of his injured leg resting lightly on the floor. Sweat was streaming down the sides of his face—the mere act of standing seemed to be draining him. His cheeks were flushed; he'd awoken with a fever, as a result of his leg infection. Flies were circling the gash across his shin, droning steadily like a fan. A trickle of pus ran down to his ankle.

"You swallowed the elixir last night before you slept, right?" Izar asked.

"Yes."

After everything he and Coralline had done to get the elixir, how could it not have worked? Izar thought. How could Zaurak's leg not be fully healed? Izar had felt certain that upon taking the elixir, not only would Zaurak's injury be cured, but his limp itself would disappear. He had imagined Zaurak leaping and skipping like a ballerina on the leg that he was currently dragging.

"Will you be able to run?" Izar whispered.

"How many times do you want me to say it?" Zaurak hissed. "*Yes.*"

There was a rattling just outside the door, and a jingle—one lackey was probably trying to balance the breakfast tray in his hands, while the other was inserting the key to unlock the door. "Shh!" Izar said, standing as straight as a soldier at attention.

The door opened. Izar was slightly off to the side, and he could not see the two lackeys, but he could see their shadows on the floor, one shadow a little more squat than the other. He saw Zaurak's lumpy shadow as well, and he heard the clang of Zaurak's pen as it hit the floor. The squat shadow jumped as the pen rolled between his feet—then there was an ear-splitting crack: The breakfast tray fell, the dishes broke. The pen was not a weapon, of course, but it was intended to alarm, and had served his purpose. The crash of dishes was Izar's cue: He leapt out of the shadows and came face-to-face with the two lackeys.

The more squat lackey stepped into the room and pointed his gun at Izar. Behind him, Zaurak collected the fallen tray and slammed it over the lackey's head, so forcefully that the tray shattered. As Izar watched, the man's eyes rolled up in his head. Starting with his feet, then knees, then hips, he collapsed in slow motion, as though a rug had been tugged out from underneath him.

Zaurak sagged down to the floor himself, shaking, huffing, exhausted.

Izar tackled the other lackey, but not before the man drew his gun. Izar expected the lackey to point the gun at him, but he pointed it at Zaurak. Before Izar could blink, a shot tore through the air. From over the lackey's shoulder, Izar saw blood diffusing out of Zaurak's chest and dripping over his sides like paint.

Izar leapt upon the lackey, and they fell together to the floor. Izar pummeled him until the lackey's nose broke twice and his jaw cracked once, and his face was so bloodied, it could no longer be recognized.

He then knelt on the floor next to Zaurak and pulled the large head onto his lap. Zaurak's lips parted—he was trying to tell Izar something—and Izar bent his head, but he heard nothing more than the rasp of Zaurak's breath against his ear. Izar prayed for the elixir to come into action now, for it to save Zaurak's life, but, before he could draw his next breath, the light vanished from Zaurak's eyes. His irises became as luminous but empty as gray pearls.

"The greatest day of your life has finally arrived! In a matter of hours, you will transform from Coralline Costaria to Coralline Elnath, hanging on the arm of the most eligible merman in Urchin Grove. Out of bed, Coralline, before he changes his mind and decides to marry Rosette instead!"

Coralline opened one eye, then the other, as though the delay could help put off her wedding. Hitting rock-bottom—that was an expression she'd heard Izar use once—and she did feel as though she'd hit her head against the bottom of a rock. Her heartache was, by now, persistent and amorphous, like general bodily pain, a complaint she'd always found difficult to treat as an apothecary. She'd hoped to die overnight, passing seamlessly, gracefully, from life to death, but here she was, her blanket being yanked off her. She turned onto her side and curled her tail up to her arms, but Abalone pulled her arms until she was in an upright position, her tailfin over the side of the bed.

"Enough with that pinched expression, darling! No one likes a bleached coralline. Now, I have a gift for you sure to create marital bliss."

Her mother handed her a book with a glossy fuchsia cover, *The Beatific Bride: Tips for a Happy Home & Husband*. Coralline skimmed the table of contents: Clean, don't be mean. Prepare good foods to avoid bad moods. Adorn yourself and your home. Be domestic, not demanding.

"You can pore over the book later, Coralline. For now, I've made you a most scrumptious breakfast as a reward for your having nibbled on nothing but ulva all week!"

Her mother handed her a bowl brimming with bushy burgundy fronds—pepper dulse, also called the truffle of the sea, an expensive treat saved for special occasions. Coralline placed the bowl on her bedside table, untouched.

"I understand, darling. On my own wedding day, I was so excited, I couldn't eat a bite either!"

Her mother was already dressed for the wedding, Coralline saw. She wore a gilded bodice with a collar that climbed up her neck and left her shoulders bare, showcasing their broad, elegant lines. Her golden hair formed a glistening sheet over one shoulder.

"Here is your wedding bodice," Abalone said.

The bodice was in the pale-pink and ochre shades of a wisp of dawn—the colors symbolic for the commencement of her new life, Coralline supposed. Thin, twirling tendrils of gauzy lace formed off-the-shoulder straps, and the neckline was low, scooped, and embroidered. Despite herself, Coralline found her hand fingering the hem of the bodice and reveling in its smoothness. She looked at her mother gratefully—the bodice was her mother's finest creation and would have taken weeks of strained eyes and stiff fingers.

Slipping into the garment, Coralline shifted with her mother to the full-length mirror behind her door. Hovering behind Coralline, Abalone laced the silky strings. Coralline found it fortunate that her mother had chosen strings as the tightening mechanism rather than buttons, for the former offered more flexibility; with buttons, the corset would have sagged loosely around her, given how little she'd eaten all week.

Abalone swung in front of Coralline and scrutinized her face, looking at her as an artist might look at a blank canvas before starting to paint. She dabbed rouge on Coralline's cheeks, until they were as pink as the tips of jewel anemones in the coral reef outside the window. Then she combed, untangled, separated, and folded Coralline's hair into a multi-tiered bun atop her head. Coralline saw why her mother had wished for her to be a waif on her wedding day—with her newly pronounced collarbone, thin shoulders, and starvation-brightened eyes, she looked as dainty and fragile as the rose petal tellin above her beating heart. She had never felt worse but never looked better.

"Now, for the final touch." Into Coralline's updo, Abalone carefully inserted a tiara, a little crown studded with shards of spirula shells that glinted silver.

"I don't need a tiara, Mother."

"But you do. Every bride wears one. It's symbolic."

"Of what?"

"Its shape, resembling a seahorse's coronet, speaks of monogamy."

Coralline flinched at the word. "I cannot marry Ecklon." She'd said the words to herself so many times that she didn't realize she'd spoken them out loud until her mother's eyes met hers in the mirror, as still as a pool of settled lava. Turning Coralline about by her shoulders, Abalone plopped her down on the corner of her bed. She perched in the desk chair herself, then, leaning forward, staring at Coralline intently, asked, "What was he like, darling?"

"Who?"

"The merman you fell in love with."

"How did you know I fell in love?" Coralline said, stunned. "Did Nacre tell you?"

"I asked her several times, but she wouldn't say a word. You seem to have quite won her over. I am your mother, though—I don't need to confirm with anyone, not even you, to know that you fell in love."

"If you knew, why didn't you say anything before now?"

"Because I was hoping there would be no need. I was hoping you would come to your senses on your own. I see now that you haven't. Who was he, darling?"

"A human."

Abalone's lips parted, and her cheekbones paled. Otherwise aristocratic and poised, she suddenly looked disconcertingly confused, as though Coralline had slapped her. "Where is this human?" she snapped.

"He returned to land. I doubt I'll ever see him again."

"Good. If you'd fallen in love with a merman superior to Ecklon—in wealth, position, prestige—he would be someone for your father and I to consider. But a human is inferior to even the lowliest of mermen."

"Love is not about superiority or inferiority, Mother."

"But it is." Abalone's eyes hardened. "I have a secret that I've never told a living soul, not even Nacre, but that I will tell you now to prevent you from making the greatest mistake of your life. Twenty-five years ago, your father wanted to marry Rhodomela, not me."

"Rhodomela!"

"Yes. Trochid, Rhodomela, and I all attended the same school. As you can imagine, I was fashionable, wearing the latest styles of bodices; Rhodomela was studious, always the top student. I had more friends than I could count; Rhodomela had none except for her sister, Osmundea. I was everything Rhodomela was not, she was everything I was not, and the only thing we had in common was Trochid. Both of us wanted to marry him. I wanted to marry him because of his family; your father never ended up making much in the way of carapace, given the do-goodery coral connoisseur profession he chose, but he came from a well-regarded family. Rhodomela wanted to marry him because they had similar sensibilities, speaking incessantly of boring scientific topics. I always assumed Trochid would choose me over her, given that I was more beautiful, but he chose her.

"One day, he confided to me that he was planning to propose to Rhodomela that evening at a restaurant, Codium. He showed me the rose petal tellin he was going to give her." Coralline's hand wrapped automatically around the shell at her own throat. "I nodded along and wished him the best, but I was crying inside from humiliation. How dare he choose her over me, with her hooked nose and plain face? Eager for revenge, I decided to take matters into my own hands."

"What did you do, Mother?" Coralline whispered.

"I bought a rose petal tellin. Wearing it at my throat, I dropped by Rhodomela's house and, giggling, told her that Trochid had proposed to me. Her chin dropped, and her face became even sallower than usual. Rhodomela was more intelligent than me, but I was more clever—she did not even think to doubt me. That evening, Trochid went to Codium, engagement shell in hand, but Rhodomela did not meet him there as planned. Confused, he eventually swam to her home. There, her parents told him that she had, without explanation, fled Urchin Grove. Over the next days, I circulated rumors that she had fled for a secret lover."

A small smile skirted about Abalone's lips.

"Disillusioned, despondent, Trochid permitted himself to fall in love with me. I hoped Rhodomela would never return to Urchin Grove, but she did in a few months, when her parents were mysteriously murdered in the middle of the night and her sister's son was abducted. Osmundea later left Urchin Grove to recover from her grief, moving to Velvet Horn, but Rhodomela remained here. By then, my lie had become reality. Trochid and I were not only engaged but married. No one ever came to learn of my deception. Rhodomela may be a master apothecary, but I turned out to be a master trickster."

A long moment passed before Coralline could find her voice. "Do you think Father would have been happier with Rhodomela?" she asked.

"Probably. They completed each other's sentences; they read the same books. Rhodomela understood him in a way that I didn't—and still don't. Even after a quarter-century of living with your father, I generally don't have a clue as to what he's thinking."

Coralline tried to imagine her father's life with Rhodomela. Their home would have been neat, minimalist, full of books, the silence broken by observations on remedial algae and coral reefs. Abalone was ashamed of Trochid's stump of a hand, perpetually reminding him to tuck it behind his back, but Rhodomela would have been no more bothered by it than Trochid was by her plainness. In fact, if he were married to Rhodomela, he would still be happily working—he would not have been pressured into a miserable early retirement.

Her father would have been much happier with Rhodomela, Coralline thought, and Rhodomela with him. And it would not have mattered much to Abalone. She would eventually have shrugged off the sting of rejection and married another merman from a well-regarded family. Then, she would have been just as happy, or unhappy, as she was now.

"Everyone assumes Rhodomela wears black because she continues to mourn the death of her parents," Abalone said, "but I alone know that it is the loss of Trochid she is mourning. She still loves him; she will love him until the last breath leaves her gills."

Coralline's heart broke for Rhodomela. At The Irregular Remedy, when Coralline had asked Rhodomela whether she'd ever loved anyone, Rhodomela had replied that she had loved once—she'd been referring to Coralline's father. She'd continued that love is a farce; now Coralline understood why Rhodomela had said so. When Rhodomela had visited the Costaria home to treat Naiadum after the black poison spill, her glance had clung to the wedding-day portrait of Abalone and Trochid on the mantel—perhaps she'd been imagining herself in the portrait in place of Abalone.

Abalone mocked Rhodomela for being a Bitter Spinster, but it was she who had made her so.

"Why did you tell me this?" Coralline asked, wishing her mother had not burdened her with the secret.

"Don't you see, darling? You're replaying the love story of your parents. In the present case, Rosette is the equivalent of me, and you are Rhodomela. Trochid was almost Rhodomela's, but I stole him away just in time—as Rosette is continuing to try to steal Ecklon away from you. And, just as I circulated rumors that Rhodomela fled Urchin Grove for a lover, Rosette has circulated rumors that you fled Urchin Grove for a lover. More importantly, you are like Rhodomela in her tragic flaw. The biggest mistake of Rhodomela's life was not that she believed me regarding Trochid's proposal; the biggest mistake was her refusal to settle. She could have married someone else, even if not the love of her life, and she could have built a pleasant enough life with him. But she had an all-or-nothing approach—and so nothing is what she got. You know how her story ends, but you can choose your own ending. I don't want you to become a Bitter Spinster, unhappy, alienated, ridiculed."

Abalone paused and stared at Coralline.

"Rhodomela did not have the options you do. Other than Trochid, there was no one in her life. But other than this *human*"—she pronounced the word derisively—"you do have someone, and not just an ordinary merman. Ecklon is the most eligible merman in the village, yes, but beyond that, he loves you in the truest sense of the word. You owe him your freedom itself; by negating your murder charge, he saved you from lifelong imprisonment. Your attitude toward prison seems strangely passive, but you would never have been able to swim outside, snip algae, marry, have children.

"Your attitude toward Ecklon is also unfair. You are taking his virtues for granted simply because he is too humble to flaunt them. By taking on a personal case, Ecklon risked his professional reputation to protect yours; by marrying you, he is not only going against his mother's wishes, but is jeopardizing his personal reputation. To the people of Urchin Grove, it does not matter whether you actually murdered someone—you will always bear the taint of an accused murderess. And with your desmarestia-sea-oak solution, you've triumphed over medical convention but have failed miserably when it comes to marital convention—everyone is now calling you the Queen of Poison. The law may be forgiving, but the marriage market is ruthlessly unforgiving."

"What do you want from me, Mother?"

"I want you to marry Ecklon."

Coralline thought of telling her mother about her death prognosis. But she wasn't quite sure she believed Mintaka's curse anymore, or at least not the abbreviated time frame of it. *You will die soon after the light dies*, Mintaka had said, but who knew what the word *soon* meant for stars, given that their life span ranged from millions to billions of years? Also, *how* would Coralline die? Urchin Grove was not Hog's Bristle; it was not overflowing with loiterers and dagger wielders. The greatest danger in this village were darts of gossip. Unfortunately, she might be alive for a while yet, Coralline admitted to herself. She'd hoped death would prevent her from having to make a decision about marrying Ecklon, but she herself would have to make the decision.

"I haven't told Ecklon about him," she whispered.

"Good. You did well to have kept the human a secret."

"But I don't want to live a lie."

"Happiness is a lie, darling. It's something carefully cultivated, mindfully pruned, like the algae in a garden—seeds of truth can ruin it all. Happiness is like the corset you're wearing—many strings must be tightened to keep it in place. Take comfort in the knowledge that time is the greatest of all healers. One day soon, when you wake up in Ecklon's beautiful Mansion, you will smile at Ecklon next to you, and you will remember the human as having been no more than a distant dream."

28

Past and Future

Izar stepped inside his Invention Chamber, his hands balled into fists before his face—Serpens or hired men could be anywhere, lurking in the shadows, waiting to pounce. But all was still. That said, it was clear someone had been here.

Long, new shelves had been carved into the walls and loaded with sheaves of iron and magnesium, as well as belts of bullets, which formed narrow, comet-shaped cylinders. And the floor, which had been hopelessly cluttered before, streaming with Izar's mementoes of his inventive work, had been tidied. Izar looked upon the space as upon a forest that had been razed. He felt as though robbers had come into his home, and, though they had not stolen his things, they had decided to make the place their own—the greatest theft of all. There was now a coldness to the Invention Chamber, a methodical aspect, a rigidness and regimentation; Izar was looking upon the first steps to mass production, he knew.

He would have to kill Castor. He had known it the moment Saiph had said it would be Castor who would kill Coralline. At that time, there'd been a distance to Izar's knowledge that he must commit murder, a distance of both time and space, and Izar had refused to think about it. Now, he acknowledged to himself that to kill Castor would be to kill a part of himself, because the robot was an extension of himself. He had endowed Castor with his own vices—apathy, violence, even the scar along his cheek.

Izar raised his eyes to Castor's home, the bulletproof tank of water. But the tank was empty. Castor was gone. Saiph must have had him loaded onto a ship—perhaps they were on their way to Urchin Grove already.

His spine suddenly weak, Izar keeled over, his hands on his knees, his eyes staring unseeingly at the floor. He listened to the rasps of his breath. His exhalations made him think of smoke—the smoke that would soon spout from Castor's arm. He would do his best to try to get to Coralline before Saiph, but there was something he had to do first: save the ocean from his creation. Saiph was clearly planning on building an army of Castors, but he wouldn't be able to if Izar destroyed this Invention Chamber, if he destroyed Ocean Dominion itself.

He strode to his shelves of combustible chemicals, clear and colored, gathered over the years from all corners of the world. He snatched a pail off a hook and emptied the contents of all the flasks into it. The pail became only half full, but Izar knew it contained the power to burn down the entire building, from the underground all the way up to the thirtieth floor. It was still early in the morning, the workers had not yet arrived, but, just in case, Izar pulled the handle of the fire alarm on the wall to ensure there would be no casualties. A strident sound like that of a police-car siren started blaring all around him.

Grabbing a set of matches off a shelf, he lit a match, admiring the golden phoenix in his hand—a tiny blaze capable of toppling a behemoth.

Kelp Cove was a large, circular arena ringed with a forest of thick, long, bright-green fronds of kelp, which acted as a curtain. Two hundred chairs sat on the pearl-white sands, facing a white gazebo with twirling pillars. Waiters wearing crisp white waistcoats erupted regularly from a kitchen along the side of the arena, bearing platters of devil's tongue, the red algae laid in finger-sized bundles on triangular limestone plates. The waiters also carted decanters of wine, which shimmered in various shades of green.

"I hope the service is up to your caliber," Epaulette said to Abalone. The comment was in reference to Abalone's complaint about the waitstaff at the engagement party.

"It is," Abalone said stiffly.

Epaulette wore a red corset, as though she was bleeding to death at her son's wedding. Her silver-gray eyes held a matching wounded expression.

Coralline saw that two plump mermaids were rapidly approaching her, Abalone, and Epaulette: Sepia, Abalone's best friend, and Telia, Sepia's twenty-five-year-old daughter. A baby was squealing at a deafening pitch in Telia's arms.

In an effort to avoid all of them, Coralline dashed away from her mother's side and started roaming about Kelp Cove alone. At her engagement party, she'd been intimidated by the presence of a hundred guests; at her wedding, there were twice the number, many of whom had seen her in handcuffs, but she felt indifferent to their stares. A whisper floated over to her ears:

"Ecklon saved his bride, but look at how ungrateful she looks, the Queen of Poison. Her lover must have dumped her, so she's with Ecklon again. I wish Ecklon would marry me instead! Maybe he's changed his mind about her, maybe that's why he's nowhere to be seen just before his own wedding—"

Pretty, purple-tailed, with an aquiline nose, the mermaid broke off upon catching sight of Coralline. Ordinarily, Coralline would have bolted away, pretending to not have heard, but now, she looked at the mermaid coldly before resuming her meander.

Where *was* Ecklon? she wondered. He was clearly not with his boss, Sinistrum Scomber, as he had been at their engagement party—Coralline could see Sinistrum grimacing by himself toward the perimeter of Kelp Cove. At her engagement party, when Ecklon had been late, Coralline had feared he'd had a change of heart; now she hoped for it.

Rosette arrived at Coralline's side. She was wearing a sleeveless silver corset, and her long red hair was swaying in a fishtail braid down to her waist. "If Ecklon marries you instead of me," she pronounced quietly, "I'll kill myself."

She and Rosette had something in common after all, Coralline realized: a desire to die. That was part of the hideousness of love—it created desires no reasonable mind could understand. Coralline patted Rosette sympathetically on the shoulder. Shrugging her hand off as though Coralline was mocking her, Rosette dashed away.

As Coralline continued to swim slowly through Kelp Cove, she noticed juvenile red crabs starting to skitter along the seabed, seeking refuge among pebbles. A long, thick gray eel sought shelter under a rocky overhang. A bush altered from green to pale gray, and a large, round eye became visible in the gray. The eye coalesced into a face, and the face bloomed into a body, and the body, with eight winding arms, sprang off upon a spurt of black ink. The octopus, a creature of three hearts and blue blood—blood that pulsed with copper rather than iron—disappeared like an apparition.

Why were animals hiding or leaving? Coralline wondered, craning her neck toward the surface. The waters above were turbulent, ripples cascading downward, but the turmoil was likely caused by the ring of kelp—currents felt more pronounced in circular arenas, just as sound had a way of echoing off curved surfaces. But then, as Coralline watched, the waters swelled measurably, and this was a swell she recognized, one that pushed her away. A white belly materialized, five times her length. Guests tripped over themselves in their rush to get away, but Coralline threw herself at the visitor, Pavonis.

"Don't you have an appointment with the grave?"

"I guess not," Coralline admitted sheepishly.

"I forgive you for your theatrics."

Abalone swam up to them in a flurry of gold, her hands on her hips. "In addition to this Ogre," she said, her chin jutting toward Pavonis, "another troll of your choosing has just arrived." Coralline followed her gaze to a reed-thin figure clad in black—Rhodomela.

"I'll see you soon, Pavonis," Coralline said, patting his side. She swam down to Rhodomela, finding that she looked at Rhodomela differently now, for she knew the reason for the grooves of grief around her eyes. On an impulse, she hugged the master apothecary. Rhodomela stiffened at first, then wrapped her arms around Coralline.

Only when they separated did Coralline notice Osmundea by Rhodomela's side. Just as Coralline had, moments ago, stared at Rhodomela with private knowledge, Osmundea seemed to now be staring at Coralline, her indigo eyes glimmering. "Do you know my son?" she asked.

"I doubt it. Who's your son?"

"Izar."

The indigo eyes, the indigo scales, the scar along the side of the mouth—an extension of Izar's own. Could he truly be Osmundea's son? Did that mean he was partly human and partly merman—a hummer? If so, why had he not told her—or had he not known it himself? Osmundea lived in Velvet Horn, Coralline remembered, and Izar had said he'd had a personal errand to tend in Velvet Horn—perhaps visiting Osmundea had been the errand.

"In your seats, please!" boomed a voice. "The wedding ceremony will commence shortly."

Rhodomela and Osmundea were ushered toward the chairs by a waiter. A centralizing current was created by the movement of the guests, and Coralline was swept along in its sway, dazed, unresisting, until someone collided into her from behind. "Cora," he said, and turned her around by the shoulders.

Ecklon.

He wore a smooth, thick, beige waistcoat, its shade matching the embroidery of her bodice. He flashed her a smile, dimples carving wedges into his cheeks. She hadn't seen such a smile on his face for a long time, she realized now, not since their engagement party. His smile steadied her as nothing could.

"You look beautiful," he said, with an admiring glance.

"Thank you," she said, returning his smile shyly.

Clasping her hand, he led her toward the gazebo. Together, they hovered below its white, arched ceiling, facing each other, holding hands. A sizable merman arrived next to them, his paunchy belly almost touching their joined hands, his jowls hanging down to his neck, making Coralline think of a bowhead whale. "I, Kombu Kasmira," he began in a sonorous voice, looking past Coralline and Ecklon at the guests, "am honored to hover here in the role of Wedded Bliss Bureaucrat of the Department of Marriage Management, part of the Under-Ministry of Birth, Marriage, and Death Events."

It dawned on Coralline only now, truly dawned on her—not in theory but in the thud of her heart—that she was getting married.

"Do you, Ecklon Elnath, take Coralline Costaria to be your partner in life?" Kombu asked.

Her mother's idea of love was based on competition: Life was a marriage mart, and a husband from a wealthy, well-regarded family was some sort of prize, like a choice dessert. But marriage should be based on connection, not competition, Coralline thought now. And, for better or worse, one could not quite control whom one connected with.

"I do," Ecklon pronounced. Sighs sounded among the mermaids in the audience.

Desmarestia and sea oak—that was the sort of potent combination Coralline and Izar were—he the acid, she the base. It was a dangerous, foolhardy blend, but, miraculously, it worked. Coralline herself had proven it.

"Do you, Coralline Costaria, take Ecklon Elnath to be your partner in life?"

Coralline's fingers tingled in Ecklon's, and her gills felt as though they were shuttering one by one. She looked out frantically at the guests, hoping they could save her from Kombu's question. But most of them were staring at her blankly, and her mother was glaring at her. In the front row, Epaulette's crab-red corset made Coralline think of Sage Dahlia Delaisi, in all her orange-red fortune teller's glory. *He is not your love*, she had said, when she'd seen Ecklon through the window.

Kombu cleared his throat loudly.

Coralline looked toward Altair, who formed a spot of orange among the holdfasts of kelp, accompanied by red—his mate, Kuda. The two seahorses bounced ever so slightly with the currents, their tails twirled around a single strand of eel-grass. Altair's color started to dull steadily, until Coralline could no longer see him. With a start, she recalled their conversation last night, while she'd been flitting between sleep and consciousness: If she spent her life with the wrong partner, she would be living in camouflage rather than glowing.

She did not want to live in camouflage. "We need to talk, Ecklon," she heard herself say.

A flurry of whispers sprouted among the guests. Kombu's eyebrows ascended into his hairline. Ecklon's face paled, but he nodded.

Despite the bright morning sunshine, the shadows of the ships in the harbor remained dense and dark, Izar was relieved to find, for they enabled him to hide in daylight. Crouched in the shadows, he looked upon his fleet of ships. The largest Ocean Dominion ship, *Vega*, designed by him last year to be virtually unsinkable, was missing from the docks. Saiph must have selected *Vega* for his Castor mission; it was a good choice—Izar would have selected the same.

To pursue *Vega*, Izar would require a vessel of speed and stealth, but something small, so it would not be detected by Saiph and his crewmen. His gaze roved over the ships to find the ideal one. His eye caught on one that did not belong, but that he recognized: Alshain Ankaa's trawler. What was the giant doing here, at Ocean Dominion's harbor?

Whatever it was, it was a good thing Alshain was here. Izar had not a moment to waste, but he wanted to thank Alshain for having saved him from Saiph and Antares earlier by tossing him overboard. He crept along the docks, half-crouching, until he stood at the stern of the fifty-foot-long vessel. His step as light as a fox's, he leapt over its rails. He remembered the first time he'd clambered onto Alshain's trawler—in the middle of the night, with rain pounding the platform and lightning cracking the sky open.

Now, as before, there was no one on the platform. Izar strode to the narrow set of stairs on the other side of the platform, leading belowdecks. Upon the top stair shone a drop of blood, red as a poppy. His heart thudding, Izar skulked down the stairs. To the side of the lowest stair, he saw Alshain's seven-foot-long frame, lying crumpled.

Alshain had been shot in the heart, and his blood was soaking into his scraggly beard. The precision of the shot and the location of Alshain's body, close to the stairs, suggested that he'd heard someone above deck and had been about to climb up, but had been shot before he'd taken his first step.

But why? Why would Saiph or Antares have ordered Alshain shot?

Saiph might have assumed that with Alshain dead, even if Izar managed to escape his underground prison, he would be unable to transform into a merman, and thus would be unable to try to kill Castor, save Coralline, or otherwise attempt to escape into the ocean. Saiph didn't know that Izar did not require Alshain's moonmumble potion to transform to a merman. Perhaps Antares didn't know it, either; twenty-five years ago, when Izar was three, he'd transformed to a human without a potion, but Antares had been transforming simultaneously, according to Zaurak's recounting of events, so had not seen it.

Squatting next to Alshain, Izar closed the unseeing eyes gently with a hand. It was his fault Alshain was dead, just as it was his fault Zaurak was dead—it was their association with him that had killed both of them. He could not let the same happen to Coralline.

Whirling around, he ran up the narrow stairs, but came face-to-face with the barrel of a gun. Serpens grinned at him from behind his red beard, his face as menacing as the spears in his earlobes. There was nowhere for Izar to go—he could not move forward, for Serpens was blocking his path, and he could not retreat down the stairs, for Serpens would simply shoot him in the back. He put his hands in the air.

Serpens pointed the gun at Izar's heart. His finger paused on the trigger—he would take his time to kill Izar, he would enjoy it as a hunter might luxuriate over a kill.

The people in Izar's life flashed before his eyes: Antares lighting a match then drowning the flame in a glass of water; Saiph handing Bumble back to him, with the teddy bear's innards streaming out; Maia tugging his hands out of the hood of her car and slapping his face; Zaurak shaking his hand on his first day at Ocean Dominion; Ascella frowning at the scar across his jaw as at chipped nail varnish; Coralline staring at him with her big blue-green eyes as she leaned against her shark; Coralline—it was her face Izar wished to hold in his mind in the moment before he died.

His smile widening, Serpens started to press the trigger—but a dark, strapping figure vaulted upon him, a mermaid tattoo on his arm. Deneb Delphinus, who'd served as derrickhand atop *Dominion Drill I.*

The gun fell out of Serpens's hands and between Izar's feet. Deneb wrestled Serpens to the ground, but Serpens, almost as sinewy, fought back and started to rise—Izar grabbed the gun, turned it around, and knocked the handle into the top of Serpens's skull. Serpens's limbs went slack, and he collapsed on the platform, his head lolling. Izar helped Deneb to his feet and shook his hand, clasping it with both of his.

"You seem to be my bodyguard, Deneb. This is the third time you've saved me. Thank you."

Deneb shrugged, as though it was simply a part of his job description.

"How did you know to find me here?"

"I saw you on the docks," he said, "and I was about to approach you—there's something I want to talk to you about—but then I saw Serpens stalking you with a gun. I figured he intended to kill you, and I decided to save you."

"I'm glad for it. What did you want to talk about?"

"I was in your Invention Chamber." He shuddered.

"Was it you who tidied it up?"

"Yes."

"And did you put in the new shelves, planning for mass production of Castors?"

"I certainly didn't! I hate Castor. To be honest, I wanted to burn down your Invention Chamber, but, somehow, I couldn't bring myself to do it."

"Me neither," Izar said quietly.

Izar looked with Deneb toward the bronze glass skyscraper of Ocean Dominion, forming an arrow to the sky. Izar had held a lit matchstick above the pail of combustible chemicals in his Invention Chamber, but he'd snuffed it out. No sane person would describe the Invention Chamber as warm or cozy but, to Izar, it had been. He had spent more time there than in his own apartment, often sleeping on the floor when the hour grew late. For all of his adult life, the Invention Chamber had served as his asylum, and Ocean Dominion as his home.

"I resign from Ocean Dominion," Deneb said.

"That makes two of us."

"I'm surprised. When we last spoke, on *Dominion Drill I*, you said that the ocean and all its inhabitants are ours to dominate."

"I said that before I fell in love with a mermaid, Coralline."

Deneb's eyes widened until they resembled black marbles. It would be a dream come true for him to even catch sight of a mermaid, Izar knew, let alone fall in love with one.

"My brother, Saiph, is on his way to Coralline's village, where he plans to kill her through Castor. Will you help me save her?"

"I will!" Deneb said eagerly.

"Thank you. Let's set forth."

Izar would have to writhe and drown in order to transform into a merman, but he would rather die a hundred deaths before Coralline died one.

Coralline and Ecklon hovered together inside the kitchen of Kelp Cove, facing each other, holding hands. The waitstaff had left as soon as Coralline and Ecklon had entered, such that the two of them were alone, surrounded by the smooth, sultry scents of wines.

Coralline's words tumbled out in a trembling, almost incoherent stream: "I fell in love with someone else."

"I know. Izar."

She blinked at Ecklon in rapid succession.

"I was a detective on your case, Cora. As such, I was following your every move from a distance."

There was no ire or indignation in his silver-gray eyes. "Why didn't you say anything before?" Coralline asked quietly.

"I was waiting for you to tell me. And I'm glad you did. Regardless of the painfulness of the truth, I couldn't bear the thought of your lying to me."

"If you know about Izar," Coralline whispered, "then you know we can't marry."

"You faced extraordinary obstacles during your elixir quest. You were not yourself."

"You're making excuses for me."

"Maybe I am," Ecklon said, clasping her hands tighter, "but we can still make our relationship work. I'm willing to let the past be the past, in favor of a future with you."

The past . . . Coralline thought of her six-month relationship with Ecklon: The day they'd met, at The Irregular Remedy, when she'd set his elbow, the time he'd gotten her a bowl of buttonweed when she'd been sick with the flu, the autographed copy of *The Universe Demystified* he'd given her on her birthday, the rose petal tellin shell he'd presented her when he'd proposed. She thought of how he'd ventured into the wave of black poison to save Naiadum, of how he'd twirled her in circle upon circle upon finding her at the Telescope Tower, of how valiantly he'd fought to clear her name of her murder charge, risking his tenured post at Urchin Interrogations for her.

There was nothing Ecklon had not done for her, nothing he would not do.

"All that matters to me now is: Do you love Izar still?"

Coralline's teeth gritted, and she tried to prevent the words, but they spewed out through her lips of their own accord: "Yes, I love him still."

She needed to remove the rose petal tellin shell at her throat—she felt as though the shell would choke her if she didn't. There was no time to whirl around and ask him to unclasp the translucent string; curling her hand around the tellin, she wrenched it off in a single sweep.

Her muscles turned unbearably weak, as though she'd removed her own heart—for Ecklon had been her heart. Tears rolled hotly down her cheeks. Sobs racked through her, shuddering through her ribs, creeping down her vertebrae. She cried for the life she would have shared with Ecklon, for the love that she had shared with him. Their foreheads together, their tears merged, even though their lives would, from this day, diverge.

29

Man and Machine

Ecklon remained inside the kitchen, saying he needed a moment, so Coralline swam out the kitchen window alone. But she stopped in her tracks: Perching on the edge of their seats, two hundred people were staring at her, their eyes inquiring whether the wedding would continue. After all the tears she'd shed, Coralline found she could no longer speak, but she shook her head emphatically.

Her mother's eyes narrowed to needle-thin slits; Coralline felt relieved at the distance between them. Epaulette clapped her hands to her mouth gleefully and hugged Rosette. The pretty, purple-tailed mermaid whom Coralline had overheard earlier, sat up straighter. Even plump Telia beamed, handing her baby to her mother, Sepia, as though she was single again.

Half the mermaids of Urchin Grove would soon be chasing Ecklon, Coralline felt certain. Her own prospects, meanwhile, were dismal.

"Let's get out of this freak show," Pavonis said from above her.

Coralline started to rise toward his white belly, when a thud sounded from the other side of the boundary of kelp. It reverberated through Coralline's tendons and through the legs of the chairs, causing guests to jump off their seats. Was it an earthquake? Coralline wondered, staring in the direction of the thud. It was impossible to tell, because the fronds of kelp formed layers of curtains, blocking all view to the other side. And yet the earthquake seemed to be approaching, for the kelp started quivering, down to the holdfasts. Coralline keened her ear; it was not an earthquake, no—it sounded like stomping. And then the stalks of kelp started falling, one by one—the creature, whatever it was, was trampling everything in its path. . . . Unmoving, every muscle of her body trained toward it, Coralline watched as the final layer of kelp collapsed, and the creature entered Kelp Cove.

Towering to three times her height, he was a demon of metal, his chest stamped with the bronze-and-black insignia of Ocean Dominion, as well as a name, Castor. With his legs, Castor was crafted in the image of his creator, man, but not just man—*one* man, in particular: Izar, for a hook-shaped scar marked Castor's jaw, matching Izar's own.

Castor pounded his left arm, which was twice as thick as his right arm, into the ocean floor. Every grain of sand in Kelp Cove trembled, every drop of water rippled, and a mass exodus of fish occurred from the kelp forest. Castor then started spewing a series of bubbles, before crooking his right arm at the elbow. A blaze shot out of his arm, hot and golden, twice the length of Coralline herself. This must be fire, she thought, but she could not be certain, for fire, to her, was not a specific thing. It was not like a rock or a whale, which she could envision precisely. It was simply something associated with the sun, something that could not exist in the ocean. And yet she was looking at it, its flame reflected in her very eyes.

Coralline had not believed Izar when he'd claimed to have invented underwater fire, but she believed him now. *Fire and water can never truly meet*, her father had said, but Izar had somehow tricked fire to burn in water, just as he had somehow tricked her into falling in love with him.

Castor's fire stopped abruptly, and his head swiveled on his shoulders—if he were sentient, Coralline would think he was looking for someone. The Ocean Dominion insignia rotated ten degrees over his chest, then a sharp click sounded, and a bullet flew out of his navel. The shot seemed experimental, but had the bullet struck someone, it would have killed like a dagger tearing through the flesh. People screamed and scrambled in all directions.

The blood rushed to the capillaries in Coralline's skin. Her former self, prior to the elixir quest, would have cowered and sought shelter, but her new self surged toward Castor. She collected a rock and hurled it at his head. The path of the rock slowed with water resistance, and it bounced off his neck as haplessly as a pebble. Castor's head rotated toward her, and his eyes seemed to register her. She had the sense there was someone there, behind the eyes, looking for her. It would be Izar, of course, controlling Castor from the surface.

Coralline spotted a tawny tail from the corner of her eye—Naiadum, approaching her. Bolting toward him, she pulled him aside—just in time, for a bullet tore past his shoulder. She tugged him into the kelp forest, such that they were both concealed among the green.

Altair and Kuda were there as well, glowing orange and red among the holdfasts of kelp but shaking so severely that Coralline could not fix her gaze on either one. And then a gargantuan shape arrived to the other side of the kelp, and her heart leapt in fear that it was Castor, but the shape was long rather than tall—Pavonis. Thank goodness for Pavonis, thank goodness for Kelp Cove itself—the ring of kelp acted as a cover.

"Pavonis, please take care of Naiadum, Kuda, and Altair," Coralline directed. Turning to Naiadum, she wagged a finger at him and said, "Don't you dare leave Pavonis's side!"

He nodded, his amber-gold eyes terrified.

"Uh-oh!" Altair screeched. "It's happening!"

"What is?" Coralline frowned.

"I spent all my life in a coral reef, hiding, meek and weak, and now here I am, in the most dangerous of circumstances—delivering my many children!"

Altair's back arched, and his belly contracted. A minuscule seahorse, the size of a fingernail but fully formed, propelled head-first out of his belly, and flew upward. Altair's belly contracted again, and a stream of little seahorses flew out like little beads, each one a miniature copy of either of its parents. With every contraction, a full cluster of seahorses erupted, dozens at a time. "They will all be killed by that monster!" Altair shrieked.

"Our babies will all die on the day of their birth!" Kuda wailed.

"Not if I have anything to do with it!" Pavonis growled.

He rotated, such that his snout pushed aside the layers of kelp and his face pointed diagonally downward above Altair. He opened his mouth wide, until it formed a dark, low tunnel. As the newborn seahorses flew up, they collided against the roof of his mouth, then bounced about within. His filtering pads, separating his mouth from his throat, meant that he would not be swallowing them, but keeping them safe in his capacious trove.

"Thank you, thank you, thank you!" Altair and Kuda cried together.

Coralline could not help but smile, despite the shots ringing outside. Pavonis had earlier known Altair only as Minion, and now here he was, protecting Altair's children. Naiadum, meanwhile, was watching the birth of the seahorses with wide, mesmerized eyes. Coralline warned him again to remain close to Pavonis, then she slipped back into Kelp Cove.

Castor stood at the center of the arena. Trampled by his feet, two hundred chairs were now in splinters, their fragments so fine that they resembled broken shells more than slate. Castor's head swiveled, and his eyes found her. The insignia over his chest rotated slightly. She knew he would shoot her, yet her gaze was riveted by the scar across his jaw. She felt as though she was looking at Izar, and, though it was a monstrous side of him she was seeing, she could not bring herself to turn away.

A sharp click sounded. A bullet tore out of Castor's navel. Coralline found herself pushed out of the way. Regaining her balance, she turned around to thank her savior. The person was Rhodomela, but the veins in Rhodomela's neck were standing out, and blood was gushing out from a hole in her black bodice, diffusing through the waters like a pot of overturned ink.

Izar awoke with a start. He touched his indigo scales and the gills fluttering along the sides of his neck; everything was as it should be. Looking around him, he saw that he was hovering midway between the surface and the seabed. The first time he'd transformed into a merman, when Coralline had found him, she'd told him it was strange that he'd been hovering midway between the surface and the seabed—it had made her think he was neither merperson nor human, for merpeople tended to sink when unconscious and humans tended to float. Izar realized now that he was midway between the surface and the seabed because he was both merperson and human.

He raised his arms over his head and swung his tail side to side, rising steadily through the waters until his head crested over the waves. His vision adjusted easily to air, for he had been human just a short while ago. Alshain's trawler formed a dot in the distance—Deneb was returning to Menkar. Izar turned his head to look at Saiph's ship, *Vega*. The bronze-and-black insignia of Ocean Dominion glistened on its side, a fishhook slashing the letters *O* and *D* in half. Izar had had the logo painted especially large on this vessel, so that all, near and far, would know the coat of arms to which the ship belonged.

Dipping his head back into the water, Izar swam toward *Vega*, figuring that Castor would not be far from the ship that had brought him. His head crested again only when he reached the ship's shadow. He was about to toss his tailfin into the air and dive down, when a voice stopped him: "Son!"

His face slackened, all tension in his shoulders released—such was the effect of the voice of his father.

Turning around, he squinted in the direction of the voice. In the shadow of *Vega* floated a little dinghy, approaching him rapidly. Antares was rowing it, his head tufty, his face flushed, his steel-gray eyes beseeching. "Don't believe anything you may have heard about me!" he called. "None of it is true. I'll explain everything. Come to me, my boy!"

Izar felt sick and hollow, as though an empty punch had landed on his stomach. He'd believed everything he'd been told about Antares—by Zaurak, by Osmundea—but now that he was looking at his father, he could hardly believe any of it. For twenty-five years, Antares had raised Izar as his son, caring for him, protecting him; at the very least, Izar owed him a chance to explain.

Izar's tail slashed through the water as a knife cuts bread. He arrived at the dinghy more quickly than he'd thought, having forgotten the power of his tail. But he wished he didn't have a tail—he wished he were the man his father recognized. He wrapped his hands around the boat's rim and extended his head over the water, while keeping his neck submerged, so his gills could continue to breathe.

He felt something in the water near him, as though someone was arriving, and he looked down. Whoever it was seemed to have shifted, such that he couldn't see anyone. He looked up again at Antares, to find that Antares's eyes had darkened to the gray of storm clouds and were glaring at him, the brows together. His hand darted forward, grabbed Izar by the neck, and lifted him out of the water. "All the wealth your Castor creates will belong only to me and Saiph!" he yelled.

Even if Izar's gills had not been flattened against the sides of his neck, he would have been unable to breathe. His father wanted to kill him. He had known it theoretically, in what Zaurak and Osmundea had said, but to see it, to feel it—it was paralyzing. He hung in the air as passively as a sack of potatoes.

Antares's other hand gripped a knife, its steel blade glinting like a mirror. It slashed toward Izar's neck.

Another hand appeared at the same time, this one from the water, clasping a half-shell; Osmundea leaned toward Antares and stabbed him in the heart.

Antares released Izar and the knife, such that both fell into the water. Upon gulping two deep breaths through his gills, Izar rose over the rim of the dinghy and looked in. Antares lay dying on the floor of the boat, unconscious, the half-shell protruding from his ribs. Izar's blood stilled in his veins, and he found himself gasping, crying, not for the loss of Antares as he saw him but for the loss of Antares as he had thought him.

"I couldn't save you from him last time, son," Osmundea said gently, "but I'm glad I was able to save you this time."

"Izar!" a voice shouted. Shading his eyes with his hand, Izar looked up toward the bow of *Vega*. Saiph was glowering down at him from the rails, his charred-kale eyes blazing.

"I'll never forgive you for this!" Saiph screamed. "I'm going to kill Coralline today, and I'm going to kill you soon after. Every day of the short remainder of your life, you're going to spend looking over your shoulder."

Izar's tailfin flicked up in the air like the flukes of a whale, and he dived down into the ocean alongside his mother.

Coralline sat concealed among the holdfasts of kelp, her tail extended in front of her, Rhodomela's head on her lap.

The bullet had torn through Rhodomela's ribs, on the left side. Coralline's hand pressed into the area to try to quell the flow of blood, but it dribbled out steadily from between her fingers. She wished there was something she could do, but a bullet to the chest, so close to the heart, was fatal, she recognized instinctively. All her life, Rhodomela had spent saving others, but now that she needed saving, no one could save her.

Her tail was bleaching fast. There was a particularly stark quality to the bleaching—the black scales were not fading to intermediate shades of gray, then white—but were switching suddenly from black to white, one scale after another, as though they were being rotated. There was something beautiful about the white scales—just as there was something beautiful about a bleached coral reef—but there was also a ghastliness to it.

Rhodomela's lips parted, a whisper emerged. Coralline bent her ear to Rhodomela's mouth. "I see you've conquered your fear of blood," Rhodomela said. Her eyes twinkled, then turned soft and smooth as a salve, as she continued, "I would be proud of you if you were my daughter."

Tears blurred Coralline's vision, and she blinked them away; she did not want her vision to cloud now, during her last moments with Rhodomela. Her face crumbling, she clasped Rhodomela's hand. Her fingers met no resistance in Rhodomela's, nor any response—she did not have the strength to clasp back. With every passing moment, Rhodomela was becoming less and less anchored to the fleshiness of life.

There was a rustle to the other side of the kelp. Coralline looked up sharply. The fronds were parting before her. Castor must have located her; he must be stomping toward her in order to kill her, but she held Rhodomela's hand more tightly—she would not leave her side, not even if Izar's monster shot her a dozen times.

The fronds parted more, then it was not Castor but Abalone and Trochid who burst through the kelp. Cringing to see Rhodomela's condition, they came to hover horizontally over her.

"Thank you," Trochid said, his dark-brown eyes moist. He removed Rhodomela's hand gently from Coralline's, and grasped the limp fingers with his own. "Thank you for saving my life when my hand was severed. And thank you for saving my daughter today, and for guiding her into becoming the lovely mermaid she is."

Coralline looked from her father to Rhodomela. The two of them could not glance away from each other; it was as though they were alone in the kelp forest. Coralline wondered whether they were thinking back to when they'd been young, when they'd held hands just like this, when they'd dreamt of a life together.

The sound of weeping broke their gaze. "I'm sorry," Abalone wailed. "I'm so sorry."

Her mother rarely cried, and Coralline had never seen her cry as she was crying now, her cheeks flaming, her eyes liquid gold. From beneath a scrunched forehead, she met Coralline's eyes. Coralline nodded emphatically—her father and Rhodomela needed to know.

"It's my fault the two of you weren't together," Abalone said. "Rhodomela, the day Trochid was supposed to propose to you, I lied to you that he'd proposed to me. I stole him away from you!"

Trochid and Rhodomela looked at Abalone, but only fleetingly. The light vanished from Rhodomela's eyes, and the final scale of her tail turned from black to white.

Abalone and Trochid sobbed, hovering to separate sides of Rhodomela. Coralline closed Rhodomela's eyes with a hand, then shifted out from beneath her. Abalone and Trochid extended a hand down in unison, such that Rhodomela's head was now cradled in their joined hands. "Where are you going—" Abalone began, but Coralline did not hear any more, for she'd darted out of the kelp forest.

Facing away from her, Castor was stomping steadily toward the kitchen; with every step he took, the pearl-white sands quivered. People inside the kitchen were screaming—they'd assumed the space a refuge, but it had become a cage—they could not escape, for he would simply shoot them if they swam out the door or window.

Castor was looking for her, Coralline knew, and he seemed to think she'd be inside the kitchen. She'd left Ecklon for Izar, and here was Izar in the form of this demon, trying to kill her—the thought made her laugh without mirth. All of this was her fault—Rhodomela's death was her fault, any other death today would also be her fault—because if not for her, and Izar's desire to kill her, Castor would not be here.

Swimming toward Castor, Coralline hurled herself at his leg from behind. It was like hurling herself at a boulder—she felt the impact more than he did, and, sliding aside, rubbed her shoulder. But the collision served its purpose. Castor began turning around with small, stuttering steps—he seemed to find it difficult to balance on the uneven ocean floor. His eyes had an easier time than his body, though, and located her swiftly. The Ocean Dominion insignia across his chest rotated ten degrees, in preparation to shoot.

"Coralline!" a voice called. Ecklon arrived beside her, his waistcoat stained, his hair rough and tousled. He grabbed her hand as though she was his bride.

A click sounded. Ecklon jerked Coralline's arm. A bullet sailed past her side, traveling so close to her skin that she felt its heat.

Pavonis and Menziesii materialized above Coralline and Ecklon. The whale shark and spotted eagle ray swam together toward Castor from overhead. Bullets exploded out of Castor's navel, but there was a confusion to them—he did not seem to know at which of them to aim, and he seemed unable to shoot overhead, for his navel could not point up, but only forward.

Pavonis stopped behind Castor, and Menziesii stopped to the side of Castor's neck. His whip of a tail flashing, Menziesii fluttered his wide, navy-blue wings next to Castor's head. The resulting ripples seemed to blur Castor's vision, for he started shaking his head side to side, as though to clear his eyes. Pavonis, meanwhile, swung his tail powerfully into Castor's back.

Castor fell to his knees. It was as though a house had fallen—Coralline felt the impact in each of her bones, even the narrow bones of her fingers. But Castor did not stay down long. Placing one leg in front of him, he started to rise onto the other.

Coralline could try to make some sort of algal paste to smear over his eyes, she thought. She could not think of the specific algae now, but if she rummaged through the kelp forest, ideas would come to her. And she was not carrying her apothecary arsenal with her at the moment, but there would be implements in the kitchen that she could use to grind algae, including a mortar and pestle. Pavonis would continue to slam into Castor from behind, Menziesii would continue to distract him through his ripples, and Coralline, together with Ecklon, would find a way to blind him—

A bullet tore through Coralline. Her chest convulsed, her tiara flew off. She looked down numbly. The bullet had struck her in almost the same location it had struck Rhodomela, among the ribs, to the left side. A red splotch was expanding through the pink and ochre shades of her bodice. A stinging pain was radiating through her, but she found that did not mind it. She'd longed to die; finally, death had found her. Mintaka had been truthful, after all, in her curse: *You will die soon after the light dies.*

Ecklon pulled Coralline into the kelp forest, as Coralline had earlier pulled Rhodomela. He settled among the holdfasts of kelp with her head on his lap. His hand landed gently on her forehead and smoothed back her hair, which was coming loose now that her tiara had tumbled off. His silver-gray eyes held an unforgiving expression, but Coralline knew their ire was directed at himself: He'd saved her from life in prison, but he'd been unable to save her from death.

Her parents came to hover horizontally over her, as they had over Rhodomela, both of them continuing to weep. Naiadum sat next to her, staring at her with a befuddled expression; though he'd come within a hair's breadth of death himself in the black poison spill, he was still too young to understand the finality of it.

Coralline felt a slight movement on her right shoulder—it would be Nacre, clambering on. Altair and Kuda, meanwhile, were somewhere on Coralline's left; she could see their orange and red colors from the corner of her eye. Pavonis's white belly started rollicking above everyone, his eye trained on her. He would have liked to speak, Coralline knew—they'd been best friends since she was two; she'd known him longer than she'd known Naiadum—but he could not open his mouth, because Altair and Kuda's hundreds of children were in it. She was glad he could not speak, for then she would cry—if she could.

She had always hoped her death would be a little like falling asleep, but it felt more like a rapidly spreading fever. Her body was paralyzing from the inside-out—first the bones, then the organs, then the muscles. Her tail was bleaching fast, the bronze giving way steadily to white, remnants of color lingering primarily around the corners of her tailfin. She could smell her blood in her own nostrils, and she felt dizzy, but not from the smell of her blood—rather, the loss of it. For what it was worth, she *had* finally conquered her fear of blood, as Rhodomela had noted. Blood was simply what her body was composed of, she saw now, just as the ocean was composed of water.

The fronds of kelp parted, but it was not Castor who burst through. It was a figure with indigo eyes and tail. She must be imagining it; she had to be hallucinating, but then he spoke: "You must be her husband," Izar said to Ecklon.

"She did not marry me," Ecklon said quietly. "You must be Izar."

Ecklon slipped aside without a further word, and Izar replaced him, such that Coralline's head came to lie on his lap. Tears sparkled in Izar's eyes. The expression on his face resembled that from Mintaka's cavern in the deep sea, Coralline saw—it was truth, in all its harshness, in all its beauty.

"I'm sorry," he said.

Coralline's anger from earlier streamed out of her as seamlessly as her blood.

The eyes Izar had thirsted all this time to see were not the eyes he recognized—their expression was dull, dying. Her eyes were his home, but the doors to the home closed—the lids shuttered, her lashes casting long, limpid shadows over her cheeks. *The celebration will be a funeral*, Mintaka had told him. He wished it were his own funeral instead of hers.

"What are you waiting for?" cried a shrill voice, startling him. He recognized the voice as belonging to Nacre, but it took him a moment to locate her: She was emerging from his satchel, tentacles waggling furiously. She must have crept off Coralline's shoulder and slipped into his bag through the partially open zip. "Give her the damn elixir! Do I have to do everything myself?"

"But I don't have the elixir."

"You do. I just saw it!"

His hands moving as fast as flying knives, Izar rummaged through his satchel. His hands slipped into an under-compartment, and there it was, the silver sphere of starlight.

Zaurak had not taken the elixir, this meant. He must have slipped it back into Izar's satchel without Izar's noticing. That was why Zaurak's leg had not healed. And that was what he'd been trying to tell Izar before he died. Zaurak had wanted Izar to save the elixir for himself, were he to require it. And he required it now. His heart bursting with gratitude for his friend, Izar placed the elixir in Coralline's mouth.

Her body, previously sagging, immediately stiffened. Her face glowed, then the glow spread throughout, becoming most prominent in the scales of her tail—which shimmered silver. She became a source of light herself, a shard of a star. Then her muscles clenched, her face scrunched, and the bullet flew out. Izar caught it in his hand, incredulous. The tear along her ribs started to close; through the gap in her bodice, Izar could see the skin joining. It joined entirely—not even a dot remained where the bullet had entered. If not for the scarlet stain of her bodice, he would not have believed she'd been shot. And then her glow faded, her scales darkened to a beautiful bronze, and her eyes flew open.

Pavonis's thirty-foot-long body rocked up and down so hard that wave-sized ripples formed, and the stalks of kelp swayed as wildly as grasses in a thunderstorm.

Placing her hands to either side of her, Coralline sat up and turned to face Izar. With her turquoise eyes and peach-pink cheeks, she looked like a fairy, he thought, his breath catching in his gills. He leaned toward her, and she leaned toward him, but just before their lips could meet, a thud sounded to his left.

Castor. He had found them among the kelp.

"*Scatter!*" Izar yelled.

Everyone bolted, spreading outward like confetti. Izar grabbed Coralline's hand and dashed away, just as bullets wrenched through the spot in the kelp forest where they'd been.

"There is a way to stop him," Izar told Coralline hurriedly, "a way that's both simple and dangerous. There's a battery in his skull—"

"Battery?"

The sound of her voice almost made Izar smile, but there was no time to smile: Both of their lives, and everyone else's, depended on his disabling Castor as soon as possible. "The battery is an object that powers him, like a brain. Its removal will paralyze him."

"All right," Coralline said. "I'll try to distract him while you remove his battery."

Izar nodded, his face set and tight. There was no other way, but he did not like this way. If Castor shot Coralline again, there would be nothing to save her this time.

They swam out of the kelp forest hand in hand. Castor stood directly before them, fire blazing out of his dragon arm. Izar could not help but look upon the golden flame with shocked admiration—how smoothly it flowed, like liquid lava. But he had only a moment to admire the fire, for Castor pointed his arm in their direction. Coralline and Izar flew apart. Castor's head swiveled as he looked between them, his confusion a manifestation of Saiph's confusion, but then he seemed to make up his mind: He turned toward Coralline. It was what Izar had predicted, for Saiph had promised to kill Coralline today, but a muscle jumped in his cheek nonetheless and his jaw clenched. He could not let anything happen to Coralline.

She swam a few feet above Castor, as a fly buzzes overhead, and she swam in circles. Castor's head started turning on his shoulders to follow her movements. But even had she been still, her upward angle would have been a difficult one for Castor—she was essentially in his blind spot, a fly who could not be swatted.

Izar approached Castor's skull stealthily, from one side, so the robot would not detect the movement. Quickly, he came to hover behind Castor's head. He recalled the moment he'd knelt above Castor in his Invention Chamber and inserted the battery in his skull. At that time, Izar would have sneered at the notion that he would ever be disabling Castor instead of enabling him. But now, Izar pressed the top of the robot's skull lightly. The pane opened on touch, but Izar drew his hand back sharply—the zinc-galvanized steel skull was as scorching as a poker. The waters directly surrounding Castor were also hot and bubbling; that was how Castor created fire, by heating water and evaporating it until the oxygen in it turned from liquid to gas. The heat was also a manner of shield for Castor; had Castor been creating fire for just a few minutes longer, the waters would have been hotter still, and Izar's skin would have blistered.

With slow, shuffling steps, Castor started to turn around, but Izar reached a hand into his skull and plucked out the battery. It was searing as an electric plate, and he dropped it immediately.

The battery floated down slowly to the ocean floor, lilting like a textbook-sized feather. Meanwhile, Castor stood perfectly still, like a man turned to stone. Then he started to fall backward, arms swinging, like he was fainting. It was a striking phenomenon to observe, and a tragic one, like a dinosaur collapsing. Castor hit the seabed flat on his back, a torrent of sands rising all around him. Izar's insides churned—Castor was an extension of him, albeit past, and now he lay dead, killed by none other than Izar himself.

From the other side of the sands, Coralline swam up to Izar, her hair framing her face in dark, loose tendrils. Izar had lost Castor, but he had gained Coralline. He wrapped his arms around her, and their lips met in a long, languorous kiss.

30

Fire and Water

From the living-room window seat, Coralline surveyed the scene in the living room.

Naiadum sat at the dining table, reading one of his children's stories, *The Magical Fairy Basslet*. Abalone sat on the settee, stitching a frilly yellow corset, Nacre on her shoulder. Trochid sat at his desk in a corner of the living room, perusing two thick volumes: *Calcium Carbonate* and *The Animated Lives of Anemones*. Coralline was happy to see him immersing himself in books from his past career, but she did not understand it. She had asked him about it, and he had demurred that he would tell her soon enough.

She turned her head and patted Pavonis's snout, just outside the window.

A knock sounded at the door. Coralline swam to the door and pulled it open. It was Izar, looking dashing in a royal-blue waistcoat, his chestnut curls smooth on his forehead.

"The hummer's here!" Naiadum announced, as Izar swam into the living room. Naiadum considered Izar an exotic creature and had asked Coralline if he could have him as his muse. With a laugh, she'd replied that he could ask Izar himself when he grew older.

Trochid smiled at Izar, got up from his desk, and joined Abalone on the settee. Abalone focused resolutely on her stitches, holding the fabric up to her nose, such that her eyes almost crossed in her desire to avoid the sight of Izar. Coralline nonetheless led Izar to the settee across from that of her parents.

"I have something to tell all of you," Trochid beamed. "I've decided to return to work as a coral connoisseur at the Under-Ministry for Coral Conservation. I start tomorrow!"

"I'm so happy for you, Father!" Coralline exclaimed, as she rose and hugged him.

"But how will you work without a hand?" Abalone asked. "How will you hold a microscope, parchment-pad, and pen, all in your one hand?"

"I'll figure it out."

"I may be able to help with that," Izar said. He unzipped his satchel, extracted a parcel bundled in twilight fabric, and handed it to Trochid.

Trochid opened it to reveal what looked to be an artificial hand, with a malleable band around the wrist, four fingers, and a thumb—so life-like that it even had veins across the back of the hand. Coralline looked at Izar quizzically, as did Abalone and Trochid.

"It's a prosthetic," Izar explained. "It won't have the full range of functionality of a biological hand, but it should be good enough to hold things like a pen or microscope and to perform most day-to-day activities."

His eyes wide with wonder, Trochid wrapped the prosthetic's band around his stump. He then flexed the fingers of his new hand, at first slowly, then fast. The prosthetic seemed flexible in all the ordinary ways of a hand—the wrist, the knuckles, the fingers, all could crook and bend. He reached for the fabric on Abalone's lap and held it up between two fingers—the grip was as steady as that of tongs. "This is a medical breakthrough in the ocean, isn't it?" he asked Coralline incredulously.

She nodded.

"How did you devise it, Izar?" Trochid continued.

"I suppose I started thinking about artificial hands years ago," Izar replied sheepishly.

Izar had constructed a whole, towering, multi-functional machine in the form of Castor, Coralline had seen with her own eyes. Compared to Castor's two arms—called the crusher and the dragon, Izar had told her—this prosthetic would have been a relatively easy feat, but it would still have taken many hours of laborious experimentation. She smiled at him gratefully.

"Given that the loss of your hand was my fault," Izar told Trochid, "this prosthetic is the least I can offer you."

The day of her failed wedding, Coralline, Izar, Abalone, and Trochid had all sat on these very settees, and Izar had told them all the truth about everything—Ocean Dominion, the coral reef dynamite blast, the black poison spill. "I forgive you," Trochid had pronounced easily, continuing, "All that matters to me now is that you make my daughter happy." Abalone had examined all of them coldly.

Now, Abalone snatched the yellow corset out of Trochid's grasp and resumed her stitches.

"I also have an announcement to make, Mother and Father," Coralline began, taking a deep breath. "Izar, Pavonis, and I have decided to move to Blue Bottle."

The fabric slipped out of Abalone's hands. Ensnaring it with his prosthetic, Trochid grinned at Coralline and Izar like a child with his favorite toy.

"Whyever would you wish to leave your family and village?" Abalone demanded.

"In Urchin Grove, it may take decades for people to get accustomed to the idea of desmarestia not as a poisonous acid kelp, but a healing algae. In Blue Bottle, I think patients will be more open-minded to the use of desmarestia, and I'll be able to truly develop as an apothecary. But more than that, I like Blue Bottle. Izar, Pavonis, and I all do."

Pavonis slammed his tailfin against the wall in agreement.

"Good for the three of you!" Nacre piped.

Altair drifted up into the window frame in front of Pavonis, a flame of orange. Were Nacre and Altair not bonded to Abalone and Trochid, they might have liked to come, too, Coralline thought.

"You don't have a job there, Coralline," Abalone said. "How will you support yourself?"

"I don't need a job. I'm going to start my own clinic."

"And how will you afford that?"

"With the one thousand carapace Rhodomela left me." Coralline and Osmundea were the only two people Rhodomela had named in her will.

"That dear, darling apothecary." Abalone sighed, shaking her head so hard that a golden lock tumbled out of her barrette.

Coralline and Osmundea had organized Rhodomela's funeral. Abalone had wept loudest, crying, "I owe Rhodomela the lives of both my husband and daughter." Abalone no longer referred to Rhodomela as the Bitter Spinster, nor did she abide by anyone else doing so—when Sepia had whispered the term at the funeral, Abalone had looked ready to slap her face.

A tear had trickled down Trochid's cheek at the funeral. Abalone had clasped his elbow, but he'd pulled his arm away.

They'd spoken few words to one another since Rhodomela's death. Today was the first time they were sitting on the settee together, Coralline noted, and that, too, only because a guest was here, Izar. As far as Coralline could tell, her father, with his forgiving nature, was trying to forgive her mother for her trickery, but the wound was still too raw. The wound would heal eventually, Coralline expected—if not for Trochid's sake, then for the sake of Naiadum, who was still young and dependent on both parents—but, like Trochid's stump, it would take months to heal, and things would never be quite the same again. Coralline hoped her parents would remain together.

"I think it's an excellent idea for you to start your own clinic," Trochid said. "What will you name it?"

"I was thinking of Coralline's Cures, but I've decided on The Irregular Remedy, in memory of Rhodomela."

"You don't want to appear irregular!" Abalone protested.

"But I do. I'm planning a full shelf called Exotic Experiments."

"You're turning your life into an exotic experiment." Abalone glanced pointedly at Izar. "A word in private, Coralline."

With a swish of her tailfin, Abalone swam into Coralline's bedroom, trailed by Coralline. Abalone closed the door behind them and turned to face Coralline, her arms crossed over her chest, her eyes blinking fiercely.

"Hummers are often unable to have children," she said. "Have you thought of that?"

"I haven't, Mother, because I'm not planning to have children."

"What's the point of marriage without children?"

"I'm not planning on marrying."

"So you're planning to be a Bitter Spinster?"

"Not bitter, no."

"Go back to Ecklon, I beg of you. Tell him you made a huge mistake and want to marry him."

"As you know, Mother, Ecklon is now with Rosette."

"He would leave her in a heartbeat for you."

"I don't want him to. I'm happy for them."

From the corner of her eye, Coralline detected a movement through her bedroom window. Turning her head, she saw that it was an oyster thief—a wispy brown algae—floating about, studded with shells. That was its mechanism: It inflated with gas, shells got attached to it, then it drifted about with the currents, carefree. Coralline admired its loose freedom, its ability to go anywhere unrestricted—that level of freedom was what she envisioned for her own future.

"I don't expect you to understand me, Mother," she said gently, "but I hope you can still accept me."

"I hope so, too!" Abalone said, amber-gold eyes ablaze.

She swung Coralline's bedroom door open, and she and Coralline returned to their seats on the settees. "If only you'd been right, Trochid," she stated, "in what you'd said that day, when Ecklon proposed, and the ship passed above."

"What did I say?"

"That fire and water can never truly meet."

The waters were dull gray. Even without looking at a sand-clock, Izar was by now familiar enough with the ocean to know that the time would be about half past six in the evening.

"I'll go do some exploring," Pavonis said, "and I'll see the two of you in the morning."

Izar smiled at the whale shark and, along with Coralline, stroked his yellow-spotted back. With a swing of his tail, Pavonis swam away, and Izar continued swimming through Blue Bottle hand in hand with Coralline.

A long shadow fell over them, even longer than Pavonis.

Izar whirled over onto his back and looked up, his heart racing. Could it be a ship, here to hunt him? No, from its splash and immense, bumpy gray shape, he identified it as a humpback whale. The whale angled up, rose straight into the air, its path straight as a dart, then crashed onto its back on the waves. The resulting swell of water pushed Izar and Coralline several feet down. Continuing to swim on his back, Izar admired the whale's sleek length, its muscular strength.

"Note that the whale's tail does not swish right and left like ours but slaps up and down," Coralline said, swimming on her back alongside Izar. "The whale tail is different from the fish tail because, although whales entered the oceans many millions of years ago, they're still outsiders. Fish have vertical tails, as merpeople do, because the slicing motion fights water resistance; whales did not evolve from fish, but from mammals who left land for water, and so their tail continues to carry the up-and-down motion of their ancestral legs. Whales look like fish, but they're not fish, just as you look like a merman, but you're not fully a merman."

Perhaps he would have a whale as a muse one day, Izar thought, for they straddled two worlds, as he did. The more time he spent with Pavonis, the more he found himself liking the idea of a muse.

Izar and Coralline drifted upon the balcony to their fifth-floor apartment. Izar opened the door and smiled as he entered the living room. It was small and shabby—furnished with little more than a pair of scratched stone settees and a low-lying bed—but all that mattered was that it was their own place.

At present, though, it looked more like a makeshift clinic than anyone's home, for all surfaces were littered with urns of algae, the size of vases. The urns were from Coralline's former workplace, The Irregular Remedy, and she would take them to her future workplace, The Irregular Remedy, as soon as she found a place to rent as a clinic. (Coralline had bundled all the urns carefully in fabric, loaded them in immense sacks, and strapped the cargo all to Pavonis, who had not complained once as he'd led Coralline and Izar south from Urchin Grove to Blue Bottle.)

Izar cleared some space on one settee, and nestled there with Coralline, her head coming to rest on his shoulder. Their first day living together had been busy but enjoyable.

They'd visited four homes, belonging to: Izar's mother in Velvet Horn (they'd all reminisced about Rhodomela); Venant Veritate, who had recovered fully from his flu; Limpet and Linatella Laminaria, who had apologized for having chased them away and had invited them for supper tomorrow evening (an invitation Coralline and Izar had gladly accepted); and Sage Dahlia Delaisi. Coralline had not spoken a word, but Sage Dahlia had taken one look at Izar and pronounced, as though in response to an unasked question, "Yes, he is your love." Izar had not understood the remark, but Coralline had giggled.

"You know, although we've just arrived in Blue Bottle," Coralline said, "I feel as though we already belong here. Don't you?"

"I do."

Izar's gaze fell on Coralline's tray of vials and flasks in one corner of the living room. It reminded him of the flasks of combustible chemicals in his own Invention Chamber. He wished he hadn't shied away from burning Ocean Dominion to the ground when he'd had the chance. He'd come to regret the decision every day since he'd returned to the ocean; at this very moment, Saiph was likely constructing an army of Castors.

"What's the matter?" Coralline asked.

"Nothing."

Izar had not told her about Saiph, and he did not plan to tell her. He had invented his way into his particular problems, and he would have to invent ways out.

Acknowledgments

W hen people ask me about writing, I tell them it's a labor of love. But it's not just the author's love—the people who love you most often end up laboring a lot along the way as well.

My husband, Aamer Hasham, encouraged me to write and accompanied me to book events. My twin sister, Sofia Faruqi, listened to me talk about *The Oyster Thief* for hours on end. Her patient questions helped me untangle plot intricacies, and her thoughts helped me devise new angles. My brother, Salman Faruqi, contributed tremendous big-picture thinking. An avid reader of fiction, he provided ideas to create more characters and enhance conflict.

Beta readers played a crucial role in the development of *The Oyster Thief*. In addition to my husband, brother, and sister, the team included: Stacey Gordon Sterling, who paid thorough attention to detail, Kristyn Nanlal Khetia, who delved into pace and emotion, and Lauren Friedwald, who focused on clarity and feeling. Without the commitment of the team of beta readers, *The Oyster Thief* would not be the same.

Acknowledgments

Sarah Krejci, Celia Kujala, Lucas Melbye, and Monisha Rahemtulla also provided feedback on early chapters, and Autumn Ladouceur and Ashley Ryan read very early iterations of the book.

My editor, Jessica Case, at Pegasus Books provided perceptive edits, contagious enthusiasm, and ambitious thinking. She was a delight to work with. Maria Fernandez provided interior design and typesetting, and Charles Brock from Faceout Studio designed a lovely cover.

Randall Abate, Jonathan Balcombe, Louisa Gilder, Lorraine Johnson, Rob Laidlaw, Nina Munteanu, and Misagh Parsa mentored and guided me in my writing career.

Friends offered a warm listening ear, including Monica Jain, Ismat Khatri, Barbi Lazarus, and Wei Su. Also, Nandita Bajaj, Barbara Center, Neel Desai, Mike Farley, Berna Ozunal, Bruce Poole, and Andrew Scorer supplied imaginative ideas for book promotion. Catherine Houle created a beautiful animated website at www.soniafaruqi.com.

I read lots of research in writing *The Oyster Thief,* but I particularly appreciated Josie Iselin's photographic books, *An Ocean Garden* and *Seashells.*

I'm indebted to my parents, Shaista and Amin Faruqi, for their love and support. I'm also grateful to my parents-in-law, Shamim and Nazir Hasham; my siblings-in-law, Erik Desrosiers and Maha Hasnain; and my extended family, including and especially Zia Aleem, Javed Aleem, Perveen Matloob, Sultana Ali, and Shireen Begum.

Reading Guide

This guide is intended for book club and classroom discussions. Please note that it contains spoilers.

1. What animal would you choose if you could have a muse?

2. Rhodomela says: "In order to heal others, you have to first heal yourself. . . . Success is an outcome not of imitation but of authenticity—of not abiding by the rules but changing them. The questions are more important than the answers." What do you think?

3. Do you think Coralline makes the right decision between Izar and Ecklon?

4. What if merpeople existed? How do you think our relationship with them would be? And how do you think their lives would be similar to and different from the depiction in *The Oyster Thief*?

5. Why do you think Abalone views and treats Coralline as she does?

6. Izar expects his discovery of underwater fire to make him rich, even as merpeople go extinct. If one person or company profits at the expense of everyone else, should it be permitted to continue?

7. "Infidelity is not an act but a feeling," Altair says. What's your opinion?

8. If there were an elixir that could save the life of someone you love, but if it were accompanied by a curse, would you try to find it?

9. Abalone says that the biggest mistake of Rhodomela's life is her refusal to settle. "She could have married someone else, even if not the love of her life, and she could have built a pleasant enough life with him. But she had an all-or-nothing approach—and so nothing is what she got." What do you think of an all-or-nothing approach to love and life?

10. How would you compare the merpeople relationship with the natural world to the human relationship with the natural world?

A Beautiful World

This section provides a behind-the-scenes look at the writing process for The Oyster Thief. *Please note that it contains spoilers.*

The idea of an underwater world fell into my mind on January 1, 2015. It was a freezing-cold morning in Canada, and I wished I could escape into tropical waters. But it was too expensive to book a last-minute flight, so I decided to escape in my mind. With a cup of tea in hand, I started inventing an underwater world.

As Izar's underwater-fire invention required several steps for completion, so did my underwater world. I describe the steps here in the hope that they are helpful to those working on their own creative pursuits.

A Discovered Culture

I pretended that merpeople already existed and that I, like an anthropologist, was simply "discovering" them.

Given that they already existed, they, like all other life on earth, would exist in accordance with the laws of science and nature. For one, merpeople would be a kind of fish, just as humans are a kind of mammal. The traits they would share with fish would include gills, scales, and a cold-blooded, streamlined body.

I would have liked for skin color to range widely in the water, as it does on land—Coralline, as I originally envisioned her, was dark-skinned—but, if merpeople did exist, they would not have dark skin. Skin color varies among humans because of melanin, a pigment that acts as a protective biological shield against ultraviolet radiation. People from the southern hemisphere tend to have dark skin because they require more melanin to protect against intense sunlight. People from the northern hemisphere, meanwhile, tend to have light skin because vitamin D is a greater concern than ultraviolet radiation, and melanin can prevent them from producing enough vitamin D. Due to a lack of direct exposure to sunlight, merpeople would lack melanin, and so they would have pale, fine, almost translucent skin.

The ocean is vastly deep—its average depth is about two miles, or three-and-a-half kilometers—but much of its life, and all of its photosynthesis, is concentrated in what is called the Sunlight Zone, a range of six-hundred-and-sixty feet, or two hundred meters, down from the waves. I would have liked for merpeople to live deeper than the Sunlight Zone—to live in the Twilight, or even Midnight, Zone—but it would have meant living in the dark.

As for merpeople clothing, I leaned originally toward flowing gowns and robes, but I came to the obvious conclusion that such clothing would be cumbersome—the fabric would tangle constantly with tails. I opted for corsets and waistcoats; they would end at the hip, and their fitted design would ensure the fabric did not fly up while swimming.

I decided on shells for currency and jewelry because some cultures on land have historically also used shells as such. The phrase "shelling out money" originates from such use.

A Scientific Setting

Over the course of snorkeling, diving, and swimming with sharks, I've been fortunate to see lots of marine animals in their natural environments. But in addition to relying on my firsthand experiences, I read books and hundreds of articles relating to the ocean, homing in specifically on algae, animals, and plot-specific topics like oil spills.

Researching the ocean is not like researching things on land, I quickly realized. Of the millions of species thought to live in the ocean, the majority are unknown to us. Even those that we know of, we don't know well—for instance, we don't know the life spans or social habits of whale sharks.

Our knowledge about the ocean is also biased toward life close to shore, because it's more accessible, of course. If we take algae as an example, what this means is that the algae we know best (including some of those mentioned in *The Oyster Thief*) grow in fairly shallow waters.

I sought to create cultural uses for algae that were in keeping with our knowledge of them. Buttonweed, dulse, pepper dulse, ulva, and undaria are eaten in certain parts of the world, so I figured they could also be eaten by merpeople. Devil's apron is a sugar kelp, so I imagined it as a dessert. Desmarestia is an acid kelp known to be poisonous, so I retained it as a poison. Sea oak has a wide variety of medicinal uses on land, so I treated it as a remedial algae. And, just as there are plants on land without any specific uses, there are algae in *The Oyster Thief* without any specific uses—like the oyster thief itself.

Several sorts of stones are found underwater—among them, shale, slate, limestone, sandstone, and olivine.

As for light, bioluminescence is common in the ocean. The compound luciferin, found in many marine organisms, including bacteria, generates light in the presence of oxygen.

I decided on the Atlantic Ocean as the setting for *The Oyster Thief* because it's the second-largest ocean in the world and is the ocean geographically closest to me. I made the decision lightly, but it meant a hefty extra layer of research—I had to ensure that every animal and algae mentioned in *The Oyster Thief* can be found in the Atlantic. (Another option would have been to set the story in a fictional ocean and to thus be able to mention any kind of algae or animal that exists.)

In addition to the setting, the story of *The Oyster Thief* is also as scientifically accurate as I could make it, where relevant. For instance, when Izar holds the scroll under tap water and it starts to lose form, that is a common phenomenon with salt water algae, due to osmosis.

A Cast of Characters

I envision Izar and Coralline as representing two polarities of the world—land and water, human and nonhuman, male and female.

I decided to have animal characters in addition to people, because animals add joy and beauty to our world.

I decided on a shark character, Pavonis, because sharks are among the most misunderstood and mistreated animals on the planet. Most people are terrified of them, but sharks kill less than ten people a year (generally mistaking them for other prey like seals), while people kill tens of millions of them a year. Sharks are often a by-catch of fishing and are also hunted for their fins, which are eaten in the form of shark fin soup.

I decided on a seahorse, Altair, because of the bizarre uniqueness of seahorses, from their appearance—they are a fish whose face resembles a horse's—to their romance—not only are they monogamous, but lined seahorses dance every morning with their partners—to their reproduction—it is the male who bears the young.

I based animal appearances on their species, from Pavonis's cavernous mouth and lack of eyelids to Altair's color changes and tail coiled around a strand of grass.

During my readings about the ocean, I kept a running list of any words I liked that I could use as names. I decided that the names of most oceanic characters should relate to the ocean, though some could also relate to the universe, and the names of all land characters should relate to the universe.

I selected the name Coralline because coralline algae play a disproportionately important role in marine ecology, cementing coral reefs together. In addition to being rosy and beautiful, their strata are strong and powerful. I chose the name Coralline also because coralline algae can be considered symbolic of the human effect on the ocean—tens of thousands of tons of these precious calcified structures are dredged out of the oceans every year. Crushed to form a powder, they are used as agricultural fertilizer.

The name Izar, meanwhile, refers to a binary star. To the naked eye, it appears to be a single point of light, but it is actually two different stars close to each other (about two hundred light-years away from us and five hundred times brighter than the sun). Giving Izar's background, I found it appropriate to name him after a binary star.

Other character names were also chosen with deliberation.

In addition to referring to a star, the name Zaurak originally derives from the Arabic word for "boat"—relevant, given Zaurak's workplace. Castor is among the brightest stars in the night sky; the name sounded right for a source of underwater fire. Antares is a supergiant star that's red in color; I found the name fitting for a character with giant ambition. Saiph is a star whose name derives from the Arabic term *saif al jabbar*, which means sword of the giant; the name seemed suitable for a character with a desire to kill. (The names of several characters in *The Oyster Thief* have Arabic origins because the names of many stars do.)

On the water side, the name Ecklon relates to *Ecklonia maxima*, or sea bamboo, a kind of kelp that's strong and steady. Rhodomela comes from *Rhodomela confervoides*, or straggly bush; the hard pronunciation of the scientific name, accompanied by the unpleasant common name, sounded right to me for a character who appears harsh on the outside. Naiadum derives from *Smithora naiadum*, a delicate kind of red algae; the fragility of the algae made it a suitable name for someone ill. The name Abalone refers to the abalone snail whose inner shell consists of shimmering, iridescent nacre. I envision the character Abalone as possessing a pearlescent beauty; appropriately, her muse is a snail named Nacre. (Pearls form when abalones and other mollusks coat irritating particles, such as grains of sand, with layers of nacre.) The name Trochid refers to a large family of snails; I chose it because it complemented the name Abalone.

Although *The Oyster Thief* is set in the Atlantic, a few character names derive from oceans other than the Atlantic, just as some human names can be found across cultures. The names of most underwater settlements relate to algae, such as Hog's Bristle, Purple Claw, Rainbow Wrack, and Velvet Horn. Blue Bottle, meanwhile, refers to a kind of peacock-blue jellyfish.

Concessions to Language

Merpeople, were they to exist, would not speak English. Their communication, in fact, might not involve speaking at all. (Sound does exist in the water, as do the other four senses, but it exists differently—it travels farther and four times faster in water than air, making its location difficult to pinpoint.) I stuck with English in the book for obvious reasons of ease and clarity.

I nonetheless grappled with words as simple as those representing color. Can Coralline describe something as olive-brown, given that she does not know what olives are? What about the word *orange*—can that be used, given that the name of the color originates from the fruit, and there are no oranges underwater? I decided to retain our ordinary usage of color, because I could not construe of equivalent terms.

A broader trouble with language when it comes to an underwater world is that our vocabulary is from land. Many ocean organisms have land-associated names. For instance, rose petal tellin, lettered olive shell, butterfly fish, lionfish, eagle ray—these names make reference to rose petals, olives, butterflies, lions, and eagles. Also, some names we've given ocean life have negative connotations, like devil's tongue and devil's apron. I saw no help for using these terms, but I shunned the word *seaweed*—because the ocean is not full of weeds.

The Elusive Elixir

The elixir in *The Oyster Thief* is symbolic. Each of us may have an "elixir" in our own lives, a goal that we're striving toward. It could be to start one's own business or to climb a mountain. My goal was to invent an underwater world. My quest toward this goal was enjoyable, but, like Coralline's and Izar's quest for the elixir, it was paved with obstacles.

I spent about two thousand hours over a period of two and a half years on the original manuscript for *The Oyster Thief,* but I decided to throw it all out, finding that I had no more than straddled the surface of my imagination. Over the next year, I ascended up to my home library every day to invent my underwater world, just as Izar descended into his Invention Chamber every night to invent underwater fire.

During this year, I became so immersed in my underwater world, and so absent-minded in my external world, that I sometimes felt as though I was in a trance. In this trance, I lost my passport. I forgot hundreds of dollars in an ATM. I routinely forgot to put detergent in the laundry. I neglected to turn on the lights when it got dark (then I would look about me, mystified by the darkness). I was on land and in the ocean at the same time—both when awake and asleep. Even upon shutting down my computer late at night, I couldn't shut down my mind. Sleepy but sleepless, I would lie in bed writing notes to myself—a particular thought Coralline might be entertaining, an observation of Izar's.

Upon completing her quest for the elixir, Coralline finds that the solution was in her all along. I found the same—the underwater world did exist somewhere in the abyss of my imagination; I just had to patiently, painstakingly haul it up to the surface.

The End and the Beginning

Over the course of writing *The Oyster Thief*, I started to think of the ocean as not just a giant ecosystem but as a giant organism. We hurt this organism constantly, sometimes without knowing it. For instance, we lather on chemical sunscreen when we snorkel above reefs, but the chemicals in the sunscreen kill reefs. *Solution*: Use mineral sunscreen instead of chemical.

Due to a multitude of factors, from chemical sunscreen and coral reef dynamite blasts to, more importantly, climate change and the resulting warming waters and ocean acidification, coral reefs are bleaching around the world.

Life throughout the oceans is threatened by human activity.

Rampant levels of fishing are resulting in the collapse of fish populations and the endangerment of species. *Solution*: Let's eat more sustainably. Trash and plastic pollution is creating immense, swirling garbage patches. *Solution*: Let's reduce plastic use, recycle more, and be mindful of our waste. Oil pollution is another danger. *The Oyster Thief* portrays a single-site spill, but such spills account for only a small portion of the total oil pollution in the ocean. Other sources of oil include ships and runoff from land. *Solution*: Let's invest more in renewable energy.

A new area of danger has opened recently. When I started *The Oyster Thief*, I construed the idea of underwater mining as fictional; it is now fact. Companies are starting to dredge the depths of the ocean for diamonds. *Solution*: Let's not go there.

Overall, let's not treat the world under the waves as Ocean Dominion does, as a set of resources to plunder. Oceans have been there always, and they will be there always, but their health has come to depend on us. We can choose to steward their depths even though we cannot peer into them.

Project Animal Farm
by Sonia Faruqi

Born out of a global expedition fearlessly undertaken by a young woman, *Project Animal Farm* offers a riveting and revealing look at what truly happens behind farm doors. It illuminates a hidden world that plays a part in all of our lives.

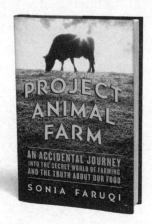

"An engaging account . . . about this most secretive of global enterprises."
—J. M. Coetzee, Winner of the Nobel Prize for Literature

"People will be talking about this book for decades."
—John Robbins, author of *The Food Revolution*

"Everybody who is interested in food policy and
animal welfare should read this book."
—Temple Grandin, author of *Animals in Translation*

PROLOGUE

THE START OF A JOURNEY

A MATERIALISTIC INVESTMENT BANKER

Growing up, I seemed almost earmarked for the financial world, as I was both studious and materialistic. I was a small mass of seriousness—a little librarian—completing my assignments early and happily. I preferred class to recess, homework to hopscotch. In middle school, I would for hours paint still lifes—a bowl of apples or a vase of flowers—feeling that my own life was a still life—a cantaloupe compressed into a teacup. My core longed for more, mentally, materially.

My wallet was wide enough to fill the well of my needs—food, school, shoes—but not the valley of my whims and wishes. I craved more clothes, more books, more boxes—dainty little tins in which to cherish my dainty little things. My mother occasionally said, "You like having things for the sake of having them; you have the joy of possession." I interpreted her comments as compliments: how sophisticated I was, I thought, to be possessed with the joy of possession.

After high school, I attended Dartmouth College, a small, liberal arts university with a campus dotted with trees. Each of its classes was an ingredient you were supposed to select, slice, and stir in the pot of your mind, toward the aim of not merely faring but flourishing. Dartmouth urged that for "bonding" purposes, its students hike together in small groups for five days before the start of school. I'd never hiked before—because I'd never wanted to, and I'd grown up in city apartments—but I decided to participate because everybody else did. Two hours into my outdoor excursion, however, I realized that it was, as I termed it then, "the biggest mistake I've ever made."

My backpack felt like a rock strapped to my back, despite the fact that I'd reluctantly unloaded my makeup and chocolates at the insistence of trip leaders. Worse, there was nothing for me to eat: I ate only meat—shunning fruits and vegetables since childhood—and there was no meat, as it would have spoiled over the course of the trip. I decided to stop eating. An even more pressing issue than food was facilities. There were no toilets; we were supposed to go in the woods like chest-pounding cavemen. I decided to hold it for days. (And I did.)

Finally, there was the wildlife: I felt sure a bear would attack me as I slept. One night, I thought I heard an animal panting and salivating right beside my ear. "GIVE ME YOUR FLASHLIGHT!" I yelled at the snoring, sleeping bag–encased form next to me, rattling him awake. I flashed his light everywhere. But there was no bear; there were only my trip members, awake and annoyed. I resolutely avoided the outdoors after that. The rugged life clearly did not suit me.

I graduated from Dartmouth College with a major in economics and public policy, and a minor in government. Degree in hand, I joined my classmates in a stampede to Wall Street. Wall Street was the money business, the fast track, a meal ready to eat, without the costly condiment of a graduate degree. I felt pleased and fulfilled when an investment bank offered me employment.

Investment banks had just one requirement of their young employees. They required that, as the moon revolves around earth, employees revolve around work. As an investment banker,

I did not work to live, I lived to work. I did not eat to live, I ate to work—and I ate at work. All of my meals—breakfast, lunch, and dinner—I consumed in my cubicle, gobbling them up rapidly so that I could continue typing, calculating, working: a machine in the form of a woman.

But I enjoyed it. I liked feeling important. I liked having a paycheck. I liked wearing a suit every day. I liked strutting across the office carpet in high heels, papers under my arm. I liked my Upper East Side apartment, only a short walk from Central Park. I liked racing my fingers across my keyboard and my eyes across my computer screen. Every morning, I awoke like a golden retriever puppy salivating to start the day, unfazed by my seventy-hour work weeks. Wall Street was where I was meant to be, I felt.

Until I was let go.

The American economy began hemorrhaging immediately after I joined, starting with the subprime mortgage sector. The pain spread outward, until the entire financial system convulsed in its throes. Investment banks decreed that it was no longer profitable for them to continue to feed the small fry they'd lured into their nets with baits of bonuses. So they cut the nets. They laid off hundreds of thousands of employees. After two years of living in my cubicle, I was forced to leave it.

I planned to apply for roles at other financial firms. I would continue to burn with the same fire, only its cinders would be raked by another bank. My life would remain the same gift basket of enjoyment, tied with the green ribbon of Excel, adorned with the red bow of PowerPoint, but would shift to a new cubicle. *After* a break, though. I'd worked nonstop on Wall Street, taking not even one sick day, and I thought a break would recharge my battery and help me recommence with renewed intensity.

During my break, I read books. I contemplated life. And I moved from New York to Toronto.

Since I had plenty of time on my hands, I decided to volunteer at a farm, imagining that the experience would be an adventure. I contacted a dozen organic and small farms with an enthusiastic offer of free assistance toward the production of their food. I was sure they'd be thrilled and grateful. They weren't. Most of them were cold and uninterested. Only one—an organic dairy farm—accepted my ambiguous offer, and only under one condition: that I volunteer with them not for a week at the most, as I'd hoped, but for two weeks at the least.

I reluctantly agreed to the duration. The dairy farm reluctantly agreed to supply accommodation.

I'd devoured the *Little House on the Prairie* books as a girl, and my mental image of organic farms resembled the pastoral, prairie-like setting of the books. I imagined that my farm stay would be both an education and a vacation, and that, shortly after, I would return to the prosperous world of suits, spreadsheets, and skyscrapers.

I had no idea what I was getting myself into.